THE DEBATERS

BARTH HOOGSTRATEN

ISBN: 978-1-4834-2682-2 (sc)
ISBN: 978-1-4834-2684-6 (hc)
ISBN: 978-1-4834-2683-9 (e)

Library of Congress Control Number: 2015902634

All proceeds of this book go to cancer research

Lulu Publishing Services rev. date: 3/6/2015

CONTENTS

1

---❖---

Erasmus: Early Years

1466–1484

Son of a priest - Decision to send him to a faraway school - Boat trip to Deventer - School of the Brethren of the Common Life - Rector Hegius - Befriends a future pope - Agricola's speech - Parents' death - Becomes a monk

The priest was reading by the light that filtered through the small window of his study when she entered with silent steps. She waited respectfully, but the man did not notice her and continued to read at his standing desk.

"I am pregnant," she whispered. When he did not look up, she said it again but louder.

This time, the man heard what she said, but he needed time to fully absorb its significance. He slowly turned toward her, rubbed his tired eyes with his fingertips, and looked at her.

"I am pregnant, Father," she said hesitantly. When he still did not respond, she said with a hint of impatience in her voice, "I am with child."

He slowly slid his fingers across his dry lips. When he saw how anxious she was, his face softened. "It is no doubt with God's blessing, dear," he said in a soothing voice. "You need not worry."

"It is you for whom I am worried. What will the people say this time?"

"They will behave the same way they did with Pieter, Margaret. They will talk a lot, snicker behind my back, and after a while, they will forget about it."

"Forget? That is easy for you to say. You don't have to go to market. The women always stop talking when they see me coming, and then they have that look—always that look, as if I am guilty of something."

With arms folded across his chest, he studied her in silence, understanding. It could not be easy for her. "What are you going to do, Margaret?"

"I can go to Rotterdam again." She sighed resignedly. "I'll take Pieter with me." Pieter was their first child, nearly three years old.

"Yes, that will probably be best," he said, and he turned back to his book.

She left his study.

Goudae conceptus, Roterodami natus,[1] he thought, and smiled.

She knew not to bother him with the details of her trip. He was a learned man, one of few priests in the diocese of Utrecht who could read and speak Latin and Greek fluently. He had spent a few years in Rome, copying and translating old religious books, and when he had returned to Holland, the archbishop had put him in charge of a church. Father Roger Gerard was the only parish priest in Gouda, a two-hundred-year-old town on the Gouwe River in the province of Holland. He took Margaret, the daughter of a physician in Zevenbergen, as his housekeeper, and over the course of a year, her respect for him had gradually changed to love. It first became apparent when she talked with him; her voice grew softer and, in a way, fuller.

One day when she brought him his morning drink, she had moved closer to him than usual, and a few days later, he had put his hand on the table next to hers so that they barely touched. The touch had grown into affection—a kiss of her hand, her lips, and then they had joined together.

She loved him, and she thought that he too loved her, but she was never quite sure. He was good to her, and he treated her with respect, which was more than could be said of most townspeople. They ignored her. They had

---

[1]   "Conceived in Gouda, born in Rotterdam."

respect for Father Gerard, however. Many priests and even monks lived with women. The people understood that. "It's only natural," they said. The Church called it *living in concubinage*. The archbishop did not seem to mind as long as the priest in question did not marry the woman, and the child was not officially recognized as being that of a clergyman. Nearly one-third of the clergy bedded women. Some bishops were even known to tax their priests for the privilege of having concubines.

Margaret went to Rotterdam to be closer to her parents, and at 3 Wijde Kerkstraat, the home of a midwife, she gave birth to a son. She came back to Father Gerard three years later with Pieter and a little boy.

"This is Erasmus," she said. The boy looked up at the strange man, began to cry, and hid behind her skirt.

"Erasmus. You named him after the holy martyr Erasmus. Good; very good. Thank you, Margaret. An unusual name for what will be an unusual boy." His head dropped to his chest, his hands flat against each other between his knees. His lips clamped together. Slowly, he lifted his head and looked at her. She noticed a tinge of anguish in his eyes.

"When was he born?" he asked with a faint smile.

"On October 28. It was a Sunday."

"That was three years ago—1466, wasn't it?"

"Yes, Father." She bravely fought back tears.

"Margaret, thank you so much for coming back to me." He touched her arm lightly and returned slowly to reading his Bible.

A year later, the boy started at the local school that his brother attended. Headmaster Pieter Winckel demanded strict discipline from his pupils but more from Erasmus and his brother, or so it seemed to Erasmus. The headmaster also tended to play favorites, and Erasmus felt it strongly because one of the favored students was his friend, Willem Hermans.

One day, while walking back from school with Peter, Erasmus was unusually quiet. Later that afternoon, Margaret found him crying in a corner.

"What is the matter, Erasmus? Why are you crying?" She stooped and gently put her arm around his small shoulders.

"They yell at me at school, and they call me names," he sobbed.

She scooped him into her lap and let him cry against her chest. She silently prayed, "Dear God, let them not hurt this innocent boy."

"What do they call you, darling?"

"They yell, 'Bastard, bastard, you are a bastard.' Am I a bastard, Mama?"

"No, you are not. You are my son, my little boy." She hugged him tighter.

"What *is* a bastard, Mama?"

She hesitated for a moment, wondering how she could answer the question without hurting him. She stroked his hair. "Why don't you ask Father Gerard? He can explain it much better than I can."

The boy opened the study door and walked up to the man standing at the desk. When the man did not notice him, he tugged on the man's long black gown. The tall, slender priest looked down at the small, sickly boy.

"Oh, Erasmus, look at you," he said warmly. "You are becoming a big boy. How old are you now?"

"I am four years old, sir," the boy answered timidly. He was always a bit shy around his father.

"Four years and already at school. You like school, don't you?"

"They call me a bastard. What is a bastard, sir?"

"Oh, I see." Father Gerard's voice dropped. "So that is why you come to me. Well, now, what is a bastard? Let me think." Unlike most of his colleagues in similar situations, he made no effort to hide the fact that he had fathered two children. The Church labeled an illegitimate child a *defectus natalis*, which cruelly translated into "birth defect." Father Gerard hoped, however, that the Church might have had a kinder meaning in mind: "imperfect birth," perhaps, or "born with a flaw."

"Listen carefully, Erasmus, because you are a big boy now. When a man and a woman are married, they have children. You know that, don't you?" The boy nodded. "For some reason, your mother and I cannot marry. Do not ask me why; it just is. But we do have you and Pieter, and we love you both. From now on, you must ignore the other children when they call you 'bastard.' Do you understand?"

"No," the boy replied in a small voice, a frown spreading across his face.

"Well, let me see. You know that boy at the end of the street, the one with the bad foot?" Erasmus nodded. "Do they call him names?"

"They call him Clubfoot."

"That's right. And that old man with the hump on his back. What do they call him?"

"Hunchback." The frown slowly dissipated as understanding spread across Erasmus's features. His eyes opened wide. "They do, they do! And they also yell at that girl with the red hair."

"Right! But the only reason why those people are yelled at is because something is different about them. But they can't help that, can they?"

The boy shook his head. He understood. He moved closer to his father and tried to put his arms around a leg, but the gown prevented him. Instead, he put his head against the smooth fabric. Father Gerard stroked his son's hair with his soft, pale hand, and with grateful relief, he silently mouthed, "Thank you, Lord," as he turned his eyes upward.

During the next two years, it became clear that young Erasmus was only a mediocre student at school. "He shows little interest," Headmaster Winckel informed Father Gerard as they shook hands at the church door after Sunday service. "He likes to read instead of paying attention."

"You do not think that he lacks intelligence, do you?" Father Gerard frowned.

"Oh, no. Quite the opposite, but he needs something that can keep his interest." Winckel knew better than to make his priest angry. He had visited Father Gerard's home not long after the priest's appointment to the local church and had seen his many books in Latin and Greek. He knew then that Father Gerard was no ordinary village priest. "Maybe you can help him, Father." With that subtle hint, Winckel turned and joined his wife.

The priest gazed at the couple. Mistress Winckel kept one proper step behind her husband and walked a bit off to his side. Several layers of garments could not hide her more than ample figure and a much-too-small bonnet strained to remain perched on her head. Her master wore a long, wide black cape that reached to just above his fashionable shoes, with square toes and silver buckles. His wide-brimmed hat was cone-shaped, one foot high, and tapered to a small circle at the top. The Winckels wore their Sunday-best black.

Father Gerard turned back into the church and headed for his study. *That schoolmaster could be right*, he thought. *Maybe it is time to pay more attention to the boys. I am their father, after all. Pieter is no problem. He is a strong boy who goes his own quiet way, is always on time for meals, and never complains. But he is not too bright. Erasmus may be slightly built and small for his age, but he is a lively, inquisitive boy whose insistence on getting answers to his many questions frequently gets him into trouble at school. Maybe he does need something to keep his mind busy. He is only six years old, but perhaps I can start by giving him lessons in Latin.*

Erasmus's Latin lessons began the next day. Father Gerard was astounded at how quickly the boy progressed. He was a natural.

Three years later, the priest turned to Margaret one day as she brought him his afternoon drink of apple juice. "Margaret, it is time for the boys to go to a good school."

"To another school? Here in Gouda?" Her face reflected one big question mark. She did not know of another school in town.

"No, I am talking about St. Lebuin School in Deventer," he retorted quickly, his face a bit sterner than usual.

"In Deventer, sir. Where is that?"

"In the province of Overijssel."

"I have never heard of it. That is not in Holland, is it?"

"No," he said, somewhat impatiently. "Here, let me draw you a map." He quickly sketched an outline of the Netherlands and filled in the most important Dutch province, Holland. "This dot is Gouda. Next to Holland is Utrecht, and east of that is Gelderland, which is bordered on the east by the IJssel River. The province across that river is called Overijssel, and this dot on the river is Deventer, a very important town."

Margaret studied the primitive map intensely, her mouth dropping open a little. She looked up, her face blank. "Why can't they go to a school nearby?"

"Deventer has a better school," he replied rather brusquely.

"But how far away is it?"

"About six times as far as from here to Rotterdam."

She gasped. "That must be many days by coach."

"You are not going by coach, Margaret. You will travel by boat."

"Me, sir? Must I go too?" Margaret pulled back, her face again one big question mark. "And leave you here all alone?"

"Yes, dear, you will go with the boys and live in Deventer. You would not want them to live there alone, would you?"

"Oh no, sir. But why can't Pieter go alone and let Erasmus stay here with us? He is only nine years old."

"Actually, it is Erasmus who needs a better school, dear. He now speaks, writes, and reads Latin fluently, and I cannot teach him more."

Margaret remained quiet for a while. They stood a few feet apart. She looked at the floor; he kept his arms folded forebodingly. The manner in which he had spoken made her feel as if he were pushing her back. Ever since she had returned from Rotterdam, he had avoided all physical contact—no bedding together, no sweet talk, only unanswered love on her part.

She looked up at him, but he avoided her eyes. "When do we leave? I have to make new clothes for the boys and prepare food for the trip."

"The boat to Amsterdam leaves on Monday."

Margaret was dumbstruck when she heard the word "Monday"—only two days away. She went toward the door but when she was halfway there, she turned around and asked, "Do the boys know?"

"I will tell them this afternoon." He did not tell her that there was a school in Gouda just like the one in Deventer, the school of the Brethren of the Common Life. His real reason for sending the boys so far away was that he felt an increasing embarrassment with his situation in town.

After their last evening meal together, Father Gerard sat down with Margaret and recounted the history of St. Lebuin School. He started at the very beginning, explaining that the school was named after St. Lebuïnus, a fearless eighth-century Anglo-Saxon monk who had preached the gospel of Christ among the pagans in Friesland. When he began to denounce their pagan gods, the pagans came after Lubuïnus with spears and chased him out of the province. He ended up in Deventer where, in or about the year 773, he erected a small church, where, in about 775, he was ultimately buried. The St. Lebuïnus Church was enlarged in the eleventh century and became the second largest church in the Netherlands.

Father Gerard continued his story with the life of Gerard Groote (1340–1384), who was born into a family of wealthy cloth merchants and became one of Deventer's leading citizens. On September 21, 1374, Groote (whose name means "great") donated his large estate to the city to house poor women; it became known as Meester Geert's House. The women were cared for by matrons, who organized their workforce, composed a governing constitution, and became known as the Sisters of the Common

Life. Groote was impressed, and in 1381 he created a larger community and called it the Brethren of the Common Life. The St. Lebuin School was founded as part of that community. Not long thereafter, other priests followed Groote's example and established Brethren of the Common Life communities throughout western Europe.

Appalled by the decadent lifestyle in which much of the clergy indulged, Groote practiced a renewed Catholic faith of life in the service of God and the salvation of the soul. It was a Christian renaissance, a "Modern Devotion" or *Devotio Moderna*. Groote planned to devote his life to spreading the word of his new faith, but to accomplish this, he needed books, which he considered essential to support effective preaching. As his own library was wholly inadequate, he traveled to Paris to buy and borrow the material that he needed. He returned to Deventer with a trunk full of books and manuscripts and invited young students of the St. Lebuin School to his home to copy them. In return for their labor, they received free room and board, which, for many, was considered priceless.

Groote began his life as a preacher, armed with a wheelbarrow full of newly copied manuscripts and several assistants to help take turns pushing it over rutted earthen roads. He traveled throughout the provinces and quickly gained a reputation as a highly effective and widely sought-after itinerant preacher. People traveled great distances to hear the pious man preach. No church was large enough to house the crowds. He became known as the "open-air preacher." His listeners were never disappointed, for his sermons lasted two or sometimes three hours. Groote's life work—his preaching, teaching, and founding of the Common Life communities— was sanctioned by the bishop of Utrecht, Florent van Wevelinckhoven, as Deventer was part of his bishopric.

Inevitably, Groote's success created jealousy and bitterness among other preachers, especially the members of the Dominican order, who considered themselves to be the proper itinerant preachers. They considered him a rival and petitioned the bishop to withdraw his approval of Groote. The weak bishop acceded to their urging. Groote had been silenced, but he was not beaten. He took to writing and translated passages of the Bible, including fifty psalms, from Latin into Dutch. When the plague hit Deventer in August 1384, Groote became stricken with the disease while nursing a friend. He died on August 20, between five and six o'clock in the afternoon and was buried in St. Mary's Church, where he had so often preached.

The school that Groote had been instrumental in founding continued to gain prominence after the great man's death. One of its most famous students was Thomas à Kempis (1380–1471), a member of the Brotherhood of the Common Life and an ardent follower of Groote's work. He became widely known for his *Imitation of Christ,* which was based on the concepts of *Devotio Moderna,* and became the most read book, after the Bible. in the Christian world.

Father Gerard had lost himself so completely in the history of St. Lebuin School that he did not notice Margaret had fallen asleep. A gentle snore distracted him, and he looked at her with affection. When he had informed her that she and his sons had to leave for Deventer, he had barely been able to keep his emotions under control, and in the process, he had been too abrupt. He longed to hold her in his arms one more time, but that would make parting even more difficult.

Early on Monday morning, Father Gerard, Margaret, and the boys walked to the Gouwe River where the boat, the *Johanna*, was moored. The children said good-bye to the priest with a handshake, after which each received pat on the head. Excitedly, they scampered on board.

"Well, good-bye, Margaret. Take good care of the boys and yourself."

"Good-bye, sir."

Their hands touched. His jaw was hard-set. He blinked once. She managed a little smile and wiped away a few tears. He turned and walked quickly away, afraid to show his emotion. They did not wave.

The first leg of the trip from Gouda to Amsterdam took about seven hours. The boat was a thirty-foot–long open barge, with benches for passengers to sit on. It was partially covered by a canopy made from an old sail, which served as a shelter in case of rain. Fortunately, it was a pleasant summer day, and the dozen or so passengers preferred to sit in the sun. The boatman's wife stood in the stern, holding the rudder. Erasmus had already figured out that her name was Johanna, same as the boat.

About ten feet from the stern of the *Johanna* stood a twelve-foot mast. A rope tied to the top of the mast was pulled by two horses, who walked seventy feet or so ahead of the boat on a path alongside the river. A second rope, leading from the top of the mast to the rear of the boat, prevented the mast from toppling forward as the horses pulled. There was no sail.[2]

Erasmus and Pieter were intrigued as they approached the first of many wooden drawbridges. "What do you think they will do with the rope?" Erasmus asked his brother, who shrugged his shoulders. At that moment, a boy about Erasmus's age who was riding the lead horse pulled a horn from his satchel blew out a single loud blast. The boy was the "chaser," and his warning alerted the bridgekeeper's wife of the boat's approach. She turned a large wheel, and the bridge slowly opened. Shortly before the boat reached it, the chaser's father unhitched the rope from behind the second horse and, holding the end of the rope, walked under the bridge on a narrow wooden platform that lined the canal. As the boat glided under the bridge, the bridgekeeper's wife, still standing next to her wheel, lowered a string with an old wooden shoe tied to its end. Johanna dropped a coin into the shoe as the passage fee. On the other side, the father had just enough slack in the rope to hitch it back onto the horse, which had not broken its stride.

Margaret was not interested in all this. She took in the beautiful landscape; the rich meadows dotted with cows, some resting and chewing their cud while others grazed nearby. A few geese squabbled over a choice nesting area on the shore. A lone fisherman in a rowboat waved. A church tower, visible above the trees, suggested the presence of an invisible village nearby. It was all so peaceful.

The *Johanna* moved at a steady pace of about five miles an hour. After two hours, she reached the Old Rijn River and crossed it before continuing on the Amstel River. Five hours later, she reached the heart of Amsterdam and entered a wider waterway called the IJ. Margaret and the

---

[2]   Traveling by boat was only possible where rivers connected towns. It was more comfortable than going by coach and, at a speed of three to four miles per hour, it was faster than walking. Most convenient of all, boats could accommodate large amount of luggage. Boat travel became so popular that the mayors of Amsterdam and Haarlem agreed to dig a straight, narrow canal, called a *vaart,* between their towns, and in 1632, the first two horse-drawn boats, called *trekschuits* (pull boats), departed, one from each city. Halfway between Amsterdam and Haarlem, the passengers changed boats and that spot place soon became a small town called Halfweg (Halfway). The venture was such a great success that eventually a network of canals developed throughout the Netherlands.

boys marveled at the many large buildings, especially the enormous church near the waterfront. Just past the church, the *Johanna* came to a stop at a dock on the side of the canal. "Your next boat is three hundred meters further on," said the boatman, two fingers touching the visor of his cap. "I wish you a safe crossing."

With their luggage in tow, Margaret and the boys walked along the waterfront to where a larger craft was docked. A middle-aged man with sailor's cap, a ring beard, and the weathered red face of a man who had lived all his life on the water, approached. "Miss, are you the people for Deventer?"

"Yes, we are," Margaret replied.

"Good. I was waiting for you. Captain Gerritsen is the name. Get right on board, and we'll be on our way."

They were not the only passengers on the sailboat *Geertruida*. Erasmus counted twenty-three, some of whom did not look too happy. They had been waiting impatiently for the passengers from Gouda to arrive. The crew of three hoisted the sails, and they were underway. Margaret settled down in a corner of the salon, but the boys stayed on deck, gazing with amazement at the hustle and bustle of numerous small boats crisscrossing the IJ. The waterway became wider and wider until they arrived in an area where enormous ships were docked at the quay or moored a short distance offshore. From there on, they could see nothing but the open water of the frigid Zuider Zee (South Sea).

"Is your wife's name Geertruida?" Erasmus asked the captain.

Gerritsen laughed heartedly. "You already figured that out, young fellow? And where are you off to?"

"To school in Deventer."

"Aye, I have heard of that school. Of the Brethren of the Common Life, it is. You are lucky that they took you, young man. I figured you for a clever boy when you asked my wife's name."

"Thank you, sir," Erasmus replied modestly. "Um, why did our first boatman look worried when he wished us a safe crossing?"

"Well, the Zuider Zee can have some bad storms, so a prayer to the good Lord is always welcome. Off you go, and say a prayer."

With a strong northeast wind, the captain stayed on a close reach, and the boat sliced through the water with impressive speed. However, after several hours, the wind suddenly shifted to the northwest and increased so much in force that Captain Gerritsen reluctantly came to a decision.

"Folks, we have a storm brewing, and it will be dark soon," he announced. "That light you see on your right is from the harbor of Harderwijk. I think we had best wait out the storm there. It will give you good people a chance for a quiet meal and some sleep."

The passengers, some already green with seasickness, wholeheartedly agreed. Margaret and her boys ate the bread with cheese and sausages she had prepared for the voyage. Shortly thereafter, affected by the long day and the fresh sea breeze, the boys fell sound asleep. When they woke up early the next morning, the *Geertruida* was once again sailing smoothly. By late afternoon, they debarked in the town of Zwolle.

"Can't you bring us all the way to Deventer?" Erasmus asked Captain Gerritsen.

"No, young fellow, I can't."

"Why not, sir?" he asked, his face serious and his voice firm.

"Well, look at the water. It flows downstream, and Deventer is upstream. That is a mighty strong current—too strong for a sailing vessel this size to maneuver on this river."

"Thank you, sir. Good-bye." Erasmus's small hand disappeared into the large, callused hand of the sailor. Gerritsen watched him go as he ran to his mother. *That is one smart boy*, he thought. *He is curious about everything.*

Margaret and the boys' next mode of transportation was a four-wheel covered wagon, which was large enough to seat eight passengers on two wooden benches that faced each other. The unpaved road was littered with potholes, and the wagon did not have springs. A few dilapidated pillows served as shock absorbers, but some experienced passengers had brought their own thicker pillows from home. The journey was rough and slow. The women and children sat in the wagon, while the menfolk rode horses alongside. It took five hours of great discomfort to cover the twenty miles between Zwolle and Deventer.

The coachman dropped Margaret and the boys off at the main building of the St. Lebuin School. She asked a passing monk where she could find the rector, and she and the boys made their way to his office. She curtsied to the man behind the desk and handed him a letter from Father Gerard. He read the letter in silence.

"Father Gerard and I met in Rome," Rector Hegius said, looking up at her as he finished reading. "He excelled in translating." He looked at both boys, making them a little uncomfortable. "Which one of the boys is Erasmus?"

Margaret pushed the smaller of the two boys forward. "This one, sir."

The rector looked at the slender boy, smiled, and asked him something in Latin. Erasmus promptly answered, also in Latin. They conversed for a few minutes, while Margaret and Pieter waited patiently. Finally, Hegius turned to Margaret and said, "Erasmus will start in the eighth grade, Mrs. Rogers, and Pieter will go to an ancillary school nearby."

Margaret curtsied again and turned to leave, thankful that the rector had addressed her as "Mrs."

Students whose parents could afford it lived in the opulent Friars Home on Papenstreet and Pontsteeg, close to the school. Margaret and the boys lived in a single room in the Clerks Home in the Krommesteeg,[3] several blocks away, where they did not have to pay rent.

Erasmus was one of approximately fifteen hundred students at the school. They came from all over Europe and England to the famous school, where only one language was spoken—Latin. The school had eight grades. Students entered in eighth grade and worked their way up to first. Each grade had at least six parallel classes led by graduate students, who were referred to as teachers. In each class, the teacher sat on a high stool in the middle of the room, and the students crowded around him, sitting on the floor. Each student had a 10 x 7-inch slate with a wooden frame, a box with slate pencils, and a round container with two compartments, one for a small sponge and the other for a piece of chamois leather, which were used to clean and dry the slate.[4]

Alexander Hegius had started his career at St. Lebuin the year before Erasmus arrived. A German humanist, Hegius had been a student of Thomas à Kempis and was considered the greatest educator of his time.

---

[3]   A *steeg* is a narrow alley, sometimes not more than two or three feet wide. The Pontsteeg and Krommesteeg still exist in downtown Deventer.

[4]   This author used the same type of slate and writing tools when he entered school in1930.

He spoke the Latin of Cicero and advocated the teaching of this "pure" Latin with the help of short verses. In his first act as rector, he threw out the old dogmatic lesson books and replaced them with the *doctrinale* written in 1199 by Alexandra de Ville-Dieu, a Minorite monk. This dismayed the older teachers, whose painstakingly slow lessons were based entirely on dogma, discipline, and early Christian writings. Hegius persevered, however, and practically overnight, the students displayed a renewed interest in their studies. Hegius was like a father to the poorer students, and he had a soft spot for Erasmus, who frequently asked for explanations and did not hesitate to disagree with his teachers.

When he was not in class, Erasmus enjoyed walking and exploring Deventer, an important harbor town that bustled with activity. He was especially interested in observing the construction of a pontoon bridge across the wide IJsel River and checked its progress whenever he could. One day, he saw a large crowd on the market square, pushing and shoving toward the center of the square. Caught up in the throng, he made his way to the edge of an open circle, where he finally saw what the excitement was all about. Chained to a post, a black bear was fending off three large dogs. With a powerful swipe of his front paw, the bear sent the smallest dog flying in the air, and the crowd howled with laughter.

"You like this entertainment?" a voice behind Erasmus asked. He turned around and recognized the owner of the voice as a more senior student at Lebuin.

"No, I do not, as a matter of fact," he replied. "How crude can people be to enjoy this barbaric show? Did you see that poor dog?"

"Oh, don't pity the dog. That bear no longer has claws," the older student answered dismissively. "Shall we look for more pleasurable entertainment? I understand that the Duchess of Guelders will soon arrive to pay her first visit to Deventer. Her entrance through the south gate will be quite a show. By the way, I am Adriaan, second grade."

"I am Erasmus, seventh grade."

"Where are you from, Erasmus?"

"I was born in Rotterdam, but my parents live in Gouda."

"I am from Utrecht. My full name is Adriaan Florenszoon Boeyens." He did not inquire why his new friend, who was at least a head smaller than he, had not given his full name or why his parents did not live in the town of his birth. Unlike Erasmus, he did not live in a squalid dormitory but in the comfortable Friars House.

As Erasmus and Adriaan reached the south gate, the duchess and her train arrived just outside the city wall. With their three-foot–long trumpets raised toward the sky, musicians played a fanfare to announce the arrival of Mary, Duchess of Burgundy and Guelders, Archduchess of Austria, wife of Maximilian, Archduke of Austria, of the House of Habsburg. Her caparisoned horse was nearly completely covered with a luxurious white cloth that left only its eyes, hooves, and silky black tail exposed. The famous Burgundy Cross, a large red "X," was embroidered on both sides of the otherwise pristine fabric. Just before the duchess rode a courtier, holding up the coat of arms of the House of Burgundy—a black lion on a yellow field, surrounded by six other colorful icons, each representing a territory belonging to the house. The duchess was dressed in a long straight gown, with a short mantle worn as a cape. The fabric of her gown and mantle was blue, green, red, and yellow, richly interwoven with gold and dotted with jewels. She wore a stiff hat with a wide brim and a long white feather that hung down to her left shoulder.

Behind the duchess, her court jester, Simon the Hunchback, rode on a miniature donkey and made all sorts of antics to the delight of the crowd. The left side of his body was dressed entirely in black, the right side in yellow. Next came the duchess' ladies-in-waiting, each wearing a cone-shaped hennin, some higher than others. A few ladies had sheer veils that covered the hennin and flowed behind. A gentle breeze caused them to flutter gracefully. Behind the ladies-in-waiting came untold numbers of noblemen on horses and young squires on foot, dressed in jerkins with cap-like sleeves. They were followed by foot soldiers armed with bows, arrows, and spears; some even carried harquebuses.

Interspersed throughout the procession were musicians with dulcimers, shawms, rauschpfeife, flutes, pipes, zinks, organettos, and viols. The spectators were enthralled by the minstrels, who sang popular songs and played their harps as they went by. It was indeed an impressive show, and the populace was well entertained. The beggars, who always crowded around the gates to the city, showed off their gross deformities and scrambled for the small change thrown to them by some of the noblemen.

"She looks so young," said Erasmus, as he gazed at the resplendit duchess.

"Well, she is," Adriaan replied. "I believe she is only twenty-four, and she is already very powerful. Did you know that they call her Mary the Rich?" He looked ahead. "Here comes her wagon train."

Stretched out as far as the eye could see was a line of heavy wagons pulled by oxen.

"What are those for?" asked Erasmus.

"They contain her household goods. They follow her wherever she goes. But come; I hear the church bell calling us for our midday meal."

"You amaze me, Adriaan. There must be at least a dozen bells in this town, and there are always two or three ringing simultaneously. How do you know which one is ours?"

"How long have you been here?"

"Nearly two years."

"Two years, and you still don't recognize the bells? You will never learn, Erasmus." Adriaan grinned.

"I hope not." Erasmus smiled, and they both laughed.

They could not know that only a year later, the horse on which Mary the Rich was riding would stumble and land on top of the duchess. With her back broken, she would die a few days later.

Not long after, while Erasmus was on an errand in town, he noticed a man struggling with a heavy load of books. There was something familiar about him.

"Excuse me, sir, did you not live in Gouda?" Erasmus asked.

"Yes, I did, young man, but that was five years ago. I now live in Antwerp." The stranger was about fifty years of age. He wore the round hat of a learned man.

"Please allow me to help you carry those books."

"Well, thank you. I can use a hand." The man stooped so that Erasmus could take some books from his back. "I am on my way to the ferry. You lived in Gouda, you said?"

"Yes, I did, sir. My name is Erasmus."

"A Latin name, no less. Do you happen to speak Latin?" asked the stranger as they began to walk.

"Oh yes, sir," Erasmus replied enthusiastically, and he instantly switched to Latin. It didn't take long for the stranger to be impressed with the boy's fluency and zeal.

"Well, now, I happen to have with me a booklet of passages from Virgil. The wife of a prominent Roman put it together in the fourth century, and Jacob Canter, who is a friend of mine from Friesland, edited it for me. You see, I am a printer. My name is Master Gheraert Leeu. Perhaps I will print a book of yours one day, if you become a writer."

The competition between printers was fierce in the Middle Ages, and the printer was always on the lookout for new authors. He showed Erasmus the introductory letter Canter had written on the first page of the booklet. The title page was empty.

"Well, here we are," said Leeu when they arrived at the ferry. "Thank you for your help, young Erasmus. I hope we will meet again."

Young as he was, Erasmus saw an intriguing opportunity. During the frequent dull moments in class, he had taken to writing poems. Mister Leeu spoke highly of his editor; perhaps he would be a useful contact in the future. Erasmus immediately wrote a letter to Canter, a member of a scholarly family in Friesland:

> My most learned James,
> Master Leeu, a charming man, narrated to my eager ears things about you, which greatly increased my regard for you. Your introductory letter to the passages of Virgil so delighted my mind and showed so much eloquence and erudition that, had not Friesland, of all places, been already honored by your birth, no one would imagine that you were born in that barbarous region. Since, dear James, you are not only a man most wonderfully gifted in literary matters, but also a most sincere patron of letters, I ought to ask you first that we entertain for each other a mutual affection. I hope that by an interchange of letters, we may relieve the tedium of absence.
>
> Farewell and please try to esteem *to me in return*.
> Erasmus of Rotterdam

In his zeal, Erasmus did not recognize that the letter was impertinent and rude—he had insulted Canter's birthplace and had addressed him not as a learned elder but by first name—and the wrong one at that—as though he were an old friend. Throughout his life, Erasmus would behave similarly, and then innocently wonder why people became annoyed with him. His effort to ingratiate himself with Canter failed. He never heard back from him and never met Leeu again.

The highlight of Erasmus's years in Deventer came in his third year, when Rector Hegius announced that a famous speaker was coming to the school. He gathered the student body in the St. Lebuin church and, speaking from the pulpit, he declared, "It gives me great honor and pleasure to introduce the man from whom I have learned all I know and what people think I know," thus invoking laughter and enthusiastic applause from the student mass. Hegius held up both arms to quiet them down. "If I may continue, young gentlemen, I bring you that esteemed humanist Rudolphus Agricola."

Agricola, eleven years Hegius's junior, was born in Baflo, a farming village ten miles north of Groningen. He was the son of Henry Huysman, the local priest, who lived with a young unmarried woman. On February 17, 1444, Huysman was elected warden of a college for nuns. Later that day, a messenger came running to him. "You have a son, Father," he announced.

"Good. This is indeed an auspicious day, for it has twice made me a father."

His son grew to become a famous humanist educated at the Universities of Erfurt and Louvain. He enjoyed a reputation as an elegant Latin speaker and superb debater, and he had lectured at the great European universities on humanism, philosophy, and the importance of dialectic over rhetoric. With a subtle wit that he inherited from his father, he had changed his surname to Agricola to remind people of his humble roots in a farming community.

Agricola climbed the steps of the pulpit and briefly surveyed his audience. He nodded to Hegius. "Thank you, Rector, for that not quite accurate introduction. Gentlemen, those who address the people below them from the pulpit above, as I do now, frequently use a great deal of eloquence in their speech and in their gestures to impress their audience with their great knowledge of the Holy Bible and the Scriptures. Their rhetoric rarely fails to awe the audience and the people leave their churches thanking the preachers for their beautiful sermons and for raising important questions. Rare is the person who notices that the preachers do not give answers to the questions. Not that rhetoric in itself is not entirely without value; however, it misses the dialectic, which adds logic to all ideas. I urge you not to accept new ideas or the long-accepted facts coming from the pulpit without asking questions and expecting to receive logical answers. When the doctrine does not satisfy you, let there be a debate between reasonable people, in which, a scholarly argument has a prominent place."

At the end of his speech, he reminded the students that their school in Deventer was one of the three most influential humanistic schools in Europe. When he was finished, the students remained silent for a moment before erupting in a heartfelt ovation.

Afterward, Hegius and Agricola had lunch together, accompanied by a few lucky students of the first grade, who were privileged enough to having been invited. Among them was Adriaan, Erasmus's friend. Remarkably, Erasmus also was invited, even though he was still in the sixth grade, for he stood out among the students for his remarkable memory and the purity of his Latin in speech and writing. When someone asked the famous guest why he had never accepted one of the many prominent positions offered to him, Agricola responded that such a situation would tie him down. "I need my freedom to do what I do best," he explained.

Meeting Agricola in person made a lasting impression on Erasmus. Years later, he wrote to the publisher Matthias Schürer, "Whenever I read anything Agricola wrote, I feel fresh admiration and affection for that inspiring and soaring mime." He would never forget Agricola's assertion that he needed freedom to do what he did best. It would be a mantra to which he returned again and again throughout his life.

In September 1483, the plague came to Deventer. Although Erasmus was spared, Margaret was not as fortunate. She developed a high fever and chest pain, two ominous signs. Erasmus wanted to go to her bedside but was kept from it—the door to their room was locked. He never saw his mother again. She died three days later and was buried in a mass grave with other victims, away from the church graveyard. Word was sent to Father Gerard in Gouda; the rector of St. Lebuin called Erasmus to his office a few weeks later.

"I have a letter from your father," said Hegius. He looked at the young man before him—seventeen years old, poorly dressed, thin as a rod, and barely five foot three inches tall. Once again, the boy's face impressed him—hollow cheeks, long pointed nose, wide mouth, and blue eyes—but Hegius noticed that the usual twinkle in the eyes and little smile were missing. "Your father wants you to come home, Erasmus."

"My *father*, sir?" His eyes opened wide, and his lips parted in surprise.

"Yes, Erasmus, your father. Does that surprise you so much?"

"No, sir. Only … yes, sir. You are the first person to ever say 'your father' to me."

"You mean because he is a priest?"

"Yes, sir." But the boy, who always was so sure of himself, no longer was.

"Erasmus, your father calls you his son in this letter." When his young charge did not respond, Hegius felt an intense wave of pity. "He never called you his son to your face, did he?" he asked softly.

"No, sir." After a short pause, he added bravely, "But that does not matter."

"Yes, it does matter, and I am glad you told me this," Hegius responded fervently. "Listen, Erasmus, the Church forbids a priest to recognize a boy or a girl as his child, yet your father did so in this letter. That took a lot of courage. Canon 21 absolutely forbids priests to contract marriage, and when a priest fathers a child, the Church forbids him to accept that child as his. Of course, that does not stop priests from having children—several popes were fathered by bishops and more than a few had children of their own. Erasmus, remember, Canon 21 was created by man, not by God. When God created a man and a woman, He meant them to have children. Keep that in mind when you see your father again. He is a remarkable man, a learned man. There are few people who can translate both Latin and Greek, and he is one of the best. You must be proud of him and of your mother. They must have loved each other very much. Now, go, my son. Go with God's speed."

"Thank you, sir, thank you." The rector noticed that Erasmus was fighting back tears. "Thank you," Erasmus said once more, and he slowly turned and left the office.

On his way to his room, Erasmus thought about what the rector had said, and he realized that Hegius may have crossed the line here and there when discussing the policies of the church. He did not know that Hegius wisely had chosen not to mention that the Church referred to an illegitimate child as a *defectus natalis*.

Father Gerard outlived Margaret by only a few months before the plague took him as well. As Pieter and Erasmus left the burial ceremony in the cemetery, their old schoolmaster, Winckels, approached the boys, now ages twenty and seventeen, and instructed, "Meet me at school tomorrow morning. We have something to settle."

"I wonder what he wants," Erasmus said to Pieter, who merely shrugged his shoulders.

When the boys entered the schoolmaster's office the next day, Winckel, flanked by two other dignified gentlemen, pointed toward two chairs. Before sitting down, Erasmus handed Winckel a piece of paper on which he expressed his desire to study at a university Winckel glanced at it, looked up, and said, "Father Gerard has asked us to be your guardians and to decide what is best for your future."

"I want to continue my education and write—"

"Well, you can forget that modern stuff they taught you in Deventer," Winckel said, cutting off Erasmus. "Things are different here. Father Gerard left you little to live on, and we think it best for you to go to school at Bois-le-Duc, where you will stay in the Fraterhouse."

Erasmus was stricken, but there was little he could do about it. He had doubts about the veracity of Winckel's words. "I bet you that Father Gerard left some money for us, and Winckel kept it for himself," he said to his brother as they left the school.

"I don't know," Pieter said meekly. "We may as well do as they say." He had no ambition and was happy as long as he got regular meals and a place to sleep.

"But it is just another school, and I want to go to a university," Erasmus complained.

"How? You can't pay, and what about me? Where would we eat and sleep?" Pieter asked impatiently. He didn't understand why his brother cared so much.

"I don't know," said Erasmus, dejectedly.

Bois-le-Duc (Forest of the Duke), or *s'Hertogenbosch* in Dutch, was a town forty miles southeast of Gouda. It was founded by Henry I, Duke of Brabant, in 1185. The school there was governed by the bishop of Utrecht and was a far cry from the St. Lebuin School in Deventer. Most of the teaching monks had little more than a grade-school education, and many did not even possess that much. They were coarse and always ready to chastise their pupils, especially Erasmus, who knew so much more than they did. Their goal seemed to be to mold their wards into docile monks who would never question authority.

After two years of drudgery, a plague epidemic caused the two brothers, now grown men, to return to Gouda, where they were not welcomed warmly by Winckel or his brother, who had become another guardian. The two men leaned heavily on Pieter and Erasmus to enter a monastery. That was good enough for Pieter, and he entered the monastery of Sion, near Delft. Erasmus, sick with a fever, was too weak to resist their persuasion for very long, and after talking to a former fellow student from Deventer who was enthusiastic about his own life as a monk, Erasmus entered the St. Gregory monastery at Steyn as an Augustinian canon. Fortunately, Winckel gave him permission to take the books left to him by his father.

2

---◈---

Luther—Early Years

1483–1505

Born Martin Luder - Hobgoblins and Witchcraft - School years - Promises to study law - Changes name to Luther - Vow to St. Anne - Rejected by his father - Enters the Black Cloister

On Wednesday, November 10, 1483, Hans Luder slowly trudged home through the narrow streets of Eisleben, Germany. Up ahead, a mangy dog sat in the middle of the street, scratching himself with one of his hind legs. The mutt slowly turned its head around as Hans approached and gazed at him unconcernedly before getting up. The dog tilted its head way back, yawned, and stretched leisurely before disappearing between two houses into a narrow alley. It was cold, almost dark, and a steady drizzle made Hans as wet as the dog.

Hans had hoped this would be the day that his wife, who was overdue, would finally give birth to their first child, but there had been no message for him at the coal mine where he worked as a foreman. He lifted the door latch of his two-room house and entered. While shaking off his wet coat, he did not notice a sturdy woman, holding a bucket of water and looking at him. A single candle lit the room.

"You must be Master Luder," she said.

He turned around, startled. "Yes, I am. And who are you?"

"I am Gretha, the midwife. Your wife is having her baby."

"Well, it's about time. How is she?"

"She is a strong woman, Master Luder, and everything is fine. You just stay out of the way and let us women do our jobs."

Hans lumbered wearily into the alcove that served as a kitchen, cut a piece of bread from a stale loaf, sliced some cheese, and poured himself a mug of milk. He ate quietly in the corner of the dimly lit room and waited, listening to the activity in the next room and hearing his wife moan now and then. It was close to midnight when the midwife woke him.

"You have a baby boy, Master Luder, and your wife is fine," she said matter-of-factly. "The baby looks healthy enough, so I did not baptize him. I'll be on my way now and be back in the morn."

Hans got up from his chair and peeked around the bedroom door. A tired but happy Margarethe looked up. "Come in, Hans, and have a look at your son," she said, smiling.

"There is not much to look at," he muttered when he saw the swaddled baby. "Thank you for giving me a son."

The incidence of infant deaths was nearly 60 percent at the time, so Hans took his son to the Church of St. Peter and St. Paul the very next morning to wash away his original sin through baptism.

"What did you name our baby?" his wife asked when he returned.

"I had him named Martin."

"That's a good name. But why? Nobody in our family has that name."

"The priest said that it is St. Martin's Day," he said simply.

Margarethe Luder, born Lindemann, was from a well-educated family of doctors, lawyers, and councilmen. Her family initially frowned upon her marriage to Hans, who was uneducated and came from farmer's stock. However, Hans was a hard worker and did not remain in the coal mines for long. A year after Martin was born, Hans moved his family seven miles north to Mansfeld, where he could make a better living working in the copper mines. Eventually, he was promoted to overseer of a foundry, and by 1491, he had saved enough money to lease a smelter, with the help of his wife's family. Her family also guaranteed a line of credit so Hans could lease one of the copper mines belonging to the Count of Mansfeld. As Hans's business prospered, his family continued to grow. Over the years,

Margarethe delivered eight more children, although only Martin and three daughters reached adulthood.

The couple lived in the duchy of Saxony, the farming and mining country of hard-working, uneducated people who believed in demons, sorcery, witches, and evil spirits. The common folk understood the pagan legends about hobgoblins, witchcraft, werewolves, and black magic. Deep down in the mines, gloomy conversations centered on the bad things that could befall a person through sorcery and witchcraft. Even Margarethe, who came from an educated family, was a firm believer in evil spirits. She lived in constant fear of her neighbor, whom the townspeople believed was a witch. Everybody knew that the old woman could cast a spell over children.

Although they believed in witchcraft, the common people were also Christians and attended church regularly. The church used the simple concepts of hell and heaven to bring the people to the sacraments. With the devil, there was hell and fear. With God, there was heaven and salvation. Both places were vividly depicted in the numerous woodcut prints and paintings sold at any of the many stalls alongside the church. One popular woodcut showed Christ on Judgment Day, sitting on His throne, surrounded by saints and angels. Below Him stretched a field of open graves. Angels tenderly helped the saved from their graves and guided them to heaven. Elsewhere, the devil's assistants dragged the doomed by their hair and threw them into the gruesome fires of hell.[5] These images were more than enough to scare the strongest of hearts.

The common people had little further understanding of their own religion. At church, they stood through mass in the long, narrow nave, far from the altar. Most could not hear the priest, but even those who could hear did not understand him, for he spoke in Latin. Common people did not own Bibles, nor could they read the Latin texts, so the Gospels remained largely unknown to them.

Margarethe Luder was a firm believer in heaven and hell. She often told her children convincing stories of the demons and the devil by the flickering candlelight in the darkened room. "Do you hear that sound?" she would whisper, and the children would cower, believing the devil was

---

[5] The woodcuts were crude copies of a 1480 cartographic scene by Hartmann Schedel, but the common people did not know that.

near. Disasters, small and large, were all believed to be the work of Satan. Belief in the devil stayed with Martin throughout his life. Years later, while living in the monastery of Wittenberg, Martin wrote, "I was sitting in the refectory going over my notes when the devil came and thudded around in the storage chamber as if he was dragging a bushel behind him. When the noise did not stop, I gathered my books and went to bed. Even then, I heard the thumping in the room above mine. It must have been Satan, so I rolled over and went to sleep, but I should have called him out with, 'I have been baptized, I am a Christian,' because that drives the Devil away for sure."

Martin grew up to be a headstrong youngster who was at times as stubborn as a mule, earning the occasional smacking from his parents. The master of the Latin school also frequently applied the rod to the boy. Martin was smart and a good enough student, but he was often involved in fights to defend his family name. *Luder* was the epithet of a bad woman, a slut. For a boy to be called a "Luder" was the worst possible insult. The other boys frequently taunted Martin, "Luder, Luder, Martin is a Luder," which, of course, led to fistfights and the teacher's rod.

Hans prospered in the copper mine business and had high hopes for his son; he wanted him to have a good education and eventually go to law school. In 1497, he sent fourteen-year-old Martin to a Catholic school in Magdeburg, where the Brotherhood of the Common Life maintained a hostel for young students. The brothers housed and supervised Martin and the other students who came from far away to attend the respected school. Gerard Groote would have been well pleased with the brethren in Magdeburg. Martin was inevitably exposed to Groote's *Devotio Moderna* while living in the hostel, and he read the writings of the brilliant Gerald Zerbolt about canon law and moral theology.

While in Magdeburg, Martin once saw a frail man in a friar's cowl begging for food. He was bent over and carried a heavy bag, while his companion carried nothing. The friar was pathetically thin—just skin and bones. Not long thereafter, the pitiful ascetic died. Martin later learned that the mendicant friar was Prince Wilhelm of Anhalt-Zerbst, who had been deceived into believing that his extreme deprivations would please God. Martin pitied the man. Somehow, he knew that the friar was wrong in his belief. A forgiving God would not be pleased.

After a year in the brotherhood hostel, Martin moved to a school in Eisenach, where, like so many other students, he sang in the boys choir as well as in a street choir, hoping for a handout. The matriarch of the Schalbe family saw Martin in a choir performance and recognized him as a relation of the Lindemann family. She convinced her son Heinrich, who was a good friend of the Lindemanns, to offer Martin room and board in exchange for tutoring his young son Kaspar and bringing him safely to and from St. George School. Martin readily accepted this arrangement, thereby saving his father from having to support him. He was also fortunate to develop a close friendship with Johannes Braun, the old vicar at the church of St. Mary. Eisenach was a good seventy miles from home, and Martin rarely saw his parents. In Braun, he found a mentor, whom he fondly called his "dear fatherly friend."

"Martin, I want you to study law," Hans instructed when his son was eighteen years old.

"Why, Father?"

"There are doctors and lawyers in your mother's family, and I want you to gain similar status in life."

"I will do as you wish, Father," said Martin, ever the obedient son. "But then I must change my surname."

Hans was flabbergasted. "Change the family name? Are you out of your mind?"

"No, Father, I am not. Our name gave me a lot of trouble with the other boys in school. Everyone knows that the word *luder* means a despicable, no-good woman."

"So what? That doesn't give you the right to change it," his father quickly retorted, visibly annoyed. "Son, that name was good enough for our family for many generations, and it is good enough for you. I won't hear of changing it."

But Martin did not give up. He remained calm and did not raise his voice. "Father, can you imagine a lawyer hanging a shingle outside the door of his office with that name on it? He'll never get clients when they see the name *Luder*."

Hans scratched his head and leaned back, thinking. "Well, I must admit, it is not a good name for a lawyer. All right. What do you suggest, son?"

"We could add an H and turn it into Ludher."

"But that still sounds the same when you pronounce it."

"What if we replace the D with a T? That would make it Luther."

"Martin Luther. Yes, I like that; it has a nice ring to it."

"And Father, I would like study at the University at Erfurt."

"Erfurt? Why Erfurt? That's sixty miles away."

"That is where Father Braun studied. He speaks highly of it."

"Then Erfurt it shall be, son," said Hans proudly. His son was going to university—that was a first in his family.[6]

Martin studied hard and was usually near the top of his university class. In the spring of 1505, he received a master's degree and made his father even more proud. Martin was ready to enter law school. On July 2 of that year, while he was making the long journey on foot from home to Erfurt, he was caught in a sudden, severe thunderstorm. Lightning struck a tree close by, and a terrified Martin fell to his knees on the wet, muddy road. "Help me, St. Anne!" he cried out. "I will become a monk!" St. Anne, the mother of the Virgin Mary, was the patron saint of miners and of people in distress during thunderstorms.

With a heavy heart, Martin told his father what had happened.

"So, you called for St. Anne's protection, just as we all do in the fields and the mines. It happens every day." Hans did not understand why Martin was making such a big deal of it.

"This is not the same, Father. I made a vow."

"And what do you think we do? You did not make a real vow. You just cried out because you were scared. That is not the same as a well-thought-out vow."

"It was a vow, Father ..."

"No it wasn't, damn it! You just blurted it out like we all do. God grant that it was not an apparition of the devil that startled you. You will go to law school as you promised, and there'll be no more talking."

---

6   Interestingly, when Martin registered at Erfurt, he wrote "Ludher" on the form. The change to "Luther" would come later.

"Father, I made a vow to God, and I will keep it," Martin declared defiantly. "I shall enter the Black Cloister of the Augustinian Hermits as soon as possible."

"And leave your family? Is that why your mother and I slaved so hard? So that you can bury yourself in a cloister? You ungrateful, selfish, no-good … Get out of here. I don't want to see you again."

Martin wanted to say more, but his father had already turned his back to him. Deeply troubled, he left the room. Later that day, he told his mother all that had happened.

"Your father is right, son. He has such high hopes for you. We worked hard and we saved so that you could study, and now you do this to us. You have an obligation to the family to help your father, to obey him."

"I can't, Mother. I made a vow, and I have searched deep in my heart. I must keep my vow."

"Then, go, son. But know that you do not go with my blessing."

Martin did not sleep that night. He tossed and turned, and every time he was close to falling asleep, the image of the storm and him on his knees on the muddy path came back to him. He saw the lightning strike, and he shuddered and again called out to St. Anne. When at last the morning came, he remained firm to his vow and left his home.

With a heavy yet resolved heart, Martin returned to Erfurt to enter a monastery. To the few friends who escorted him to the door of the Black Cloister, he said, "This day you see me and then never again." Martin began his life as a monk on July 17, 1505.

3

---◆◆◆---

The Reluctant Monk

1484–1498

Life in a monastery - Love for fellow monk Servatius - Ordained a priest -
Secretary to a Bishop - James Batt - Lady Anne - Pauper in Paris - Becomes a
tutor - William Blount - First publication

Much to his delight, Erasmus found that the St. Gregory monastery
offered him the academic freedom he had missed in Bois-le-Duc, where
the students were forced to fit into a mold of mediocrity. He also found
a reasonably good library, which included some of the ancient Greek
and Latin texts he had missed during his St. Lebuin days. Among the
many other canons, he made friends with two kindred spirits: his former
schoolmate Willem Hermans of Gouda and Servatius Rogerus from
Rotterdam. He also found a friend in Cornelius Gerard, a monk in the
monastery of nearby Lopsen, who visited St. Gregory whenever he had a
chance. The four friends shared their experiences of monastic life, gave
reports of the books they read, and drank a stein or two of beer together
while they socialized. They also wrote and read poetry, such as the love
poems written by Jean Meschinot, the fifteenth-century French poet. One
of Erasmus's poems of that time reads:

Nec si quot placidis ignea noctibus (Neither as many as the
ardent stars that sparkle)
Scintillant tacito sydera culmine (On silent eminence
through the gentle night)
Nec si quot tepidum flante Favonio (Nor as many roses the
warm spring causes to well up)
Ver suffundit humo rosas (From the earth in the West
wind's breath)
Tot sint ora mihi ... (So many hours would be mine ...)

The friends shared moments of intimacy and eventually developed
strong feelings for one another. When they were temporarily assigned to
another monastery or were traveling the country as assistants to the bishop,
they often sent passionate letters to each other—they lived a poetic dream.
Erasmus was especially attracted to Servatius and wrote several passionate
letters to him.

"I miss you dearly and long for you to return to me. I cannot live
without you; I want to touch you, feel your arm around me, and kiss your
face."

"What do you want from me? Stay away from me," Servatius wrote
back. "What is wrong with you?"

Erasmus was deeply hurt. He did not feel that he had spoken out of
line, as such sentimentality was not uncommon among friends in the
Middle Ages. Alone in his cell, he wept, for he missed his friend dearly.
He did not finish his meals and began to lose weight, noticeably. During
this time, he wrote Servatius a long letter:

Is there something which you take hard ... which makes
life a misery for you. Whence come these sorrowful
downcast eyes, whence this perpetual silence, so unlike
you ...? It is certain then, my Servatius, that there is
something which troubles you ... Why do you hide
your pain from me as if we did not know each other by
this time? I suspect what the matter is: you have not yet
convinced yourself that I love you so much. So I entreat
you by the things sweetest to you in life, by our great

love, if you have any care for your safety, if you want me to live unharmed, not to be at such pains to hide your feelings, but whatever it is, entrust it to my safe ears. I will assist you in every way I can with help or council. But if I cannot provide either, still it will be sweet to rejoice with you, to weep with you, to live and die with you. Farewell, my Servatius, and look after your health.

Servatius did not reply, and Erasmus went through a period of deep soul-searching. He knew that some brothers in the monastery had paired off, and more than once he had seen one leave the cell of another in the middle of the night. The existence of this sexual behavior was common knowledge in the monastery, and the abbot seemed to tolerate it.

"Am I like those brothers?" Erasmus wondered. "Is what I feel for Servatius the same? Is it sexual in nature?"

It took weeks for him to conclude that this was not the case. But he realized that some men might have the wrong impression of him. He was just over five feet tall and spoke with a soft voice, and for the first time, he became aware that he walked with short steps, giving him an almost feminine gait. From then on, he taught himself to extend his stride a bit.

He came to recognize that he had wronged his friend Servatius with his limitless outpouring of emotions and had given cause for a terrible misunderstanding. "I will never again write with such passion," he decided, not knowing that later, the great Thomas More would begin his letters with "My darling Erasmus."

Erasmus would always cherish the friendship among men. He realized that the poetic words that men shared could be expressions of love, and that they often sufficed, in lieu of the love between a man and a woman. He engaged in many fervent friendships that were so common of the Modern Devotion preached by Gerard Groote and the Brethren of the Common Life. The Devotion promoted not only seeking an intimate relationship with Christ through meditation, but also sharing an inward communion with others.

Erasmus turned his attention entirely to the books of classic antiquity, held both in the library at St. Gregory and in the more modest collection he'd inherited from his father. His interest in humanism grew stronger with every volume he read. This set him apart from the other monks, who were devoted solely to the religious duties and the practices of life in the monastery. Erasmus never achieved that level of fervent and strict degree of piety; he spent his time reading and corresponding with friends in letters and poetry. In the long run, however, not even St. Gregory fulfilled him completely.

"I am growing bored of this confining monastic life," he wrote to a friend. "I have read all the books in this library and yearn for more knowledge that only can be found in great universities. I feel imprisoned here and hate the long mealtimes where the discourse is loud and crude. Most of the monks are illiterate and are recruited straight from the farms. Only one or two speak and write Latin; they are the only ones who can read the Vulgate. I long for a chance to leave St. Gregory and, when that chance comes, I will never again go back to monastic life. I must have my freedom back so that I can write what I will and not only what I am permitted to write."

On April 25, 1492, he was ordained a priest by the bishop of Utrecht, David of Burgundy, an illegitimate son of Philip, Duke of Burgundy. Erasmus hoped that his ordination would afford him a chance to leave St. Gregory, and he didn't have to wait long. Opportunity found him when Henry Bergen, bishop of Cambray, came to Utrecht to visit his superior, David of Burgundy. Bergen's family had long worked in the service of the bishops of Utrecht.

"I must congratulate you, Henry, with your appointment as chancellor of the Golden Fleece," said the bishop of Utrecht.

"Thank you, David, for the honor of mentioning it. I do hope to meet our Holy Father when I visit Rome in the near future." He did not add that he hoped to obtain a cardinal's robe while there. His host, however, understood him all too well.

"Oh, you expect to go to Rome? A beautiful city, if I may say so, but I must advise you that fluency in Latin is essential."

Henry realized that his host had just implied that his Latin was less than adequate for a journey to Rome. He bowed slightly and said, "Perhaps a secretary can assist me on my travels."

"That is a good idea. Do you have anyone in mind?"

"No, indeed, I do not. Perhaps Your Excellency can recommend one?" He had the feeling that his host did not welcome being addressed by his first name.

David of Burgundy smiled. "I highly recommend an Augustinian canon called Erasmus, whom I recently ordained. His Latin is excellent, and he is well read. You will find him in St. Gregory in Steyn. My secretary will give you a letter authorizing the young man to leave the monastery."

"I am most grateful for your assistance and will leave at once for Steyn," Henry said graciously, realizing that his colleague would not extend an invitation to stay for lunch.

The general of the Augustinian order readily accepted the bishop of Utrecht's letter and approved a leave of absence for Erasmus. The next morning, the prior of St. Gregory, Nicholas Werner, called Erasmus to his office.

"Our bishop has plans to go Rome, and he has selected you to accompany him on his journey," the prior announced. "I have consented."

Erasmus struggled to conceal his elation. "Does the prior know how long the trip will take?" he asked, curious to know about this new adventure.

"No, but I venture to say that it may last many months. Let me remind you, however, that your home is at St. Gregory. I expect you to return after the bishop no longer requires your service," Werner asserted sternly. "And you are to wear your canon's dress at all times."

Early the next morning as he left the monastery, Erasmus was met at the gate by Prior Werner and a young monk whom Erasmus had never seen before.

"This is Francis Theoderik. He will accompany you and be of service to you at all times. Farewell, and return in good health."

A few months later, Erasmus received a letter from his friend Willem Hermans, in which Willem expressed his disappointment at not being chosen to accompany Erasmus. "I begged the prior, but he refused and instead gave you Theoderik. He is not too smart, but he will be useful in domestic matters, and he is a good cook."

Erasmus's elation at being free from St. Gregory gradually turned to disappointment and frustration as he realized that the bishop's trip to

Rome was by no means finalized. First weeks and then months went by as the bishop and his secretary waited for approval to visit the pope to come from above. Possibly, David of Burgundy had something to do with that, but whatever the reason, approval was not forthcoming. In the meantime, Bishop Henry became restless and constantly moved between his many residences. Erasmus quickly became bored with his mundane duties as secretary to a man who did not need one.

Relief came only when the bishop visited the monastery in Groenendael, a suburb of Brussels. There, Erasmus found a library well stocked with the works of St. Augustine (354–430), and he read them day and night.

"You know, our monastery also houses the mystical treatises by Jan van Ruysbroeck, one of our former priors," one of the older monks informed Erasmus one afternoon.

"Yes, I do know. Thank you for reminding me." He was too involved with St. Augustine to waste his time with a local hero.

The old man was clearly disappointed. "But I do not see you reading any of it."

"Esteemed brother, I never know when the bishop will leave. I have little time, and right now, my interest lies with the classics. Where else will I have a chance to read the books of St. Augustine?"

"I understand." The old man appeared taken aback by Erasmus's neglect of their treasure. "Perhaps we concentrate a bit too much on Ruysbroeck. But you must realize that he had a great influence on the religious practices in Belgium and Holland."

"Forgive me, Brother, that I do not have more time," Erasmus replied, hoping to appease the old monk's wounded pride. "However, I look forward to another visit to Groenendael soon, when I will honor the great man."

After he finished reading the treaties of Augustine, Erasmus was torn between his loyalty to the great religious icon and what Augustine had published during the last decade of his life. Before adopting Catholicism at the age of thirty-three, Augustine had a mistress for fourteen years who bore him a son. At thirty-seven, he became a priest and lived nearly all of the remainder of his life in North Africa, far removed from Rome, at a time when the Church was wobbling on its foundations. During the last years of his life, he went to the extreme of declaring in his treatises that, without God's help, the will of man is impotent and the vast majority of mankind would be eternally punished by an omnipotent God. Only the souls of a chosen few would be saved for eternity in the kingdom of heaven. He did not predict where his own soul would go.

As an Augustinian monk, Erasmus was greatly disturbed by these last two dogmas, especially because, through his extensive writing, Augustine, who eventually attained sainthood, had such an enormous influence on the formation of Christianity. Several questions came to Erasmus's mind. Had not Augustine severely critiqued his own earlier writings, and did he not continue to be his own critic during the rest of his life? Had he not searched and never found conclusive answers? If he had lived longer, would he have retracted his extreme stances?

"Erasmus, we are leaving early tomorrow morning," Bishop Henry announced abruptly at the evening meal one day. "You had better start packing."

"May I ask where we are going, sir?"

"To my country home in Halsteren. You will enjoy it there. It is my favorite house, and it has a beautiful new church. It was finished thirty-seven years ago."

"Where is Halsteren?" Erasmus asked.

"Just outside Bergen op Zoom, about six hours on horseback north of Antwerp. You can invite some of your old friends to visit while we are there."

When they arrived the following afternoon, Erasmus, who hated the confining monastery walls, was delighted to see that the large, well-kept garden of the huge country home looked out on the Eastern Schelde River. He befriended the local schoolmaster, Jacob Batt; the town doctor, Joost van Schoonhoven; and the burgomaster of Bergen, and the four met frequently in the castle. Erasmus was especially pleased when his old friend Willem Hermans showed up at the house one day.

"Willem, dear, how delightful to see you again," he exclaimed, rising to greet his friend.

"My dearest Erasmus, when I heard that you were in Halsteren, I took the first opportunity to rush over and embrace you. How have you been? Oh, how I envy your travels. If only I could have joined you."

"Well, why not join me now? A group of four of us meets almost every evening. Why don't you come?"

When Willem arrived that night, Erasmus introduced him to the other three and explained to Willem that during each get-together, one of the friends gave a presentation, which was followed by a discussion. The discussions were fueled with the aid of good wine that flowed generously from the bishop's cellar. That night, James Batt gave a speech in defense of literature as an important tool for learning.

"I don't think it is necessary for me to give an introduction in front of such learned friends," he declared. "With you considerate, attentive, and sympathetic listeners, I can already claim victory. But do not expect magnificent oratory from Batt or that will you be entertained."

"Excuse me; can we interrupt you during your presentation?" Erasmus asked.

"Certainly, interrupt me as often as you like. We are not speaking by the clock."

"I just thought that you were well on your way with an introduction."

"Erasmus, that is just like you," Batt came back at him. "You have all those subtle rhetorical tricks, of which I have none. Let me continue by saying that there is a new attack on the old way of learning by people who want to destroy the Republic of Letters. The enemy is made up of three groups. The first group consists of uncouth people who detest all literature. The second group accepts study as a means of learning, as long as it does not include the humanities, which we all know are essential. They hate humanists more than snakes. The people of the third group admire and approve all kinds of literature, as long as they themselves are considered the finest orators and poets. It is this last group that is the most harmful, because these people are so full of their own importance and are such zealots that they have appointed themselves the jury of what constitutes high-class literature—namely, their own."

"I will make use of your permission to interrupt you," said Joost. "You show yourself quite a skirmisher. I think you are rightly called Batt."

"What do you mean?" asked the burgomaster.

"Well, he has listed the tricks of the barbarians so well that I almost think that he is a transformation from that legendary stone."

"Refresh my memory," said Willem. "What was that myth about again?"

"Oh, according to Greek mythology, Battus was tending his sheep when he saw Hermes stealing cattle from Apollo. He promised to keep his mouth shut, but he told others anyway. So Hermes then turned him into stone."

"And you cleverly made use of poor Battus," Erasmus said with a laugh, delighted with his friend's quick wit.

"Actually, Joost is right," Batt replied. "I do challenge these people by showing their own stupidity and ignorance, and that will rouse their rage, just as Hermes became angry." He concluded his lecture by encouraging his friends to study the literature of the pagans and to separate good books from the bad. After the discussion, the five friends drank more wine. It was then that the burgomaster and Batt extolled the hospitality of the Lady of Veere.

"You must meet her, Erasmus. She is not only charming, but she is also wealthy, and she may be able to help you if she takes a liking to you," encouraged Batt.

"Her family is from Borssele on the island of Walcheren, and the town of Veere is part of the Borssele domain," said the burgomaster. "She is married to Philip, one of the many lesser members of the House of Burgundy. He is quite a bit older than she is."

"They usually reside in Tournehem, but right now they are in Veere," continued Batt. "We can pay our compliments tomorrow."

"I look forward to it," replied Erasmus. "And Jacob, your talk gave me food for thought. Thank you. I am thinking of writing a book about the enemies of pre-Christian literature, the barbarians, as you called them. I may call it *Antibarbari*."

The next day, they arrived at the castle in Veere after an eight-hour ride, and Erasmus could barely climb off his horse. He and Batt shuffled bow-legged to a small door within the massive outer doors of the castle wall, and an attendant led them into the great room, where a young woman was seated next to a window.

"This is a pleasant surprise, Master Batt," she said as she touched his hand. "And who is your friend?"

"Lady Anna, may I introduce Father Erasmus?"

The lady looked at the Augustinian monk and smiled. "Welcome to Veere, Father. From where did you two gentlemen come?"

"From Halsteren, my lady," said Batt. "Father Erasmus is the secretary of the bishop of Cambray. He is also, I may add, an accomplished poet."

"Then I look forward to hearing you recite, Father." She pulled a cord behind her, and a servant entered almost instantly. "You must be tired. Joseph will show you to your room. The evening meal will be served at the fifth bell. I look forward to seeing you then."

In their bedroom, Erasmus exclaimed, "Lady Anna is beautiful, the most beautiful woman I have ever seen."

"We all think so!" Batt said with a laugh.

When they entered the dining area, Erasmus was amazed at the sumptuous feast laid out before him. Mountains of pheasant, rabbit, deer, fish and shellfish, cheese, and fruit—enough to feed dozens of people— were piled on the long, wooden table. At one end, places were set for four diners, each with a tankard of beer on one side of the plate and a goblet of wine on the other. With a graceful wave of her hand, Lady Anna invited her guests to take their seats on one side of the table while she sat opposite them. The chair at the head of the table remained empty. They proceeded to dine while a musician softly plucked the strings of his zither at the other end of the large room.

All at once, a man sauntered in, sat at the chair at the head of the table, and began to eat and drink. "Good day, Batt," he said without looking up. "And who are you?" he inquired, pointing at Erasmus.

"This is Father Erasmus," said Lady Anna, "He is the secretary to Bishop Henry."

"Can he talk for himself?" With that rude remark, the man left the table. At the door, he abruptly turned around. "I want to see you before you leave," he said, pointing at Erasmus once more.

Early the next morning, their horses were saddled for the long trip back to Halsteren. Batt was ready to depart, but Erasmus had left to meet with the duke.

"I understand from the bishop that you are talented in languages," Duke Philip said haughtily. "I want you to translate this stuff into Dutch." He handed Erasmus a stack of papers. "When you are finished, return it to me by messenger." He turned and left abruptly, without mention of remuneration.

"That duke is one nasty individual," Erasmus said after he and Batt had left the castle.

"Would you believe that he behaved better than I have ever seen him before?" asked Batt. "Wait until he acts really tough. He'll scream his lungs out."

Eight months after Erasmus entered Bishop Henry's employ, it became apparent that the bishop would never to travel to Rome and that Erasmus's services as a Latin tutor were no longer needed. Upon dismissing him, the bishop inquired, "Will it be back to Steyn for you?"

"I had hoped not, sir, but I am afraid that I have no other place to go."

"Have you given any thought to going to Paris to continue your studies?"

"Oh, I would love to go there, but will the monastery permit it?"

"Father, you have served me well, and you have been faithful," replied Henry, kindly. "I will straighten out that matter with the abbot and provide you a stipend for a while."

"I am so grateful to Your Grace, and I will pray for you to our good Lord," exclaimed a relieved Erasmus.

"Before you leave, see Jacob Batt. He studied in Paris, and he can give you good advice," said Henry, pleased to see Erasmus's obvious enthusiasm. "I want you to go to the Collège de Montaigu. The rector there is Jan Standock, who, just like you, went to a school of the Brethren of the Common Life. He will help you. Here is a letter of introduction. Farewell, Brother Erasmus."

Erasmus gratefully took the letter. On the way to his room, he realized how lucky he was to have been assigned to the service of the bishop. During his time working as a secretary, he had gained a much clearer understanding of the power of the Church, of the clergy, and of the monks.

With his newly acquired worldly knowledge, Erasmus entered Paris on foot in 1495, carrying his meager belongings in a bag over his shoulder. Included were the many pages of *Antibarbari* he had already written. He was nearly thirty years old and as poor as a church mouse. He was dressed in his Augustinian monk garb—a black ankle-long habit with a cowl and a simple rope belt, which unraveled at the ends. His habit was covered with food stains and was faded gray from years of exposure to the sun and dust. His sandals were so worn out and filthy that he should have thrown them away long ago. He was small and thin, with long dirty hair, yet he almost constantly wore a nearly imperceptible smile. His eyes were bright and inquisitive, not those of a beaten man. Thus, he entered the office of Jan Standock, a fellow Dutchman and the current master of the Collège de Montaigu of the University of Paris.

Seeing a poor monk standing before him was nothing new to the rector. He, too, had come from a humble family; his father had been a cobbler with a large brood of children. He was used to the meager meals and the cold dormitories at school. Strict, austere habits had been bred into him from a young age and remained with him throughout his life. He had worked his way through the Universities of Louvain and Paris, and he liked to emulate the draconian policies of St. Francis of Paola, who had visited the college in May 1483. Upon his appointment as the new dean of the college, Standock immediately instituted a regime of strict discipline, which included the requirement that students be informers and report each others' behavior to the school authorities. Physical punishment was severe and frequent. When he was promoted to rector in December 1485, the students protested but to no avail.

Standock read Erasmus's letter of introduction.

"I went to the school of the Brethren of the Common Life in Gouda. You are from Gouda, so why did you go to school in Deventer?" he asked with a frown.

The existence of the school in Gouda was news to Erasmus, and the question took him completely off guard. He stood there, bewildered, wondering why his father had broken up his family by sending him to school in Deventer. Standock looked at the disheveled figure before him, read the letter again, and made up his mind.

"Although you won't be a student here, you can stay in our home for the poor students and eat and sleep with them. Since you are already a priest, you are free to leave to go to other parts of the university, but you must return before nightfall. Wash your habit; it is disgusting. Go."

The home, which the students referred to as *domus pauperum* (pauper's house), was filthy. The straw mattresses were lumpy and saggy, and there was no fireplace. Meals consisted of one piece of stale bread per day, which the students had to supplement by scrounging for leftover food at the door of a nearby monastery, although that usually was still not enough to quell their hunger. The drinking water was often contaminated, and students were frequently ill. A fair number died and were buried in a small churchyard adjoining the college. The citizens of Paris referred to these sickly, emaciated students as *les pauvres capettes de Montaigu* (the poor capes of Montaigu), referring to the dark rose-colored cowls they were required to wear.

"How am I supposed to survive?" Erasmus wondered after being at the school for a week. The almost daily thrashings of students who were guilty of the slightest infractions turned his already weak stomach. Despite these horrible conditions, however, the college had an excellent academic reputation, and Standock was famous throughout the western European countries.

In addition to the harrowing experiences inside the college, Erasmus also encountered one in the outside world. He wanted to be proper in this new country, and so he wore a white linen scapular over his habit, as he had seen French priests do in smaller towns during his trip from Holland. One day, he saw a noisy crowd armed with sticks and stones coming down the street toward him, and he wondered what was going on. "Kill the dog!" they yelled. Not knowing the French language, Erasmus did not understand what the rushing mob was chanting. He looked around and, seeing no one behind him, suddenly realized that the mob was after him. All at once, a door behind him flung open, and a well-dressed young man pulled Erasmus inside. The crowd surged past.

"Let me tell you something," said the young man. "If you value your life, you had better take that scapular off and hide it."

"But why?" Erasmus asked incredulously. "I don't understand. It is very common for priests to wear scapulars."

"That may well be, but some doctors wear a white cloth over their shoulders to warn people to avoid them because they've been treating plague victims."

"You mean they thought I was a plague doctor?"

"Right. And that can be dangerous. People are scared to death of the plague, and they think doctors may spread it."

"Oh, dear God. I can't thank you enough for helping me, young sir. You put yourself at risk. Permit me to introduce myself. I am Father Erasmus."

"My name is William," the man replied. "Now, if you'll please excuse me, I was about to leave for an appointment."

Erasmus had come to Paris to study for a degree in theology. He attended lectures at the Sorbonne, only to find out that the teachers dwelled endlessly on minutiae and constantly quibbled over interpretations of meaningless small points. He quickly classified them as pseudo-scholars who insisted on teaching the doctrines of the early fathers of the church, while rejecting the classics of Cicero and other Greek and Roman philosophers as being poisonous to the brain. He called them "Scotists," after Duns Scotus, a twelfth-century Scottish philosopher who kept theology and philosophy strictly apart in his doctrines. For the remainder of his life, Erasmus despised the Scotists. Years later, in a letter to his friend John Colet, dean of St. Paul's School in London, he referred to them as "an invincible race of men most successful in pleasing themselves."

When Erasmus questioned whether the Hebrews had written the Epistles and whether all of John and the Apocalypse originated with the apostles, the professors universally declared that he was wrong to question the authorship of the Bible. He countered, "Study Greek and Hebrew, and you will find out for yourself what is correct." This somewhat haughty answer found a sarcastic retort from Conrad of Hersbach: "They found a language called Greek, the mother of all heresies … As for Hebrew, it is certain that those who learn it will sooner or later turn into Jews."

While studying at the Sorbonne, Erasmus sought out the company of Parisian humanists, eventually meeting Robert Gaguin, the elderly general of the Order of the Holy Trinity, which was affiliated with the Church of Saint-Mathurin and whose followers were commonly referred to as the Mathurins. Gaguin was the leader of the literary community in Paris, and he had just finished writing a book titled *History of France*. When Erasmus noticed that the last two pages of the printed copy were blank, he seized the opportunity to write a letter of praise to the great author. The printer used it to fill the blank pages and credited Erasmus as Herasmus Roterdam. Those two short pages were enough to spread his name and were the beginning of his fame. They also demonstrated that Erasmus could be an opportunist.

Erasmus quickly learned that the stipend that he received from Bishop Henry did not stretch very far. He had become weary of the inhumane conditions of the *domus pauperum*, and he badly wanted to free himself from living in those quarters. To do so, he needed funds, so he convinced Antoine Denidel, one of the numerous Parisian booksellers and printers, to print his collection of poems, *Carmen de casa natalitia Jesu*. The book was published in January 1496, but despite Denidel's promise to pay Erasmus, he never did; the printer kept the proceeds of the few copies that sold.

Shortly thereafter, Erasmus became ill. He knew that he would not recover in the godforsaken *domus pauperum*, so he left Paris and dragged himself back to Halsteren, where his beneficiary, Bishop Henry, welcomed him back with open arms. He rested in a real bed, ate nutritious meals, and steadily recovered. He went to see his old friends Willem Hermans, Cornelius Gerard, and Jacob Batt, but he avoided Servatius. He told them how disappointed he was with Paris and that he wanted to stay in Holland, but all three were against that plan.

"From what you have told us, you have every right to be disappointed," said Batt. "No wonder, when you lived in such squalid quarters."

"Don't blame all of Paris, Erasmus. You were just in the wrong place. You must try to make some money," added Willem.

"With what?" Erasmus objected. "I have no trade."

"With your brains," said Cornelius. "Of all of us, you are the smartest by far, so teach and get some well-paying students. There must be many in a city like Paris," he added encouragingly.

"Yes, of course, and through them and their parents, you will make some good contacts," Jacob joined in. "I'll explain your situation to the Lady of Veere and ask her for some money to tide you over for a few weeks after your return. That'll give you a chance to attract enough students."

His friends were much more enthusiastic than he was about returning to Paris, but together, they persuaded him follow their advice.

"Can you do me a favor?" Willem asked Erasmus the night before he left. "I have here a letter for Gaguin and collection of poems that I have dedicated to him. Can you give it to him and see what he thinks of it?"

"Nothing will give me greater pleasure, Willem," Erasmus replied. "And now, my friends, shall we share a last bottle of wine?"

In Paris, Gaguin briefly scanned a few poems in the collection, read Willem's flattering letter, and took notice of the dedication. Erasmus, too, had added a poem dedicated to the great man, as well as a long letter in which he praised him. Gaguin was struck by its beautiful Latin. He studied Erasmus for a moment. "From your lyrical letter, I can see that you are a scholar. My friendship is at your disposal. You know, as an old man, I still appreciate a little flattery. However, do not be so profuse in your praise that it becomes too obvious." He smiled somewhat benevolently at the younger man.

"Thank you, sir," said Erasmus, blushing a bit at the master's insight.

"Now, let's see. I suggest you pay a visit to Mr. Guy Marchand, the printer," Gaguin instructed. "Tell him that I sent you."

Upon hearing that he was recommended by the leader of the Parisian literary community, Marchand readily accepted Willem's collection as well as Erasmus's added poem. He didn't pay much for it, but even a little bit helped. With it, Erasmus was able to rent a room not far from the university.

Next, he sought out a new friend in a fellow student, Faustus Andrelini, who, like almost every student, had Latinized his name and was called "Andrelinus." Faustus was a young man of some means who enjoyed the lighter side of life during his studies. He, too, was a humanist who frequently visited Gaguin.

"I need to make some money," Erasmus explained to Faustus. "I left that pigsty Standock calls student housing and have rented a room. Now I need to take on some students to help pay the rent, but I don't know how to go about getting them. Do you have any suggestions?"

"That's simple. Just tack a message on the board next to the door of your room and wait," said his new friend. Erasmus took Faustus's advice and before long, two brothers, Christian and Henry Northoff from the German town of Lübeck, knocked on his door. They were followed by Augustine Vincent Caminade of London, Robert Fisher, and Thomas Grey, who later became the second Marquess of Dorset and one of the richest men in England. And there was one familiar face.

"I remember you. You are William, the one who helped me escape from that rowdy bunch," Erasmus said happily when he saw the young man at his door. "What a nice surprise."

William Blount, who unbeknownst to Erasmus would become the future Lord Mountjoy, smiled. "I see that you no longer wear the scapula."

"Not quite. Now I wear it under my habit, out of view."

Erasmus's young students paid him handsomely for his efforts, which included spicing up the often dull, stiff letters they sent to their families back home. In turn, Erasmus learned to appreciate the *joie de vivre* of the French, the fluency of their language, the languid gestures of their hands as they talked, and their *à demain*—"until tomorrow"—which set the tempo of their lives. He, too, could appreciate a more leisurely existence.

One day, Erasmus was approached by a twenty-year-old English priest who wanted to hire him. He offered Erasmus one hundred gold *scudi* to teach him for one year and a loan of three hundred *scudi*, to be paid back later. It sounded too good to be true, so Erasmus turned to William for advice.

"Do you know Father James Stuart?"

"Yes, I do," Blount replied with a careful tone.

Erasmus told him what Stuart had offered him. "Do you think that it is a legitimate offer?"

Blount remained silent for a while. Finally, he said cautiously, "Before you do, you should know something about the man. His brother is James IV, king of Scotland, and he supports Perkin Warbeck in his claim for our crown."

"I have never heard of Warbeck. Who is he?" Erasmus asked.

"Well, he is about twenty years old, was born in Belgium, and he claims to be the younger son of King Edward IV. Evidently, he looks a little like the king. Margaret of Burgundy supports him in his ridiculous claim. She paid to outfit the small army that Warbeck landed in Kent last year. He was immediately thrown back, of course, but he escaped to Ireland. He tried to take the town of Waterford there, and that was his second mistake. Now he lives in Scotland, where he has the support of King James, who always likes to be a thorn in England's side. As you can imagine, that does not sit well with our king."

"That is some story" Erasmus replied slowly as he tried to absorb the importance of what William had just said. "Is there any basis for Warbeck's claim?"

"Not really," replied William dismissively. "The man is a fraud. Since you asked me, I think you should tread carefully."

"Thank you, William. I will reject Stuart's offer tomorrow," Erasmus assured him. "By the way, where do gold *scudi* come from?"

"They're used in Italy and Sicily."

"Can they be used here in Paris?"

"Father Erasmus, it does not matter where coins come from as long as they are made of silver or of gold. It is the weight of the coins that counts. They can be used in every country, no matter what their origin is."

Because Erasmus's students were likely to play important roles in society, it was necessary that they become fluent in Latin. Erasmus, therefore, wrote short practice exercises intended to be used in social settings, such as greeting friends, family, and important people. He also wrote instructive pieces in how to improve one's manners, including refraining from sneezing, burping, and laughing too loudly during dinner, and how to maintain a conversation with dinner guests. He recommended common phrases, such as "Pleased to meet you," "Thank you for a lovely evening," and "How do you do," as useful tools for maintaining polite relations. The exercises were given in the form of two-person dialogues. Thus, Erasmus, a man who had lived only in poor settings, wrote a book about good manners for use in high society, essentially instructing his social superiors in proper behavior.

"Faustus, do you have any other suggestions of how I can make money?" he asked once again.

"Well, publish or starve, I always say, and you have the capability to publish," his friend replied with a smile.

"That is easier said than done," Erasmus sighed wearily, thinking of the many nights he stayed up, trying to think up another topic for a book.

"Come, come, my dear Erasmus," Faustus replied comfortingly. "Have you not written those little booklets for your students to make the study of Latin easier for them?"

"Yes, but they are for just a few students," Erasmus complained.

"Nonsense. I hear that your students value these exercises enormously. Publish them, my dear fellow."

Erasmus was not convinced. Moreover, he did not possess the confidence to sell himself. Nevertheless, he contacted a fellow Dutchman, Dirck Maertensz, a printer in Leuven who published a limited edition of Erasmus's instructional writings in 1497 and titled them simply *Colloquies* (Conversations).[7] The selection of the colloquies included such pieces of wit and wisdom as:

> The truth is not always to be spoken.
> Popes and bishops have invented too many feast days.
> Christianity has come down to the point where "love thy neighbor" is less important than abstaining from butter and cheese during Lent.
> The costly offerings on the tomb of St. Thomas might better be devoted to the charity dear to the saint.
> Those who never try to imitate St. Francis want to die in his cowl.
> Men's minds are so unsteady that any new dogma, however absurd, will find disciples.
> Those who want to ward off the devil's spirit put their trust in a garment incapable of killing lice.
> Christ should be adored but not while carried around or on horseback in processions.
> There are too many special masses, such as the mass for the foreskin of Christ.

"I have been called back to England," Blount abruptly announced to his friends in September 1497.

---

[7] One copy somehow made its way to Basel, Switzerland, where in November 1518, the famed publisher Johann Froben, a friend of Erasmus's, used it to print an eighty-page book titled *Familliarium colloquiorum formula* ("Prescription for Familiar Conversation"). Initially, Erasmus was annoyed, because he had not given permission for Froben to publish it, nor had he edited the volume. However, the book became an enormous success, and the money he earned from the sale quickly evaporated his annoyance.

"That is rather sudden, isn't it?" said Erasmus. "I hope your family is well."

"Quite well, thank you," William assured him. "But the king has ordered me to serve in the army. That pest Perkin Warbeck is at it again. This time he has landed an army near Land's End in Cornwall, where the rebellious Cornish now call him Richard IV. I must leave posthaste to serve my country."

"Travel safely, my young friend. I do hope that we will meet again," Erasmus said, putting his hand firmly on Blount's broad shoulder.

"We will for certain, Father. I will be back in Paris as soon as this is over."

Blount kept his promise and returned two months later.

"How did you fare in England?" asked Erasmus, happy for his friend's safe return.

"Quite well, thank you," Blount said heartily. "When I arrived in London, General Giles appointed me a lieutenant and gave me a command in his army. We went to Cornwall, where our spies reported that Warbeck had taken the town of Taunton with an army of six thousand. We anticipated a spirited battle, but when we got to within fifteen miles of Taunton, the coward fled, and his army surrendered. We executed the leaders and let the rest go. I thought for sure that Warbeck would flee to Land's End and from there to Scotland, and so did everybody else. Instead, the rascal hid in Beaulieu Abbey close to Southampton, from where he hoped to charter a boat north. But we found him, and he is now safely in the Tower of London." He finished his report with a great deal of satisfaction.

"Well, you had an exciting two months!" exclaimed Erasmus. "Welcome back."

A few days later, Erasmus surprised his friends by informing them that from then on, he wished to be known as Desiderius Erasmus Roterodamus.

"Isn't that a bit long?" asked Christian Northoff. "Where did you get the 'Desiderius'?"

"Is that after St. Desiderius?" Thomas Grey wanted to know.

"Who was that?" still another student inquired.

"He was a bishop somewhere in the south of France in the early seventh century," Thomas explained. "He built several churches and monasteries, and when he died, he left all his possessions to the church."

"That should be enough to make him a saint," Erasmus said dryly.

"I like the choice of Desiderius," said Blount, looking at Erasmus with a twinkle.

Erasmus was grateful that Blount understood. Ever since he had learned of the circumstances of his own birth, Erasmus could not erase the illegitimacy of it from his mind—the fact that his Church regarded him as a *defectus natalis.* On the other hand, he could not forget the words of Master Hegius: "Your father and mother must have loved each other very much." He knew that his own creation was the inevitable outcome of their love and that he was desired in their minds and in the eyes of God. He wanted so badly to belong that he added the Latin *Desiderius* for "desire" to his name, and he then felt more complete.

4

Erasmus Visits England

1499–1502

Visits Lord Mountjoy - Meets Crown Prince Henry - Oxford intellectuals: More, Colet, Wolsey - Rejects a job offer - Loses his savings - Tells Batt to lie for him - Fallout with Servatius - Studies Greek - Jean Vitrier at Saint-Omer

By December 1498, Erasmus had had enough of the University of Paris. His teachers were too narrowly focused for his taste, and he yearned to explore the world outside the university. His friend Jacob Batt invited him to accompany him to Tournehem (Tower on the River Hem) to visit Lady Anna of Veere, who had asked Batt to give private lessons her young children. Erasmus eagerly accepted the invitation, especially since Bishop Henry had given notice that he intended to terminate Erasmus's stipend. Perhaps Lady Anna could be persuaded to become his patron, if only she were not married to such a rude man.

Before he left Paris, he wrote a letter to the Prince Adolph of Veere, Lady Anna's nine-year-old son:

> I believe that intelligent men, who well understood the nature of the universe and human nature, too, could scarcely hope that the lion's proud spirit lurks in every royal breast ... fortune bestowed on you the gift of a lineage

distinguished on both sides by famous ancestors ... on your father's side from Philip, Duke of Burgundy and from your mother's side, the House of Bourbon ... your mother has joined to her womanly sex a man's strong mind ... the invincible prince, your father and that supremely modest and dedicated lady, your mother.

He knew, of course, that this flattering letter to the young boy would reach the Lady of Veere and hoped it would make a good impression. He and Batt departed on horseback in early January 1499, and upon arriving in Tournehem, Erasmus described the journey and his hosts in a letter to his friend William Blount, who was back in Paris.

Dear William,

The god of the wind, Aeolus, beat down upon us with hail, and rain, and wind. After the storm came snow that mixed with water and quickly froze into lumps and sheets of ice ... Our horses crunched through the crust with every step and cut their fetlocks as if with glass. Your friend Erasmus sat bewildered on a steed as astonished as himself and I cursed myself for trusting my life and my learning to a dumb beast. When the castle came in sight, the wind blew furiously. I got off and slid down the frozen slope. Fortunately, we were not in fear of robbers in this ghastly weather. When we reached the castle, of the lady's graciousness I cannot say enough.

Duke Philip joined the party for the evening meal and again maligned himself. He never paid me for my earlier translation service and now he did not bother to thank me. Instead, he treated me as if I were a piece of dirt. I detest the man, but, for the sake of the hostess, I ignored him. However, I have decided never to serve the man again.

Lady Anna's goodness to us was as much beyond what we deserved as the old man's malignity was below it. She loaded me with good offices and offered me a present. I shall soon be in Paris again. Meanwhile, believe that you have no heartier friend than Erasmus.

Farewell, Tournehem, January 1499

William Blount had been an admirer of Erasmus's ever since their first meeting in 1496. Blount quickly learned that the small Dutchman was not only a superb teacher of Latin but also possessed an unsurpassed memory. He never saw Erasmus angry, although when someone annoyed him, Erasmus could cut down the offending person with just a few choice words. When Blount read the letter, he devised a plan.

"You have to get away from your miserable existence here in Paris and come with me to England," he proposed to Erasmus upon his return from Tournehem. "I will introduce you to the splendid minds at Oxford and Cambridge."

Erasmus did not need much persuasion. He'd had his fill of Paris and had no intention of going back to St. Gregory's monastery in Steyn. "When can we go?" he asked eagerly.

William smiled. "Is tomorrow soon enough? My servants will assist you with packing your books and belongings, and we will be on our way early in the morning."

Four days later, their chartered boat glided around a bend in the River Thames, and Erasmus saw a magnificent mansion with lovely gardens spread along the south bank. Several servants rushed down the lawn toward the dock, followed by a distinguished-looking gentleman, whom Erasmus took to be William's father. He was surprised to see the gentleman bow to William and say, "Welcome home, Master William."

"Thank you, Bates. It is good to be back. This is Father Erasmus, a very special guest. Take good care of him."

The man turned to Erasmus with a measured bow. "Welcome to England, Father." Erasmus quickly surmised that the gentleman was the butler of the enormous estate.

A young lady dashed down the lawn toward them, hitching up her skirts as she ran. She threw herself into William's arms and kissed him ardently. Eventually, William managed to free himself from her arms and turn her attention toward his friend. "Elizabeth, this is Father Erasmus. Father, this wild creature is my wife, Lady Blount."

She brushed her hair from her eyes, blushed, and curtsied slightly. "Forgive me, Father. It has been a long time since I last saw my William."

"My dear lady, your enthusiasm is quite understandable," Erasmus replied kindly. "Knowing your husband, I would not be surprised if you two absconded forthwith."

"But not before you meet my mother," said William, and he waved at a woman who had appeared in one of mansion's several glass doors facing the river.

They walked up the hill, and William warmly embraced his mother. "I would like you to meet my tutor from Paris, Mother. This is Father Erasmus."

The stately yet simply dressed Lady Mountjoy extended her hand and said, "Welcome Father. I have heard much about you from William, and I am grateful to you."

Erasmus felt compelled to bow slightly to the elegant woman, take her hand, and kiss it lightly.

It was Erasmus's first introduction to the lifestyle of the English upper aristocracy. Remarkably, for a poor monk with a habit as his only piece of clothing and not a penny in his pocket, Erasmus adapted to his new surroundings in no time and immensely enjoyed the attendant luxury. He took up hunting, rode an excellent horse instead of a mule or a sagged-back old nag, and openly flirted with the pretty women dressed in their finery. Without hesitation, he adopted the English habit of kissing the ladies and enjoyed it. His amazing ability to learn passable English very quickly made him comfortable in social circles. The English loved his wit, which was always accompanied by his knowing smile. They admired his brilliance, the quickness of his mind and, above all, his sense of humor, which had a Dutch flavor that amused his new friends.

"Father, tomorrow we have been invited to a picnic at the palace. I believe that it is a birthday party," said William as he and Erasmus walked in the garden on the morning of June 27.

"The palace? Does that mean the—"

"Yes, it does, the royal family. Actually, it is not so much a palace; it's more like a royal villa." Erasmus looked down at his only habit. Although it was newly cleaned, he did not feel entirely comfortable for such a visit. William noticed. "Come, it is time for you to dress a bit more appropriately for the occasion. I am sure that your abbot will excuse you for one day."

"You don't know my abbot," Erasmus said with a laugh. "He is stricter than the pope, but let's do it anyway."

"Good. Bates will help you select something. Oh, by the way, we will have a guest this afternoon who I would like you to meet." The guest turned out to be Thomas More, a quiet, reserved scholar who was twenty-two years of age and would become one of Erasmus's dearest friends.

At breakfast the next morning, Erasmus appeared in a simple ankle-long, light grey garment made of the finest linen. Rather than draping his usual scapular over it, he instead wore a dark brown buttonless jacket, its wide sleeves bordered with reddish fur. His ensemble was complemented by a cap made of the same material and fur. His legs were covered in long stockings, and for the first time in his life, he wore real shoes with silver buckles.

"That outfit looks quite becoming on you, Father," said Lady Mountjoy, as a somewhat sheepish Erasmus entered the breakfast room. "That jacket is just the piece to wear at a picnic."

"Thank you, my lady. I must say that after all those years in a habit, I feel quite different. It is rather comfortable, I must say."

"Are we all ready? Then let's go," said William, taking charge of the party.

"Where are the horses and carriage?" asked Erasmus.

"We will be walking."

"Walking?"

"Yes, walking," William repeated and off he strode toward a tree line to the right of the estate. He led the party to a path through the trees and a few minutes later, the woods opened up to a huge lawn and flower garden, with Greenwich Palace standing majestically in its midst. It seemed to Erasmus that all members of the royal household, including many children, had gathered on the lawn. In the center of all the attention stood Prince Henry, the future King Henry VIII, who was celebrating his eighth birthday. His two little sisters played off to the side, while a nurse, carrying a baby boy in her arms, looked on.

"We did not bring any gifts," Erasmus whispered to William.

"Oh, we never do. It is customary—or rather, the wish of the queen—that all gifts be delivered early in the morning."

"But I did not give anything."

"Don't worry; the party came as a surprise to you," William assured his friend.

The Mountjoys appeared quite at home among the royal gathering, and William took his tutor and Thomas More to meet the crown prince. With a graceful sweeping motion, William removed his richly feathered hat, bowed, and said, "Your Royal Highness, may I introduce Father Erasmus? And you may remember Master Thomas More."

"Thank you for coming to my birthday party, Father." The boy looked up at him. "From what country do you come?"

"From Holland, Your Highness. I was born in Rotterdam," Erasmus replied respectfully.

"Ah, yes. Are you a prior?"

"No, Your Highness. I am a simple monk."

"You do not look like a monk," the boy said.

"Father Erasmus is a learned man, Highness," William added. "He has been my tutor—"

"Well, thank you for coming to my party." And with that, the young prince turned to other visitors.

That night, Erasmus, still ashamed that he had not brought a gift, wrote a poem in which he lauded England. He gracefully dedicated it and sent it to the young prince, who sent him a thank-you note in return.

Erasmus continued to write while he was a guest at the Mountjoy house, but toward the end of the summer, he became restless. He did not have access to a good library, and he longed to be back in a place where there was an abundance of study material. William, who, between his frequent trips to London, had kept an eye on his friend and sensed his frustration, decided that it was time to introduce Erasmus to the academic environment of Oxford University. "I want you to meet John Colet," William announced to his friend one afternoon. "He is quite an authority on St. Paul's Epistles. You two should get along well."

John Colet, whose father was the former lord mayor of London, was about Erasmus's age. While visiting Paris and Italy, he had read the works of the Greek philosopher Plato and the Roman philosopher Plotinus. He was knowledgeable in scholasticism, mathematics, law, history, and the English poets, though expert in none. He settled at Oxford, where he first became a deacon and, a year later, a priest. In his lectures on St. Paul, he disregarded the extensive commentary on which other theologians typically focused and instead concentrated on St. Paul the person and on his pure text.

"Father Erasmus, we meet at last," Colet said, when they were introduced during afternoon tea.

"Meet at last? How so, Father?" Erasmus asked incredulously.

"Well, while I was in Paris, I read and admired your letter of praise to the great Gaguin that was printed at the end of his *History of France.* Ever since, I have wanted to meet you."

"You flatter me, sir. I am merely a humble priest and an author who has yet to write anything worthwhile."

Erasmus's humility struck Colet, who regarded him as an equal. Colet looked at his new acquaintance, the smallish young man with a fair complexion and unruly reddish hair. He took notice of the monk's eyes, which were a mixture of blue and gray, and of the small upward folds at the corners of his mouth that gave the impression of a permanent smile. Colet observed that Erasmus's voice was a tad soft, which made the listener pay attention, and his speech was concise, clear, and charming.

Colet was amazed at the incredible memory and breadth of knowledge of his new acquaintance. However, even though he recognized Erasmus's brilliance, Colet noticed that in his writings and speech, Erasmus sometimes tended to touch only the surface of some subjects, without digging further. One day, when they had a disagreement about the origin of Jesus's fear of personal suffering, Colet urged Erasmus to rethink his opinion. "You should delve more deeply into your studies and thought before reaching conclusions," Colet gently urged. Those words, a mixture of encouragement and critique, were not lost on Erasmus, who throughout his life had never feared uncovering the truth. Their disagreement led to an extensive correspondence, which Erasmus finalized in the form of a pamphlet titled *A little disputation concerning the anguish, fear and sadness of Jesus.*

Whereas Colet clearly and vigorously defended his position in his writings and discussions, Erasmus always kept something in reserve.

Although he wrote in elegant Latin with a poetic, sometimes witty slant, he maintained a certain ambiguity that sometimes drove both his friends and enemies mad. They were seldom able to pin down Erasmus on his exact opinion. Erasmus, however, remained careful not to step on the toes of the clergy or the nobility.

In November, Richard Charnock, prior of St. Mary's College, Oxford, who had heard about Erasmus from Colet and wished to meet him, gave a large party in Erasmus's honor. Those assembled included William Grocyn, who, at age sixty-three, was the most senior of the company. He had studied Latin and Greek in Italy for three years and was the first Englishman to teach Greek at Oxford. Also present was Thomas Wolsey, dean of divinity at Magdelan College. Next was William Lily, who had made a pilgrimage to Jerusalem and had traveled to Rome and throughout Italy. Thomas More, the youngest of the company, remained mostly silent; he preferred to listen to the others.

Last but not least was Thomas Linacre, who at age twenty-four had been chosen to accompany King Henry VII's envoy to the court of Pope Innocent VIII. He never reached Rome, however, and instead remained in northern Italy, where he studied the writings of Aristotle, as well as Galen's *Methodus medendi,* a textbook of medicine, which although written in the second century was still in use. At the invitation of a senior doctor in Padua, he once participated brilliantly in a faculty discussion and was awarded a doctorate in medicine on the spot. He did not practice or teach medicine but nevertheless was appointed as a king's physician. He received the priest's orders, was a rector and holder of many clerical benefices, translated Galen into English, and founded the Royal College of Physicians.

Erasmus felt remarkably comfortable in this illustrious company and participated enthusiastically in the animated dinner conversation. However, after dinner, a dispute arose between Erasmus and a late-arriving guest, to whom Erasmus had not been introduced. When the man, who considered himself a theologian and insisted on continuously splitting hairs about minute interpretations of the Bible, became too hot under the collar, Erasmus diplomatically changed the topic. He recounted a fable about Cain, who asked the angel in charge of the vegetable garden in paradise for one ear of corn. The angel refused to give him one. "Look, I am not asking for a forbidden apple," Cain told the angel. "God will not mind your giving one ear." The angel stood firm, with his sword in front of him. Cain continued to sweet-talk the angel until he received his single ear of corn. Planted on earth, the corn grew fabulously, but just before the harvest, God set fire to it.

All except the theologian enjoyed the story. Some wondered whether it was a true fable or an on-the-spot product of Erasmus's imagination. After the party broke up, the guest of honor approached Grocyn. "Sir, I understand that you studied Greek and Latin in Italy."

"True. I was there for three years. However, before I left for Italy, I had already studied some Greek here at Oxford under Vitelli."

"I hope to go to Italy in the not-too-distant future. Perhaps you can recommend a good Greek teacher."

"Well, I really do not know. Vitelli left Oxford, and my first tutor in Padua, Demetrius Chalcondyles, may have died by now. I am quite sure that my other tutor, Politian, is also dead."

"That is too bad, I had hoped—"

"Don't despair, my dear Erasmus. You will find excellent tutors in Padua and Bologna. The best Greek teachers outside of Greece can be found in Italy."

"Thank you, sir." He looked around the room at the assembled learned men and considered himself to be the luckiest man on earth.

It was not the first time that Erasmus had expressed an interest in Greek. A few years earlier, he had written to Antoon van Bergen, abbot of St. Bertin:

> Latin scholarship, however elaborate, is maimed and reduced by half without Greek. A knowledge of Greek is indispensable to the study of the Scriptures … Leading universities should engage persons capable of giving complete instruction in the Hebrew, Greek, and Latin tongues.[8]

---

[8] Eighteen years later, Erasmus would be severely attacked by the theologians at the University of Louvain for his assistance in making that university trilingual.

Toward the end of his visit to England, Erasmus began to show more interest in the study of religious matters. Thus far, he had thought of himself as a poet and a man of worldly letters, but at Oxford, he began to pay more attention to theology. Colet may have played an important part in this conversion. Erasmus noticed that Colet's dissertations about St. Paul's Epistles were based on Colet's own interpretation of a Latin version of the text—the original Epistles were written in Greek, a language Colet could not read. Erasmus also had thus far based his scholarship of the Vulgate entirely on the version translated by Jerome in the late fourth century. The more he thought about it, the more he felt the need to seek knowledge of texts directly from original copies, rather than relying on others' translations. He needed to learn Greek, and for that he planned to take Grocyn's advice and go to Italy.

"Why don't you stay at Oxford as a lecturer and study the Old Testament or the prophet Isaiah?" Colet urged. "Just as I do with the Epistles of Paul."

"John, I understand your interest in Paul, but I would rather concentrate on the New Testament."

"But you gave me the impression that you were interested in teaching and working with me here at Oxford," Colet retorted.

Erasmus realized that his friend was hurt, and he proceeded carefully. "My dearest Colet, I could not possibly do that; I am not qualified. In the words of the Roman playwright Plautus, *that would be like trying to get water from pumice stone.* How can I dare to teach that which I have not learned myself? It was never my aim to interpret the prophet Isaiah or books of the Old Testament, as you recommend. I humbly ask you to forgive me, for it was not my intent to deceive you."

Now it was Colet's turn to notice the dismay in his friend.

"Dear, dear Erasmus, it was the beauty of our friendship and the desire to remain in your company that gave me a false hope. Go, dear friend, and find what you are looking for, but you may never find a permanent place of content, for you are a restless one."

"No one has ever found my weakness and expressed it as well as you, John. Thank you for understanding." He was deeply touched by Colet's love for him.

"By the way, tomorrow there will be a celebration at the shrine for Thomas Becket in Canterbury Cathedral." Colet's voice lightened. "You may be interested."

The next morning, the abbot, surrounded by a large entourage, opened the shrine. Many kneeled, raised their hands to heaven, and showed great reverence. When they began kissing the shoe of a marble statue of the saint, Colet could not restrain himself. "The fools," he muttered derisively.

"What on earth are they doing over there?" Erasmus asked.

"They're probably looking for the statue's handkerchief," Colet said sarcastically. "I cannot abide the impiety of those miserable priests, of whom this age of ours contains a great multitude, who fear not to rush into the arms of some foul harlot in the temple of the church, to the altar of Christ, to the mysteries of God." Colet's disgust increased with each word. "Did you know that concubinage is now used by the bishops in Germany to raise money? They charge a tax of five florins for every child born to a priest, and I have been told that the diocese of Bamberg raised fifteen hundred florins that way."

Colet did not know the circumstances of his guest's birth. Erasmus kept quiet.

Later that day, Colet asked Erasmus about his travel plans.

"I feel that I must visit Italy first and seek a good Greek teacher. Also, I have always been interested in Jerome. Of all Christians, he is the most learned and most eloquent. I intend to go over his early work and perhaps even look into whether his translation of the New Testament needs some revision."

"That is a lofty idea, indeed. Does that mean that you find fault with the Vulgate?"

"Not necessarily. I understand that there is a printer in Venice, Aldus Manutius, who is seeking philosophers and authors who have studied the old languages—Greek, Hebrew, and Latin—and can revisit the old translations of the Bible. I may be interested in that."

"That'll be a large undertaking, my friend, but if one man can do it, it is you."

"Thank you for the compliment, John. If anything comes of it, I'll send you a copy." Erasmus smiled.

"I have a better idea. Gather your material in Italy and come back to England to work on a revision."

"With God's will, I certainly shall."

Before he left England, Erasmus went to say good-bye to William Blount. "I am ever so grateful that you brought me to England, William. I cannot thank you enough for the splendid hospitality that you and your family have given me and for introducing me to the academic world at Oxford." He bowed graciously.

"It was my pleasure, my friend," said William. "You must promise me to come back and stay a longer time, so that I can introduce you to Canterbury as well. Oh, by the way, you remember that scoundrel Perkin Warbeck, the pretender? He managed to escape from the Tower three days ago. They just caught him again, and they're going to hang him tomorrow."

Erasmus did not like the idea of hanging a man, and his face said so. "May God be the judge of his soul," he said softly.

Erasmus retired to the library and penned a quick letter to Faustus Andrelini, who had been his fellow student in Paris.

> To Faustus Andrelini, greetings:
> Your humble servant is now a fair hunter and he can act the courtier with the best of them. If I were you, I would visit Britain as fast as I could; the girls here are divinely handsome, unreserved, and wherever you go, may kiss you for the slightest pretense, like when you are coming, leaving, meeting the first time, and every time thereafter. My dear fellow, you have no idea how delicious their kisses taste and how they enjoy your embrace.
> I will leave for Paris tomorrow morning and look forward seeing you again soon.
>
> Farewell, London, 5 December 1499

Obviously, Erasmus was quite enamored of the English propensity for kissing and had not behaved quite like a man of the cloth during his time in London. That letter, combined with reports of the many evenings that Erasmus spent in Paris with the jolly Andrelini, eventually reached the ear of the bishop of Cambrai and his superiors in Steyn. Consequently, Erasmus received stern admonishments from both.

The next morning, William saw Erasmus off in a fine carriage, pulled by a horse driven by one of his servants. During the sixty-mile trip to Dover, Erasmus had time to reflect on the previous months. He had immensely enjoyed living outside the confines of monastic walls. He loved the company of like-thinking men, enjoyed wearing clothes other than the Augustinian habit and cowl, and delighted in meeting interesting women, especially those who were quite beautiful. He liked eating good food and drinking fine wine. He especially enjoyed writing whatever he wanted to write, without first obtaining the approval from the prior of a monastery. Above all, he enjoyed being free—free to go where he wanted, when he wanted. The world was open to him, and he intended to address that world. He had never really been a monk at heart, although he was faithful to his Church and wanted to study more theology.

He realized that in order to continue leading a monastic-free lifestyle, he needed money. The Lady Veere had given him a small sum, and Henry of Bergen still paid him small amounts, although his regular stipend had dried up. In addition, John Colet had donated a few pounds. From all this, he had saved about twenty pounds, a nice sum that he could use to rent a decent room in Paris. He had no intention of going back to Jan Standock's *domus pauperum* at the Collège de Montaigu.

Seven hours later, the carriage reached the Dover customs house, and William's servant helped Erasmus unload his luggage, which was composed almost entirely of books.

"Well, let's see what we have here," said a heavyset officer.

"Mostly books, I can assure you," replied Erasmus.

"Heavy, aren't they? Anything else? How about gold or silver? You can't take that with you, you know."

"Nothing other than some money."

"Show me, please."

Erasmus opened his purse, displaying the twenty pounds in coins.

"Sorry, I have to confiscate these," said the officer.

"Lord Mountjoy and Master More told me that I could take them with me," Erasmus replied, panicked. "I saved them!"

"Father, the problem is that you have only English money. Last month, King Henry reenacted the law set by the old King Edward. You can take out only foreign coins now."

"What am I going to do without money? I am only a poor monk," Erasmus pleaded.

The officer scratched his three-day beard and looked sympathetically at the little man before him. "You wait here, and I'll see what my boss says."

He went into the station house and after what seemed like an eternity to Erasmus, he finally returned.

"I am sorry, but we can only help you a little bit," the officer apologized. "Here are six angels. They are gold pieces, all right, but together they are not more than one pound. It is the law, you know."

Erasmus fought back tears. "What am I going to do?"

"For what it is worth, you don't have to worry about robbers on the road between Calais and Paris," the officer said half-heartedly.

"Slight solace that is."

The movable-type printing press was invented in the late 1420s by Laurence Janszoon Koster, who held the position of *koster* (sexton) of the famous St. Bavo Church in Haarlem, Holland. Koster printed several books before dying of the plague in 1440. After his death, one of his assistants, Johann Fust, stole the type and the presses, brought them to Mainz, and began a partnership with Johann Gutenberg, who later became famous for printing the first Bible in 1455. Over the next fifty years, printers set up shop all over Europe and anxiously waited for the few authors of importance to submit manuscripts for publication.

It was this explosion of the presses that ultimately saved Erasmus from the poorhouse. He had returned to Paris with barely a penny to his name and had to earn some money quickly if he wanted to keep the two rooms he had rented in the heart of Paris. He could have lobbied for a benefice from a Church, but he feared that would tie him down. Indeed, the archbishop of Canterbury had offered Erasmus a handsome benefice, contingent upon his return to England, but Erasmus politely demurred; he wanted to retain his freedom. Instead, he took in some new pupils, but that was not enough. If he were ever to be successful, he had to write and publish, just as so many other aspiring authors in Paris were trying to do. However, he had no idea what to write.

He had completed much of *Antibarbari* back in 1495, during his time at the St. Gregory monastery in Steyn, but he had lost track of the manuscript. Before going to England, he had left it with a friend, who had given it to a countryman for safekeeping, and that countryman had given it to yet another person. Even if he could find the manuscript, Erasmus did not dare publish it under his own name; it was controversial and could cause him trouble with the clergy.

One day, an idea came to him as he was leafing through a folder of proverbs and sayings of the early Latin authors that he had collected over the years: why not publish his collection of old proverbs in the form of a book? Working day and night, it did not take him long to put some eight hundred proverbs together in a small volume. He annotated many of them briefly for the benefit of those readers interested in elegant Latin. He also added a poem, in which he described the loss of his money in Dover, but he was careful to add that he was not angry; he wanted to stay on good terms with his English friends.

When he finished the book, he dedicated it to his former pupil and friend, William Blount. In return, Blount granted Erasmus a pension of twenty pounds for life. The book was published in Paris in 1500 with the title *Adagiorum Collectanea*; in short, the *Adages* or *Adagia*, a collection of old proverbs and sayings that over time have been accepted as truths. Unfortunately, it did not sell well and therefore did not solve Erasmus's financial problems.

Throughout the sixteenth century, the plague continued to erupt in western Europe. Fortunately, the majority of the outbreaks were limited to smaller towns and the countryside. When rumors spread of an outbreak nearby, however, it was enough to scare Erasmus into temporarily fleeing Paris for the south of France. His fear, which dated back to witnessing his mother's death from the plague, was perhaps a bit overblown. In the end, Paris was safe.

"I think you are a coward," teased Faustus Andrelini upon Erasmus's return.

"If I were a Swiss soldier, that remark would be an intolerable insult, my friend. However, that I am but a poet's soul, loving peace and shady places, is proof against it."

Actually, news of the frequent burials of plague victims frightened Erasmus exceedingly; He was on edge. He often reminisced with fondness about his stay in England; he had felt safe there and had enjoyed the scholarly company of John Colet and his circle of friends. He kept his connection with Colet, writing him frequently. He not only admired but also seemed to envy his friend.

> This England of yours has many charms for me, most of all because it contains so many men of high intelligence, of which I count yourself to be chief. Theology is the mother of science and you have taken arms against the dull and sordid who do not understand this. Yours is a hard task, a noble one, and you will succeed and will not pay attention to the clamours of fools. You will not stand alone.

Colet replied, lamenting, "Why, then, has one of the wisest of the Bench of Bishops censured my lectures as useless and mischievous?"

Erasmus was not a man without flaws. He could be petty, quick to judge, even envious. This is evidenced in a string of correspondence from the year 1500. In June he discovered that his friend and former schoolmate Willem Hermans had been devoting a great deal of attention to the Lady Anna of Veere, whom Erasmus had long hoped would become his patron. Jacob Batt had assisted Hermans in his attentions to Lady Anna, and Erasmus was jealous.

> I remember how coldly and indifferently you suggested that I might seek refuge with you. I do not know whether even literature interests you since you have fallen into a new kind of love in which flattery warms desire ... It is no secret to me that you have developed a preference to Willem and that you have devoted your entire attention

to assisting him. My Lady provided magnificently for Willem's travel expenses: me, she sent away empty. He hastened back to his carousing while I was going back to my books. You know well the airy siftings of women's minds.

But if my suspicions are false, as I truly hope they are ... make my Lady do what she promised and in addition to this, move her to give me a benefice ... I want to see you and my friend Willem somewhat oftener.

Paris, June 1500

Batt was deeply wounded, and he forwarded Erasmus's letter to Hermans, who immediately replied. Batt then penned a withering letter to Erasmus and enclosed Hermans's response. Erasmus received the letter just before leaving Paris on horseback for a two-day journey to Orleans. From there, he wrote Batt a contrite reply:

Dearest Batt,

I see that I have made you angry ... you consider my letter cross, while I rather call it a joke. However, I acknowledge my error, for it is not proper for me to appear facetious or petulant and much less should I be sarcastic, especially to those whom I am indebted in many ways ... I thought that I could say anything to my Batt with impunity for I have hitherto loved you so much that I was not afraid. But a truly blind love drew me a little further than was proper, and I see my fault ... Henceforth, I will love my friend Batt as a friend, as a benefactor, as a scholar ... I will be thankful, my patron, that you have brought me to a recollection of myself and have made me realize my good fortune ...

Farewell my dearest and sweetest Batt, Orleans, July 1500

While in Orleans, Erasmus was the guest of Augustine Vincent Caminade, who had been one of Erasmus's first students in Paris.

Caminade's household also hosted several boys as lodgers. Erasmus had sent one of the boys to deliver some books to Batt but became suspicious of Caminade when the boy did not return in a timely manner. He fired off another letter to Batt.

> Dearest Batt,
>
> I hope you are enjoying the best of health. A young man whom I sent to you loaded with books promised to be back in four weeks but he has not done so after eight weeks. I fear that there may be fraud in play.
>
> I have often wondered what was the reason for Augustine's sudden flood of generosity. He was ever want to filch other people's goods. I recognized the animus of an enemy, of a traitor, of a robber. I perceive that he is meditating perfidiously and that he is want to employ deceitful measures. Believe me, Batt, I expect from him only what one might expect from such a scoundrel, this wolf Augustine.
>
> New Orleans, August 1500

A few days later, the boy messenger returned, and Erasmus's opinion of Caminade took a complete reversal. He picked up his pen once more to inform Batt that he had restored his friendship with Caminade. Following that, he sent Caminade a flowing missive:

> I have always acknowledged your zeal to my fame and praise it anew … where there is perfect love, such as I opine exists between us two, what is the use of figures of speech. Take care of your health, dear Augustine, and love me as ever.
>
> Dated the day after the Conception of the Virgin Mother, September 9, 1500

These letters reveal Erasmus to have been an impulsive man. Within the span of a few months, he had harshly accused his friends Batt and

Caminade and then swiftly reversed himself and professed his love for them. Perhaps Erasmus had a touch of paranoia as well. In yet another incident, he accused his benefactor Bishop Henry of telling Standock to handle him harshly when he arrived at the University of Paris back in 1495. Yet Erasmus could not or would not recognize these flaws in his character. He once wrote, "I do not understand why some people dislike me so. I have never written a line to blacken any man's fame."

In the beginning of 1501, Erasmus was still desperately in need of funds. With a near total lack of shame, coupled with a strong sense of superiority, he instructed Jacob Batt to intervene on his behalf in an attempt to obtain the patronage of Lady Anne.

> I am at a loss to understand why you suspect me of playing the "logodaedalus"[9] in my letters to you, that is, of being uncandid and insincere. Pray, dearest Batt, fix this once and for all in your mind, that I hate hypocrisy more than anything ... Now it is plain that you suppose the letters which I wrote from Orleans about my poverty, are equally fictitious. If I am thought to be playing the fool, I see no reason why I should write you at all.
>
> If you are heartily interested in my fortune, this is what you must do. Plead my shyness before my Lady of Veere. You must write her that I am now in a state of extreme poverty ... that Italy is the place for me to take the Degree of Doctor and that it is impossible for a fastidious man to travel without a large sum of money. Explain how much greater fame I am likely to bring to my Lady ... A man like myself is hardly to be found once in many centuries, unless perhaps you are too scrupulous to tell a few fibs for a friend ... Let her know that I need two hundred francs as next year's payment now ... Employ a few harmless lies to help a friend ... Persuade her, in the most amusing words at your command, to send me some

---

[9] In Greek mythology, Daedalus was the craftsman who built the labyrinth of Crete, from which he escaped with his son, Icarus, by means of wax wings.

sapphire or other gem wherewith to fortify my eyesight … Also, urge her to look out for a benefice for me.

Let me tell you what else I want you to attempt still further– to extract a grant from the Abbot of St. Bertin … Say that I have a great work in view to restore the whole of Jerome and for this purpose I shall want a supply of books, and the assistance of Greek scholars. All this, my dear Jacob, does not seem to me too formidable … Trust me, if you handle the matter cleverly, all will go well. Lose no time, my dear Batt.

Farewell, my best and dearest Batt, and put your whole self into this business. I mean Batt the friend, not Batt the dawdler.

Paris, January 1501

Erasmus did not know it at the time, but it was to be one of his last letters to his friend. Batt remained true and did as Erasmus asked, writing, "Lady Anna is receptive to the idea of supporting you, but she is waiting for the customary compliments and flattery. I urge you to do so handsomely and you will find her generous." Erasmus immediately wrote the lady a long, outrageously flattering letter, in which he cooed:

> *From the time when I was a child I have been a devoted worshipper of St. Anne. I composed a hymn to her … the hymn I now send you, another Anne, as well as a collection of prayers to the Holy Virgin … for as a virgin I hold you … I place you among St. Jerome's Queens.*

The letter did its work, for Lady Anne sent Erasmus a handsome sum. However, it was a one-time sum only. In the next year, 1502, Lady Anne remarried and was no longer inclined to be so generous. At the end of that year, Jacob Batt died, and Erasmus never mentioned the loss of the friend who had helped him so much.

Erasmus resolved to leave Paris and travel to Holland, the homeland that he had not visited in many years. While en route, he heard that his old friend Servatius Rogerus, whom Erasmus first met in Steyn at St. Gregory monastery in 1494, had been appointed as the new prior of that monastery. Erasmus was delighted and immediately went to see his friend. To his surprise, he received an icy welcome. As prior, Servatius was Erasmus's superior.

"Who gave you permission to leave Paris, Brother Erasmus?" he demanded.

"Nobody, Brother, I—"

"You will address me as Father Superior," Servatius interrupted sternly, his eyes cold and hard.

Erasmus did not reply immediately. *So that is how it is going to be*, he thought. This was a potentially dangerous situation. By law, a prior had the power to arrest an errant monk and lock him up for life. It was imperative that Erasmus tread cautiously. "Please accept my humble apologies, Father. It will not happen again."

Servatius smiled ever so slightly. "Proceed."

"I fled from Paris when a rumor spread that the plague had returned," Erasmus explained, hoping the half-truth would suffice.

"That was only a rumor and only few people left the city. Why you?"

"I trust that Father will forgive my fear in light of the death of both my parents from the dreadful disease." Servatius merely nodded. Erasmus silently thanked the Lord that Servatius did not seem to know about his trip to England. He continued, "With your permission, I would like to study Greek, in the hope of better understanding the Vulgate. I intend to revisit the work of Jerome. I came to Steyn to beg you, Father Superior, for permission to continue my study outside St. Gregory for another year. I will be extremely grateful for your permission." Erasmus practically groveled at the feet of his former friend.

"You have my permission," Servatius said dismissively. "You can go now."

When the heavy door of the monastery closed behind him, Erasmus vowed never to enter through it again.

He next went to Haarlem to visit Willem Hermans. There, he received a warmer welcome from his old friend, despite their earlier dispute over the attentions of Lady Anna of Veere.

"Willem, I am going to study Greek. Why don't you learn it with me?"

"Oh, no, dear Erasmus, not me," Hermans replied. "Languages are not my strength, and I prefer to stick to Latin."

"Oh, come on. We can correspond in Greek and help one another."

"My dear Erasmus, I am not nearly as smart as you. I am sorry, but Greek shall always remain for me what it is—foreign. I prefer to study the history of Holland."

Whether it was due to his nature or the fact that he had lived in Paris for too long, Erasmus no longer appreciated the Dutch way of living, the lack of *joie de vivre*. He once commented, "If the story is not witty, remember it is a Dutch story." He discovered that Hermans was a dull person, that nothing exuded from him. With this and his altercation with Servatius, Erasmus felt he had lost his last Dutch friend.

He longed to travel to Italy and find a Greek tutor, but that was not financially or otherwise possible. Instead, he returned to Paris and started studying Greek with the help of a dictionary in the University of Paris library and a volume of Homer that he had borrowed from Augustine Caminade's personal collection in Orleans. After a year of dedicated study, Erasmus began to feel comfortable enough to declare that he was well versed in the language. However, he had overestimated himself, for when he turned to Jerome's text, Erasmus realized how little he really knew. Two years later, he finally had achieved a higher level of competency, and he began to give lessons in Greek to college students and private pupils.

During those years, he moved around quite a bit, taking his Greek books with him wherever he went. In September 1501, he paid a visit to the Saint-Omer monastery in northern France, with the intention of making the acquaintance of its warden, a Franciscan monk named Jean Vitrier. Erasmus knocked on the door of the warden's house, which was opened by a man dressed in a gray Franciscan habit.

"Are you the warden, Jean Vitrier?" Erasmus asked.

"Yes, I am," the monk said as he looked over Erasmus and his Augustinian habit. "And who may you be?"

"I am Erasmus of Rotterdam, and I am anxious to meet the infamous Vitrier, about whom I heard so much—but not all good, I may add."

"And I am equally happy to meet you, Erasmus!" the warden exclaimed. "Come in, please, and rest your weary bones. Let's enjoy some wine together."

While Vitrier left to get the wine, Erasmus looked around. The room reminded him of his father's office in Gouda. It contained a simple cross on the wall and the bare essentials of furniture. Vitrier, however, allowed himself the luxury of two comfortable chairs situated near the fireplace.

"And pray tell, what did you hear about me?" asked Vitrier upon reentering the room with two tumblers of wine. "It could not have been much good, I dare say."

"Indeed, it was not," Erasmus said with a smile. "I was at the Sorbonne in Paris when you were almost tarred and feathered for your sixteen supposedly heretical propositions. As I recall, you preached that it is a mortal sin to listen to the mass of a priest who lives in concubinage. You rejected the mediation of saints and declared that pardons and indulgences were the offspring of hell. And even worse, you claimed that indulgence monies are used to maintain the brothels."

"Guilty as charged, Brother Erasmus," Vitrier acknowledged with a wry smile. "I must say that there is nothing wrong with your memory. And what are your thoughts about all this?"

"You mean about the theologians in Paris condemning the sixteen propositions? My thoughts, dear Vitrier, are that their actions were nothing more than smokescreen that culminated in not punishing you."

Vitrier laughed. "You know, I still cannot believe that I was made warden here last year. By the way, I studied in at the Sorbonne also, as well as at Louvain University, but that was ten years before your time. Two good places, I might say, if only the Dominicans were not so dominating."

"I understand that you had something to say against monastic life?" asked Erasmus.

"Well, you lived in a monastery long enough to know what I was talking about." He leaned back in his chair. "Not only are monks frequently licentious, but they also dominate the church and life in the outside world. Even kings and princes are scared of those devils."

"Agreed. And I must say that I admire a priest, such as you, who preaches the word as it is derived from scripture, who refuses to give credence to ritual acts, and who keeps everyday life as simple as our Lord Jesus lived it. Warden—"

"Call me Jean, please," Vitrier interrupted.

"Thank you. I believe that you abhor as much as I do the adulation of the saints and the burning of the candles in church. I also think that Rome has gone too far in its promotion of the Holy Virgin, to the extent that the son of God, Jesus Christ, has dropped into the background. I wish our Church to return to the fundamentals, to the Church of St. Paul."

Vitrier smiled. "I could not have said it better. Tell me, my friend, what is in your future?" He sensed in Erasmus an unrest, a drifting of his brilliant mind. He felt that his guest was seeking his advice but was hesitant to ask.

"I want to study the writings of Jerome and the Vulgate that he produced. I want to go to the source and read for myself the original Greek, with Jerome's Latin translation side by side."

"That will be a massive undertaking, dear Erasmus. May I make a suggestion?" Without waiting for an answer, Vitrier continued. "Before you start on it, you must read Origen's comments on Paul's Epistles."

"I never heard of Origen. Who was he?"

"He was an early Christian whose family lived in Egypt. In the year 202, when he was twenty years old, the legions of the Roman emperor Severus killed Origen's father because he refused to denounce our Lord Jesus and make offerings to the Roman gods. Origen became such a fanatic ascetic that he took Matthew's third definition of the eunuchs literally—he castrated himself."

"That *is* extreme. Why did he do it? Was it really for the sake of the kingdom of heaven, as it says in Matthew?" asked Erasmus.

"I doubt it. No, he was a teacher of women and supposedly, he was afraid that the townspeople would think badly of it. Anyway, in those early years, there were quite a number of clerics who had their own religious ideas. Origen managed to change the minds of a few bishops, and like him, they became strict adherents of the Bible. Actually, his philosophy was much like that of Plato. I know that you, too, must admire that old Greek. My advice to you is to study Origen's comments on Paul's Epistles before you start with Jerome."

"You are the second person to give me advice about the Epistles. John Colet was the first," said Erasmus.

"I am sorry that I never met him," Vitrier commented. "He must be quite a man."

"Yes, he is, and I am lucky to know both of you."

"Well, that is enough of that. Come; let's see whether we can clean out the brothel."

"Clean the brothel?" Erasmus was shocked. "What brothel?"

"Oh, the nearby convent of St. Marguerite is under my jurisdiction. It is time for me to clean out the stable, because some nuns have a habit of, shall we say, spreading their personal assets too liberally."

"I understand you, but count me out," Erasmus said in disgust. "That is your business. That's why they call you the warden."[10]

Erasmus stayed in Saint-Omer for nearly a year, giving him ample time to study Origen and delve deeper in theology. He enjoyed the company of his new friend. He and Vitrier shared common ground not only in their respective life experiences but also in several philosophical frames of mind. Both men were devoted to their church while, at the same time, they leaned toward humanistic thoughts. However, while Vitrier willingly and openly attacked what he perceived as the wrongdoings of the Church from the top tiers of ecclesiastic power on down, Erasmus preferred to remain cautious in expressing his views.

---

[10]   Approximately a year after leaving Saint-Omer, Erasmus received word that Vitrier was no longer the warden. He had narrowly escaped with his life after the nuns tried to kill him during one of his stable raids. The mother superior went over his head to the bishop, who told him in no uncertain terms to stay out of the convent. Disillusioned, he resigned from his position as warden in 1502 and died as a village priest in 1521.

5

---◈◈◈---

Father Martin

1505–1507

*Brother Martinus - Monastic Life - Mortification of the flesh - Ordained a
priest - Says his first mass - Hans Luder shows his pride and temper*

Martin pulled the bell cord next to the door of the Black Cloister of the
Observant Augustinians and waited. To find a monastery to his liking, he
did not have to look far, because there were six to choose from in town. He
also could have become a Benedictine, Carmelite, Franciscan, Carthusian,
or Dominican. Only the Augustinians, however, kept contact with the
outside world via the leading citizens of Erfurt. As a result, the townspeople
had some idea of what life was like inside the monastery's forbidding walls.
Martin considered this when he made his choice. He also took into account
the facts that the Order of Augustinian Hermits did not reject Groote's
Devotio Moderna and, most important, that the Black Cloister maintained
a fraternity in honor of St. Anne, to whom Martin had made his vow.

A small shutter in the heavy door opened and a voice asked, "What
do you seek here?"

"God's grace and thy mercy," Martin replied, giving the answer that
Father Braun had advised.

"Wait." The shutter closed, and the door opened just wide enough to let him through. "Follow me." A monk led him through a few hallways, opened a door, and motioned for Martin to go inside.

He entered a sparsely furnished room with a desk near the window.

"I am Prior Winand von Diedenhofen," said a monk who was seated behind the desk. "And who might you be?"

"Martin Luder, Prior."

"Sit down, Martin, and just call me Father," the man said with a warm smile. "Is it your desire to become a monk?"

"Yes, Father."

"And how long have you had that desire?"

"Two weeks, Father."

"Fourteen days. Well, now, that is not a long time, is it? What made you decide?" Prior Winand seemed a little amused.

Martin told him the story of the thunderstorm.

"Did you consider entering a monastery any time before you made that vow?"

"No, Father. I was studying to become a lawyer."

"Well, at least you give a straightforward answer." The prior leaned back and studied the young man, while Martin, who was quite at ease, looked around the room. The walls were unadorned but for a small wooden cross on the wall behind the desk. Two other walls were covered with bookcases from bottom to top, and a small ladder stood in a corner.

The prior continued, now businesslike. "Are you married, Martin, and are you healthy?"

"No, Father, and yes."

The prior smiled. "Well, Martin Luder, we will accept you into our monastery for a month of observation. That also will give you time to reconsider your decision. Go now, and I will meet you after you have changed your clothes."

As Martin exited the prior's office, a tall monk appeared out of nowhere. "Follow me," he instructed and led Martin through a long corridor lined with doors on either side. One of the doors was open, and when Martin glanced inside, he saw a narrow, sparsely furnished room. His guide, who had not introduced himself, turned to Martin. "These are our cells," he explained and walked on, until at the end of the corridor, they reached a room with a wider door. The monk opened the door and led Martin into a larger room, where monk habits hung on hooks lining the walls.

Only then did the monk introduce himself. "I am Father Marcus. You can change clothes here. I'm sure that you will find a habit that will fit you. Can you remember your way back to the prior's office?"

"I think so," replied Martin.

"When you're dressed, you must go back there. Welcome to the Black Cloister."

When Martin returned to the office wearing his novice monk habit, he saw that another monk was visiting the prior.

"Let us pray," said Prior Winand, and the three men kneeled. "Lord, save Thy servant and grant him Thy mercy. Admit this servant whom we have given our habit in Thy name. Give him Thy blessing so that he shall be worthy to gain eternal life through our Lord Jesus Christ."

The prior turned to Martin, placed a hand on his shoulder, and said, "Not he who begins but he who perseveres to the end will be saved." He turned and added, "This is Brother Johann Graffenstein. He will help you in spiritual and material matters. Welcome, Brother Martinus."

After leaving the prior's office, Martin turned to Brother Johann, who was about twice his age. "The prior called me Martinus, not Martin. Was that a mistake?"

"No, he just changed your name into Latin. You will find that many of our fifty or so brothers have Latin names. Now, let me show you around and give you an idea of our daily routine. We'll start with the church."

Martin's eyes widened when he saw the size of the church. It could easily house three hundred people. The altar at the far end of the long and narrow nave was not high enough for people near the entrance to see. He wondered whether much of the congregation could even hear the priest during services. Martin and Brother Johann made their way behind the altar and passed through a small wooden door.

"We call this the *Kreuzweg* (Crossway) because it crosses the inner courtyard," explained Brother Johann. "It is so peaceful in this little garden that I love to come here to meditate. It is not big—maybe sixty feet square—but it is cozy. The graves of the departed brothers are at the opposite end, and the building here on this end is where we congregate and have our meals. Those windows up on the first and second floors are our cells. Come; I'll show you yours."

The cell was five by seven feet at most. A pallet filled with straw lay on the floor. At the far end of the cell stood a small table with a washbasin, jug, and chair. "It will be cold in the winter months, sleeping like that," said Brother Johann.

"I won't mind," Martin replied cheerfully. "At least I have a bed of my own. At home, I shared a pallet that size with my brothers." He walked to the window and looked out onto the courtyard below.

"You are lucky to have that window. Not every cell has a view," said Brother Johann, and he clapped his hands together. "Now, let me go over the daily routine. You will do a lot of meditating and reading of the Bible. We go to the church to worship and pray together seven times each day. The first time is called *matins* and is at two o'clock in the morning. That is followed by *lauds* at five, *terce* at nine, *sext* at noon, *nones* at three in the afternoon, *vespers* at five, and *compline* when we retire. We each have a job—the prior will assign one to you. Do you think you can remember all that?" Brother Johann asked with a smile.

"No, but I am sure that you will remind me."

"Yes, I will. Any questions?"

"Just one. Where can I pee?"

Brother Johann laughed. "Sorry. I forgot the most important part. It is at the end of this corridor." The sound of a bell interrupted him. "Time for *nones*. Let's go."

Prior Winand was not quite sure what to think about the new arrival. After all, just two weeks prior, Martin had been a law student, and he only vowed to become a monk in a moment of fear. Instead of accepting Martin as a novice monk, the prior decided to consider him as a guest for five or six weeks. During that time, the "guest" would learn how difficult monastic life was and have a chance to reconsider his decision.

Martin slept on his straw-filled pallet on the cold, hard floor and ate only two simple meals a day. Wherever he went and whatever he did, there was always a proctor at his side to guide and encourage him. He confessed his sins daily, often multiple times, and became somewhat of a bother to the priests, because his lengthy confessions took so long. But he worked hard and was a fast learner, and in the first week of September, he took the vows of a novice monk, and his head was tonsured.

"You now understand thoroughly how rigorous our life is," said Prior Johann. "Are you ready to renounce your self-will and accept the shame of begging, poverty, and mortification of the flesh?"

"Yes, with God's help," answered Martin in a firm voice.

"Then let your novitiate begin."

Mortification of the flesh, or the control of all physical desires, caused anguish in the novice monk. Martin was deeply disturbed when he experienced normal manifestations of sex, such as an erection and the discharge of semen in his sleep, which he thought sinful in the eyes of God. He had those experiences before he entered the cloister and at times had even used his hand to bring them on. He had refrained from such action since entering the monastery, but try as he might, he could not control his body's other impulses.

"Is there anything else you need to confess?" asked Brother Johann one afternoon during their daily session.

"No, Brother," replied Martin, looking uneasy.

The priest noticed Martin's hesitation. "I sense that there is more. I'll wait for you to tell me."

After a pause, the novice monk confessed his trouble.

"Brother Martinus, listen carefully. Erections and what we call 'wet dreams' are not sinful in the eyes of the Lord. Most brothers had them in their prior lives, and some probably still do. After all, we are all men. It is only an incubus—"

"What does that mean?" Martin interrupted.

"It is a nightmare in which an evil spirit has intercourse with a woman. It can cause erections. But it is only a sin if you consciously use your hands or think about using them to induce an ejaculation. You must clear your head of such thoughts and wait for the effects of the incubus to pass."

Martin constantly thought about of sins of all sorts. No matter how hard he tried, his mind eventually slipped into it. It was not an urge, not a temptation, not something he could fight. He used the German word *Anfechtung* (temptation) to describe it, but that did not cover it fully. He tried to cleanse his mind by fasting for two to three days, but it did not help. Other monks had tried that before him, he was told, and they also had failed. In his deeply troubled state, he once tried to make a confession in the middle of the night, but Brother Johann had had enough of Martin's never-ending sins.

"But I feel that God is angry with me," Martin cried anxiously.

"You are wrong, Brother Martin. God is not angry with you; you are angry with God," his confessor said calmly.

With that simple answer, Martin was dismissed. To his amazement, the abruptness of it brought him comfort—for one night. His mind later resumed the disturbing thoughts. When the prior encouraged him to study for the priesthood, Martin eagerly immersed himself in study to keep his mind occupied. Eventually, he succeeded to the point where he could consider himself a good monk. "If anyone could have gained heaven as a monk, then I would indeed have been among them," he said once, later in life.

In September 1506, Martin's testing period ended, and he took his vows as an Augustinian Hermit. Three months later, the prior ordained him subdeacon, and he was promoted to deacon on February 27, 1507. Bishop Johann Bonemilch von Lasphe ordained him a priest on April 4 of the same year. To Martin, it all seemed to happen so quickly. When the time came for Martin to say his first Mass, he invited his father and his old vicar Father Braun to come to the Black Cloister for the momentous event.

Hans Luder requested that the occasion be postponed to the second day of May, for he had to ride over fifty miles on horseback over the winding dirt roads from Mansfeld to Erfurt. He invited several friends to accompany him on the journey. They started the trip the day before, stayed overnight at an inn, and arrived, twenty men strong, in time to celebrate the Mass. Upon their arrival, Hans made a sizeable donation of twenty gold florins to the cloister.

Martin had studied every detail of the Mass and came to the church well prepared. Yet he was shaking with nerves because he knew that even a slight mistake in the ritual would be considered a serious matter. He was close to being overwhelmed, and his hands shook so much that he nearly dropped the communion bread and wine. He began the Consecration with "*Te igitur, clementissime Pater*" (Therefore, O most merciful Father) but could go no further. At that moment, Martin felt that he faced God all alone, and he was overcome, momentarily stumbling backward. Fortunately, his two assistants had been forewarned that this might happen, and with experienced hands they guided Martin back so that he could continue, *"Per Jesum Christum, Filium tuum, Dominum nostrum* (Through Jesus Christ, your Son, our Lord). He offered the bread and wine to God and called upon Him to transform it into the body and blood of Jesus Christ.

After the Mass, the participants and guests attended a celebratory meal in the dining hall. Hans and his friends occupied a long table on one side of the hall, while his son sat at another with the bishop, the prior, and several monks. Hans was in a good mood, fueled by the consumption of several steins of beer, filled to the rim. Prior Johannes walked over to thank him profusely for his generous donation. "Think nothing of it, Father," Hans replied with the sweep of a hand, but then he added rather audaciously, "My boy became a priest in record time, didn't he?" It was an awkward way of expressing how proud he was. The prior nodded curtly and returned to his table.

Martin crossed the room to where his father sat. It was their first meeting in two years. They started off well enough, but then Martin made the mistake of reminding his father of his vow to St. Anne.

"Son, I still think that you were only scared. How do you know it was not the devil testing you? You should have gone to law school."

"Dear Father, is it not better for me to be a priest than a lawyer?"

That was too much for the quick-tempered Hans, who had been on his best behavior. He stood up and in a loud voice yelled, "No, it is not! Have you not read in the Bible where it says 'Honor thy father and thy mother'? You should have been a lawyer." Hans turned to his friends. "It's time to go," he ordered angrily and stomped out.

"I can do more good with my prayers," a deeply hurt Martin called after him.

6

━━◆◆◆━━

Handbook of a Christian Soldier
and Travels in Italy

1502–1509

*Louvain University - Handbook of a Christian Soldier - Discovers manuscript
by Laurentius Valla - Second trip to England - Travels to Italy - Receives a
doctorate degree - Aldus Manutius's printing shop in Venice - Meets Jerome
Aleander - The Adagia - Travels to Rome - Reads St. Thomas Aquinas - Stigma
of illegitimate birth*

During his long stay in Saint-Omer, Erasmus made several trips to the
Castle of Tournehem, accompanied by his friend Jacob Batt. It was during
one of those visits that a woman approached the two men. She made the
sign of the cross and bowed to Erasmus.

"Gracious Father, may the Lord Jesus bless you," she said hesitantly.
Her long black dress covered her feet and sandals. Her hair was hidden
under a white cap, and the left side of her face showed a large bluish
discoloration. "I fear that my husband has lost his way and that he will not
gain salvation. Please help guide him back into the arms of the Church."

"Who is your husband, dear woman?" asked Erasmus.

"He is John, the master of arms of the castle, Father."

"I know of him," Erasmus said. "He has little respect for priests. He often gets drunk and into fights." He did not add that he suspected the man was also a wife-beater. "So why do you think I can help?"

"He told me that you are the only priest he respects," the woman replied. "Can you please write something that can show him the way back to the Church?"

Erasmus paused, thinking. He had never before faced a situation like this and did not readily know what to do. With an air of heavy resignation, he said, "I will try, dear woman. However, there is no guarantee that it will work."

Later that day, Erasmus passed the hordes of vendors selling religious trinkets on the steps to the church, and he reflected that just inside the church doors were monks who habitually sold indulgences to believers. Erasmus had witnessed enough wrongdoings of the Church and the decreasing attendance at services to realize that eventually he had to write something substantial to change those conditions. The episode with the woman and her errant husband was the catalyst he needed to get started.

Thus, Erasmus began work on what would become one of his most influential books, *Enchiridon militis Christiani* (Handbook of a Christian Soldier). Although it took only a few months to write, Erasmus's work was interrupted when the plague popped up once more in several nearby towns, and he was forced to leave Saint-Omer. He fled to the University of Louvain, just east of Brussels in the Dutch-speaking part of Belgium. When he arrived, he learned, to his pleasant surprise, that Adriaan Florenszoon Boeyens, his old schoolmate from Deventer, was the dean of the university. The teaching staff consisted of scholars and theologians of stature, and with the exception of a few, they were conservative. They came from many countries, but most were Dutch or French. The reputation of the university exceeded that of the University of Paris.

"Tell us about your travels, Brother Erasmus," one of the more liberal professors asked during that evening's faculty dinner.

"Before you do that, tell us why you are not in your monastery," a senior member of the staff rudely demanded.

"Yes, try to explain that," other members joined in. Jealousy and outright hostility by some, as well as ignorance by several, threatened to dominate the otherwise polite conversation.

"Brother Erasmus and I were schoolmates in Deventer," Dean Adriaan quietly interjected. "We had the privilege of listening to a speech by Brother Agricola." He turned to Erasmus and smiled. "We also spent a pleasant afternoon together when the Duchess of Guelders made her grand entry into the city." One could hear a coin drop in the dining hall. Erasmus sat bent over, trying to keep a straight face.

"Brother Erasmus did me the honor of showing to me a portion of the manuscript of his latest book, which I understand will be published next year," Dean Adriaan continued. "He intends to put the final touches on it during his stay with us, and I look forward to reading it," he said with a nod to Erasmus, who tried not to blush but did not quite succeed. The older professors looked indignant, while the younger ones tried to suppress smiles.

As long as Adriaan was dean, even the most conservative members of the staff remained civil. Adriaan offered Erasmus a teaching position at the university, which Erasmus politely declined, for fear that it would demand too much time and effort, distracting him from his studies. He hung around because the university had an excellent library, which gave him a chance to translate Lucian and Euripides from Greek into Latin while he continued to finish the *Enchiridion*.

The first edition of the *Enchiridion* was ready for publishing in 1503. The title of the book was not to be taken literally—it was not intended to address common soldiers, who could not read Latin, but rather to enlighten and inspire well-educated readers. The introduction read, "What I write will be for you a source of strength and determination."

Part I consisted of seven chapters, and the first began ominously: "We must always be on guard in our lives." Erasmus argued that we were at war against superbly armored enemies in a raging world that shook the confines of our minds. The enemy was numerically superior, better armed, and more experienced than we were. He used imagery intended to scare the wits out of his readers, such as "a hell of stinking corpses and evil-smelling souls." He did not identify the enemy, other than to refer to it as vile and deadly pleasure. He warned the reader not to become complacent and to stay on the middle of the road, because the enemy lurked on either side. "They are like Scylla and Charybdis," the mythical sea monsters that guard the strait between Italy and Sicily. It was a chapter full of terror, but Erasmus concluded it by quoting God as having said, "Have confidence, I have conquered the world."

In the second chapter, Erasmus described the two weapons of Christian warfare: prayer and knowledge. Prayer to heaven subdued passion, and knowledge fortified the mind. He warned, however, that one should not overdo praying, because God the Father already knows what we need. He urged his readers to read the scriptures carefully, to study the philosophy of Plato, and to read Origen, Ambrose, Jerome, Augustine, and especially St. Paul.

In the third chapter he stated that "the crown of wisdom is to know yourself." Jesus Christ is the author of wisdom and is Himself wisdom. Erasmus rambled on and on, yet he knew that rambling was one of his weaknesses; at one point, he stated, "Perhaps I am more verbose than necessary ..."

Throughout this and other chapters Erasmus acted both as a preacher and a teacher. "Go back to the Scriptures and live as the Scriptures teach us," he insisted to his readers. He warned that many of the rituals and ceremonies practiced by churches only fed the outer frames of men but did not touch their inner souls. Therefore, he reasoned, they had little value. He admonished monks for the deterioration of the faith, for seeing the world only in black and white, for their intolerance, and for their illogical superstitions.

In the final chapters of Part I, Erasmus proclaimed that the only road to happiness was to know oneself, and he warned that one must not allow passions to lead one to excesses. He pointed out that the authority of the ancient philosophers rested upon the fact that they had stated the same ideas, although in different terms, that are found in the scriptures. Finally, he outlined the three parts of man, beginning with *spirit*, which represents us as a reflection of our Creator and therefore is closest to God. *Flesh* is the farthest away from God; it is what Satan preys on as he leads us to evil. In the middle is the *soul*, which is neither good nor bad; it is the battleground where the struggle between good and evil urges occurs. The *spirit* can make us divine, the *flesh* brings out the animal in us, and the *soul* is what makes us human.

In Part II of the *Enchiridion*, Erasmus enumerated the twenty-two rules of living a Christian life. In his opening, he mentioned that the majority of mankind considered the existence of heaven and hell as some kind of myth. That daring statement directly contradicted the Church's interpretation of the Bible. Erasmus, however, dabbled in Hebrew and knew that the word "hell" did not actually appear in the original scriptures.[11]

Erasmus bluntly warned that man can only walk one of two paths: the first, where he gratifies his physical desires and thus loses his soul; and the second, where he controls his physical desires and gains eternal life. Man chooses his own path, and any excuse that claims he cannot do so is invalid, because Jesus did it before man. Other rules covered much of life and its relation to Christ—have no fear that is unfounded; make Christ the only goal in your life; stay free of vice; use Him to keep from temptation.

The twenty-first rule contained another short warning: "Life is sad and miserable, short and quick. Death lies in wait on every side, haunting us. We do not know when it will come and it can come unexpectedly, so it is foolish to live a life that leads to damnation."

It is the fifth rule, however, that is considered the most important: "Turn away from visible things … seek the invisible." Here, Erasmus reached back to his old teacher Alexander Hegius and, through him, to Thomas à Kempis, who in his *The Imitation of Christ* urged people to live like Christ, be devoted to Christ, show piety, and move from the outer man to the inner man, from the body to the soul.

Erasmus stressed that man is frightened by the death of his body, but he should fear the death of his soul. Erasmus undertook a difficult task, to turn man from what he understands—his body—to what is foreign to him—his invisible soul. While it was easy for him to give advice—"As for dying or living, leave that in the hands of God"—it was a great deal more difficult to convince people to adhere to that advice.

In the *Enchiridion*, Erasmus professed what he believed was the true meaning of sound Catholicism. He warned the reader against embracing

---

[11]   The closest word in the Bible is "Sheol," Hebrew for "to dig," as in Amos 9:2.

the trappings of Christianity in lieu of embracing the Christ and the true meaning of the scriptures. Among his assertions, he declared that it was not enough to merely dress like St. Francis or burn candles at his shrine if one did not live like him. He asked his readers why some people revered what was merely purported by clerics to be the shroud of Christ, while at the same time, they neglected to read the actual oracles of Christ. He pointed out that a sliver of the cross did not make one richer and that it was not enough to admire a painting of the family of Christ if it did not fill one with the Holy Spirit. Basically, he advocated for a simple church, based on the life of Christ and the scriptures.

Finally, Erasmus could not resist including a warning that monasticism did not necessarily mean holiness and that life in a monastery could be either useful or useless, depending on the individual.

Theological historians have expressed diverse opinions about the *Enchiridion*, but on one point, most agree—it is too wordy and entirely too long, but it is classic Erasmus. The first person to warn Erasmus about his verbosity was Gaguin, who after reading the early *Antibarbari*, wrote, "One thing, Erasmus, and I know that you will accept this from a friend— you drag the introduction out a little too far ... I would be a bad mentor for you if I were to add beauty to Venus. It will suffice if you eliminate what is redundant and supply what is lacking." However, in the *Enchiridion* and his other books, Erasmus seldom followed this advice. Once he took up his feather pen, he wrote on and on in the most elegant Latin, as if it were a dance, stringing the words together so quickly that he could not be bothered about small errors. He admitted, "I have never been able to stomach the tedium of revision."

The first edition of *Enchiridion* was printed in 1503 by Dirck Maertensz, a well-known printer in Antwerp. Unfortunately for Erasmus, it turned out to be a financial failure. Eventually, however, it was reprinted many times, and ultimately became one of the world's more important religious works for centuries to come.

Meanwhile, Erasmus's financial situation continued to deteriorate. The previous year had not been a good one for him. Not only had Jacob Batt died and Anna of Veere's generosity dried up upon her remarriage, but Bishop Henry, Erasmus's main benefactor, had passed away in the fall. Shortly after Bishop Henry's death, Erasmus wrote to a friend: "I have celebrated the bishop of Cambrai in three Latin epitaphs and one in Greek. I received six florins only, so that even in death he was like himself." The bishop, having passed away, of course had nothing to do with this small payment, yet Erasmus could not resist being petulant and ungrateful.

Erasmus had to earn an income and was presented with an opportunity to do so in 1503, when he was chosen to deliver a lengthy laudation in honor of young Philip the Handsome, Prince of Burgundy and Archduke of Austria, upon the occasion of his return to Holland as the new king of Spain. "I hate to write this nonsense," Erasmus confessed to a friend. "Normally it would take me one day, but I just couldn't put my mind to it." It may have been the worst piece he had written thus far, but he was paid one hundred florins for it—a handsome sum indeed.

One summer day in 1504, Erasmus heard that there was an old manuscript written by Laurentius Valla (1407–1457) in the nearby abbey of Parc. The name Valla was not new to Erasmus; while at the monastery of St. Gregory in Steyn, he had read and admired Valla's *Elegantiae Linguae Latinae* (Elegance of the Latin Language). The abbey's old manuscript turned out to be a copy of Valla's unpublished notes on the New Testament, the *Annotationes in Novum Testamentum*, and Erasmus arranged to have it published by Jodocus Badius in Paris in March 1505.

In the same library, Erasmus found another book by Valla titled *De Voluptate* (On Pleasure), in which Valla asserted that it was not only good but acceptable to indulge in one's natural appetites. Valla had found the basis for his daring statement among the teachings of the Greek philosopher Epicurus (321–270 BC), who, according to Valla, had stated that while it is acceptable to indulge, one must not overdo it. Valla also proved that the *Donation of Constantine*, the document by which Emperor Constantine I donated Rome and the western regions of the Roman Empire to the papacy, was a fake. Valla continued his rebellious streak by vilifying monastic life and even accusing St. Augustine of heresy. Despite all this, Erasmus found much to contemplate in Valla's works, which spurred him on in his own work and thoughts for years to come.

For several years Erasmus maintained a correspondence with an Augustinian priest in Gouda named Cornelius Goudanus. It began when the priest sent a poem he had authored to Erasmus and asked for his opinion on it. Erasmus had never met the man and did not want to disappoint him with a negative opinion. Instead, he wrote a cordial reply, and this led to their somewhat regular correspondence. Later, Goudanus sent him a full collection of poems he had written, and again, Erasmus did not have the heart to say that they were of poor quality. However, he did bring up the topic of Valla's writings and praised Valla's elegant style of writing, immense memory, and intelligence. Goudanus did not appreciate this:

> If I say so in jest, I don't know what you have done with your eyes that you propose that I take as an example a man against whom so many men of learning wage war. He is denounced by the whole world as a defamer.

Erasmus was not pleased, and the friendship between the two men dissipated in subsequent letters. Then, one day, they met by chance.

"At long last, we meet, my sweetest Erasmus," Cornelius said with a big smile.

"Indeed, it is a pleasure," replied Erasmus. "From your last letter, I take it that you did read Valla after all."

"Did you sense that from an improvement in my style of writing?"

"Yes, indeed."

The old priest was visibly pleased. "But that does not mean that I admire the man," he insisted, betraying a stubborn streak. "I remind you of what Poggio wrote in his epigram:

> *Since Valla wet the trembling Shades to seek,*
> *No word of Latin Pluto dares to speak;*
> *Jove fears to call him to the blessed abodes,*
> *Lest carping censure vex the blameless gods."*

"I know the poem well, dear friend, and Valla was not the last of Poggio's victims, although I must immediately add that Valla neither feared nor recognized the man as a true humanist. Poggio censured Valla in an openly hostile and acrimonious spirit."[12]

"That does not alleviate the fact that Poggio was right. Remember what everyone says about your Laurentius Valla."

"Oh, I know what they say, but you went a step further. You called him a croaking crow and a jester but not an orator. You provoked me into defending my literary friends, for in striking Laurentius, you have wounded all men of letters."

Cornelius was clearly upset. "Now, this time do you not think that it is you who have gone too far?"

"No, sir, and if it were not for our acquaintance, I would have spoken in even stronger words. But I hate wars, even civil ones. Let us remember Horatio: 'As wolves and lambs are born to disagree, A fatal discord severs you and me.' So let us not quarrel and make peace, shall we?" Erasmus continued. "I have only three conditions: First, instead of calling Valla a croaking crow, you must call him the 'marrow of persuasion.' Second, you must learn his *Elegances* until you have them at your fingertips. And third, you must let me borrow your books."

Erasmus was greatly relieved when Cornelius laughed. "Dear Erasmus, they warned me that your tongue could be as sharp as a rapier and as smooth as silk. You just confirmed that in a few sentences." After this exchange, Erasmus addressed his friend as "My sweetest Cornelius" in his subsequent letters.

Not long thereafter, Erasmus moved back to Paris, from where he wrote a long letter to John Colet:

> To my friend Colet, greetings:
> I am a little afraid that our friendship might have failed ... I have no right and no wish to find fault with your silence ... I beg and entreat that you will steal some moments to greet me now and then with a letter ... I am surprised that none of your commentaries on Paul and the Gospels have yet seen the light ... If you want to

---

[12] Poggio Bracciolini (1380–1459), an Italian humanist and secretary of the Curia, was famous and feared for his personal invectives.

91

see your work printed, just send a copy to me and I will attend to the rest … All my extremities pull me to the Holy Script and I detest all that that prevents me—I only wrote *Enchiridion* to heal the errors of he who usually seeks the essence of religion in ceremonies and rites, while he neglects devotion.

I am ready to devote myself to the sacred literature study of the Scriptures. I am now competent enough in Greek to do it with the Greek version close at hand. I beseech you to do what you can to help me in my craving for sacred studies.

Farewell,
Paris, January 1505

John Colet did not fail him; he wrote to Erasmus and offered him a job teaching Greek at the university.

In the spring of 1505, Erasmus sailed to England for a second time, and he was welcomed with open arms by his old friends. "I have read Valla's unpublished notes on the New Testament," Erasmus announced with some pride.

"I did not know that Valla made notes," said Colet dryly.

"I do hope that you do not mind if I have some doubt about the value of such notes," said Thomas More. "I have heard enough about that man to wonder whether he can be believed. His reputation is not too commendatory here."

"I understand your doubts, friends," Erasmus assured them. "Valla was not exactly a diplomat, and he has ruffled many feathers. But I have brought you a copy of his notes, and I would greatly value your opinions about them."

That evening, Colet introduced Erasmus to William Warham, the archbishop of Canterbury. Erasmus presented him with a copy of his Latin translations of *Hecuba* and *Iphigenia*, two plays by Euripides that he had published by Jodocus Badius in Paris.

"Thank you, Erasmus. I'll treasure these. Now what did I hear? You have become an admirer of Laurentius Valla?"

"You may say that. While I was at Steyn, I read his *The Elegance of the Latin Language*, and I think it has led to a major improvement in the style of Latin writing."

"Not everybody agrees with you on that, my friend."

"True, but then not everybody is well versed in Latin," Erasmus insisted. Around the room, a few eyebrows went up.

"Did not Valla severely criticize St. Augustine?" asked More. "I believe he even called him a heretic."

"Yes, he did, and perhaps rightfully so. Augustine was not nearly as saintly as people are led to believe." He paused, surveying the skeptical faces around him. "For instance, he believed that the vast majority of mankind will be eternally punished by God and that few souls will be worthy of entering the kingdom of heaven. Is that not a form of heresy?"

"But he came to that conclusion during the last decade of his life," challenged More, unconvinced.

"Thomas, that is no excuse. Moreover, I have another reason for admiring Valla. As I have already told you and John, I have read the notes that Valla made on the Vulgate. While I lived in Louvain, I paid a visit to the nearby abbey of Parc and one of the monks drew my attention to a long-forgotten manuscript. It turned out to be those notes. When you place them side by side with the Vulgate, it is clear that Jerome's New Testament leaves a lot to be desired. I have arranged for Jodocus Badius to print the notes."

"So you think that Valla's good side outweighs his bad side?" asked Warham.

"Yes, sir, I do. Oh, I know that he sometimes used the foulest of language and that he fulminated against the power of Rome, but that did not prevent Pope Nicholas from making Valla a secretary of the Curia and Pope Calixtus from welcoming him. Laurentius was extremely outspoken and too critical of religious establishments, especially the monasteries, for the taste of his many enemies. He shook the rafters and blew the dust off."

The lively conversation continued until someone brought up the name Thomas Aquinas. Colet interrupted, saying, "That man has corrupted the whole teaching of Christ with his profane philosophy." The discussion continued into the night, but Colet was silent. After his visitors left, he sat down with Erasmus at the open fire with a glass of wine.

"Tell me, Erasmus," he began. "What about your original plans to revisit the writings of Jerome? Did you abandon them?"

"Before I answer you, John, please tell me what you have against Thomas Aquinas."

Colet looked intently at his guest, seeking an indication of whether he had spoken in jest or in earnest. Erasmus looked back, his face questioning. Colet rested his head in the palm of his hand for a while before looking up. "My dear friend, I prefer not to answer you at this moment. When you visit Italy—and I am sure you will one of these days—favor me and read the *Summa Theologica* [*The Substance of Theology*] for which Aquinas is so famous. I believe that you will find your answer there."

It was then Erasmus's turn to remain silent as he considered his friend's words. After a few moments, he looked up and continued. "To go back to your question about Jerome, no, John, I have not abandoned him. However, Valla has convinced me that Jerome's Vulgate, as it has been copied by the many scribes over so many years, contains numerous errors. Remember, those scribes were not always well versed in Latin and a few could have interjected their own ideas while writing."

"That may well be possible, but nevertheless, Jerome's version is the best we have."

"There is another thing that came to my mind while I read Valla's notes. Jerome worked from the Hebrew and Greek versions of the Vulgate, three centuries after Christ was born. Could the copyists also not have made errors in those texts in all those years?"

"That, too, could well be. However, you know of course that by publishing those notes you sail into dangerous waters. Many in the church and in monasteries will henceforth be your enemies. We here in England can accept it better, but from what I know of other countries, there will be trouble. You had better cover your back."

"I know that, John, but I am not afraid of creating controversy. It often leads to progress."

"Let us hope so. And now, my friend, what do you intend to do? Write another New Testament?"

"No, I just want to study and make notes and perhaps publish them at a later time."

"I wish you well in your noble effort, my friend, and I will lend all possible help. Do not hesitate to ask."

"Thank you, John."

"Erasmus, how would you like to finally go to Italy?" asked Colet a few days later, knowing his friend would leap at the chance.

"Italy? You are joking, aren't you?" exclaimed a surprised Erasmus.

"No, I am not, my friend. The king's court physician is looking for an experienced traveler to guide his two sons to Bologna, where they will attend university. I immediately thought of you."

"I still do not understand. Why does he want his sons to study in a foreign country? England has excellent universities."

"Because the physician is Giovanni Boerio, and he is Italian," Colet explained.

Erasmus was too excited to sit still. He got up, threw up his hands, and paced the floor with such unusually long steps that Colet could not help but grin with amusement.

"John, I am dumbfounded by this sudden gift from heaven. Yes, of course, I would love to go!"

"Then you had better get ready. They are leaving in two days. And do not forget to read at least part of the *Summa Theologica* while you are in Rome."

When Erasmus met Giovanni Boerio the next day, he was immediately struck by the ebullience of the great Italian doctor.

"Thank you, thank you, Master Erasmus, for agreeing to take care of my boys. They are good boys—maybe a little wild sometimes, but they are good."

"I understand that I am to guide your two sons, Doctor." Erasmus again was so excited that he could hardly sit still. "What will that entail?"

"Guidance, illustrious Father, just guidance. An English teacher, Master Clifton, and a courier-caretaker will look after my boys. You will please make the journey easy—how do they say? Smooth. Maybe show them a little of Paris on the way."

The party left London in the first week of June 1506 and arrived in Paris on June 11. Erasmus found himself welcomed not only by his old friends but also in several salons. He was by then considered a famous author, and his wit and charm made him the center of attention. With his blond hair and light blue eyes, he stood out among the darker French. The ladies surrounded the seemingly ever-cheerful man, and he thrived on their attention. While in Paris, Erasmus arranged for Jodocus Badius to print his translations of Lucian and Euripides, as well as a new edition of the *Adagia*, the book of proverbs he originally published in 1500. Two months passed by before he knew it, and in the first week of August, the traveling party was on its way again.

The two boys were well behaved, but their teacher and the courier were constantly arguing with one another. They were often drunk and fought to the point of drawing knives, only to become pals again the next morning. Such behavior was too much for the delicate Erasmus, and he withdrew, not to enjoy the magnificent mountain scenery in which he had no interest but to compose and store his thoughts in his mind. Via Orleans and Lyons, the party crossed the Alps into northern Italy and then stayed a while in Turin, where Erasmus was instantly adopted into the academic circles.

"Welcome, Doctor. Welcome to our city," the dean of Turin University warmly exclaimed as Erasmus entered the auditorium where the faculty was gathered.

"Thank you, sir," Erasmus replied graciously. "However, you give me too much honor. I am just a simple monk without a doctorate."

"What? No doctorate? Gentlemen, your attention please." The dean turned to the assembled group. "I just heard that our honored guest does not yet have a doctorate. It will be an honor for our university to bestow the degree of doctor of theology on him, don't you agree?" Everyone applauded, and cries of "*Salutem Doctoris*" reverberated off the walls of the old auditorium. The next day, on September 5, 1506, Erasmus received the proper document, which was dated the previous day. It read:

> I, Baldassare Bernezio, Archbishop of Lodi, declare that Father Jacopino de Prato has presented you, Desiderius Erasmus, to us as a sufficient and worthy Bachelor … We have solemnly decreed you fit and suitable for obtaining the degree of Doctor and Master in the faculty of Sacred Theology … and according to custom are accorded a

Master's chair, an open and a closed book, a cap on your head and a kiss.

Erasmus did not possess a bachelor's degree, but when he read the document, he noticed that it also declared him a bachelor at the university. Two months later, he wrote a letter to Servatius—"I have obtained a doctorate in theology"—leaving out that it was an honorary degree from a university far less important than the prestigious University of Bologna.

From Turin, Erasmus planned to go to Bologna, but that city was under siege by an army led by Pope Julius II. He wanted to add the city to his papal states, but it was ruled by the despotic Giovanni II of the Bentivogli family. The battle did not last very long, because the citizens had had enough of the shifty Giovanni and forced him to leave the city in the middle of the night. The next morning, November 10, 1506, Erasmus and the boys walked into Bologna and witnessed Julius the Conqueror enter with great fanfare upon a magnificent white stallion. Erasmus, who hated war and all those who waged it, was not impressed. He escorted his charges to the university gates and left to roam Europe as free man.

Near the end of 1507, Erasmus made his way to Venice to seek Aldus Manutius, who had established a printing shop in 1495 and was famous for his beautiful, very fine type. Upon his arrival in Venice, Erasmus approached a teenage boy, loitering at a lantern post, and asked, "Young man, do you know where I can find the printing shop of Master Aldus Manutius?"

"Yes, sir," the boy said. After catching the coin that Erasmus flipped to him, he added enthusiastically, "I will lead you to it."

When the pair reached the shop, Erasmus paused to admire the lettering above the door before he entered. The sound of the bell announced his presence, but no one came forward. He looked over an assortment of prints on display, smelled the ink, heard the sound of presses, and intuitively knew that he had found the place he wanted to be. There was nothing else to do but wait until, finally, a man approximately Erasmus's own age emerged from the back room.

"What can I do for you?" he asked while wiping his ink-stained hands on a full-length apron that he wore over his naked upper body. A cap partially covered his shoulder-length hair. His long nose stood out; his jaw was firmly set; and he had a few ink smears on each cheek.

"Are you the famous Aldus Manutius?" Erasmus replied. He had his doubts whether this dirty man could be the man he was looking for.

"Well, I don't know about the 'famous' part, but yes, I am Aldus. And who might you be?"

"I am Desiderius Erasmus Roterodamus."

Aldus looked at him. His eyes grew larger as he clapped his hands not once but twice, his face animated with excitement.

"Father Erasmus, you do honor me. I hope you didn't wait long." He stuck out his ink-stained hand in greeting but pulled it back, looked at it, and with a grin added, "I had better not."

"Quite some time, I would say," said a bemused Erasmus.

"Oh, forgive me, I am all, eh … Oh, forget it. Welcome to Venice, Father. Now let me see. You brought your luggage, yes?"

"I left it on the quay."

Aldus called out to the back room, and a sturdy young man appeared in the doorway. "Guido, go to the quay and bring Father Erasmus's luggage to the house of Mr. Asolani." He turned back to Erasmus. "You, sir, will be staying with my father-in-law, Andrea Asolani, whom I regard as my partner. I, by the way, live next door to him. I trust you will find the accommodations quite convenient."

Over dinner later that evening, Aldus asked, "Now, what brought you to Venice, my friend? Do you have something for me to print?"

"I would like you to publish my translation of the two dramas of Euripides."

"Didn't Badius just do that?"

"Yes, but they are already out of print, and I am not happy with his work," Erasmus informed his new friend. "There are too many errors, and I also do not like the type."

"I see, but that is not much, is it? I'll do it on one condition."

"And what is that?"

"I want to publish a new edition of your *Adagia*. I believe that there is a market for the book, but I would like to expand it. Your original contains only eight hundred proverbs, but there must be many more out there."

"My dear Aldus, I have been collecting proverbs for years. I must have a couple of thousand by now. Reworking the *Adagia* will take a long time."

"I know, and I propose that you stay with us during that time. I'll give you a place where you can write, and I'll assign my best corrector to you full time."

Erasmus did not have to think twice about the offer. A major book published by the famous Aldus Manutius meant instant fame to the author.

"Your generous offer is more than I expected. I look forward to working with you."

"How about a glass of my finest Chianti to seal the deal?"

"Good idea." Erasmus waited for his host to finish pouring before continuing. "By the way, who is that young man I saw coming out of my room earlier?"

"He calls himself Jerome Aleander. I think he will have a promising career. He is staying with us for a while. You two will share a room and a bed. You will soon learn that Jerome is fluid in Latin and Greek. He may assist you in some manner, should you so desire."

The room was small, the bed was narrow, and the air was stifling. That evening, as they lay side by side, Erasmus asked, "Jerome Aleander, is that your birth name?"

"No, that was Girolamo Aleandro. I was born in a little village nearby."

"Well, you picked two famous names. The only letter missing is an *X.*"

"I am a modest man," Jerome chuckled.

"I understand that you translated the works of Galen and Hippocrates. What made you decide to do that?"

Aleander laughed. "My father made me do it. He is a physician, and it was purely for his benefit."

"And now you give lessons to the archbishop of Nicosia. How is that possible?"

"That is what everybody asks, and it is a mystery to me as well. The man came all the way from Cyprus to learn Greek and Latin."

"My compliments, Jerome. Your reputation already reaches far."

They turned back-to-back and fell asleep.

When Erasmus entered the printing room the next morning, Aldus motioned him to a table and chair in a corner of the noisy room, and Erasmus went straight to work. From the depths of his memory and the many pages of notes that he had scribbled while sitting none too comfortably on the horseback journey from England, Erasmus wrote one page of text after another, without bothering to check for errors.

"How can you write so fast with all that noise and bustle around you?" Aldus asked several times.

The corrector, Pieter Gilles, carefully went over each page and returned it to Erasmus with suggested changes. The completed pages went off to the typesetter, but not before Aldus also had a peek at them.

"Why do you look at the proofs after Pieter already has made his corrections?" Erasmus asked one afternoon.

Aldus smiled. "Because I am learning as we go along."

Erasmus was impressed by his friend's desire to learn. "Do you do that with every manuscript?"

"No, only with the good stuff."

"I'll take that as a compliment."

Erasmus stayed with Aldus for eight months and worked unceasingly on the new *Adagia*. He enjoyed the task and was surprised and gratified when several citizens who had heard about the new project brought him old books and manuscripts containing proverbs, most of which he had never seen before. As he buried himself in his work, he neglected to drink enough liquids, and he gulped his food; as a result, he experienced his first painful kidney stone attack. After that, he let up a bit and took some time each day to play with Aldus's two-year-old son. The little fellow climbed up on Erasmus's knees whenever he could and demanded one horsey ride after another.

The finished book contained 3,260 proverbs and was titled *Adagiorum Chiliades Tres.*[13]

Unlike his first edition of the *Adagia*, in which he had merely copied the proverbs, with the addition of a sentence or two of commentary in some cases, in this edition he frequently elaborated extensively. He opened

---

[13] It is possible that Erasmus had read the twelfth-century book *Chiliades* by John Tzetzes and had borrowed the word, which means "thousands."

himself to the world and made the reader privy to his inner feelings and thoughts.

The title page of the book was a magnificent example of the art of fine printing in the early 1500s. Aldus cleverly arranged the text of 136 words in the form of what looked like a martini glass, complete with a stem and foot. The bottom line on the foot read *Nam, quod dicitur,* which could be translated as "As an example of its use." Aldus meant to illustrate how Erasmus's elegant Latin could be molded into a fine piece of art.

Erasmus was well pleased when Aldus presented him with the first completed book. They celebrated with a bottle of Chianti, and for the first time in eight months, they both could relax.

"Aldus, you never told me why you wanted to print this book so badly. They are only proverbs."

Aldus laughed. "If they are just proverbs, why did you bother to write the book?"

"Actually, it was more of a hobby. I have long been interested in the origin of the proverbs, especially some of the old Greek ones."

"And that is why I became interested also."

"But that still does not explain why you printed them. It must have cost you a small fortune to spend eight months on this project."

"Ah, my friend, you must understand that I am not in this business for philanthropic reasons. I am going to make a lot of money from this book—and, I might add, so will you."

"But Aldus, was it not a gamble for you?"

"I don't think so. As a matter of fact, I know it wasn't. Look at what is being published these days. Practically everything is about religion, God, and how one must live like a good Christian. I think that true scholars are desperate to read something entirely different for a change, something that will allow them to be entertained and learn at the same time. Reading your translations and interpretations of these proverbs will be a great learning experience for every scholar and even non-scholar who can read Latin. You, sir, will soon be the most famous Dutchman in the world."

Erasmus remained quiet for a while. He had become used to the constant flattery from people who hardly meant it, but the printer was the not type to give empty praise. Erasmus realized that Aldus had just stated a fact.

"Thank you," was all he said.
"You are welcome." And with that the two friends raised their glasses.

Adagiorum Chiliades Tres left the presses in September 1508, and as Aldus had predicted, it immediately became an enormous success. At least forty new editions were printed in the course of the following century. Not everyone was pleased with the new book, however. Erasmus was accused of plagiarism by his friend Polydore Vergil (1470–1555), who in April 1498 had published *Liber Proverbiorum* (Book of Proverbs), which he later called his *Adagia*. Erasmus and Vergil, who had changed his surname to Virgil after the famous Roman poet, had become friends when Vergil moved from Italy to England in 1501. Erasmus explained to his friend that he did not know of his book at the time that *Adagiorum Chiliades Tres* was written. Fortunately, the men's friendship survived the disagreement.[14]

At Aldus's urging, Erasmus stayed in Venice until the end of October and translated the works of Plautus and other ancient playwrights. The market for books about old plays and historical events had exploded with the advent of the printing press. The rulers and the members of the prosperous merchant classes in Europe had one language in common— Latin—and they were eager to read newly published works. There was fierce competition among printers to find good writers. Erasmus was highly sought after for his prolific pen and ability to produce works in elegant Latin. In no time, he became a well-to-do man, and his clothes were evidence thereof. The man who once roamed Paris in a filthy monk's habit and cowl now, without permission from the church, roamed Venice in a new full-length dress coat made of fine material and a cap, as was fashionable among leading citizens of the time

From Venice, Erasmus traveled to Padua, where for a few months he tutored eighteen-year-old Prince Alexander, the illegitimate son of King

---

[14] A few years later, Erasmus asked Vergil, whose Latin he admired, to translate *De Perfecto Monacho* (*The Perfect Monk*) by St. Chrysostom (347–407). In 1528, Vergil wrote Erasmus to tell him, "Everyone is saying that your unrivalled learning has made you immortal already."

James IV of Scotland[15] and his mistress, Marion Boyd. Three years earlier, Alexander had been appointed by his father as archbishop of St. Andrews. Erasmus liked his new pupil, but unfortunately, the prince was severely myopic, which required the two to work sitting close together. Wherever they walked through the city, Erasmus had to describe everything to his pupil—the architectural style of the buildings, the antics of the pigeons who ran after bread crumbs in the town square, and, to Erasmus's amusement, the appearance of any fashionable young ladies. Erasmus did not mind, because the young prince was an intelligent student and moreover, the job paid well.

Alexander returned to Scotland at the end of 1508, but before he departed, he gave his teacher a ring, set with a stone carved with the likeness of the Roman god Terminus, the protector of the boundary markers. Erasmus had the ring engraved with either *Cedo nulli Terminus* ("Grant no limits" or "Respect no boundaries"), according to some historians, or *Concedo nulli Terminus* (Yield only to death), according to others. Latinists have debated the meaning of the two possible inscriptions for centuries, and Erasmus's true intent is still not clear. Four years later, Erasmus mourned the loss of Alexander, who, along with King James and most of the Scottish noble class, was killed in a disastrous battle versus the English army in the field of Flodden, about fifty miles southeast of Edinburgh. Three centuries later, Sir Walter Scott memorialized the battle in his poem *Marmion: A Tale of Flodden Field*:

> They close, in clouds of smoke and dust,
> With sword-sway and with lance's thrust;
> And such a yell was there,
> Of sudden and portentous birth,
> As if men fought in upper earth,
> And fiends in upper air.

In February 1509, Erasmus left for Rome, arriving in the papal city in early summer. While there, he received a letter dated May 27 from his English friend William Blount, informing him that King Henry VII had

---

[15] The same James IV who supported Perkin Warbeck's claim to the English throne.

died on April 21 and that his successor, Henry VIII, whom Erasmus had met years earlier on his eighth birthday, expressed an immediate desire to attach Erasmus to his court, although his official coronation would not take place until June.

> If you could have seen the tremendous enthusiasm and pride with which the people embraced their new king, you would weep for pleasure. Soon, you will receive a letter from his majesty written under his own hand, an honour which befalls but few. … Archbishop Warham is so charmed with your *Adagia*, that I cannot get it back. He sends you five pounds for the expenses of your journey, and I add as much more.

Blount's letter included a message from the new king:

> Our acquaintance began when I was a boy … The regard which I then learnt to feel for you has been increased by the honourable mention which you have made of me in your writings … So far you have borne your burden alone; give me the pleasure of assisting and protecting you … Come to England and assure yourself of a hearty welcome … name your own terms. We shall ask nothing of you save to make our Realm your home … Come to us, therefore, my dear Erasmus, and let your presence be your answer to my invitation.

Erasmus did not immediately reply to the king's invitation. First, he wanted to explore Rome.

Erasmus had arrived in Rome with a fistful of letters of introduction from various notables, but he could have saved himself the trouble of obtaining them, as he was welcomed with open arms by the Roman Catholic hierarchy. He met Cardinal Rafael Riario, who was a nephew of Pope Julius II and would become one of Erasmus's strongest protectors. He was also introduced to Cardinal Giovanni de Medici, the future Pope Leo X.

Cardinal Domenico Grimani, a Venetian, was especially eager to meet Erasmus, having heard much about the Dutchman from his sources in Venice. After ignoring several invitations from Grimani, Erasmus finally relented and rode his horse to the courtyard of Grimani's grand palace, where a servant took charge of his mount and directed Erasmus to an antechamber.

"Can you direct me to the study of Cardinal Grimani?" he asked the only person in the chamber.

"His Eminence has an important guest right now. May I ask why you wish to see him, sir?"

"I would like to pay my respect to the cardinal, but I can come back another day."

"Please give me your name, so that I can tell His Eminence that you have called."

"I am Desiderius Erasmus."

The man stood up straight, his eyes opening in alarm. "Ah, please wait here, sir," he said with sudden urgency and ran away. Within a few minutes, he returned and ushered Erasmus into the cardinal's office. The great man arose from his chair, spread his arms open in welcome, and walked around his desk to meet Erasmus in the middle of the room. For a moment, the slender Erasmus feared that he would be asphyxiated against the cardinal's more than ample stomach. Fortunately, the cardinal finally released him, and Erasmus could breathe again.

"Father Erasmus, you have no idea how much I have longed to meet you. It is a great pleasure, indeed, sir. Come, let us sit down, and we can talk at leisure."

And talk they did for nearly two hours, after which Grimani showed Erasmus his library, the second best in the city. At one point, the cardinal offered his guest a position in Rome, but Erasmus confided that he had been sent for by the king of England. When it was time to leave, the cardinal rested his chin on the upper fold of his neck and looked sideways at his guest.

"You know, Erasmus, I have read your *Adagio*. You show great insights, and you are not afraid to express them. That is a rarity these days, and I urge you to continue. My door will always be open to you, and you can forever count on my assistance, should you need it. Do come back, please. I mean that sincerely."

At that point, an elderly man entered the chamber, and Grimani smiled. "This is my dear father," he said, without adding that the old man had recently escaped from the island of Chios, where he had been exiled by the doge of Venice after losing two sea battles against the Ottoman fleets.[16] "Now, before you leave, is there anything I can do for you?" Grimani asked eagerly.

"Yes, please," Erasmus replied. "I would like to study the *Summa Theologica*. Do you think that you could help me gain access to a copy?"

"Of course. Give me a moment to write a note to Paulus Bombasius, the Vatican librarian."

The next day, with Grimani's note in hand, Erasmus entered the great library of the Vatican, where Bombasius met him. "It is a great honor to welcome you, Erasmus. How can I help you?"

"I would like to study Thomas Aquinas's *Summa Theologica*."

"By all means, sir. Which part?"

"The whole book."

The librarian frowned. "Pardon me, but there seems to be a little misunderstanding. It is not written in the form of a book. It is a collection of folio pages. More than a thousand, as a matter of fact."

"Oh, I did not know." Erasmus paused. "Perhaps you can give me his writings about God."

"We certainly can, but I warn you, I believe that numbers eighty-three folios. More like a book by itself, with more than 150,000 words."

Erasmus stared at the librarian in amazement. He became even more astonished when he later read the prologue to the folio: "The purpose of this book is to treat those things that pertain to the Christian religion as a manual for beginners—to treat those things, so far as the subject will permit, with brevity and clearness."

Erasmus's favorable opinion of St. Aquinas, which was based entirely on what he had heard from others, evaporated when he read the prologue.

---

[16] Not long after his father arrived in Rome, the cardinal managed to have the exile order removed. In 1521, at age eighty-seven, his father was elected doge of Venice.

As he continued to read, his admiration quickly changed into indignation. This was not the work of a teacher; it was more akin to that of a pretentious person, a pedant, a dictator. It did not surprise him that the bishop of Paris had condemned the teaching of the Dominican friar and that the bishop of Oxford did the same a few months later. How could this enormous mountain of paper, safely put away in the Vatican, possibly be useful for the clergy at large, let alone for beginners? He finally understood why, in 1505, John Colet had not explained his objection to Aquinas and urged Erasmus to read the *Summa Theologica*. "Thank you. That was quite an education," he said to a broadly smiling Bombasius on his way out.

Just as he had ignored the magnificent vistas of the Alps, Erasmus was uninterested in what Rome had to offer in the form of architecture, museums, and churches. He was only interested in libraries; years later, he was reported as having remarked, "There is no Rome, except her ruins and rubbish, the scars and vestiges of her former disasters. Take away the pope and the cardinals, what then would be Rome?" To him, the pontifical court was not much more than the world's largest peddler's office—and he had learned how to peddle.

Rome presented Erasmus with everything he desired. Several cardinals invited him to their dinner tables, rich and influential citizens clamored to be his friend, and scholars opened their libraries to him. He received many offers of important positions within the Church and the civil offices. With Cardinal Grimani as his protector, a rapid advance within the hierarchy of the Church would have been secure. His would-be benefactors did not know that he could not accept their offers. Doing so would mean that he would have to reveal the secret of his birth.

No matter how high he rose in the world, Erasmus was always plagued by the fact that he was a bastard child. Illegitimate children did not have the same rights or protections as other citizens. For example, they were barred from giving testimony in a court of law, even in their own defense. Furthermore, they could not hold political office—the Dutch Charter of 1417 clearly stated, "Towns shall never have a bailiff who is not an honest man or who is a bastard."

Erasmus was painfully aware that he was not even an ordinary bastard but the illegitimate son of a priest, the worst kind of all in the eyes of the Church. The Church allowed such men to become priests, but they could never be promoted to a higher rank within the Church or receive benefices without dispensation from the pope. When the bishop of Utrecht ordained Erasmus, he surely did not know the circumstances of his birth, and Erasmus had purposely neglected to inform him.

All of this weighed on Erasmus. From early on, he resolved to excel and rise above the circumstances of his birth. His ambition explains why he hated living in monasteries—he felt that the institution was keeping him down. He aspired to rise higher in the world, and in order to do so, Erasmus realized, he would one day need to resolve the issue of his birth.

The Church in Rome had already been made aware of Erasmus's illegitimacy but not its extent. Several years earlier, King Henry VII had promised Erasmus a Church benefice, which Erasmus could not accept without permission from Rome. On January 4, 1506, Pope Julius II issued a dispensation allowing Erasmus to hold and keep any ecclesiastical benefice, but Erasmus received the dispensation under false pretenses. In his application, he revealed that his father was a single man and his mother a widow. He did not mention that his father was a priest. That crucial omission would continue to haunt him.

7

---❯◆❮---

Professor Luther

1507–1516

Delegate to Rome - Sent to Wittenberg - Johann von Staupitz - Secretary to Frederick the Wise - Doctor Luther - Of the Devil, shit, and piss - Meets Waldensians - Researches early church heretics

Martin discovered, to his dismay, that not everything was peaceful within the monastic world. A significant rivalry existed between the various orders. His Augustinian brothers sometimes ridiculed the Dominicans by calling them *Domini canes* (dogs of the Lord), but Martin paid little attention to such rivalries. However, an even larger struggle was brewing within the Augustinian order itself between the "reformed" and "conventional" monasteries. Martin continued to immerse himself in his studies and tried to keep to himself.

In the midst of the struggle, Johann van Staupitz, the vicar general of the Augustinian order in Germany, visited Erfurt. He and the general of the order in Rome had decided to bring all twenty-seven German Augustinian cloisters under one administration, which would impose strict rules of conduct over the order. Erfurt had long been the power center of the Observant Augustinians and was largely responsible for the election of von Staupitz as the new vicar general. It was therefore somewhat of a surprise to Martin when the Black Cloister and six other monasteries resisted the new arrangement for unification.

The seven cloisters that opposed the plan met in Nuremberg to plan a course of action. Luther was in attendance, representing the Erfurt Black Cloister. The decision was made to send two friars to Rome to appeal to Pope Leo X. A senior negotiator was selected, and Luther was chosen to accompany him as a member of the delegation.

Winter was a difficult time of year to travel, and trudging through the snow on foot across the Alps made the trip longer than expected. When Martin and his companions arrived in Rome after three weeks of hard travel and asked for an audience with the pope, the weary travelers learned that Leo X was wintering in southern Italy, where it was warmer. The general of the order, Egidio of Viterbo, refused to grant the delegation an audience, and the mission became a complete failure.

Nonetheless, Martin used his time in Rome well; he visited the catacombs, saw many shrines, and celebrated Mass wherever he could. One Saturday morning, he tried to say Mass at one of Rome's sacred chapels but found the altar crowded with so-called Mass priests, who were each assigned to say a number of masses on behalf of the dead. When his turn finally came, Martin tried to savor the moment, but he was much too slow for those waiting behind him. "*Passa, passa!*" (Hurry up!), they prompted, and poor Martin was forced to do so.

On his last day in Rome, he went to the *Scala Sancta*, the twenty-eight steps Jesus climbed on his way to his trial before Pontius Pilate. The stone stairway had been brought to Rome in 326 by St. Helena. Martin climbed the stairs on his knees, stopping on each step to kiss it and say a short prayer. With each step, Martin gained indulgences, which, because his own parents were still alive, he dedicated to his mother's deceased father, old Mr. Lindemann, whom Martin thought might still have been in purgatory. When he finally reached the *Sancta Sanctorum*, Martin was captivated by its treasures. A few years later, Pope Leo X ordered them locked up, away from public view forever.

Martin and his fellow delegates returned to Erfurt to report their failure to the Brothers of the Black Cloister. The brothers decided to mount another appeal, but Martin had had enough. "I will submit to the orders of vicar von Staupitz," he informed his colleagues.

"Then you are no longer welcome here," ordered the prior after hearing Martin's decision. "You can go to Wittenberg."

Martin was filled with disappointment when he saw Wittenberg for the first time. Built on a slight elevation of sandy soil, it was not much to look at. A quarter-mile-long narrow square separated the church and cloister from the castle and its church. The town of two thousand citizens was famous for brewing beer. Years later, Martin wrote a short poem describing his impression of the town:

> *Little land, little land,*
> *You are but a heap of sand.*
> *If I dig you, the soil is light;*
> *If I reap you, the yield is slight.*

Fortunately for Martin, Wittenberg was also home to the University of Wittenberg, founded in 1502, where Johann von Staupitz was dean of the theology faculty.

Martin had left Erfurt in a such hurry that he had not had an opportunity to say good-bye to Father Braun. After settling in his accommodations in the cloister at Wittenberg, Martin wrote his friend and mentor a letter to make amends:

> To the most honorable Johann Braun, devoted to Christ and the Virgin Mary, priest in Eisenach. My lord, dear Father!
> Brother Martin Luther, Augustinian, wishes you salvation and the Savior Himself, Jesus Christ. My lord and father, whom I esteem highly but love even more. Please stop wondering why I have left you clandestinely without saying goodbye, how I could bring myself to do such a thing, as if there were not the closest bond between us, as if ungrateful forgetfulness had blotted all memory from my heart, as if a cold withering storm had extinguished every spark of love in me. There is absolutely no truth in this. Things did not go according to my own plans.

It is true that I went away; but no, in actual fact the most and best part of me stayed behind with you and will always stay with you. I am absolutely convinced that I mean enough to you, since your faith in me did not arise from my merit but from your goodness, so that you will not allow me to lose for no reason what I received without reason. For you were never like that.

Thus we are separated in space, but have come even closer spiritually. And you agree—if I am not totally mistaken.

The letter continues at length in the same vein and in the poetic style that was common at the time, but the warmth of Luther's tone exceeded common convention.

Fortunately, Martin found another friend and father figure in Vicar von Staupitz, who kept an eye on the energetic monk and guided him in his studies. He also became the father confessor to the young monk but may have wished that was not the case. Martin still confessed excessively—so long and so often that an exasperated Staupitz finally exclaimed, "You want to be without sin, but you don't even have a sin. Murder, stealing, adultery, and such are the type of awful sins that Christ may forgive. You are blowing your imagined sins way out of proportion. Don't come back unless you commit a real sin!"

After this admonition, Martin shut himself in his cell, where he contemplated the impurity of his conscience, his lack of sufficient contriteness, and the many awful deeds that he had neglected to confess. Back he went to Staupitz, but before Martin could begin enumerating his new sins, the vicar stopped him.

"Now listen carefully, because I'm not going to say this again. Christ only forgives real sins. I want you to make a long list of actual sins that men commit, and when you feel the need for confession, I want you to look at that list and see whether your sin is on it. Don't come back to me without your list, because I will check it, and your so-called carnal sins had better not be on it."

Staupitz was a busy man, who, with his many responsibilities, negotiations, and travels, had little time for teaching and preaching at his university, but he always made time to have a talk with his protégé, as long as it was not for another confession. On a crisp October day in 1512, he took Martin out for a little fresh air in the garden that graced the front of the monastery.

"Let's sit on the bench below the pear tree," he suggested, and Martin, who loved the tree, eagerly agreed.

"Now, Brother Martin, I want you to obtain your doctor's degree and start preaching."

For a moment, Martin was flabbergasted. "Why me?" he blurted out. "I'm not ready. I'm too busy."

"You are as ready as you'll ever be. I want you to take over my Bible lectures."

"I can't do it. I need time to meditate, to think."

"You mean time to obsess about your imaginary sins? Well, son, this job will keep you from it."

Martin was desperate. "It will kill me. I won't even survive three months," he cried out.

"Brother Martin, the Lord has many great matters to deal with. He needs intelligent people in heaven." The vicar pulled a piece of paper out of his pocket and handed it to Martin. "Here is a license, making you a candidate for the doctorate. You will go to Leipzig to study and get your promotion."

Resigned, Martin knew that there could be no further argument. He bowed his head slightly and escorted the older man back to his office. On October 19, 1512, Vicar von Staupitz personally placed a woolen doctor's cap on Martin's head and a silver doctor's ring on his finger. Martin gave his first Bible lecture in Wittenberg on October 25. Although he was now a teacher, he felt that he still had much to learn, and he told his students, "I sense with certainty the weight upon my neck of this task … And I confess simply that to this day I cannot understand some of the psalms and unless, as I hope, the Lord will enlighten me through your talents, I cannot interpret them."

Over the next five years, Professor Luther devoted his lectures to the Psalms, the Epistles, and the Romans. He was given a small room above the front entrance of the monastery in which he could study and prepare his lectures without being disturbed. He turned out to be an excellent speaker, so much so that the young students looked forward to his lectures. Martin did not teach by merely repeating that which he had been taught; instead, he prepared his lectures by delving into the written word of others so that he could better understand the most difficult of all books: the Bible. Martin also urged his students to commit themselves only to good deeds, even though good deeds themselves were neither qualitatively nor quantitatively sufficient for salvation. Salvation could only come from the Church.

Frederick the Wise, the founder of the university and elector of Saxony, heard Luther preach every Sunday and was so impressed that he appointed Martin chaplain of his court and, shortly thereafter, his personal secretary. In his new role, Martin translated Latin and Greek literature and documents into German and accompanied the elector to important meetings throughout Saxony. At the same time, he maintained his professorship at the university.

When Martin preached, he did not mince words. When invoking the devil, he used graphic, sometimes even filthy language, such as, "If that is not enough for you, you Devil, I have also shit and pissed; wipe your mouth on that and take a hearty bite." On May 1, 1515, Staupitz assigned him to give a ceremonial sermon to the decision-making body of the Augustinian Observants in Gotha. His subject was the sin of slander, which he attributed to the work of the devil:

> A slanderer does nothing but ruminate the filth of others with his own teeth and wallow like a pig with his nose in the dirt. That is also why his droppings stink most, surpassed only by the Devil's. And though man drops his excrements in private, the slanderer does not respect this privacy. He gluts on the pleasure of wallowing in it and he does not deserve better according to God's righteous

judgment. When the slanderer whispers "Look how he has shit on himself," the best answer is "You go eat it."

Rather than being shocked, Martin's illustrious audience approved of his choice of words—they were used to such language. Indeed, rough language was not uncommon in sermons. Only a few weeks earlier, the cardinal of Mainz declared in open forum, "I know very well that without God's grace there is nothing good in me, and that I am as much a piece of useless, stinking shit as anyone else, if not more."

Martin continued to struggle with his "sexual impurity," a centuries-old problem for some Catholic clergy. Priests were advised not to say Mass after having had a seminal emission the night before. Martin, who wished to say Mass daily, was distraught. Staupitz sympathized with his protégé and prescribed what all parents and doctors prescribed—exercise, by which he actually meant more work. In May 1515, he arranged for Martin to be elected district vicar of ten monasteries, one of which was the Black Cloister. Martin's problem, however, persisted, and he returned to his mentor for advice.

"I, too, used to confess every day and resolved to remain devout," Staupitz told Martin. "My boy, I failed every time and finally, I gave up trying to deceive God. I was going to wait for God to come to me."

"How, then, can I repent for my sin?" Martin cried.

"Do you not know that repentance begins with the love of God?"

With those seven simple words—"repentance begins with the love of God"—Staupitz put Martin on the right path. He finally found peace with himself with respect to sexuality, but he continued to have what he called his "spiritual temptations," and Staupitz could not help him with those. Martin continued to fear that he was not contrite enough in the eyes of the Lord, that he did not appease God, and that God was angry with him.

"God is not angry with you. You are angry with God," Staupitz told him, repeating the exact words that Brother Johann had used years earlier in the Black Cloister.

The words stayed with Martin. Gradually, he came to understand that Christians could aid their own salvation by using the powers and gifts that God had given them.

The library of the monastery had a limited collection. There were not enough books to go around, so Vicar Staupitz asked Martin to read aloud to the other monks. After exhausting the monastery's collection, Martin received permission from Staupitz to go outside the walls of the cloister and walk to the nearby university library. There, he not only selected books to read aloud in the monastery but also had a chance to choose books for his personal reading.

Martin especially enjoyed *Exposition of the Canon of the Mass* by Gabriel Biel, as well as *Via Moderna*, written by the English philosopher William of Ockham, whom he considered a great dialectician. Reading meant learning for Martin, and learning meant going beyond the church doctrine as it applied to the Mass, the seven sacraments, and church ceremony. Through his reading, Martin gradually joined the ranks of those who placed their trust in the Bible and in God, the all-powerful. Instead of questioning and debating God's intentions, he asked himself, "Why not leave God alone and accept His goodness?"

Martin continued to read voraciously and retained that what made sense to him. He read several sermons given by Johannes Tauler (1300–1361), a Dominican philosopher from Strasbourg who believed, "The state of the soul is more affected by a personal relationship with God than by external practices." Tauler preached that "God in His wisdom has decided that He will reward no work but His own," a concept that Martin found difficult to comprehend. He found more clarity in another Tauler quote: "Never believe that true prayer consists of mere babbling, reciting many psalms and vigils, turning your beads while you allow your thoughts to roam." That was just the type of simple truth with which Martin could associate, and he incorporated it in his own teaching.

Martin found other simple truths in several works by Erasmus, who, in beautiful Latin, wrote down-to-earth messages in all his books. He nodded approvingly over Erasmus's assertion, "As far as practical piety is concerned, theologians are hardly recommended."

While Martin's readings continually enriched his mind, it also raised more and more questions, some of which dismayed his colleagues at the university. "The righteousness of God—can someone explain to me what that means?" he asked his colleagues one day.

"What is there to explain?" replied one of the other professors. "The Gospel is the power of God unto salvation for everyone that believeth; to the Jew first and also to the Greek. Romans 1:17 says, 'For therein is the righteousness of God revealed from faith to faith: as it is written, the just shall live by faith.' That is it, brother. Simple."

"It is not simple to me," said Martin. "Romans 1:18 continues 'For the wrath of God is revealed from Heaven against all ungodliness and unrighteousness of men, who hold the truth in unrighteousness.' It does not say what is and what is not righteousness."

"I think that it means doing that which is right," another brother said.

"I realize that," said Martin, "but Paul says that the righteous live by faith. Does that mean that I must be righteous to gain faith? What comes first?"

"Just read the Bible, and you will understand soon enough," the first professor said and walked out of the room. The others followed, one by one.

Martin never liked the word "righteousness"; he found it forbidding, exclusive, and harsh. The longer he thought about it, the more his dislike changed into anger. *If the righteousness of God means that He punishes the unrighteous sinner, who already is lost by his eternal sin, then this is not a loving God*, he thought. *This is a God with righteousness and wrath. Only God is righteous and I, Martin Luther, am not; I am a sinner. How can I love such a God who, according to Paul and St. Augustine, has already predetermined the destiny of man? This is a cruel God, a God I hate.*

"Have you never had this feeling?" he asked Staupitz, after explaining his thoughts to his learned and trusted mentor.

"No, I have not. I'm beginning to think that you cannot live without constant doubting and trying to find a reason for everything you read in the Bible. You thrive on it," Staupitz said wryly.

"I seek the love of God, and I can't find it through all that talk about righteousness, sin, wrath, and damnation. Where is the love?"

"It is there all around you, but you have closed your eyes and mind to it. You only see the ugly because that is what you want to see. Remember, Jesus himself doubted and cried out, 'My God, why have You forsaken me?' Go and seek love, Brother Luther."

Martin returned to his small room and opened the Bible to prepare for his next lecture. He turned to Psalm 72 and read all that God will do for the poor, the children, and the needy, the earth, the waters, and the seas. He stopped reading and leaned back and reflected, "This is not a harsh God; this is a God of love." The longer he thought, the more he realized how self-centered he had been, how he had lived without true faith, not recognizing that Jesus had died to save all. "Jesus has died for me, has made my sins his own, has freed me." It was as if a heavy burden had lifted, and he found himself smiling.

One day, on his way to the university, Martin's attention was drawn to a few strangers praying in the street. They were obviously very poor, and he asked them who they were.

"We are Waldensians, Father," one replied.

"I have never heard of that," Martin said. "Where do you come from?"

"We are disciples of Peter Waldo, Father."

Martin had never heard of Waldo and assumed he was not a man of the cloth. Nevertheless, he was curious enough to do some research and discovered that Peter Waldo (1140–1217), or Pierre Vaudès, as the French called him, was born in Lyon, the son of a wealthy merchant. One day, Waldo asked a priest how he could come closer to God and was told, "You will find your answer in Matthew 19:21—Jesus said unto him, if thou wilt be perfect, go, sell what thou hast, and give it to the poor, and thou shalt have treasure in Heaven, and come, and follow me."

Waldo promptly gave his fortune to the poor and began preaching in the streets of Lyon about the word of God and voluntary poverty. He appealed to the common people and quickly gained many followers. None could read the Bible, however, so Waldo commissioned a translation of portions of the Bible into vernacular French. In 1179, Pope Alexander III and the Curia summoned him to Rome to explain his actions. They were enraged that the Holy Book had been translated into common, plain language. Waldo and his followers, the Waldensians, were subsequently driven out of Lyon. In 1184, Waldo was officially excommunicated by Pope Lucius III, and the persecution of the Waldensians began in earnest.

Martin wondered why translating the Bible into a language accessible to common men was considered such a horrible, excommunicable offense. What was Rome afraid of? The longer he thought about it, the more his curiosity was piqued. If Waldo could be excommunicated for actions that Martin himself did not deem offensive, perhaps there were others as well. He decided to learn more about the histories of men who were branded heretics by the Church.

He began with Eckhart von Hochheim (1260–1328), who was Johannes Tauler's teacher. Hochheim was a Dominican monk in Erfurt who preached in German to lay groups such as the Friends of God. He inspired his listeners to do good works and eventually earned the moniker "inspirational layman." The archbishop of Cologne opposed Hochheim's unorthodox methods and accused him of heresy. Pope John XXII agreed with the archbishop and issued a bull against the monk's "heretical" statements. Shortly before he died, Hochheim was forced to withdraw his offending statements. From what Martin could discover, however, there never were "heretical" statements.

Martin next turned to the life of John Wycliffe (c. 1320–1384), an Oxford scholar who translated the Bible into vernacular English in 1381. Martin admired Wycliffe for advocating a clear separation between the church and the civil authorities. He was impressed by Wycliffe's condemnation of the immorality within the Church, especially the manner in which popes and archbishops appointed their family members to important Church positions in which they did little more than collect money. Martin himself hated to see teenage bishops and archbishops.

Jan I Ius (1369–1415) was yet another religious thinker who fascinated Martin. He preached against the amorality of the clergy, the episcopate, and the papacy. In 1406, two students brought him a document eulogizing Wycliffe, and Hus read it from the pulpit. Later, when Pope Alexander V, who resided in Avignon, issued a bull declaring that all of Wycliffe's writings be burned, Hus refused. Instead, he burned the bull and continued to defend Wycliffe. Hus wrote, "One pays for confession, for mass, for the Sacrament, blessings, funeral services, and for prayers. The very last penny which an old woman has saved will not be safe from the villainous priest."

In 1414, despite having received a promise of safe conduct from the pope, Hus was imprisoned and tortured, and on July 6, 1415, he was condemned to be burned alive. His jailers took him to the stake. He knelt and prayed but was denied a confessor. He forgave his enemies, and while standing on the pyre with his hands tied behind his back and a chain around his neck and the stake, he uttered his last words: "God is my witness that I have never taught that of which I have by false witnesses been accused. In the truth of the Gospel which I have written, taught and preached, I will die today with gladness." Martin not only sympathized with much of what Hus had preached, but he also could identify with the man who was caught at a time when the leadership of the Church was in total disarray.

When he finished his research, Martin came to realize that the men the Church had branded as "heretics" were not necessarily evil. Rather, they were men who believed in God but had offended the Church.

8

---◆---

Five Years in England and
the Praise of Folly

1509–1514

*Leaves Italy - Reads The Ship of Fools - Houseguest of Thomas More - The
Praise of Folly - Relies on the charity of friends - Andrew Ammonius - De
Ratione Studii - Colet's sermon - Satirizes Pope Julius II - Reconciles with
Servatius*

There is no country which has bred me so many friends,
so sincere, so learned, so devoted, so brilliant and so
distinguished by every kind of virtue, as the single city
of London; every one of whom has so vied in loving and
assisting me, that I know not whom I should prefer to
another, and am bound to return an equal affection to
them all. I hope it will soon come to pass that I shall meet
them again, not to part until separated by death.

Erasmus had written these words several years earlier to his friend John
Colet, but it was not until the late summer of 1509 that he finally had
a chance to return to the country he loved. He climbed onto his horse
and embarked on the long journey from Rome to England. His servant

followed behind on a mule, pulling a second mule loaded with Erasmus's luggage and books. They traveled via Florence and Milan, followed the east shore of Lake Como, and went straight north toward the Splügen Pass and into Switzerland. From there, they swung northwest to Zürich and Basel. They spent their nights in small inns, slept on straw mattresses, and ate food that more often than not was quite miserable. Only in the larger cities did Erasmus's reputation make him the welcomed guest of a bishop or the ranking nobleman.

During the first night after he left Rome, his never-idle mind pondered over his experiences in France and Italy, trying to discern the people who had left a meaningful impression on him from those who did not interest him. He recognized that the people in the second group lived mostly artificial lives, full of false pride and deceit. They were fools, and Erasmus decided to expose their folly. The movements of his horse made writing impossible, but when they stopped overnight, he wrote copious notes, first by the light of the setting sun and then by candlelight.

He also wrote about the hardships of his travels. The long hours on horseback provided little physical exercise, and he adopted a habit of scratching his groin to provoke bowel movements. The area became inflamed and swollen, and a hard lump appeared higher up the groin. "The awkward gait of my horse twisted my kidneys extraordinarily. The trip was an incredible torture of my whole body. I couldn't eat the scantiest of lunches, but nevertheless ate some German *stockfisch*.[17] It was a mistake to eat the fish, for my stomach became so upset that I had to stick a finger in my throat, and out came the fish."

Later, he developed a large ulcer on his buttock, which fortunately burst, and a surgeon put a hot compress on it. But when a second ulcer appeared on his back and then a third, the surgeon, scared that Erasmus had the plague, refused to see him again. Erasmus next saw a Jewish doctor who made a superficial examination and declared, "I wish my body could be as healthy as yours," before leaving in a hurry.

"Does he think I have the plague?" Erasmus asked his servant.

---

[17] The German word *stockfisch* means "stickfish." Erasmus mistakenly explained that the *stockfisch* was named after the stick with which it was beaten. Instead, the fish was named after the sticks it was hung on to dry.

"Yes, he does. He found three buboes on your backside."

Erasmus tried to laugh it off, but he was actually very worried and sent for yet another surgeon, who examined him thoroughly. "I would not be afraid to go to bed with you," he said when he was finished. "And if you were a woman, I would have sex with you as well."

The great hypochondriac, remembering his mother's death from plague, was still not satisfied. He summoned a fourth doctor and tried to explain his entire story. The moment Erasmus mentioned his ulcers, however, the good doctor backed off. Erasmus gave him a gold coin for his efforts and finally commended himself to Christ the Physician. The ulcers healed with time.

At long last, Erasmus reached the Rhine River at Basel and began a more comfortable trip by boat for the remainder of the journey. In Strasbourg, the captain of the barge declared a twenty-four-hour layover, giving Erasmus a chance to stretch his legs. He disembarked to take a walk in town, and a book stand near the door of the cathedral drew his attention.

"Do you have anything written by a local author?" he asked the owner.

"Are you familiar with our Sebastian Brant, sir?"

"No, I'm afraid I have never heard of him."

"Well, then, you may be interested in this booklet, *Das Narrenschiff* [*The Ship of Fools*]. I also have it in Latin, but some of its charm is lost in the translation."

"I'll take the Latin version, please," said Erasmus, who was competent but not fluent in German. Brant was a lawyer, humanist, poet, and religious conservative who did not hesitate to expose the abuses in his church. His booklet was written in the form of an allegory, telling the tale of a ship filled with fools on their way to Narragonia, a fool's paradise led by St. Grobian, the patron saint of vulgar people. The author represented the helmsman of the ship.

Upon his arrival in England, Erasmus traveled to London, where he became a welcomed guest at the home of his old friend Thomas More. More was a busy lawyer, a member of Parliament, and one of only two undersheriffs of London, yet he found time to write and to study humanism. In his letters, Erasmus described More as an *omnium horarum homo* (a man of all seasons). Erasmus was delighted by More's happy family—he was especially touched by the devotion with which Thomas taught his uneducated wife and the time he spent with his four young children. At least a dozen birds chirped and sang away in the various rooms of the cheerful household, and a monkey had the run of the place.

The two men got along famously, so much so that their friends maintained that they fed off of each other. They spoke softly, but their words carried far. During his second stay in England, they had translated the work of the Greek satirist Lucian together, and Erasmus later had it published in Paris, he had been looking forward to working with More again.

"Well, my friend," began Thomas after he and Erasmus settled down by a log fire, Erasmus with a glass of wine in hand, his host with water. "Are you working on something interesting these days?"

"Thomas, I have just spent two months traveling by horse and boat. I couldn't see myself wasting that time in idleness or on meaningless writing. In the last couple of years, I have spent a lot of time in castles and palaces, and I had to endure and observe so much flattery and empty conversation that I decided to make some sport with the praise of folly."

"Hmm, an interesting project. Knowing you, you already have a title for it, don't you?"

"Indeed I have, and I hope you will find it worthy of you." Erasmus paused before continuing. "I call it *Moriae Encomium*."

"Now, wait a minute. That is not proper Latin."

Erasmus smiled. "Only you would pick that up. You are right, of course. It is actually a liberal translation of the Greek *Morias Enkomiom*, which is 'Praise of Folly' in English."

"Clever. Only you could get away with something like that." Thomas chuckled heartily.

"You, in particular, might want to know how I came up with it, because I was inspired by your surname, which is so close to the word *moriae*. In fact, the title could be read as 'Praise of More,'" Erasmus teased his host, "but the whole world knows that you are far from a folly. Wherefore you must not only accept this small recognition with good will but take upon yourself the defense of it; for as it is dedicated to you, it will not be solely mine but yours also. I think you will appreciate the book when it is finished."

"I certainly hope so," Thomas replied, smiling. "By the way, are you familiar with Nigel Wireker's satire *Speculum stultorum*?"

"Never heard of him."

"His real name was de Longchamps, and he lived about three centuries ago. The hero in his book is Burnellus, a foolish ass, who wants to grow a longer tail. It is a satire about the Church. He even goes so far as joining a religious order."

"It is interesting that you mention him," Erasmus said. "And it intrigues me, because in Strasbourg, I came across a German satire written by a man called Brant. Actually, I wouldn't be surprised if there are other people like Brant and Wireker in every country. It seems that the time is ripe to expose the excesses of the Church and of the princes."

"Yes, you may be right." Thomas leaned back as he looked pensively at the fire. Suddenly, he changed the topic, "By the way, did you hear that while you were traveling from Rome, King Henry married his brother's widow?"

"But that is against canon law!" exclaimed Erasmus with a deep frown. "How is that possible?"

"Well, as you may remember, back in 1489, after the war with Spain ended, old King Henry VII and the king of Spain signed the Peace Treaty of Medina Del Campo. To solidify the treaty, the two majesties married off their children, Prince Arthur and Catherine of Aragon. But it was only by proxy, as they were only three and four years old at the time. The actual marriage took place twelve years later, on November 14, 1501. Prince Arthur died on the second day of April the next year. There is some doubt that marriage was ever consummated."

"Let's see. That leaves … 111 days, more than enough time for teenagers to consummate, don't you think?" Erasmus asked, his lips pressed together to suppress a smile.

"Don't you get me involved in that stuff, you rascal," Thomas said, wagging his finger. "Anyway, Henry, who was still a prince at the time, had his eye on his much younger sister-in-law. Just before the old king's death in April, he and the king of Spain encouraged Henry and Catherine to get married, thus preserving the connection between the two countries."

"But what about the canon law forbidding such a marriage?"

"That was the easy part. Pope Julius II issued a bull of exemption, no doubt after a healthy contribution to his coffers," Thomas said with a laugh.

As he started to write the *Moriae Encomium*, Erasmus realized he had a much larger task ahead of him than he had originally anticipated. It was not a work that he could finish in a week or two. He visited the library at Cambridge and researched how the ancient philosophers used satire, wit, and comedy to expose the many wrongs of society. Homer, Virgil, Lucian, and even Jerome used the literary technique of personifying animals with the characteristics of humans. Rats, hogs, crabs, and gnats were some of the most popular. Erasmus believed that these satires could be quite effective, provided that "the foolery is so handled that the reader, provided he is not altogether thick-skulled, may reap the benefit."

In the early summer of 1511, the plague broke out in London. The English called it the "sweating sickness," but regardless of what they named the disease, the symptoms and outcome were the same: violent headache, pain in the neck and extremities, extreme weakness, and short periods of teeth-clattering cold spells, followed by a prolonged period of sweating, delirium, collapse into a deep sleep and, finally, death. Jane Colt, the beloved wife of Thomas More, contracted the harrowing disease and died in less than forty-eight hours. Erasmus, too, developed the early symptoms, but fortunately it was only a mild attack.

More, although grief-stricken, did what every practical man did when left with a brood of young children; he remarried. His new wife, Alice Middleton, was a rich widow several years his senior. "She is not what you would call a beauty, and she is not a girl," he said to Erasmus.

"Thomas, she is nearly in her old age," Erasmus teased him.

"Now don't exaggerate, my friend. She is thirty-nine and a good housewife."

"That I have noticed, and I have also heard her play some instruments. She will be good for your children." Erasmus did not mention her somber demeanor or her ugly nose, which a friend later described as "the hooked beak of a harpy." He could not help wondering how much pleasure she could offer his friend.

"Erasmus, what about you? You are moping around here, and I don't see you writing."

"I don't feel like working, Thomas. I am still too weak."

"Nonsense. You are just being lazy. What about the *Moriae*? You did start that, didn't you?"

"Yes, but I am beginning to wonder if anybody will be interested in it."

"Oh, but you are so wrong. Colet, Warham, and I all think that only you have the wit and the ability to fuel the type of satire needed to expose the ills of the church and the government. You must continue where you left off, Erasmus. You must finish it and publish it."

Erasmus remained silent for some time. He plucked a loose thread from his vest, rocked back and forth in his chair, put his hands between his knees, and at last looked up and nodded. "You have pushed me enough, Thomas. I'll do as you say, but you must promise me to read what I write as I go along."

"I will be glad to do that, my friend." It was More's time to smile. He knew that once Erasmus got started, there would be no way of stopping him, and he would not need help from anyone.

Erasmus continued to work diligently on the *Moriae* but never showed any drafts to Thomas. Finally, near the end of 1511, he handed his friend a completed manuscript. The book was written in the form of a fictional speech given by Folly, in the form of a woman. It read, in part:

The Praise of Folly
Moriae Encomium

An oration of fainted matter, spoken by Folly in her own person

The reason why I appear before you in this unusual outfit will soon be clear to you, because I am about to present to you an eulogy of myself, the one person most qualified to do so; you might say that I am blowing my own horn. I was born in Fortune Islands and I suckled the breasts of two jolly nymphs, Drunkenness, the daughter of Bacchus, and Ignorance, daughter of Pan. I am the giver of wealth whom the Greeks call Moria, the Latins Stultitia and our plain English, Folly ...

She pauses to take a sip, and continues by stating that philosophers are useless for real life. Socrates measured how far a flea could leap, how a fly made a buzzing sound, and he never meddled with common life. He was accused of wisdom only, and for that, he drank hemlock. Philosophers spoil a party with morose silence or troublesome disputes and a cow can dance better than they can. No city ever accepted a law of Aristotle or Plato or the precepts of Socrates.

Now look at how people behave—what greater folly than when some go to see a wooden or painted one-eye Christopher so that one shall not die that day or the soldier saluting a carving of Barbara so that he shall return safely from battle. Plant a small wax candle for Erasmus and say the right prayer and one will be rich. One saint is good for a toothache, another for a moaning woman, one to cure the sheep of rot. But chiefly, the Virgin Mother, to whom people attribute more than to the Son. Your priests allow and encourage such nonsense because it brings profit. Add to this those who during their lifetime make elaborate funeral arrangements and specify how many pallbearers must be hired and how many singers, how many candles must be burned. They might as well have planned a banquet. Yet those fools never build a temple for Folly—such ingratitude.

Perhaps it is better to remain quiet about the theologians, because if I do, they may attack me en masse and force me to retract that what I said, for, if I refuse, they will declare me a heretic. They are happy in their self-love and, as if they dwell in the third heaven, they look down on all others. They hide behind so many definitions, conclusions, corollaries, and arguments that not even Vulcan's net can catch them. They have an explanation for everything—how the world was created, how long Christ lay in the Virgin's womb, and how accidents subsist in the Eucharist without their substance. But ask them some offbeat questions and they have no answers—is it possible that God the Father hates the Son; could Christ take the likeness of a woman, a devil, an ass, or a piece of flint, or a gourd and then how that gourd should have preached or be hung on the cross? The apostles knew the mother of Jesus, but who among them has explained just how she escaped the stain of original sin as our theologians have done? They taught the gospel, "God is a Spirit and they that worship Him must do so in spirit and truth," but they never knew that a drawing on a wall ought to be worshipped as though it were Christ Himself, as long as two fingers are held up, the hair is long and uncombed, and three golden rays appear from the crown of the head. Theologians also know everything about Hell; that it is large enough to house all comers, has footpaths for the walkers, entertainment at dinner, and, yes, a field on which to play football.

Then there are the "religious" or "monks," two deceiving names, because, for the most part, they stay far away from religion. Most people detest them so much, that accidentally meeting one of them is considered bad luck. They reckon it one of the main points of piety if they are so illiterate that they cannot read. Some of them make a good living with their uncleanliness and beggary from door to door. They think they are setting an apostolic example by it. They take great pleasure in conceiving names such as Benedictines, Bernardines, Carmelites, Augustines and Jacobins as if it were not enough to be called "Christians." No wonder Christ will ask himself, "Where does this new kind of Jew come from?" Folly can dwell a long time on the monks and find little good in them.

Sciences have crept into the world with the other pests of mankind and among these sciences only those that come nearest to common sense, that is to say, folly, are valued. The theologians are half-starved, the naturalists out of heart, the astrologists laughed at and the logicians slighted. Only the physician is worth more than all the rest. And among them the more unlearned, impudent and ignorant he is, the higher he is esteemed among princes. Physics as it is now practiced by most men is nothing more than the art of flattery no less than rhetoric is. In the second place behind the doctors come the lawyers, whose profession most people laugh at as the ass of philosophy. However, they become rich, while the theologians eat radishes and fight a losing war against lice and fleas.

It now pleases me to expound kings and the nobility who sincerely worship me. Consider, a righteous king or prince has such responsibility that it is not worth perjuring himself or poisoning someone else to become a sovereign. All his time and effort I devoted to his public; he must follow all the laws and he is exposed to the public at all times. Instead of following my advice, kings live extravagantly; they hunt, raise fine horses, sell high offices and drain the wealth of their citizens into their own pocket. Their noble courtiers address them as "Your Grace," "Your Lordship" and "Your Majesty," while they practice the skill of flattery. They amuse themselves with dice, cards, clowns, fools, whores, and drink and they dwindle their lives away.

Our popes, cardinals, and bishops have diligently followed the example of the princes. They are too busy eating and leave the care of their sheep to their subordinates or to Christ Himself. However, when it comes to money matters, they truly act the part of the bishop; they oversee everything and overlook nothing. Cardinals should realize that they are the stewards, not the lords of spiritual affairs. Just look at their vestments: does the white upper garment not symbolize purity? Is not the scarlet or crimson of their lower garment the emblem of burning love and desire of

God? What about their outer garment that falls around His Reference's mule and is large enough to cover a camel? If they truly consider these questions, they would lead the weary and pious life lived by the ancient Apostles.

As for popes, if only they would remember the meaning of the name "pope," that is "father" or "holiness," who would purchase that post with all his substance or defend it with swords, poison, and all the force imaginable? If there be anything that requires work, it is handed over to Peter or Paul to do at their leisure, while anything of honor or pleasure is taken care of by the popes, they who insist that kings, no matter how great, bend and kiss their slippers. Although Peter said in the Gospels, "We have left all and followed Thee," the popes in our time insist on profanely attaching Peter's name to territories, cities, taxes, wages, and all money. Instead of defending the Church in the way that is necessary, the popes make war their only duty. They refer all apostolic work to the bishops, the bishops to the vicars, the vicars to their brother mendicants and they again throw the care of the flock on those that take the wool.

I do not intend to explore fully the lives of the popes and priests and let no one think that I reproach good clergymen when I praise the bad ones. Remember, man can only be happy when he possesses my favor, for Fortune favors me, while she always is hostile to the wise, because she rewards the fools. If anyone is in genuine need of wealth or ecclesiastical power, he had better be an ass or a buffalo than a wise man.

I could go on indefinitely with my praise, but my oration must come to an end. Lawyers will not be able to slander me that I have proven nothing. Following their example, I shall free my proofs from legal difficulties by admitting that my presentation contains nothing to the point, but rather to the wit. Remember, there are many annotations in the Bible about fools. Solomon in

Chapter Fifteen states, "A fool delights in his folly," and Ecclesiastes, whoever he was, wrote, "A fool walking along the way, being a fool, considers all men to be fools." Paul admitted, "I speak as a fool; take me as a fool." Saint Paul even ascribes folly to God, writing "The foolishness of God is wiser than man."

And now, lest I go on and on, let me sum up. Christian religion seems to have a certain relationship with folly, but fails to agree at all with wisdom. The majority of people gives greatest importance to riches and bodily comfort and believes in little beyond that; leaving last place to their soul, because they can not see it with their own eyes.

If I have said anything more boldly or impertinently than I ought, please remember that it is Folly and a woman who has spoken. You are mistaken if you think that I can remember anything I have said. The old saying goes, "I hate a drinking companion with a memory." Let me add a new one of my own, "I hate a student with a memory." Therefore, to your health, cheers, live and drink, my most celebrated disciples of Folly.

Erasmus had exposed the weak underpinning of society as none other could have or dared to. In some parts, he had crossed that fine line between satire and hard-bitten critique, but he was careful to make sure Folly's speech could be interpreted as a mere jest. Thomas noticed that Erasmus had not signed his name to the manuscript, although Folly mentioned his name in the text.

Erasmus hoped to have the *Moriae* published by Jodocus Badius, the respected Parisian printer, whom he had used in the past. Badius passed on the offer, however, and Erasmus instead gave the manuscript to a twenty-one-year-old agent, Richard Croke, who sent it to Gilles Gourmont, an obscure printer in Paris. Only a dozen books were printed, but they were of poor quality. Years later, when Erasmus finally saw an original copy, he thought it "in most villainous type and form." Erasmus did not earn a single penny from the first printing. In January 1512, a second edition was printed in Antwerp by Thierry Martens, and a third was printed by Schürer in August of the same year.

Another revised edition, printed by Johann Froben in Basel in 1515, was illustrated with a drawing by the seventeen-year-old Hans Holbein the Younger. The drawing depicts Folly, who has just finished her speech, descending the pulpit steps wearing a fool's cap that has donkey's ears with bells at their tips. With a fine sense of humor, young Holbein draws her audience of seven men likewise dressed as fools. Yet another edition contains a charcoal drawing by a Dutch contemporary of Erasmus, depicting Folly on a throne, six feet above a much larger audience milling about below. In the foreground are a bishop, several women, a nobleman with a side sword, a businessman, and a rotund monk speaking to Erasmus, whose finger is raised to make a point.

"Well, what do you think of the reworked *Moriae*?" Erasmus asked More one evening in the summer of 1514. Erasmus was leaving England the next day and wished to get his friend's opinion before departing.

"To begin with, it is far better than what you showed me three years ago. In a few places, your critique may be a bit too sharp, and there are also times that you may be too frivolous to some people's taste. But on the whole, it is excellent."

"From which corner do you think the greatest backlash will come?"

"From the theologians, of course. You really went after them with your sarcasm."

"They deserve it, don't you think?"

"What I think is not important, Erasmus." Thomas leaned forward and put his finger on the booklet. Looking very serious, he continued. "You have given the world something that only you could write and get away with, and yes, there will be many good people who will be offended."

"Funny that you say that, because I think that the good ones will take it in stride."

Thomas leaned back again. "You may be right. Nevertheless, you can expect some strong criticism from that corner."

"If there is, let them remember that I am not the first to write in this vein. Homer is at the top of a long list of famous authors who have ridiculed society and religion. As far as sarcasm is concerned, I think that is part of all satire, as long as it does not go to extremes. Remember, Folly was merely the narrator, and she never mentions anyone by name. But Thomas, my dear friend, why do I say all this to you, the defender of good causes? Remember, I dedicated the *Moriae* to you, and now it is yours. Good night, eloquent More, and don't forget to stoutly defend your Folly!"

Thomas More was right when he told Erasmus that there would be a backlash from the theologians. They, together with the monks, were upset and offended by Erasmus's fierce attack, but they took no action. Erasmus received only one negative letter about the *Moriae*, and it came from the University of Louvain. The faculty there had selected Maarten van Dorp as their spokesman, perhaps because he, like Erasmus, was a Dutchman. Dorp, a professor of divinity who was about twenty years younger than Erasmus, wrote:

> I am, most importantly, your fellow-countryman, admirer of your genius and a herald of your fame beyond all others. So now what I am going to write to you comes from the heart. You should know what the men here think of you in your absence. "What is this but madness, even if what he wrote were mostly true ... no one can read it without being offended ... to hear Christ and His Holy Life spoken of as nothing but a crazy notion?"
>
> Formerly, most members of the faculty of theology used to admire you and read your works: now, this unlucky *Praise of Folly* upsets everything. Is it not better to be praised? Does it not please us when even little dogs give us a flattering wave of their tails as a sign of friendship? "What can I do about it, what is done cannot be undone." You could accomplish this by writing and publishing against your *Praise of Folly* a *Praise of Wisdom*.

Erasmus replied:

> My dear Dorp, your letter gave me no offense because you advise me so sincerely, admonish me so amiably, and rebuke me so lovingly ... I value your single vote in my

favor more than a thousand votes of other men ... to be perfectly frank, I am almost sorry that I published my *Folly*. It has earned me a little notoriety. I spoke in the form of a joke, not rebuke, of advice to do good, not injure. You must have noticed that I never criticized by name ... I showed my *Folly* to several friends and they encouraged me to continue ... So, if all this, my dear Dorp, is ill-judged, your culprit owns up, or, at least, puts up no defense. However, does not St. Paul say, "Rebuke, reprove, exhort, in season, out of season?" Paul wants faults to be attacked in every possible way.

Tell me, why are theologians more offended than bishops, cardinals, popes? Since I published *Folly*, I have lived in many universities and great cities and not one theologian was annoyed with me. You write that your theologians are offended to hear Christ spoken of as nothing but a crazy notion, but why are they not offended when they hear Paul speak of the foolishness of God and the folly of the cross? How much better for peace and suitable to Christians' fairness of mind to take our exercise in the Scriptures without hurting one another and for theologians to study Greek, or Hebrew, or Latin, at least! Knowledge of these is so important for our understanding of Scriptures that it seems to me impudent for one who knows none of them to expect to be called a theologian. I do not believe that writing a *Praise of Wisdom* will affect a handful of prejudiced, uneducated people and I had better "let sleeping dogs lie." A fond farewell to you, my friend, dearest of mortal men.

Maarten van Dorp responded with a short, pleasant letter in which he thanked Erasmus for his lengthy reply.

There was, however, also much positive reaction to the *Moriae*; never before had a well-known person been so bold in exposing the many ills of society and the Church. Praise came from every corner of Europe, especially from those who recognized the genius in the author. Erasmus was not yet fifty and had already caused quite a stir in the Christian world.

The Church hierarchy in Rome remained silent.

Erasmus greatly enjoyed his time in England and was in no hurry to leave. After finishing the first version of *The Praise of Folly* in late 1511, he left Thomas More's house, and his other English friends took turns hosting him. He stayed with John Colet and William Grocyn, as well as John Fisher, the bishop of Rochester, and William Warham, the archbishop of Canterbury. These four gentlemen knew full well that their guest had no income to speak of, and each tried to help Erasmus as best as he could.

Erasmus had befriended William Warham during his second visit to England in 1505 and had dedicated his translation of *Hecuba* to him. Warham was eager to help his new friend establish himself financially. He knew that in 1509, the king had written to Erasmus, offering him a position at court, but it had not come to fruition. Later in the same year, Warham wrote to Erasmus, who was in Italy at the time, to convey a generous offer: "I desire your consent to accept from me 150 nobles on your arrival in England under the condition that you agree to spend the rest of your life in England and have the privilege of visiting your native country and your other friends at opportune times." However, living anywhere permanently was not appealing to Erasmus; he enjoyed his freedom too much. He politely refused the offer.

Now that Erasmus was in England, Warham decided to make him a second offer to stay in the country. He invited Erasmus to lunch and began, "My friend, I know that life has not been easy for you these last two years."

Erasmus smiled; he could not agree more. "I am rich in golden promises, and meantime, I am starving bravely."

"Now, now, my dear Erasmus. It is a good thing that I know of your tendency to exaggerate. But I have some news that may cheer you up. The king has asked me to give you fifty Henry VII gold angels, and I have been waiting for an opportunity to present them to you. Moreover, a vacancy presented itself in the parish of Aldington in Kent, and I would like to appoint you as the new rector, with an annual income of thirty-six pounds, six shillings, and eight pence. What do you think?"

"You overwhelm me, sir. I don't know what to say."

"Well, take a few days to think it over, and let me know."

He is throwing me a lifeline, Erasmus thought after Warham left. He was really not interested in the job, however, especially after asking around and learning that Aldington was a hamlet ten miles outside Oxford at the crossing of Bank and Forge Hill Roads. The parish population was less than a thousand. He would be buried there. He had to find a diplomatic way out.

"No words can describe my gratitude to Your Eminence," he said four days later, when he visited Warham again. "Unfortunately, I fear that my command of the English language is not sufficient enough to communicate effectively with the parishioners."

"I appreciate your honesty, dear Erasmus, but if you cannot converse with the parishioners in their own vernacular speech, then perhaps we can make another arrangement. Your command of Latin and Greek is such that I may have to make an exception in your case."

"Perhaps there is another solution?" Erasmus ventured. "I do believe that canon law permits for a substitute to take over my parish duties." He paused before continuing. "Would it then be possible for me to receive a pension? A smaller amount, of course."

Warham smiled. "I see that you came prepared, my friend. Indeed, that is a possibility. I may be able to convince John Thorton, prior of St. Martin's, to step in as rector of Aldington. Your pension would then be twenty pounds annually, half to be paid on September 29 when we celebrate the archangel Michael, and half on March 25, on what we call Lady Day."

Erasmus threw up his hands. "That is much too generous. I do not think that I can accept."

"Nonsense, sir. It is the least I can do for your love of England, and it will help you in your work. After all, who has a fairer claim to live off a church income than you?"

Erasmus accepted the generous offer. Five weeks later, he dedicated a larger edition of Lucian's *Dialogues* to his new benefactor.

The small pension became Erasmus's only source of income, but although it was supplemented when several of his friends occasionally gave him small sums of money, it was not nearly enough to support the comfortable lifestyle to which he had become accustomed and insisted on maintaining. He simply could not live without good French wine, two decent horses, and a student server.

Fortunately, he was able to find a comfortable and affordable living arrangement. He had been invited to share rented rooms—initially without sharing the burden of rent—by Andreas Ammonius, an Italian by birth who had changed his name to Andrew upon arriving in England. He had secured a position as the Latin secretary of William Blount, on Erasmus's recommendation, and he wished to repay Erasmus's kindness.

"Did you know that all those beautiful letters that Lord Mountjoy sent to you over the years were actually written by me?" Ammonius asked shortly after his new friend moved in.

"You forget, my dear Andrew, that his lordship was one of my pupils in Paris and that he is well versed in Latin. Nevertheless, I had my doubts that he had written such beautiful letters."

"I also write poetry," Ammonius ventured. "I have a few poems right here, if you would care to look at them … please?" He had a silent hope that with Erasmus's help, the poems could be published in a short volume.

"They are well written. You should publish them," Erasmus said after he had read Ammonius's work.

"I was hoping that you would help me with that. You must know some good printers."

"Yes, I do, and I will help you. However, I would suggest that you dedicate your poems to someone before you print them."

"I already did so," Ammonius replied, handing Erasmus a handwritten sheet.

Erasmus took one quick look at the length of the dedication and handed it back. "That is much too elaborate. I am sure Lord Mountjoy will deeply appreciate the honor, but you have overdone it." Erasmus was right, for he knew his friend well. William Blount did not like the original dedication and accepted the honor only after Ammonius sent him a much shorter, revised version for his approval.

A few days later, Erasmus had lunch with John Colet in his garden. It was spring, and the magnolias were in full blossom. The sun played through the first light-green leaves of an old oak tree.

"I love to sit here and look at the leaves while they still have that youthful shine," Colet sighed. "Don't you think it is beautiful?" Erasmus was looking at the ground. "Look up my friend." When his guest did not respond, he asked, "Are you colorblind?"

"No, John, it is just one of my shortcomings. I am sorry, but I never had an eye for that sort of thing."

"That's a pity, because you miss out. What is on your mind?"

"I want to congratulate you on your work in founding St. Paul's School."

"Thank you, Erasmus. I wonder … can you do me a favor? I need to select a Latin grammar book for the school, and I have decided not to use Linacre's. Our headmaster, William Lily, is working on writing a new one, and I would greatly appreciate it if you would give him a hand."

"But of course, John. I would be glad to."

"Thank you. Now, how about you? Anything new coming up?"

"I have been working on a book titled *De copia verborum ac rerum*, or 'On the Abundance of Expressions and Ideas.' I started it in Paris, and it is nearly finished."

"Who is your intended reading audience?"

"Students. I am thinking of dedicating it to young Prince Henry."

"Why not dedicate it to my school?"

"Now, John, you know that your school does not have any money yet. I need to see a little cash for my efforts." When Colet laughed, Erasmus persisted, "I am serious, John. I have two years of work and expenses invested in it."

Colet leaned forward; he drummed the fingers of his left hand, and he pulled on the skin below his chin with his right. "I can give you fifteen angels to offset your cost."

With raised eyebrows, Erasmus asked, "Do you think that is enough?"

Colet leaned forward. "All right … I will *gladly* give you fifteen."

Now it was Erasmus's turn to laugh. "Dear John, if you put it that way, then I will *gladly* accept." And with that, the two friends shook hands.

Erasmus enjoyed helping Lily produce the grammar book. When he was finished, he also presented Colet with a small booklet titled *De ratione studii* (Upon the Correct Method of Instruction), which outlined the correct way of teaching Latin and Greek. Colet loved it. Erasmus then made a short trip to Paris for a meeting with the printer Jodocus Badius, who had previously declined to print the first edition of the *Moriae*.

"You still do not want to take my *Moriae*, do you?" Erasmus asked Badius impatiently.

"My dear Erasmus, I cannot but believe that it will hurt your reputation and your career. Please do not ask me to print it." Badius looked unhappy.

"Well, how about a revised and updated edition of the *Adagia*? Will that interest you?"

Badius's face lit up with pleasure. "I am very interested! As a matter of fact, I had every intention to ask you for it."

"But that is not all. I have here a book of poems by Andreas Ammonius, which I think are worthwhile for you as well."

Erasmus left Paris with an advance for the new *Adagia* and a promise of reimbursement for Ammonius.

Erasmus returned to England with his advance in his pocket, but even when coupled with his pension, it still did not amount to what he considered a livable income. He continued to rely on the generosity of his friends and spent some time at Queen's College, Cambridge, at the invitation of John Fisher. He was an insufferable beggar, especially from Colet, whom Erasmus regarded as a rich man. "Oh, this begging. I hate myself for it. I must either fall into some good fortune or imitate Diogenes and live in poverty," he wrote, hinting to Colet.

Colet did not bite—perhaps he had heard about the pension. He chastised Erasmus somewhat, writing:

> You do well to imitate Diogenes and, taking pleasure in poverty, consider yourself the king of kings. But I am smiling at your innate simplicity, Erasmus, and at the same time charmed that in this odious begging habit of yours, you can plead the cause of others ... How often have I wished that you were a teacher at my school ... for

the students as well as for our teachers. If you beg humbly, I have some money of my own to share with you. Ask without shame, and poverty shall in a poor way come to the aid of poverty. Farewell, and pray write often to me.

London, October 1511

Colet himself did not lead a lavish lifestyle, although three years earlier he had inherited the wealth of his father, who had twice been elected lord mayor of London. He used his inheritance for the establishment of St. Paul's School and lived humbly, without feasts or fancy clothes. He was not always inclined to help Erasmus who, by contrast, was born poor but was determined to spend the rest of his life in some comfort. Colet was aware that Erasmus had rejected several well-paying positions from kings and princes, cardinals and bishops, who all offered him positions in their courts. Erasmus, however, required his freedom and refused to be tied down, even if it meant that he had to beg off his friends.

Erasmus was annoyed by Colet's response. "If you have fun with my role of playing Diogenes, I am indeed glad to give you that pleasure," Erasmus wrote back to Colet with a certain sarcasm and arrogance.

That phrase of yours has rankled me considerably even if it was a joke—if you will humbly beg. Perhaps you mean that it is false pride on my part that makes me bear my lot so poorly ... I ask you, who can be more impudent or abject than I, who has so long begged openly in England? ... I hate my ill luck, because it does not even permit me to feel ashamed. However, if need be, I will end this letter as immodestly as possible. I am not brazen-faced enough to ask you under any pretext, but to reject a gift, freely offered by such a friend, especially in my present circumstances. Farewell.

Cambridge, 29 October 1511

The abruptness of this farewell was most unlike Erasmus, and Colet no doubt felt it. Their friendship soured, but fortunately, the animosity did not last long. Erasmus was the first to make a move. In a November

26 letter to Ammonius, he mentioned that he had written to Colet, and he continued, "If you happen to see Colet and he says anything about me, offer him your help if he wants to write anything to me." He was calling out for reconciliation.

On February 6, 1512, Archbishop Warham presided over the convocation in St. Paul's Cathedral, where an audience of over four hundred bishops and priests of the archdiocese of Canterbury had gathered to hear Colet's sermon. Colet stood quietly, waiting for the last voice in the audience to die down before beginning:

> Nothing has disfigured the face of the Church as has the faction of secular and worldly living in clerks and priests … How much greediness and appetite for honor and dignity is nowadays in men of the Church … Carnal concupiscence has grown and waxed in the Church as a flood of lust … All corruptness, all the decay of the Church come from the covetousness of priests.
>
> Secular evil is the occupation wherein priests and bishops nowadays are busy … The beautiful order and holy dignity in the Church is confused when the highests in the Church meddle with vile and earthy things …
>
> Go now in the Spirit that you have called on … ordain only those things that may be profitable to the Church … praise unto you and honor unto God. Unto whom be all honor and glory forever more. Amen.

Colet had spoken calmly during his hour-long sermon and never raised his voice. He had shown his audience the error of their ways and made them ashamed of their unchristian lifestyles. The chastised audience filed out in complete silence.[18]

In March, Colet extended an olive branch to Erasmus by sending him a copy of the St. Paul's sermon along with a note:

---

[18]   This sermon led the famed British historian Frederic Seebohm (1833–1912) to call John Colet "one of the Reformers before the Reformation."

Indeed, dearest Erasmus, I have not heard anything fresh concerning you since your departure. I have been in the country with my mother to console her on the death of a servant … on the night when I returned, I received your letter … Please let me have the second part of your *Copia*.

Erasmus wrote back:

He is no friend to England that will not do his best to aid such enterprise. I am well aware how much I owe to England generally and how greatly I am obliged to you privately … to assist in the furniture of your school, I will place its name on two Commentaries de Copia … Farewell, most excellent Colet.

Six months later, Colet paid Erasmus the equivalent of the fifteen gold angels he had promised him for *De copia verborum ac rerum*. The payment was made in the form of French crowns.

In January 1513, Erasmus had another attack of what he called "the stone." The passage of the kidney stone was extremely painful, but there was not much that could be done about it. He wrote to William Warham, lamenting, "I have fallen into the hands of doctors and apothecaries, in other words of butchers and harpies." He continued, "I am still in labor and it is uncertain when and what I shall bring forth."

Warham wrote back: "What business do you have with stones? You are busy working on great buildings, are you? To make it easier for you, I have changed thirty angels into ten gold pieces. A gold physic will help cure you."

"You know, I should have stayed in Italy," Andrew Ammonius moaned one day after Erasmus's crisis was over. They had just polished off dinner and were well into their third bottle of wine. "Coming to England didn't turn out as well as I expected."

"I sometimes feel the same way," sighed Erasmus. "These Englishmen can be such undisciplined bulls, such miserly dung-eaters."

"The common sort of people at Cambridge surpass all these inhospitable Britons in barbarity. They ignore all obligations and are completely devoid of any refinement. Do you not agree?"

"I cannot agree with you more, dear Andrew. I have translated Lucian and Plutarch and offered them as bait on the first of January, but I am pretty sure that it will be a waste of time. And what kind of university is this? There is not one of them who can write a decent piece."

Ammonius got up to refill their glasses. "I wish you would show me a way out."

"You must put up a bold front, my friend, and never be ashamed of anything. Push everybody who obstructs you out of the way, and give nothing unless you know that you will get something in return. You know how vain and jealous the English are. Make use of it. Start using two horses instead of one to demonstrate your importance. Threaten to leave and start packing. Show them letters in which you are invited to go somewhere else and take a few days off, so that they will miss you. Fake it."

"Thank you, Erasmus. As always, you give good advice. By the way, yesterday I heard someone joke that so many heretics have been burned at the stake that there may be a shortage of wood for our fireplaces during the winter months."

"I don't think we have to worry," said Erasmus. "Torture has been refined so much that fewer and fewer heretics are being burned. They all 'confess' under torture and are welcomed back into the church."

On February 21, 1513, Pope Julius II, who was also known as the Warrior Pope, died, leaving a full money chest for his successor. Cardinal Giovanni de' Medici, whom Erasmus had met briefly four years earlier while he was in Rome, was elected as the new pope at the age of thirty-seven; he took the name Leo X. At the time, much of Europe was in a state of war, fighting over various cities and borders. Erasmus, who was living safely in England at the time, was full of contempt for warring kings and popes, declaring, "We are set upon by the plague and threatened by robbers. The embargo of French wine forces us to drink inferior wine, but hooray, we are the conquerors of the world." His disgust prompted him, in deep secret, to write *Julius exclusus*, one of the finest satires ever written, which reads, in part:

Julius arrives at the closed door to heaven and bangs on the door with both fists. A peephole in the door opens and a face appears.

P [St. Peter]: Who are you and what do you want?

J [Julius]: I want you to open this door forthwith.

P: You still have not told me who you are.

J: Don't you see my crown, man, and the letters PM.

P: I suppose that means Pestis Maxima. (Big Troublemaker)

J: Of course not! Pontifex Maximus. (Supreme Pontiff)

P: So what? I still won't let you in unless you are holy.

J: Everybody always called me "most holy." There are thousands of bulls ...

P: "Cock-and-bulls," you mean! You really do not see the difference between being holy and being called holy, do you? I begin to suspect that you are that pagan Julius returning from Hell in disguise to mock me.

J: Enough of that talk. If you do not open quickly, I'll excommunicate you with this bull especially prepared for this purpose.

P: Christ never told us anything about excommunication and bulls.

J: So what! You are not even a priest and you have no power to consecrate.

P: That's because I am dead, I suppose.

J: Exactly.

P: You are dead, too. But tell me, why were you an outstanding pope?

J: In the first place, I am a Ligurian and not a Jew like you. I was the nephew of Sixtus, a truly supreme pontiff. And I raised an immense amount of money by using my wits.

P: What do you mean by that?

J: I promised benefices in return for cash and ...

P: (Interrupting) Who are those youths with that blond, curly hair behind you?

J: They are for my personal pleasure.

P: And the dark men with the scars?

J: They are my soldiers who died in battle for the Church. I promised them that they would go straight to Heaven.

P: I can assure you that I do not let any of them in. Now, tell me, why do you wear a sword?

J: You don't want me to fight naked, do you?

P: When I was Supreme Pontiff, I did not carry a real sword. My sword was the word of God. By the way, you mentioned Sixtus; no such person ever arrived here.

J: He was a Franciscan, no less.

P: But was he poor?

J: Of course not. After Benedict, all pontiffs were wealthy.

P: Is that now the only way to become a pope?

J: Has been for hundreds of years.

P: I see. Now something else, about those battles of yours. Why did you go after Bologna?

J: Because our treasury was nearly empty and Bologna was a rich town. After I conquered it, I appointed several new cardinals and bishops to run the city and to make sure that all the revenue went to us in Rome.

P: And what did the Venetians do wrong to attack them?

J: Same story.

P: And the Duke of Ferrara; was that also the same story?

J: No, that was different. He was a good man. The Vicar of Christ Alexander even gave his younger daughter in marriage to him. No, it was simple. I needed that duchy as a present to the husband of my daughter.

P: What?? Supreme Pontiffs with wives and children?

J: Sure, but those wives were not their own. What is so strange about having children? We are men, not eunuchs.

P: Can a sinful and pestilent pope be removed?

J: Absolutely not; not even for the most hideous crimes.

P: Now another; what did you do with all those riches you took?

J: I used it for the magnificence and the enlargement of the church.

P: In what way?

J: I adorned the church with magnificent ornaments and dressed the cardinals and bishops with gold and jewels. We have fine horses, many servants, well-trained troops and dainty courtiers.

P: I think I am looking at one of the worst tyrants in the world, the enemy of Christ and the ruin of the Church.

J: You are talking nonsense.

P: Did your preachers not teach you anything?

J: They never gave me anything but pure praise. They declared that there was something truly sublime about me and much more in the same vein.

P: I assume that they didn't dare say something different. The true role of the apostle is to preach Christ to others in the purest possible way. You did not do anything like that.

J: I take it that you will not open the door.

P: A pestilent fellow like you? Oh, unhappy Church.

Peter shook his head and closed the peephole.

After finishing *Julius exclusus*, Erasmus showed it to the man he trusted most, Thomas More.

"It reminds me a little of the story of Cain and the angel who refused to give him an ear of corn. But that was in jest, my dear Erasmus. This is different and dangerous."

"Do you think I went too far?" asked Erasmus anxiously.

"You can best answer your own question with another question—why didn't you write this while Julius was still alive?"

"You go right to the tender spot, don't you? Well, to be truthful, it is because I feared that Julius would have gone after me."

"Are you going to admit to authoring it now?"

"No, I am not in a hurry. When it comes out in print, my name will not be on it."

For the rest of his life, Erasmus denied authorship of the steaming satire. The exact year of publication is not known. He did not give the manuscript to one of his usual printers but instead selected Andreas Cratander, an obscure German printer.

Both in speaking and in writing, Erasmus frequently interrupted his line of thought when a new thought entered his active mind. He simply switched gears to an anecdote or a short story and blissfully entertained his audience. Always witty and charming, he delighted his listeners. These digressions made him exceedingly attractive as a speaker and author. People came from afar to hear him, and readers bought his books, expecting to be entertained. Frequently, however, only the more intelligent ones would hear or read the hidden meaning of his words.

By 1513, Erasmus's fame was already such that when a false rumor spread that he was on his deathbed, Europe's top publisher, Johannes Froben, printed a new edition of the *Adagio* with a short eulogy on its title page:

> What a great loss to good learning is this great man! He would have brought more luster not only to his native Germany, but to the whole of Europe; and would have edited many authors who must now continue their struggle with the corruptions of worm and moth.

Froben had never met Erasmus and moreover was incorrect in stating that he was a native of Germany. Erasmus enjoyed telling the story of his premature death. He later befriended Froben and for many years afterward teased him quite a bit about it.

Erasmus never gave up his aversion to war. Although the protracted war on the continent took place across the Channel, it impacted his life in England severely. Ammonius was in France, acting as Henry VIII's secretary. William Blount was off fighting the war, which was marked by few battles between long, dull waits. Erasmus had not seen John Colet since their exchange of letters in March 1512, and even More seemed a bit removed. Erasmus began to feel lonely, and in the spring of 1514, he took the first steps to leave England.

At about the same time, Ammonius finally returned, along with the "victorious" King Henry. Shortly thereafter—and in greatest secrecy— Pope Leo X sent a legate to England to discuss peace terms. In June, Ammonius invited Erasmus to a dinner party that was also attended by Cardinal Leone Ludovica da Canossa, who, unbeknownst to Erasmus, was the Pope's legate traveling incognito as a Mr. Canossa.

"Who is that man?" Erasmus asked Ammonius in Greek as they sat down for dinner.

"Oh, he is a leading merchant in Italy."

"He certainly looks like one." Erasmus paid little further attention to the man. "Is there anything to the rumor that the pope has sent a secret legate to England?"

"It's possible."

"Well, if he had asked me, I would have advised him differently."

"In what way?"

"I think it is too early to discuss a peace treaty. As soon as the soldiers hear the slightest rumor of peace, they will forget all discipline. It is much better to make a truce first and then take the time to forge a lasting treaty."

"I agree with you, my friend, and if there already is a legate here from Rome, I believe that will be the object of his visit."

There was something in the way Ammonius spoke that caused Erasmus to nod toward Mr. Canossa. "Is he from Rome?"

"I don't know; maybe."

Up until that point, Erasmus had heard Mr. Canossa speak to other guests only in Italian with a sprinkling of Latin mixed in. However, the Italian suddenly turned to Erasmus and said in perfect Latin, "I am amazed that you live in this barbarian nation, sir. A man with your education would rank very high in Rome."

For a moment, Erasmus was completely taken by surprise. Then he looked at Canossa and in a stern voice protested, "This is hardly a land of barbarians, sir. England has been most hospitable to me. This kingdom has a larger concentration of excellent scholars than any country in Europe, including Italy."

Three days later, Ammonius revealed Mr. Canossa's true identity. Erasmus was furious. "Why didn't you stop me? I must have displeased the man to no end."

"To the contrary, he much appreciated your frankness and insight, and he hopes to meet you again."

In early July 1514, Erasmus left England and sailed across the Channel to visit his friend Lord Mountjoy, who, as governor of Normandy, resided in Hammes Castle in the outskirts of Calais. While there, he was surprised to receive a letter from his superior, Prior Servatius from the St. Gregory monastery in Steyn. The letter was written on April 18 and by some miracle had found its way to Calais. It had been opened and read by several strangers, but it was still intact. When they had last met in Steyn, Servatius had treated Erasmus most severely, and Erasmus therefore hesitated to open the letter, fearing the worst. Rather than containing the dressing down that Erasmus anticipated, it contained a plea from Servatius, who extended Erasmus an olive branch.

> I fear for the salvation of your soul; your constant travels can not be good for a spiritual life. Why not come back to our community of like souls and I will guarantee you a position with emoluments and total freedom to follow your literary avocation. You must wish to die amongst your brethren. We are all proud of your many achievements and long to see you.

The remainder of the letter continued along the same cordial vein, although Servatius did question why Erasmus had shed his monk's garb. Erasmus was greatly relieved. His initial reaction was to reply to Servatius and tell him in no uncertain terms that he would never return to Steyn, but after he slept over it for a night, he knew that he should be contrite, which was difficult for him. He wrote to Servatius:

> Most humane father, your letter has afforded me unbelievable delight, as it still breathes your old affection for me … My own feelings are that I want to follow what is best to do, God is my witness … I have realized

that I am not fit for monastic life, both physically and psychologically ... So, had I come back to you, all I would have achieved would be to bring trouble on you and death on myself ... You want me to settle on a permanent abode ... but the travels of Solon, Pythagoras and Plato are praised; the Apostles were wanderers ... I have been commended by the most highly commended and praised by the most praised ...

It now remains to satisfy you on the question of my dress. When I was at Louvain, I received permission from the Bishop of Utrecht to wear a linen scapular instead of a complete linen garment ... On my journey to Italy, seeing all monks wearing a black garment, I took to wearing black as well to avoid giving offense ... I obtained a dispensation from Pope Julius II allowing me to wear the religious dress or not, provided I wore clerical garb ... In England I was warned by friends that that would not be tolerated there.

There you have an account of my whole life ... You guaranteed emoluments and I cannot begin to imagine what this can be, unless you intend to place me in a community of nuns to serve them ... Your letter went far astray and was read by many persons ... I am on my way to Basel to have my works published and shall perhaps spend the winter in Rome ... On my return, I'll see to it that we meet and talk somewhere. Do not forget to commend me to Christ in your prayers.

Farewell, once my sweetest companion, now my esteemed father.

Hammes Castle, 8 July 1514

In the letter, Erasmus referred to the dispensation that he had received from Pope Julius II on January 4, 1506. He had always felt slightly guilty that in his application for the dispensation, he had purposely omitted the fact that his father was a priest. He realized that his conscience would never be clean until he cleared up the matter, and he vowed not to let it wait too long.

9

⟸⟩◆⟨⟹

Erasmus and the Bible

1514–1516

From Torah to Bible - Jerome's Vulgate - Translates the New Testament into Greek and Latin - The Reuchlin Affair - Outrage in Louvain - The story of John Wycliffe

In 1514, Erasmus was living in Basel, Switzerland. He was amazed at the cleanliness of the streets and the orderliness of the houses, and he enjoyed the friendliness of the citizens. While there, he stayed in the home of his friend, the renowned printer and publisher Johann Froben. It was Froben who finally gave Erasmus the push that he needed to complete his famous translation of the Bible.

Erasmus had been working on the project on and off for years, repeatedly laying it aside for extended periods only to take it up again. His work traveled with him on his many journeys through western Europe, and in every library he visited, he searched for books about the Gospels.

In July, Froben chastised his friend. "Erasmus, don't you think it is time for you to become serious about publishing your translation of the Bible? You have been working on it for how long now—five, ten years?" His jocular yet strained tone betrayed his exasperation.

"Longer than that, Johann. More like fifteen years," Erasmus replied nonchalantly. "Why are you in such a hurry?"

"Because Cardinal Ximenes has had a small army of scholars in Alcalá, Spain, working on a translation for at least ten years, and he will finish it fairly soon."

Erasmus was surprised. He wondered why he had not heard this news before. "How do you know?"

"That is a trade secret, my friend. Believe me; he will be ready soon."

What neither man knew was that Cardinal Ximenes had finished his translation earlier in the year. It was an enormous work of parallel translations of the Old Testament into Hebrew and Greek and the New Testament into Greek and Latin. It was called the Polyglot Bible to plainly indicate its multilingual quality. However, Ximenes needed permission from Rome to publish, and Rome withheld such permission until 1520. This gave Erasmus the time he needed to complete his own translation.

The Bible and its translations into Greek and Latin have a long history. The Old Testament originated with the Torah, the Hebrew Law, during the Persian Period, which lasted from 559 BC, when King Cyrus the Great of Persia conquered much of the then-modern world, until 330 BC, when Alexander the Great defeated the Persians. The Hebrew Law was eventually translated into Greek in a volume known as the *Septuagint* (Seventy), although the origin of the translation is unclear. One story states that around 320 BCE, Demetrius Phalereus, the director of the famous library of Alexandria, Egypt, asked King Ptolemy II of Egypt for a translation of the Hebrew Bible into Greek for the greater glory of the library. The king agreed wholeheartedly and sent gifts to Jerusalem, requesting that in return, scholars who could perform the translation should be sent to Egypt. Seventy scholars were chosen to do the work and they completed their task in seventy days. The translators worked on Pharos, a small island in the harbor of Alexandria, and their work varied from good to barely acceptable.[19]

---

[19] This story was based on the fictional *Captivi* (*The Captives*), by the Roman playwright Plautus (254–184 BC), in which the translation of the Hebrew Law into Greek is described in a letter from the Jew Aristeas to his brother Philocrates.

In AD130, another Greek translation of the Hebrew Law was produced. Its author was Aquila, who although born a pagan in Pontus, Asia Minor, first converted to Christianity and then to Judaism. He completed a word-for-word translation of the Old Testament from Hebrew into Greek and called it the *Vetus Itala*, or the *Itala Vulgate* (Old Latin Bible). A century and a half later, the leading clerics in Rome deemed Aquila's translation too rabbinical, and Pope Damasus (c. 305–385) encouraged Jerome to revise Aquila's work.

St. Jerome was born in AD 347 in Illyria, a country along the northeastern part of the Adriatic Sea. He was baptized thirteen years later in Rome, traveled extensively through Asia Minor, and settled for several years in and near Antioch, a harbor town in the southern tip of Turkey. His travels included time spent in the desert of Chalcis, a favorite place for hermits. There, he learned Hebrew from a converted Jew and became interested in the Gospel according to the Hebrews. In 382 he moved to Rome and became Pope Damasus's personal secretary.

Jerome was a towering figure with a substantial following; he tended to be arrogant and to belittle his many rivals with biting sarcasm. The wealthy widow Paula became one of his most devoted followers. Shortly after the death of Pope Damasus, Jerome's rivals chased him out of Rome under a cloud of improper behavior with the lady. He returned to Antioch, followed by Paula, his brother, and a few other ladies. Of women he once said, "They paint their cheeks with rouge and when they share a tear it makes a furrow through the paint. Older women load their heads with other people's hair, enamel the wrinkles of old age and fake maidenly timidity." After Helvidius, one of his competitors, wrote him a letter in which he claimed that celibacy was inferior to marriage, Jerome wrote back, "I praise wedlock, I praise marriage, but it is because they give me virgins."

Although he never returned to Rome, Jerome continued his work on the Bible and went much further than simply revising Aquila's translation. He examined not only the Latin *Vetus Itala* but also the Greek *Septuagint* and the Hebrew Bible. However, he did not use the original Torah from the third century (350 BC). Despite that weakness, his was an enormous undertaking that took years to complete. Although it took the Church two centuries to adopt it, Jerome's Latin Bible ultimately was accepted as *the* Vulgate. The Vulgate continued to be tinkered with by several self-appointed revisionists, each with their own ax to grind. Alcuin presented his version in 801, Lanfranc in 1089, Bishop Theodulph of Orleans in 1134, St. Stephen in 1134, and Cardinal Nicolas in 1150.

Armed with his copy of the Vulgate, along with the other materials he had collected over the years, and with the help of two young assistants provided by Froben, Erasmus went to work in a space provided by Froben in the summer of 1514. He had studied Jerome's Vulgate extensively before starting his own translation. He especially admired Jerome's ability to speak both Hebrew and Greek, and referred to him as the *vir trilinguis*—"the man with the three tongues." For his own translation, Erasmus concluded that since the Old Testament originated with the Torah, it should be translated into Latin from that original Hebrew text. As for the New Testament, which consisted of twenty-seven books written in Greek during the first and second centuries, Erasmus decided that in order to understand it fully, he would use as many original sources as he could find.

He wrote a letter to Pope Leo X to inform him about his project.

> We now find that the writings of Jerome so depraved by others after him that they cannot be understood even by the learned. It is my earnest endeavor to bring Jerome back to life … The glory of Leo is incomparable brilliant and Jerome will be more widely read by all be he approved by the favorable mark of so great a Pontiff.

> After a long delay, Leo replied in a letter dated July 10, 1515, approving Erasmus's proposal to dedicate his translation to him.

After a year of intense study, Erasmus completed a work of nearly seven hundred pages: a Greek New Testament and a parallel Latin New Testament. He had uncovered many inaccuracies in Jerome's Vulgate, which Erasmus attributed to the fact that during the twelve centuries since Jerome, scribes, church authorities, and popes included their own interpretations and "corrections" and thus had corrupted Jerome's work.

In his New Testament, Erasmus purified the Vulgate without corrupting it with new and manipulative additions.

Erasmus, however, was not happy with his finished product.

"Why not?" asked Froben, as a gloomy Erasmus sat with him in his shop.

"Johann, I have tried to stay as close to the text of the Vulgate as possible, but in some areas, I find that the research is too … flimsy."

"Flimsy? What does that mean?" asked Froben incredulously.

"That is a good English word. It means 'weak' or 'thin.' It is not deep enough. I have a feeling that there is more information out there somewhere." Erasmus kept shifting on his chair, further betraying his discomfort.

"Erasmus, this is a good book. What more do you want?" Froben was used to Erasmus's perfectionism, but that did not make dealing with him any easier.

"A better book, Johann. I want a better book. This one is the best I could do under the circumstances, but it's not what I wanted."

Against Erasmus's wishes, Froben went ahead and published the New Testament in the beginning of 1516. It was a rush job and contained typographical errors, which annoyed Erasmus greatly.

Erasmus added, deleted, altered, and shaved his New Testament for the remainder of his life. He examined manuscripts everywhere he went—Antwerp, Brugge, Gent, Constance, and myriad other places. Eventually, he produced four new editions of the translation in the years 1519, 1522, 1527, and 1535, only a year before his death. He apologized for deficiencies in his original translation and made changes to bring it even closer to the Vulgate, for it was not his intent to replace the Vulgate, as his enemies charged him. To him, the Bible was a living document and should thus rightly be made available in those languages that could easily be understood in modern times.

While Erasmus was working on the original translation in 1514, he kept his eye on a conflict that had been broiling in Germany for some time and eventually became known as the Reuchlin Affair. Johann Reuchlin (1455–1522) studied Latin in a Dominican monastery school where his father was an official. He studied Greek in Paris, law in Orleans and Poitiers, and in 1492, he commenced a six-year study of Hebrew. Eventually he became the center of Greek and Hebrew studies in Heidelberg. Without a doubt, he was the most linguistic humanist in Europe, and this led him to become the primary victim of Johannus Pfefferkorn ("Peppercorn," in German).

Pfefferkorn, born a Jew in Nuremberg, was a butcher by trade and had spent time in prison for burglary. Upon his release at age thirty-five, he converted to Catholicism, together with the other members of his family. Jacob Hoogstraten, an inquisitor and the prior of the Dominican order in Cologne, took him on as his assistant. Pfefferkorn began to attack the Jews in defamatory pamphlets written in German. In *Der Judenspiegel* (The Jewish Mirror), published in 1507, he demanded that the Jews give up the practice of usury, attend Christian sermons, and discard the Talmud. This was followed by *Judenbeicht* (Jewish Confession) in 1508 and *Judenfeind* (Jewish Enemy) in 1509. "Who afflicts the Jews is doing the will of God, and who seeks their benefit will incur damnation," he concluded. "The only way to get rid of the Jews is to burn their Talmud and to expel or enslave them."

The Dominicans, led by Hoogstraten, supported Pfefferkorn and took his cause all the way to the imperial palace of the Holy Roman Emperor. On August 19, 1509, Emperor Maximilian ordered the Jews to hand over to Pfefferkorn all books in which Christianity was opposed in any way and to destroy all Hebrew books, except the Hebrew Bible, as it was the Old Testament. The Jews appealed to Maximilian to establish an independent committee to investigate the accusations against them, whereupon the emperor asked Reuchlin for his opinion in the matter.

Reuchlin argued that most Jewish books were of great historical value for Christianity, but he recommended burning books in which the character of Jesus was attacked. However, the widespread destruction of Jewish books was averted when the majority of universities came out in support of the position of the Jews. On May 23, 1510, Maximilian suspended his verdict of the previous year and ordered Pfefferkorn to return the confiscated books.

Despite those setbacks, Pfefferkorn was undeterred. With all the vehemence of a recent convert, he began a vicious, largely self-serving attack against Reuchlin, whom he blamed for Maximilian's reversal. He was proud of his new journal, *Der Spiegel* (The Mirror) which he used as a vehicle against the famous humanist. Reuchlin defended his position in *Speculum Oculare*, which Hoogstraten translated into German as *Augenspiegel* (Eye Mirror) for the benefit of his henchman, who did not read Latin. Hoogstraten damned the booklet and burned it in front of Heidelberg University. He summoned Reuchlin to appear before the court of the church in Mainz, to be tried on charges of heresy and favoring the Jews.

Hoogstraten acted both as accuser and judge, finding Reuchlin guilty. The archbishop of Mainz informed Pope Leo X about the miscarriage of justice at Mainz, and Leo appointed the bishop of Speyer to settle the issue. On March 29, 1514, the bishop ruled in favor of Reuchlin; he ordered Hoogstraten to pay the court expenses, which amounted to a hefty sum of 111 gold florins. The Dominicans had had enough of these disruptive incidents; they fired Hoogstraten as prior and inquisitor. The pope, however, had yet to give his blessing to the bishop's ruling.

After his trial in Mainz, Reuchlin wrote to his fellow humanist Erasmus in April 1514:

> I have been attacked by some professors of theology in Cologne in language unbecoming to doctors– with most violent personal insults and abuse like the meanest buffoons ... I send you a summary of the court proceedings in Mainz to satisfy the kind interest that you feel in all lovers of good letters ... I shall now by your defense be reinstated as against these incendiaries of books.

Erasmus was still in England when he finally received Reuchlin's letter in August. He responded:

> My learned friends here laughed when they read your letter and demanded to see a copy of your condemned book ... When I read those heretical, irreverent and impious letters of yours, I could not suppress a laugh ... take the trouble to send the book to England, either to John, Bishop of

Rochester, or to Colet, Dean of St. Paul's. Farewell, sole glory and incomparable ornament of Germany.

He also sent Hoogstraten a short epistle: "What could ever be written at all so carefully that it could not be twisted by an angry opponent into some sinister meaning?"

Erasmus kept his friends in England up-to-date about the struggle in Germany, and he encouraged Reuchlin to correspond with people like John Fisher, bishop of Rochester; Colet; and More. He campaigned for Reuchlin with his cardinal friends in Rome as well. Thus, a fight between two camps took place; the Dominicans represented the conservative clerical wing of the Church and the more liberal humanists were represented by Reuchlin and Erasmus.

In a November 15, 1514, letter from Louvain, Erasmus wrote to Reuchlin, referring to Pfefferkorn:

> This circumcised creature, who from a wicked Jew has become a still more reprobate—I will not say Christian— has published a book, and that in the vulgar tongue, so as to be intelligible to his own class of people—in which, I am told, he tears to pieces all the learned, naming them by name ... Good heavens, that one man, half-Jew, half Christian, has done more mischief to Christianity than a whole sink of Jews ... It is for us, my Reuchlin, to turn our backs upon such portents, and to find pleasure in Christ, and in the enjoyment of honourable studies.

In the meantime, the stubborn Hoogstraten refused to give up; he hastened to Rome and obtained an audience with Leo X. "Your Holiness, I am distressed by the situation in Germany between the church and the Jews."

"So am I. So am I, dear Prior." Leo had yet to hear the latest news and waited for Hoogstraten to bring him up-to-date. "Has the bishop of Speyer made a ruling in the Reuchlin matter?"

"I believe he has, Your Holiness, but there are still some issues to be solved."

"Oh, I see. How unfortunate. Do the Jews not wish to see the problem solved?"

"Yes, they do, and they are helpful indeed, but Reuchlin insists on asking for a most favorable decision."

"Well, you know all about the situation. What do you recommend?"

"I think that Your Holiness will be well served by temporizing somewhat with a final solution. That will allow the situation to cool down."

"An excellent suggestion," agreed Leo X, who was not a particularly decisive man.

Hoogstraten had successfully bought time to create more trouble, and he knew where to find it in the person of the king of France. When King Louis heard that his enemy Maximilian had ruled in favor of Reuchlin, he immediately joined the anti-Reuchlin side of the dispute. Shortly thereafter, at his prompting, the theologians in Paris and the faculty of the University of Cologne declared that Reuchlin's *Oculare Speculum* contained heresy. The Dominicans celebrated—but not for long.

In 1515, a group of six authors who supported Reuchlin satirized the dispute in a publication titled *Epistolae Obscurorum Virorum* (Letters of Obscure Men), in which they lampooned members of the faculty of the University of Cologne. The letters laid bare the baseness of the clergy and exposed their contemptible moralities, lies, and foolishness. More threateningly, they were written in such a way that even the half-educated majority could understand them. The authors of the *Epistolae* used fictitious pseudonyms, such as Nicolaus Caprimulgius or Country Bumpkin, Simon Wurst, Berthold Häckerling or Scarecrow, and Conradus Unckebunk. In reality, Crotus Rubeanus and Ulrich von Hutten were the best known of the six authors, who also included a young Philipp Melanchthon, whose great-uncle happened to be Reuchlin.

Erasmus read the *Epistolae* and wrote, "If it is Christian to hate the Jews, are we then true Christians?" People throughout Europe enjoyed the satirical letters immensely and wondered who authored them. Ulrich von Hutten gave the only plausible reply: "God Himself." Hoogstraten and Pfefferkorn were completely neutralized. In a letter to Maximilian, Count Hermann von Neuehaar called Hoogstraten "the pestilence of

Germany." After Hoogstraten died, one of the authors of the *Epistolae* wrote his epitaph:

So here lays Hoogstraat dead as a stone;
The bad he made glad, but the good to groan;
And when he found he could live no longer,
His wish to harm waxed all the stronger.

Johann Reuchlin quietly retired to his small estate near Stuttgart. The Reuchlin Affair had ended.

Meanwhile, the monks in Louvain University were in a quandary over what to do about Erasmus. Not only had he the audacity to publish the damnable *Praise of Folly* but even worse, he had published his own Latin version of the New Testament. This new text was considered by many ecclesiastical authorities to be a major danger to the Church. They were especially alarmed by what Erasmus had written in the preface:

I could wish that every woman might read the Gospel and the Epistles of St. Paul. Would that these were translated into each and every language so that they might be read and understood not only by Scots and Irishmen, but also by Turks and Saracens ... Would that the farmer might sing snatches of Scripture at his plow, that the weaver might hum verses of Scriptures to the tune of his shuttle, that the traveler might lighten with stories from the Scripture the weariness of his journey.

The monks were outraged. Women *read* the Gospel? Impossible. Translating the Gospel into the vernacular of each country? Heretical! The New Testament read by enemies—the Turks and the Saracens? Outrageous! Common laborers singing or humming portions of the scripture at work? Revolutionary!

"Erasmus is nothing more than a radical," the monks of Louvain proclaimed. The Vulgate was written in Latin and thus was readable only by members of the clergy and the few well-educated outsiders—and they wanted to keep it that way. As long as they were the only ones who read the Vulgate, they possessed unbounded power over the common people, who had to rely upon them to understand religion and what it meant for the way they lived their lives.

For nearly a thousand years, the translation of verses of the Bible into vernacular language was strictly forbidden by the Church, with only one exception—the English translation of the Gospel of John, which the monk Bede (672–735) is reputed to have dictated on his deathbed.[20] A few unauthorized translations did surface, however, including a German version of the Gospel of Matthew in 748. In 900, the Saxon king Alfred the Great had several passages of the Bible, including the Ten Commandments, translated, and in 990, a translation of the four Gospels appeared in Old English. The veracity of Pope Innocent III's ban of unauthorized translations of parts of the Bible in 1199 is in dispute, but he did ban their use in the Church.[21]

Nearly one hundred years before Erasmus was born, an unauthorized translation of the Bible into English had been made by John Wycliffe (c. 1320–1384), a theologian and outspoken critic of the Church hierarchy.[22] While a young student at Oxford University, Wycliffe became convinced that the Roman Curia exerted too much power in the daily life of the people and in the politics of their countries. Wycliffe concluded that the Church needed reform, because its temporal rule was incompatible with the teaching of Christ. He stated that the king stood above the pope in worldly matters, and the English Parliament agreed, declaring that the Curia should stay out of politics. Wycliffe also condemned the collection of annates—the value of one year's profit of spiritual benefices given to the pope—as well the sale of indulgences.

"The Church must not have worldly possessions," he preached in London's churches to the delight of his listeners and of the first Duke of Lancaster, John of Gaunt. Reverberations hit Rome before the clergy in

---

[20]   Unfortunately, the manuscript is lost; Bede is remembered as the father of English history for his great work, *The Ecclesiastical History of the English People*.

[21]   The ban was made partially in response to Peter Waldo's translation of portions of the Bible into French in the 1170s, which led to the Waldensian movement.

[22]   Luther had studied the life of John Wycliffe in 1515–16 when he was researching church heretics.

England woke up; the Curia accused Oxford University of being too lenient with Wycliffe and ordered the English bishops to get rid of him. William Courtenay, Bishop of London, ordered Wycliffe to appear before him on Wednesday, February 19, 1377, to explain himself. On the designated day, the pontifically dressed bishop was waiting, surrounded by dignitaries of the Church. He was surprised to see a large crowd gathering in the church and was even more surprised when John Wycliffe entered, followed by John of Gaunt and Sir Henry Percy, the earl marshal.[23]

"John Wycliffe, you are summoned to appear before me to explain your recent preaching that has harmed the Church," declared Courtenay loudly, in the hope of instilling fear and awe among the crowd.

"Before he does, I want to know what charge is made against John Wycliffe," declared John of Gaunt, his voice echoing clearly throughout the church.

"Who may you be, sir, that you so rudely interrupt these proceedings?" retorted the provoked bishop in clipped tones, although he already knew the answer.

Gaunt was not intimidated. "I am John of Gaunt, Duke of Lancaster, Duke of Aquitaine, son of King Henry III."

"Your titles, grand as they are, do not give you the right to interfere, sir," Courtenay declared dogmatically. "I beg you to sit down and hold your tongue."

"I will do no such thing," replied Gaunt to the enthusiastic applause of the audience. The spectators sensed a fight coming on.

"You, John of Gaunt, are in the holy church where I, bishop of London, rule." Courtenay's voice betrayed his poorly controlled anger. "You will remain silent unless asked to speak."

It was then that Sir Henry Percy stood and declared, "The Church, through its clergy, has long stepped outside its proper realm and is interfering with worldly matters."

The assembly burst into riotous cheering, as the bishop flushed red with rage. John Wycliffe had yet to say a word, but the crowd was already unruly in its support for him, even though most did not understand what the charges against him were about.

---

23   Earl marshal is a hereditary office and title. It is the eighth of the Great Officers of State in England (since 1800, in the United Kingdom).

"Bishop, you and your fellow clergymen have gone too far outside your Church, and I intend to divest you of the land you have unlawfully appropriated," John of Gaunt bellowed.

"This hearing is closed," thundered William Courtenay as he gathered the folds of his robe around him and hurriedly left, desperately trying to keep his dignity.

On May 22, Pope Gregory XI issued a bull against Wycliffe and sent copies to King Edward III, the archbishop of Canterbury, the bishop of London, and Oxford University. The king died a month later and was succeeded by his ten-year-old nephew, Richard II, who was guided by John of Gaunt. Wycliffe continued to speak out, knowing that Gaunt and Parliament stood behind him. The bishops, in a futile gesture, forbade him to speak further on the controversy. Wycliffe replied that the truth resided only in the holy scripture, which came from God, the only authority, not from popes or bishops. Wycliffe was especially critical of the numerous monasteries in England, which during the previous centuries had gained large tracts of land. "The Bible knows of no monastic orders. They should all be abolished, together with their possessions," he wrote.

He next turned to an issue close to his heart: the language of the Bible. Throughout Europe, the Bible was directly accessible only by those who could read Latin; namely, the clergy and the nobility. Wycliffe fervently believed that the common people also had a right to read the Bible, and he proceeded to translate the New Testament from Latin into English. Eager scribes copied his manuscripts, and his Bible was distributed throughout the country. With the new Bible in hand, many scribes became itinerant preachers. They walked in pairs, wearing long dark-red robes while carrying long staffs in hand, and they reached into the far corners of the land. The pope called them Lollards, because they mumbled their prayers as they went. The name was supposed to be derisive, but the preachers themselves considered it a badge of honor.

On December 31, 1384, John Wycliffe died from complications of stroke that he'd suffered three days earlier, while hearing Mass in a small parish church. He had not been excommunicated by the Church during his lifetime and therefore was buried in consecrated church ground. Forty years later, Rome finally exacted its revenge. On the orders of Pope Urban VI, the English bishop had Wycliffe's body exhumed. His remains were gathered in a jute sack, burned to ashes on the banks of the River Swift, and spread into the waters. A poem by William Wordsworth (1770–1850) describes the event:

> Wycliffe is disinhumed
> Yea his dry bones to ashes are consumed
> And flung into the brook which travels near
> Into the Avon—Avon to the
> Main ocean they—this deed accursed
> An emblem yields to friends and enemies
> How the bold Teacher's Doctrine sanctified
> By truth, shall throughout the world dispersed.

Wycliffe had written: *"If a man believes in Christ, and makes a point of his belief, then the promise that God hath made to come into the land of light shall be given by virtue of Christ to all men that make this the chief matter."* Over a century later, this would become a doctrine of the Reformation.

After studying the life of John Wycliffe, Erasmus wrote, *"I utterly disagree with those who are unwilling that the sacred Scriptures should be read by the unlearned translated into their own tongue."* Fortunately, his stature in Europe had reached such height that he did not need to fear any repercussion from the Church for his own New Testament.

10

⟫◈⟪

The Ninety-Five Theses

1516–1517

Frederick the Wise - Georg Spalatin - Preaches against indulgences - Indulgence sellers Albert of Brandenburg, Jacob Fuggers, and Johann Tetzel - Nails Ninety-Five Theses to the castle church door

By 1516, Martin had read several of Erasmus's works, but he did not quite know what to think of him. He greatly admired Erasmus's translation of the New Testament and used it many times in the preparation of his lectures. However, Erasmus's other works troubled him. Although he considered some of Erasmus's ideas to have merit, he disagreed with Erasmus's mode of expressing them. In a letter to his dear friend Johann Lange, the prior at Erfurt, Martin confided:

> I am at present reading our Erasmus, but my heart recoils more and more from him. One thing I admire is that he constantly and learnedly accuses not only the monks and the priests of a lazy, deep-rooted ignorance. Only I fear that he does not spread Christ and God's grace sufficiently, of which he knows little. I warn you not to read blindly what he writes.

The *Moriae Encomium*, however, elicited a different reaction. In a letter to his new friend Georg Spalatin, who had been appointed the secretary of Frederick the Elector, Martin gushed:

> I decided to tell nobody of the dialogue with Erasmus's *The Praise of Folly*. My sole reason is that it was so delightful, so clever and woven together in such an Erasmus-like manner that the reader is tempted to laugh and enjoy the failings in the Church, which ought rather to grieve all Christians and be borne before the Lord in prayer. But noticing you plead so earnestly to see it, here it is and after perusing it, return it to me.

Never before had he read such cleverly constructed satire. Erasmus had exposed the excesses of the Church, the clergy, and the nobles, but because he cloaked his criticism in satire, he had gotten away with it. Erasmus's writings gave Luther food for thought.

In 1516, Duke Frederick the Wise of Saxony was fifty-three years old, and he had ruled over Saxony for thirty years. During that time, he had done much to improve the lives of his people. He had built new schools and hospitals, improved the roads, and built bridges across the major rivers in his territory. He was determined to transform lowly Wittenberg into an important town. He founded the University of Wittenberg and hired young, bright professors such as Andreas Karlstadt, Albrecht Dürer, Martin Luther, Johann Lange, and Christoph Scheurl, who, in turn, attracted bright students to Wittenberg. In addition, he constructed the castle Church to house his collection of thousands of religious relics, which included a tooth from St. Jerome, a strand of Jesus's beard, a hair from the Virgin Mary, and nearly twenty thousand holy bones, each carefully mounted. The pope granted the castle church the right to dispense indulgences, granting the full remission of all sins.

Frederick was an elector, which meant that he, together with three other German princes and three German archbishops, was responsible for electing a new Holy Roman Emperor upon the death of the previous one. Since the beginning of the fifteenth century, only rulers from the

Austrian House of Habsburg were elected, but it was no secret that Frederick, although not a Habsburg, aspired to become the next Holy Roman emperor. It was even rumored that his election would be favored by Pope Leo X.

Frederick showed great wisdom in selecting Georg Spalatin as his personal secretary. Spalatin was born Georg Burkhardt in Spalt but changed his name to Spalatinus upon being ordained to the priesthood. Martin found a new friend in the red-haired Spalatin, with whom he had three things in common—they were only two months apart in age, both had studied in Erfurt, and both were studying at the University of Wittenberg.

"It is impossible for an indulgence to grant full remission of sins," Martin announced abruptly to Georg after Church on one beautiful autumn day. The congregation had dispersed, and the two friends had just stepped out into the crisp air.

"What brings that up so suddenly?"

"I have given much thought to indulgences lately, and I am now convinced that there is a lot of evil in them."

"Knowing you, you are probably going to give a sermon about it, but before you do, please remember that the elector uses them," said Georg, a look of worry crossing his furrowed brow.

"I know, and I have no intention of making trouble for him. At least he uses his indulgence income for good causes, like rebuilding bridges and supporting the university and church. Georg, you will soon discover that our Frederick is very wise in worldly things, but in those pertaining to God and to the salvation of souls, I consider him sevenfold blind. But back to the indulgences," Martin said, striding briskly as they rounded the church lawn. "It is wrong to claim that they can grant full remission of all sins."

Georg was astonished. "Even indulgences issued by the pope?"

"Especially those coming from the pope. The pope should not need to issue indulgences. He can simply forgive the sins of all people, including those who cannot afford to pay for it."

Georg remained quiet during another turn around the small lawn. "There is truth in what you say, Martin," he said in a concerned voice. "But be careful, will you?"

"I promise, Georg, and thank you for listening."

On October 31, 1516, the eve of All Saints' Day, Martin gave his first sermon questioning the legitimacy of indulgences. He asked his audience, "When that seller of the indulgence gave remission of your sin, how did he know that the remission was complete?" He slowly surveyed the attentive parishioners and continued. "Only God knows—and that seller is not God. How did he know whether you were contrite and gave the true confession required by the Church before you bought that indulgence?"

At a second sermon, he continued his argument. "I tell you, the sale of indulgences is the bane of our society. It drains the poor of their last pence. It makes you complacent. It gives you temporary self-satisfaction, but if you are truly honest in the face of God, it does not give you inner peace." Martin further criticized Church practices by questioning a pope's ability to deliver souls from purgatory. "If it were true that he could deliver one soul, why does he not release them all? Why would he be so cruel? Why is he more concerned with the dead than with the living?"

At his third and last sermon on the subject, Martin briefly faced Elector Frederick, who sat near the altar, before turning to the crowd that had squeezed into every last square inch of the church. He pointed to the open Bible before him and began. "Not many of you can read the scriptures. Instead, you have to rely on what your preacher tells you is in the Holy Book. I now tell you that the word *purgatory* is not in the Book and that the word *indulgence* is not in the Book. But I do believe that a sinner, who did not fully pay his penance before God while he was alive must complete that penance after death before he can go to heaven, before he has satisfied God. And I believe that the place where he completes his penance, where he purges himself, may be called *purgatory.*"

Again he turned to the elector, looked him straight in the eye, and said for all to hear, "When I speak of the evil of indulgences, I do not mean to say that the intentions behind all indulgences are evil." Turning back to his parishioners, he continued. "We all know that our beloved town needs to repair its bridge across the mighty River Elbe, and we know that our church needs funds to help the poor, and we know that our university needs money to grow. But there is a better way of obtaining those needed funds than through the sale of indulgences." He stretched his left arm out toward the people, index finger pointing. "I say that instead of wasting your hard-earned money on a false indulgence, you must freely give that money in your love for God. Our town will be grateful, and God will reward you with His grace. Let us pray."

Martin descended from the pulpit, walked down the aisle, and stood at the door to bless the people as they left the church. He was amazed to see that the first man to approach him was the elector, who normally left through a private side door.

"You skated on thin ice for a while there, preacher, but you came across safely—barely."

Luther was by no means the only one to speak out against indulgences; many of his colleagues did so, as did most university students.

Every time a student presented and defended his graduation thesis, Martin listened, learned, and made notes. The notes piled up, and from them he began to distill common threads. He followed with great interest the proceedings of the Fifth Lateran Council, where Cardinal Egidio of Viterbo, the superior-general of the Augustinian order, had announced an urgent need for Church reform—"Men must change through sacred things, not sacred things through men." A few years earlier, the cardinal had described the world of Pope Alexander as "No law, no divinity: gold, force, and Venus rule." It was time for a major change but not one acted.

The unsavory lifestyle of the clergy in Rome was no secret to the Church or the well-meaning princes of the land. Much of the blame rested on Pope Leo X, who was born the second son of the fabulously rich Lorenzo dé Medici. In 1513, Leo inherited a rich papal treasury from his predecessor, Pope Julius II, but he was a spendthrift and in two years had managed to spend it all—and then some. He tried to refill his empty coffers by selling indulgences, and when this was not enough, he resorted to pawning palace furniture and treasures.

All over Europe, the common people, who heard continuous sermons about sin, purgatory, hell, and penance, willingly paid for indulgences, because their priests urged them to do so. This angered Martin more and more. He began to keep a record of indulgence sales and of other wrongdoings of the Church—and his list grew longer every day. In his opinion, the Church atrocities formed a fuse for reform, which only waited for a spark to light it.

The German House of Hohenzollern and the Italian House of Medici strove toward two common goals—control of civil life first and of ecclesiastical life second. Each clerical rank came with a benefice; the higher the rank, the more the benefice paid. Therefore, the goal was to accumulate as many ranks as possible, which would translate into vast revenues. The Hohenzollerns sought to increase their ecclesiastical control of Germany through the personage of Margrave Albert von Brandenburg.

In 1514, at twenty-three years of age, Albert was already archbishop of Magdeburg and administrator of the Diocese of Halberstadt. He aspired to become archbishop of Mainz as well, because that would also make him an elector. The people of Mainz accepted his appointment, but the parish did not have the funds to pay for the installation fee, in large part because its three prior archbishops had died in a span of ten short years. Albert could not pay the fee out of his own pocket, because his wealth consisted largely of land and buildings. However, he knew where to procure the necessary funds.

Albert approached Jacob Fugger, the head of Fugger's Bank, the largest banking firm in Europe. The plan was to borrow the installation fee from Fugger, who would be responsible for negotiating its amount with the pope. Both Albert and Fugger were aware that Pope Leo needed money to complete the construction of St. Peter's Basilica, which his predecessor, Julius II, had started. Fugger traveled to Rome for the negotiation.

"Holy Father, Margrave Albert sends you his greetings," began Fugger, after kissing the pope's ring.

"Thank you, dear friend. And what message do you bring today?"

"The margrave has entrusted me to discuss with you the installation fee for the archbishopric of Mainz. What does Your Holiness have in mind?"

"Nothing less than twelve thousand gold ducats, Mr. Fugger," said Pope Leo, putting forth his best stern look.

Fugger, who was used to these negotiations, smiled. "Is that one thousand for each apostle?"

It was then Leo's turn to smile. "You could say that."

"That is much more than the usual fee," resumed the banker. "May I ask why?"

"I have to overlook a few things about your Albertus von Brandenburg. He is already archbishop of Magdeburg and administrator of Halberstadt, and by asking for Mainz as well, we have a case of pluralism. That is forbidden by canon law. And by that same law, he is too young, only twenty-three. I will have to give him a special dispensation. So, you see, my fee is not really that high." Leo leaned back in his chair and folded his hands across his ample lap. "Lastly, the man is no theologian," he continued, confident in the legitimacy of his reasoning.

The banker, who knew little about canon law, had lost the first round. "My client is prepared to pay seven thousand ducats," he offered, and added, "One thousand for each of the seven deadly sins."

The pope was not amused by Fugger's second biblical reference. He remained quite resolute and ignored the banker's next bid of eight thousand, waiting patiently for a better offer. Finally, when Fugger reached nine thousand ducats, Leo made his counterbid.

"Ten thousand, cash in advance. That is my final offer."

"I do believe that will be acceptable to the margrave," said the old banker, with a satisfactory nod. He gathered his papers and added, as if it were an afterthought, "Perhaps, for mutual benefit of course, Your Holiness would grant my client permission to dispense an indulgence."

Leo looked up, just a little too fast, and Fugger knew that he had hit the mark. His host thought a few seconds and said, "Yes, I will. Of course, it will only count for the Hohenzollern territories and for a period of eight years. I expect to receive half of the money from the sale—for construction of the new basilica, of course."

Jacob Fugger smiled. He did not care as much about negotiating the amount of Albert's installation fee as he did about obtaining Leo's permission to dispense indulgences. Not only would the sale of indulgences provide the funds to repay Albert's loan but in addition, the bank would receive 5 percent of each sale for the full eight-year period, even after the loan was fully repaid. All Fugger needed was a top salesman, and he knew just the right man: Dominican friar Johann Tetzel, who, it was rumored, could sell an indulgence to the devil himself.

Tetzel was fifty-two years old when he reported to Albert von Brandenburg. "They tell me that you are the best," said Albert. He knew that the man could get results, even though his only academic qualification was a bachelor's degree in theology.

The friar ignored the compliment and went straight to business. "I have brought you some samples of indulgences I have handled in the past," he said, putting a bundle of documents on the table and unrolling them. "I recommend this last one. I prepared it for your consideration." It was an imposing document that began with the name Albertus and left space for the name of the person who bought the indulgence, as well as the date and the amount "donated" for the construction of St. Peter's Basilica.

"Your document looks fine, Friar. We will make the necessary corrections and the special instructions to go with the distribution. Now, how will the collections be handled?"

"Well, Highness, we will travel your entire territory and visit as many towns as possible. It could take a few years. In good weather, we will set up business in front of the town church and when it rains, we will work inside. The money will be handled by a representative of Fugger's Bank. He will put half the money in a strongbox for Rome and the other half in a second box. At the end of the day, he will pay me my expenses out of the Rome box and take 5 percent interest from the Fugger's box. The rest will be used to pay off the loan."

"That does not leave anything for me, does it?"

"No, sir, it doesn't—at first," Tetzel said matter-of-factly. "But you will receive 45 percent of all of the indulgences sold after your loan is paid off."

"And when will that be?" asked a wary Albert.

"With an important indulgence such as this, it can very well be after three … four years."

"Well, then, you had better get started, Friar."

When Tetzel informed Albert that Fugger's interest rate was 5 percent, neither man knew that the bank would make even more money off the loan in another way. In 1507, Fugger had made a secret deal with the pope, by which the bank received up to half of the total amount of all installation fees financed by Fugger's Bank. In Albert's case, the bank received 20 percent.

Five days later, the town crier of Mainz and his helpers spread through the town, announcing that in two days a very special indulgence granted by Pope Leo X would become available. At every church and large building, they mounted large posters advertising the graces of the indulgence:

The first grace is a plenary remission of all sins, of which one might say no grace could be greater, because a sinner deprived of grace through it achieves perfect remission of sin and the grace of God anew. By which grace the pains of Purgatory are wiped out.

The second grace for sale is a confessional letter allowing the penitent to choose his own confessor.

The third grace is the participation in the merits of the saints.

The fourth grace is for the souls in Purgatory– a plenary remission of all sins.

It is not necessary for those contributing to the fund for this purpose to be contrite or to confess.

"What does it say?" curious townspeople asked again and again. They could not read the Latin text and had to wait until a learned man walked by. He was immediately surrounded by the inquisitive crowd, anxious for him to translate the news. The last sentence, especially, intrigued them. "Can you imagine—no confession? That'll really make it easy. I am going to get one." The speaker's declaration was followed by enthusiastic nods throughout the crowd.

Tetzel arrived at the main gate of each successive town with great fanfare. Flags flew, while trumpets and other musical instruments sounded celebratory peals. One helper carried the pope's magnificent coat of arms while another carried the coat of his papacy, with silver and gold keys forming a cross held together with a golden cord. He was followed by an assistant carrying a copy of the indulgence on a purple velvet pillow. Tetzel, decked out far more regally than a simple friar, brought up the rear. It was a sight to behold. People gave little gave notice to the bank clerk or the two men carrying heavy strongboxes who followed behind Tetzel.

While his assistants made the arrangement for the sale in front of the church doors, Tetzel gave his standard speech to the crowd:

> Listen, good citizens, and think of the salvation of your souls and of the immortal souls of your departed loved ones. Don't you hear them crying out to you from purgatory? "Free me, free me from these torments." Only you can do that for them with this letter of indulgence, which our Holy Father Pope Leo has blessed. You, farmer, hear the plea of your departed wife who blessed you with your children, and you, virgin, listen to your mother crying out to you, she who bore you. Are they not worth saving? How can you be so cruel as to not to help them? Listen, I say! Hear them screaming in agony, begging you to have pity. "Have pity on me! Rescue me with your alms!" I guarantee you that when you buy this indulgence, the souls you care for will be freed from Purgatory and enter Heaven.
>
> You can trust me, good people, these are the best indulgences you'll ever see in your lifetime. As a matter of fact, they are so good that I, too, will obtain one for my dear departed father.

Tetzel demonstratively strode over to the table where the Fugger's clerk was waiting. "Listen," he said, and with an elegant gesture, he dropped coins into the empty lockbox. "You hear that sound? On your way home, you, too, will sing this little jingle: *As soon as coin in coffer rings, the soul from purgatory springs.*"

It was easy for the smooth-tongued monk to convince his poorly educated listeners to part with their money. They crowded around the table, paid the bank clerk, and moved on to collect their indulgence from his assistant. The assistant filled in each indulgence document with the name of the purchaser, date, and the amount they had paid. He then murmured, "Praise the Lord," and handed the purchaser the precious piece of paper, which the buyer could not read, as it was in Latin.

Tetzel traveled from town to town, repeating his carefully orchestrated event, eventually approaching the border of Saxony. In January 1517, he came near Eisenach, and four months later, he brought his business to Jüterborg, a mere twenty miles from Wittenberg. At that point, Elector Frederick became nervous. He consulted with his confessor, Martin Luther, and showed him a copy of the poster enumerating the graces of Albert's indulgence.

"This is obviously a big deal if the pope sanctioned it," the elector reasoned. "I would like to learn more about indulgences. I know that I have used them often enough, but if it is not in the Bible, as you say, how did the practice get started? Tell me, Martin, where do all these graces come from?"

"I believe it was Alexander of Hales who started it."

"Never heard of the man," Frederick grunted.

"I believe he came from Hales, a town somewhere in England. He was the theologian responsible for the foundation of the school of theology at the University of Paris. Around 1220, he was the first person to use some of Aristotle's principles in teaching theology—"

"What has that to do with indulgences?" interrupted an impatient Frederick.

"Well, he became a Franciscan monk, I believe in 1233, and soon thereafter he introduced the idea of the Treasure of the Church, which consists of the surplus merits of Christ, Mary, and of the saints. It is a sort of bank of merits that is kept in heaven. When the pope grants an indulgence, he dips into that bank and gives merit to the person who buys the indulgence."

"Hmm, I see. And that is now legal?"

"It has been since 1343, when Pope Clement VI made it a doctrine."

"Amazing. Truly amazing." Frederick shook his head as he spoke. "Well, I don't want that Tetzel fellow selling any indulgences in my Saxony." Frederick was permitted to issue his own indulgences and did not want any competition. "Thank you for your explanation."

"Can I have that poster, please?" Martin gestured to the rolled-up document that Frederick so tightly clenched.

Martin was astounded when he read the four graces of Tetzel's indulgence, especially the final grace, which stated that it was not necessary for purchasers to be contrite or confess. He was furious. Did canon law not require a person to be contrite and confess before he was eligible for an indulgence? According to Church practice, only the pope could grant a plenary remission of all sins, so that no further expiation was required in purgatory. Martin had trouble with this. How could the pope remit penalties that he himself had not imposed? Did a penitent not have a right to choose his own confessor? Why should this privilege be for sale? How did the pope know which souls were in purgatory, or did that not matter? Did people have to pay for the construction of a chapel roof in order to receive remission of their sins? These and many other questions swirled in Martin's mind. He wondered whether the message on the poster was the complete instruction or only an abstract prepared by Tetzel.

His answer came a few weeks later when he laid his hands on *Instructio Summaria*, Albert's instructions authorizing the sale of the indulgence. It was about 1,300 words long and in Latin, so few citizens could actually read it. Before distributing the instructions, Albert had submitted them to the pope for approval. He instructed the confessors to ask those making confession how much money they would conscientiously give for full forgiveness. He then fixed several price levels for the indulgence:

25 guilders—For kings, queens, princes, archbishops and bishops
10 guilders- -For abbots, prelates of cathedral churches, counts, barons, and others of high nobility
6 guilders—For lesser prelates and nobles, rectors of famous places, and all others who took in a steady annual income of five hundred gold guilders
3 florins—For citizens with an annual income of two hundred florins per year
½ florin—For all others

Tetzel added that people who were too poor to pay any amount could say a prayer as a contribution, for the kingdom of heaven was open to the poor no less than the rich. If poor wives and sons were able to beg gifts from the rich, they were to put those gifts into the chest. As far as the general public was concerned, the most important requirement of the indulgence read: "It is not necessary for those contributing to the fund for this purpose to be contrite or to confess."

By the time Martin finished reading the lengthy instructions, he was furious. A few days later, he met a few of his parishioners, who were carrying rolls of indulgences.

"Where did you get these?" he asked.

"In Eisenach," said a man.

"In Jüterborg," replied an old woman. "That nice friar Tetzel convinced me to buy them."

"Did you not hear me preach against indulgences in Church?"

"Yes, but when I heard that the holy pope had issued these, I had to get them," said a second man. Others nodded.

"Throw them away," Martin growled. "They are worthless." And he stomped off.

Alone in his cell, he prayed fervently and then hurriedly dug up the notes about indulgences that he had written while he was a university student, searching especially for those concerning the power of the Church. After he finished reading, his mind was made up—he would challenge the practice of granting indulgences and openly condemn it. He enumerated his grievances in a document titled *The Disputations of Martin Luther on the Power and Efficacy of Indulgences*, which was printed by John Grünenberg and eventually became known as the Ninety-Five Theses.

On October 31, 1517, Martin nailed his Ninety-Five Theses on the door of the castle church in Wittenberg, a location that was commonly used as a place for posting public announcements. It was the eve of All Saints' Day and precisely one year after his first sermon challenging indulgences. Martin also announced that the Theses would be publicly debated at Wittenberg under guidance of the "Reverend Father Martin Luther." Those who could not attend the debate were invited to contribute by letter.

The Ninety-Five Theses begin with the subjects of penance and repentance, drawing largely on Matthew 4:17. Luther maintained that the penalty of sin remained until the man's entrance into the kingdom of heaven and could not be bought off before that time. The fifth thesis stated that the pope could only remit those penalties that he personally imposed or that were authorized by canon law. Neither the pope nor canons could impose penalty on the dead; the pope had no power over souls in purgatory. Priests who reserved penalties for purgatory were ignorant and wicked. Indulgence preachers were in error when they said that a man could be freed from every penalty and saved by papal indulgence. People were deceived by that indiscriminate and high-sounding promise. Those who were certain of their salvation because they had indulgence letters would be eternally condemned, together with their teachers. Every true Christian had the right to full remission of penalty and guilt, even without letters of pardon.

Luther argued that Christians should be taught that he who passes by a needy man and yet gives money for indulgences does not buy indulgence but the wrath of God. He implied that the pope was not aware of how indulgence preachers deceived the people. In a swipe at Tetzel, Theses 55 and 59 stated that "certain hawkers" who use parades with bells and ceremonies to sell indulgences were committing blasphemy. In Thesis 61, Luther presented the limitation of the power of the pope. Theses 75–78 strongly condemned the conceived strength of papel pardons and pointed out that even St. Peter could not bestow greater graces. While the pope distributed indulgences from the Treasure of the Church, Luther declared that the true Treasure of the Church was not one that the pope could distribute. The true treasure was the holy Gospel and the glory and grace of God.

To Martin's surprise and disappointment, no one showed up to debate the Theses during the subsequent weeks. He invited Tetzel to come to Wittenberg and debate, but Tetzel declined. Martin sent a copy of the Theses to the bishop of Brandenburg, who was his local bishop, but did not receive a reply. He sent another copy of the document to Albert, who had been recently appointed the new archbishop, but he too had no interest in Luther's Theses; he considered the monk an impudent dilettante. Yet he asked his professors of theology in Mainz to form an opinion about the Luther's document.

"Well, what do you men make of it?" asked Albert when he met with the professors a few days later.

"The man is only a young monk at Wittenberg, Your Highness, and—"

"Nevertheless, he holds a doctorate of theology," Albert interrupted.

"True, but from Wittenberg! That is a second- or third-rate university. We are of the unanimous opinion that this man Luther attacks the power of the pope and questions the competence of our Holy Father. It smacks of heresy."

Albert was well aware of the disdain his Dominican professors had for their Augustinian colleagues in Wittenberg. At the same time, he wanted to avoid a scrimmage with the man he despised most, Frederick the Wise, in whose lands Wittenberg lay.

"Since you indicate possible heresy, I will send the documents on to Rome for His Pontifical Holiness to deal with. Is there anything else I should know?"

"Your Highness, we do not believe that there is much to worry about. The Theses are written in Latin, and the common people are illiterate," one of the professors pointed out. "We will investigate Luther's experience and—"

"There is no time for that. Tetzel must be made a doctor as soon as possible. Meanwhile, make sure that there are no other publications about indulgences."

The professors bowed and left without another word.

None of the professors in Mainz offered to support Tetzel's promotion. However, Albert found a man eager to do it: Conrad Wimpina, rector of the recently founded university in Frankfurt. Wimpina saw a rival in the University of Wittenberg and was envious of Luther's sudden fame. With permission from Leo X, he promoted Tetzel to doctor of theology and helped him write 106 counter-theses. In essence, they defended the doctrine of indulgences and supported the authority of the pope.

Tetzel had eight hundred copies printed and employed a bookseller in Halle for their distribution. When the bookseller showed up at Wittenberg University, a group of undergraduate students surrounded him. They pushed and pulled and ran away with the copies and burned them in the square. This greatly annoyed Luther, who abhorred violence. He became depressed because there had been no reaction from Elector Frederick, but he then realized that it was his own fault—he had neglected to give a copy of the Theses to the man who would become his principal protector.

"What on earth were you thinking by excluding him?" asked Spalatin.

"I did not want to make any trouble for him. You know, he ... eh ... he would find out sooner or later anyway," Martin responded sheepishly.

"Well, he sure did find out, and he is not pleased, I can tell you that."

"But I only wrote the Theses to invite a debate, not to make trouble," Martin said unhappily.

"Martin, it is going to be a huge trouble, you'll see. Someone is going to translate this into German, and before you know it, it will spread throughout the country. Maybe even throughout Europe."

"What can I do?" Martin cried out, feeling utterly helpless.

"Nothing. If you take my advice, do nothing. Just lie low, and don't leave town."

But it was too late. Martin had sent copies of his Theses to his friend Johann Lange, as well as to friends at the priory and the university. Canon Ulrich von Dinstedt forwarded a copy to Christoph Scheurl, a jurist in Nuremberg, who immediately had the Theses translated into German and printed with one useful addition—the printer numbered each of the ninety-five theses, something Luther had not deemed necessary. From that moment on, the document became known as the Ninety-Five Theses of Martin Luther. Within a few weeks, the German translation became available throughout Germany. Translations also appeared in several other countries, and in no time the Ninety-Five Theses was on the lips of everyone who could read. A bright light had exposed the darkness of the sixteenth-century church.

It did not take long for Tetzel, Albert, and Fugger's Bank to notice a sharp decrease in revenue from the sale of indulgences. The pope, who initially had not reacted to the Theses, was alarmed when he was notified that church revenue from indulgences had dropped considerably. He directed Aegidius of Viterbo, the superior-general of the Augustinian order, to "Put the lid on a monk in your order by the name of Martin Luther. We must smother the fire before it becomes a conflagration."

11

━━━◆◆◆◆━━━

A Church in Trouble

1516–1517

Secret letter to Rome - Teases friends about their names - The need for reform - More's Utopia - Receives early warnings - A bastard no longer - Returns to Louvain

With his Bible translation work behind him, Erasmus once more became restless. He missed England and his many friends there, and in the summer of 1516, he decided to take a short trip back to London to visit them. His first stop was at the door of his friend Ammonius. Erasmus felt guilty that he had not yet fulfilled his vow to clarify the circumstances of his birth with the Church, and he asked Ammonius to help him write to Rome.

Together they composed a "secret" letter, in which Erasmus thinly disguised himself by using the pseudonym "Florentius." He addressed the letter "Lambert," a fictional character who was one of seven prothonotaries, the papal notaries who recorded pontifical events. By doing so, Erasmus knew that the letter would be read in the conclave of the pope and cardinals. The content of the letter was largely autobiographical. It recounted the loss of his parents, his schooling, and how he was forced to enter a monastery. He detailed the role of Bishop Henry Bergen in his life and how he eventually realized that monastic life was not for him, a youth of fine intelligence. He included an account of how, after many years of travel to the finest institutes of learning, he had laid aside his habit by the authority of a dispensation from the supreme pontiff, and he explained that, unfortunately, there were still forces that compelled him to put it on.

The body of the letter did not include mention of the circumstances of his birth, the most potentially damaging detail of his identity. However, at the end of the letter he added an appendix written in code, the key of which he had sent in a previous, separate letter. In the appendix, he requested the chancery to free him from the impediment of his birth—the fact that his father was a priest. The letter was hand delivered by the bishop of Worcester, who went to Italy to attend the Lateran Council.

After the letter was sent, Erasmus felt as if a great burden had been lifted from his shoulders. That evening, John Colet organized a get-together for dinner and conversation. All of Erasmus's old friends were there: Warham, More, John Fisher, and Cardinal Wolsey. Even Lord Mountjoy somehow managed to come to what they intuitively knew would be their last meeting together.

Erasmus was in a jovial mood, and during dinner he tapped his glass, looked up, and made an announcement. "Dear friends, when I look around this table, it occurs to me that there is definitely something wrong with your names." He paused for dramatic effect.

"Our names?" said Fisher. "What is wrong with them?"

"Well, for one thing, they are too short." He paused again.

"Too short?" asked More. "What on earth are you talking about?"

"Just count the letters. More has only four, Colet is five, and with one exception, the others barely stretch out to six letters. William, you do not count."

"Thank you for leaving me out of this," said Mountjoy wryly.

"What are you driving at, Erasmus?" said Wolsey.

"Simple. You people are not modern. You are too English. Now, take the names of your colleagues in Europe. Other than the Italians, most have Latinized their names. There is Andrelinus, Stephanus, Servatius, Marcus Musurus. My friend Gerard Hermans went all out to Gerardus Noviomagnus. Of course, I am the exception; I received my 'us' when I was born. You good people simply have got to get up-to-date; don't you think so, Colettius?"

After the laughter died down, John Colet said, "No way. We will remain simple Englishmen, thank you." He then became serious. "Now fill us in about the Church in Europe. Is it true that there have been some rumblings?"

"Yes, and they are coming from more than one angle but mainly from Germany." Erasmus's face lost its humor and betrayed his concern; his eyes turned downcast and his brow wrinkled.

"Why is that?" Colet asked.

"Well, it has to do with the way Germany is put together. You see, it really is not one unified country and does not have one king in whom power is concentrated. Here, you have a king, just like in France and Spain. Germany consists of many principalities, each headed by a king, a prince, a duke, or someone with a similar title, and they are all rather independent. And—"

"But they have the Holy Roman emperor," interrupted Warham.

"True, but that is just an empty title. There is no power behind it, and it is not hereditary. He is elected by the princes, and when he dies, they, not the pope, elect a new one. Some of the princes are not happy at all with the hierarchy in Rome. Germans are, by nature, down-to-earth people; they abhor the loose living that is going on in Rome."

"You are German, aren't you?" said Watson.

"No, sir, I am not," Erasmus exclaimed rather indignantly. "Germans may claim that I am one of theirs, but I am a Hollander and proud of it. Anyway, there is a new class of merchants and educated people who are beginning to call for a change in the Church. They want to loosen the tight grip that the clergy exerts over them, and a few of the younger clergymen are beginning to feel the same way. As I see it, the reason why there is no unrest here in England is because most leaders of the Church are, like you, honest and pious but not overly so. You maintain good contact with the people and respond to their religious needs. Discussion like we have here would be impossible in a Europe where the bishops consider themselves to be princes."

His listeners were silent for a moment. Then Warham, the archbishop of Canterbury, spoke. "I think we all feel a need for reform, but it seems that no one wants to take the bull by the horns." He turned suddenly and looked directly at Erasmus. "How about you, Erasmus? With your

Enchiridion militis christiani, the *Moriae,* your edition of Jerome, and above all, your New Testament, your authority in the Christian world is recognized even by the highest princes of the Church and by the papal seat. Are you not the best-qualified person to initiate reform?"

The others in the room nodded.

"Gentlemen, qualified? Yes, but am I the right person? No." Erasmus's face suddenly changed; the folds around his mouth that always gave the impression of a slight smile flattened out, giving his face a serious expression that his friends had never seen before. "I am fiercely attacked by many in the Church and hated by others." Even his voice had changed and was more assertive than before. He continued. "Besides, my strength comes from being a writer and a free thinker, not as an orator. Look at me; physically, I do not look like a strong person, and psychologically, I know that I do not have the strength for it. After many years of thinking otherwise, I now believe that what is needed is a new face, someone who is not afraid to make a radical change. Reform has to come from outside the Church, not from within, where the resistance to change is so strong that any attempt at reform will surely fail. It must be someone unencumbered by a thick layer of Roman lawyers and Roman authoritarians. I can only give opinions, not decisions."

For a while, all was quiet around the dinner table.

"Erasmus knows himself best." Thomas More broke the silence and pushed his chair back. The others followed his lead. It was time to say good-bye to their dear guest. When Erasmus shook the hand of John Colet on his way out, he thanked him for everything. Smiling again, he added, "By the way, you were so right about Thomas Aquinas."

Colet nodded and then turned serious. "Can I ask you one last question?"

"What is it, my dear friend?"

"Are there any leaders of the Church who realize that a reformation, a change of the Church, is badly needed?" John Colet looked concerned, almost dismayed.

"John, I think that they are everywhere, and they are looking for Rome to start working on reform. The trouble is that all of the leaders close to the Vatican are Italians. They are beholden to the Church and do not want to lose their cushioned positions. They are afraid to rock the boat. They will continue to vacillate until it is too late. The clouds are forming, John, and the storm will start any moment." Erasmus laid his hand firmly on Colet's shoulder in a reassuring gesture. "Farewell, my friend. Farewell."

Colet slowly closed the door behind him and returned to the other guests.

"Gentlemen, *nomen Erasmi nunquam peribit* [the name Erasmus will never perish]."

"Hear, hear."

In late September 1516, Erasmus arrived in Antwerp, where he received a disturbing letter from Wolfgang Faber, whom he had met in Basel, where Faber was a preacher. Shortly after their meeting, Faber had changed his name to Fabritius Capito. The letter was dated September 2, 1516. After the usual pleasantries, Capito continued in strict confidence:

> Up to this time, you have nobly undertaken the risk of speaking for the truth, but be aware of giving a handle to jealousy. She will certainly play you a shrewd turn whenever the opportunity presents itself. You know what a spirit the false conviction of learning and religion has assumed among us. Do not add a single word—unless guarded by that careful circumlocution of yours—about Penance, the Sacraments, the popular error in relations to the saints or the weekly onslaughts upon heretics founded merely on a forced interpretation of the Scriptures. Given an opening, the virulence of envy will hit with full force and pious Erasmus will be condemned and execrated as the common enemy of Christendom.

This warning from Capito was the first distant rumble of a major storm that was beginning to take form in the Christian world.

The following day, Erasmus received a parcel from Thomas More containing a manuscript of his new book, *Utopia*, which was subtitled *On the best state of a republic and on the new island of Utopia*.[24] Just as Erasmus had used Folly in his satire *The Praise of Folly* to address the ills of the church, More used his protagonist, Raphael Hythlodaeus (Dispenser of Nonsense), to address the many ills of the world. He discusses the evils

---

[24]   One may wonder whether it was More who invented the word *utopia* by combining the Greek word *ou* (not) with *topos* (place) and adding the letters *ia*.

of war-making kings and the theft of huge tracts of land by princes and monasteries.

After Erasmus edited the manuscript and More made corrections, it was published in Basel in November 1518. Although the book was well received, it did not make More a wealthier man than he already was.

In a letter accompanying the *Utopia* manuscript, More mentioned that a copy of Eramus's New Testament, intended for the Venetian ambassador in London, had been intercepted by "the Carmelite." That mysterious figure turned out to be Nicolaas Baechem Egmond, a Dutchman who detested Erasmus and would later become the self-appointed leader of the conservative faculty faction at Louvain University.

On October 31, 1516, coincidentally the same day that Luther gave his first sermon about the evils of indulgences, More wrote another, warning Erasmus:

> There are people among us, who have conspired to read your writings in a different spirit and whose formidable intentions make me uneasy ... with the utmost confidence and with all the anxiety which I feel on your behalf, I do beg and beseech you to lose no time in revising and correcting your New Testament so as not to leave the smallest possible room for calumny anywhere.

The conservative faculty at the University of Louvain followed Erasmus's career very closely and never missed an opportunity to attack him. After *The Praise of Folly* was published, they had delegated to one of their younger members, Maarten Dorp, the task of writing to Erasmus to convey their displeasure. In the same letter, Dorp also had warned Erasmus about translating the New Testament.

> I understand that you are proposing to correct the Latin New Testament into Greek, but if I show that the Latin version has no falsehood or mistakes, will you not admit that such a work is unnecessary? It is not probable that so many Fathers have been mistaken and the General

Councils, which, it is admitted by most theologians as well as lawyers, are not subject to error in matters of faith.

The letter took a long time to reach Erasmus, who finally responded in March 1515, a year before his translation of the New Testament was first published:

> While you approve of our studies in the restoration of Jerome, you already deprecate the publication of a New Testament before it has seen the light of day ... that may be your own conception, or instilled into you by persons who have suborned you to write in order to play their own game under mask of another.

He added that he would soon come to stay in Louvain for an extended period. Dorp, realizing that he would soon meet Erasmus in person, contritely replied:

> Do not believe that any oblique or slandering or suspicion of which some persons are guilty comes from me. Whatever has arisen to separate us, I trust that we may put it away and cultivate a sincere friendship. For my part, I will show myself to be a Christian friend. Farewell.

Erasmus discovered, however, that Dorp continued to speak about him behind his back in a less than favorable manner. In a letter to a friend dated October 17, 1516, he mentioned Dorp's duplicity. Dorp, perhaps sensing that Erasmus was informed about him, wrote again in January 1517, repeating that he would show himself to be a Christian friend if only Erasmus did not believe that calumny or suspicion that may have arisen had proceeded from him.

In the meantime, to his enormous relief, Erasmus received a liberating letter from Rome. It was written by Lambertus Grunnius, the papal secretary, in response to Erasmus's request for a papal dispensation clearing the circumstances of his birth:

Dearest Erasmus,

I have never undertaken any business more willingly than that which you have entrusted to me and have scarcely ever concluded any with more satisfaction. I read your letter from beginning to end to the Pope in the presence of several Cardinals and other eminent persons ... The Holy Father has ordered your bull to be prepared forthwith and that without charge. Nevertheless, I have given the clerks and notaries three ducats to obtain it more quickly. You know what a voracious pack it is ... a safe man will deliver you the bull with the exemplification and the Pope's signature. Farewell, and greet Florence lovingly in my name. He is now my Florence as well as yours.

Shortly thereafter, on January 26, 1517, Pope Leo X issued a dispensation bull to *Erasmo Rogerii Roterodamensi*, referring to—and thus recognizing—Erasmus's father's first name, Roger. On the same day, the pope wrote to the papal nuncio to the English court:

Erasmus suffers from a defect of birth, being born of an illicit and an impure and condemned connection. You shall remove from him every mark or stain of disability or infamy contracted by him by reason of the aforesaid circumstances.

In the eyes of the Church, Erasmus was no longer illegitimate.

On August 19, 1517, Erasmus arrived in Louvain, where his many friends warmly welcomed him. He stayed for a while in the home of Johannes Paludanus, a fellow Dutchman and the master of the university. One evening, Paludanus hosted a dinner, at which the vice chancellor of the university declared that he approved of Erasmus's New Testament. Martin Dorp also attended the dinner and was exceedingly civil.

"Did you hear that the pope has promoted our countryman Adriaan to cardinal?" Paludanus asked Erasmus during the evening meal.

Erasmus looked up from his plate and smiled, remembering his old schoolmate from Deventer. "That's indeed nice to hear. No one deserves the red hat more than he."

"He was one of thirty new cardinals, all chosen in one day."

"Are you sure about that? Why so many? It must be a record."

"Well, there is more to the story." Paludanus leaned over conspiratorially. He clearly enjoyed gossip. "Pope Leo suffers from an anal fistula that refuses to heal. While his personal physician was out of town, another doctor came to treat him, but Leo noticed how nervous the man was. With so many assassinations in Rome lately, the pope became suspicious, and he called his guards. After a minimum amount of torture, the doctor confessed that he was going to poison Leo."

Erasmus looked incredulous. "Who on earth would want to poison the pope?"

"Well, it turned out that the instigator of the plot was Cardinal Alfonso Petrucci. But he was not alone; three other cardinals were also involved."

"So that's why Pope Leo appointed new cardinals. You can be sure that most of them are from the Medici clan." Erasmus shook his head in amazement. "What a story. What happened to Petrucci and the others?"

"Petrucci was strangled, and the other three were pardoned after they paid enormous fines. Rome and the Vatican are in a sad state of affairs, if you ask me."

"The trouble is widespread, Johannes, especially in the cloisters. The church and Rome have no idea how dissatisfied people are with the debauchery they see all around them. Something is bound to happen."

Although Erasmus did not realize it, at the very same time that he was enjoying dinner with Paludanus in Louvain, his friend Andrew Ammonius was being put to rest in London. He had died of the sweating sickness. Thomas More later wrote that, ironically, on the day of his death, Andrew had told him that he thought himself protected against contagion by his temperate habits. Erasmus received the sad news of his friend's death a few days later, when a letter arrived from their mutual friend John Sixtin:

> Although how grievous a message I am sending you, still I think that I ought to write what you will be so

much concerned to hear. Our friend Andrew Ammonius has been buried today, having been carried off by this Sweating Sickness of which so many persons of note have perished. May God be gracious to his soul! On the day he died, we were to have gone into the country together … But he, as I hope, has been born on high, and has left me to follow when it shall please God.

Two days before his death, I had a most agreeable and cheerful dinner at his house, but the news of his death, arriving before any intelligence of his illness, was brought me, just as I was rising, and before I was dressed. So fragile, tottering and uncertain are human affairs!

Farewell, London, 19 August 1517

12

---◆◆◆◆◆---

The Diet at Augsburg

1518

Phillipp Melanchthon - Disputation at Heidelberg - The Vatican responds - Protected by Elector Frederick - Summoned to Augsburg - Duels with Cardinal Cajetan - Support from Staupitz - Escapes into the night - Pope issues bull on indulgences

In his ambition to enhance the reputation of the University of Wittenberg, Frederick the Wise had, for some time, given thought of adding scholars in Hebrew and Greek to his faculty. He originally tried to hire the famous linguistic and humanist Johann Reuchlin, but Reuchlin declined. Luther, however, had heard superior reports about Reuchlin's great nephew, who was a twenty-one-year-old prodigy. He was born Philipp Schwartzerd ("black earth," in German), but his uncle persuaded him to adopt the Greek translation of his name, Melanchthon. At twelve years of age, Philipp Melanchthon entered the University of Heidelberg, where he studied Greek, astronomy, and rhetoric. After being informed that the university deemed him too young to receive a master's degree, he switched to Tübingen University, where he studied philosophy, humanity, and mathematics and obtained a masters degree in 1516. Although Luther had never met Melanchthon, he convinced Elector Frederick and Staupitz to offer the young man the Greek professorship, based on his excellent reputation.

Martin could not believe his eyes when Philipp finally arrived in Wittenberg—the teenager was so emaciated that Martin referred to him as the "scrawny shrimp." He kept his eye on the boy and a few months later, when he noticed Melanchthon was still as thin as a rail, he wrote a letter to his friend Spalatin, who was Frederick's secretary:

> I fear that our coarse food does not suit his delicate constitution and I fear that he is getting too small a salary. I believe that [the elector's budget director] Herr Pfeffinger as usual has been too faithful a steward by giving Philipp as little as possible. Dear Spalatin, see to it that, despite his youth and boyish appearance, he is worthy of all honor. I do not wish that our university should do such a mean thing, thereby causing our detractors to speak evil of us.

Frederick didn't have to look far to fill the Hebrew professorship position. Andreas Rudolph Bodenstein von Karlstadt, better known as Andreas Karlstadt, was a Hebrew scholar who studied at the University of Erfurt before receiving a doctorate in theology from the University of Wittenberg in 1510. He was awarded the chair of the Theology Department and a year later became chancellor of the university at age twenty-five. The elector was fortunate that Andreas accepted the Hebrew professorship in addition to his other tasks.

Although neither Frederick nor Luther had any way of knowing it at the time, both Andreas Karlstadt and Philipp Menachthlon would play important roles in Luther's life during the coming tumultuous years leading to the Reformation.

On a beautiful afternoon in early April 1518, Staupitz, who had been promoted to vicar-general of Germany, asked Luther to join him on a stroll through the monastery garden. It was obvious that he had something on his mind. "You know, Martin, the triennial meeting of the Augustinian order will be held in Heidelberg in three weeks and as district vicar, you are expected to give a report."

"Yes, Father, I know. Can you give me an idea of how long such a report should be?"

"Ten minutes will do. It's just a formality. Don't make a big deal of it. But I want you to do something else, something very important. It is also a tradition at these meetings for someone to defend the theology of St. Augustine. I want you to do that too."

Martin felt uneasy. "But there must be far better-qualified brothers than I."

"True, true, but this will be your chance to explain yourself. You have created quite a ruckus with your Ninety-Five Theses, and I don't think the Church hierarchy will ever allow you to defend why you wrote them. This may be your only chance."

"But that is not exactly defending St. Augustine."

"I know, but that is not important. The defense of Augustine has been done so many times that everybody already knows what to expect; they are bored of it. I want you to take some time off to prepare a thorough presentation. And when you leave for Heidelberg, take somebody with you."

Martin was so excited that he could have jumped. The trip to Heidelberg was not without danger. Martin was warned that he could fall victim to a possible assassination or kidnapping attempt once he left the safety of Wittenberg and Frederick's protection. Nevertheless, he decided to travel on foot, and as his companion and assistant, he chose twenty-three-year-old Leonhard Beier, who had just finished his studies at Wittenberg. Actually, they had little to fear, because unbeknownst to them, Elector Frederick had taken some measures to make certain that they had a safe journey. After Martin arrived in Heidelberg, Elector Palatin invited him to dinner as guest of honor.

Staupitz, who presided over the order's meeting, introduced Martin to the assembly the next day. "Our main speaker tonight is Brother Martin Luther, master of sacred theology, who will defend the theology of our St. Augustine. He is assisted by Brother Leonhard Beier, master of arts and philosophy. Please join me in welcoming our guests."

The audience gave a short, polite round of applause and then settled down to hear what they expected would be another dull presentation about St. Augustine.

Luther began, "Distrusting completely our own wisdom and in accordance with council of the Holy Spirit 'Rely not on your own insight,' we humbly present for your judgment these theological paradoxes, so that it may become clear whether they have been deduced well or poorly from St. Paul, the especially chosen vessel and instrument of Christ, and also from St. Augustine, his most trustworthy interpreter."

Martin then proceeded to present and discuss twenty-eight theological and twelve philosophical theses. The first twelve were mostly generalities, but with thesis thirteen, he challenged his audience: "Free will, after all, is nothing but a word, and as long as it does what is within it, it is committing deadly sin." Those words made his listeners sit up straight—they had been taught precisely the opposite. Luther hit his listeners with a second surprise in thesis sixteen: "Anyone who believes that he can obtain grace by doing what is in him adds sin to sin so that he becomes doubly guilty." And with thesis eighteen, he added, "It is certain that man must utterly despair of his own ability before he is prepared to receive the grace of Christ." He finished with, "The theology of glory calls the bad 'good' and the good 'bad.' The theology of the cross says what it really is."

He had spoken with a calm and clear voice; he had attacked no one and had not mentioned a word about indulgences. He started to descend from the podium but did not get far before the audience came to its feet and showered him with a long and warm applause. To his amazement, a young monk in Dominican robes approached him in the corridor.

"Doctor, I am Martin Bucer. Allow me to congratulate on your disputation."

"Thank you, Brother. But you have taken me quite by surprise. I did not know that a Dominican monk was welcome at this Augustinian affair. And for you to congratulate me—amazing."

"I just want to thank you," said Bucer with a rueful smile.

Later that day, in a letter to a friend, Bucer wrote: *"Luther responds with magnificent grace and listens with insurmountable patience. He presents an argument with the insight of Apostle Paul. What Erasmus insinuates, Luther speaks of openly and freely."*

After his return to Wittenberg, Luther continued to write a lengthy explanation of his Ninety-Five Theses. He had started the work the previous

November and hoped to publish it in book form once it was finished. He intended to dedicate it to the pope, but he first needed to obtain permission to publish from his diocesan bishop Schulze of Brandenburg, and the good bishop let him wait. In the meantime, the Dominicans geared up for an all-out assault on the defiant monk in Wittenberg.

Rome's reaction to the Ninety-Five Theses was slow in coming, largely because Pope Leo X had a major problem on his hands—the Holy Roman emperor Maximilian was ill and was expected to die in the near future. Maximilian had been scheming for some time to assure that his grandson, King Charles V of Spain, would succeed him, but Leo opposed the idea. He talked the situation over with three of his closest advisors.

"That boy, Charles, is too young. He is only eighteen years old," Leo began.

"We have had archbishops younger than that," one advisor reminded him.

"True, but we must also consider the political consequences. An election of Charles would grant too much power to the kingdom of Spain."

"What about King Francis of France?"

"Then we would have the same problem with France. Let's face it—electing either one will cause friction with the other, and I can ill afford that. We need them both on our side for the stability of the papacy."

"Does Your Holiness have another suggestion?"

"I can live with Frederick of Saxony. Sooner or later, I have to deal with that monk Luther, and I can do that more easily if I appease Frederick first."

They discussed the idea at length and settled on Frederick as their choice for next Holy Roman emperor. "Why don't you three prepare the Curia in all secrecy?" Leo instructed, and dismissed the advisors with a wave of his hand.

Pope Leo then instructed his Master of the Sacred Palace, the Dominican monk Sylvester Prierias, to prepare a response to Luther and his Ninety-Five Theses. Prierias could not wait to attack the Augustinian Luther and took only three days to compose his response, which he had written in the form of a *Dialogus* (Dialogue). He addressed Luther as a heretic and treated him accordingly. He started with four axioms, or *fundamenta*. In the first, he described the world as a large circle, with the church as a small ball in the center and the pope as the center of the ball. The second axiom represented the universal Church and the council with the pope as its infallible leader. The third and fourth axioms stated that in the Church of Rome and in the pope, the believer experiences the truths of the scripture, doctrine, and authority.

> He who does not accept that the doctrine of the Roman Church and of the Roman Pontiff is an infallible rule of faith from which sacred Scripture derives strength and authority is a heretic. He who declares that in the matter of indulgences the Roman Church cannot do what it actually does, is a heretic.

Prierias carefully avoided any mention of theology and stuck strictly to the legality of the Church, the council and the pope.

Luther received the *Dialogus* in the first week of August, together with a summons to appear in Rome. He did not reply to Prierias until August 31, well past the deadline to appear, and as usual, he did not mince his words:

> I regret that I despised Tetzel, because, as ridiculous he is, he is more accurate than you are. You cite no Scripture, give no reason, and, like an insidious devil, you pervert the Scriptures. You say that the Church consists virtually of the pope. What abominations will you not have to regard as the deeds of the Church? Look at the ghastly bloodshed by Julius II. Look at the outrageous tyranny of Boniface VIII, who, as the proverb declares, "came in as a wolf, reigned as a lion, and died as a dog." If the Church consists representatively in the cardinals, what do you make of a general council of the whole Church? You call me a leper because I mix truth with error; I am glad there is some truth. You make the pope into an emperor in power and violence. Emperor Maximilian and the Germans will never tolerate this.

Spare me your threats. My Father, Christ lives. The censure of the Church will not separate me from the Church if the truth joins me to the Church. I have nothing to lose for I am the Lord's. Seek therefore somebody else whom you may terrify.

Martin had no intention of going to Rome. He did not mind the prospect of a meeting with a deputy of the pope, but not in Rome, where he would undoubtedly become a permanent prisoner—or worse, be killed. Martin appealed to his friend Spalatin to discuss the matter with his employer, Elector Frederick. Could the elector intervene?

In the meantime, Emperor Maximilian, who had recovered from his illness, had written to Cardinal Cajetan, the papal legate in Germany, demanding Luther's excommunication, and stated that he, the emperor, would carry out the sentence. Cajetan was born as Jacopo Vio in Gaeta, a small harbor town between Rome and Naples. He had entered the Dominican order at age fifteen, and when he was thirty, he earned a doctorate of theology in Padua under his new name, Thomas Cajetan. In 1508, he was made superior-general of the Dominican order. He publicly defended Pope Julius II on two occasions, first after the Council of Pisa and second during the Fifth Lateran Council. Pope Leo X made him a cardinal in 1517.

Cajetan was in Augsburg, attending the meeting of the Imperial Diet of the Holy Roman Empire, when he received Maximilian's letter. Leo X had sent Cajetan to the Diet to obtain a crusade indulgence and a crusade tax—he was in dire need of money to stop the Ottoman army that was closing in on Vienna. Unfortunately, Cajetan's please fell on deaf ears. Maximilian did not fear the distant Turks; he was more concerned about punishing Luther.

Cajetan's presence in Augsburg gave Elector Frederick the opening that he needed to aid his protégé. He fired off a dispatch to Pope Leo, suggesting that rather than requiring Luther to travel to distant Rome, the pope should allow him to travel to nearby Augsburg, where Cajetan could examine him immediately after the Diet closed. He, Frederick, would guarantee Luther's appearance.

The pope wholeheartedly agreed. He wrote a letter to Cajetan, ordering him to give Luther a fair hearing and an opportunity to recant. If Luther did recant, Cajetan was to fully reunite him with the Church; if not, Cajetan had two choices: he was either to arrest Luther and send him to Rome, or ban Luther and all of his sympathizers from the Church. Separately, the pope wrote a letter to Frederick:

> Beloved son, the apostolic benediction upon you.
> We recall that the chief ornament of your most noble family has been devotion to the faith of God and the honor and dignity of the Holy See. Now we hear that a son of iniquity, Brother Martin Luther of the Augustinian eremites, hurling himself upon the Church of God, has your support. Even though we know it to be false, we must urge you to clear the reputation of your noble family from such calumny. Having been advised by the Master of the Sacred Palace that Luther's teaching contains heresy, we have cited him to appear before Cardinal Cajetan. We call on you to see that Luther is placed in the hands and under the jurisdiction of this Holy See lest future generations reproach you with having fostered the rise of a most pernicious heresy against the Church of God.

Frederick realized that Rome had already decided Luther's fate. He summoned his secretary and advisor, Spalatin, and showed him the pope's letter. "I want you to tell Luther not to talk to Cardinal Cajetan without a safe conduct letter from Emperor Maximilian. I'm sure he is behind all this."

"Are you going to defend him?"

"That will not be necessary, as long as he has the safe conduct. Just make sure that Luther gets the message."

Frederick was not called "Wise" for nothing. When he faced a problem, he took his time to study it from all angles. Luther had his supporters. He was enormously popular at the University of Wittenberg; his disputation at Heidelberg had been a great success and had advanced his reputation through most of Germany and even beyond its borders. Vicar-General Staupitz, who knew Luther better than anyone else, always spoke highly of his protégé and supported his theses. Frederick decided to keep a close watch on future developments by going to Augsburg and attending the meeting with Cajetan. He summoned Luther to inform him.

"I have decided to go to Augsburg for your meeting with Cajetan, but first you must meet Karl von Miltitz, a papal nuncio sent to us by the pope."

Karl von Miltitz was of low-level Saxon nobility, twenty-seven years old, and a man with limited learning capacity. Despite that, he had managed to rise to a position as one of many papal chamberlains. Miltitz had been instructed by the pope to present Frederick with the Golden Rose, a token of esteem and paternal affection, which actually was intended as a bribe of sorts for Frederick to give up his protection of Luther. But Miltitz did not have the Rose with him; it was still safely tucked in the vault at Fugger's Bank. Frederick suspected that Miltitz was stalling in the hope of securing a promise to deliver Luther, but Frederick had no intention of making any such promise; the presentation of the Rose would have to wait. He did, however, arrange for the Nuncio to meet with Luther before he left for Augsburg. Their first meeting ended without resolution.

"So, what do you think of young Miltitz?" Frederick asked Luther afterward.

"He's a lightweight if ever there was one."

"My thoughts exactly. Meet him again, but make no firm promises."

"Why did the pope send someone like him?"

"Don't ask me, but it doesn't speak well of Rome."

Luther and Miltitz met again in the first week of January 1519. Miltitz did most of the talking, but in the end, they worked out a tentative agreement.

"Let's see now. Martin, you agree to lay off on the indulgences, you will write a letter of apology to the pope, and you will publish an article supporting the pope's authority. Is that correct?"

"That sounds about right." Martin noticed that Miltitz had deliberately addressed him by his first name.

"All right. I'll see to it that your opponents remain silent, Tetzel especially. Now, about your recantation—"

"I will recant nothing."

"How about if we phrase it a little bit differently?"

"Such as?"

"That you will not recant your position without specifying what that position is."

"I'll go along with that," agreed Martin, realizing that the dull Miltitz had been unintentionally vague.

Miltitz left the meeting thinking that he had Luther in his pocket.

Martin, who enjoyed walking, covered the two hundred miles between Wittenberg and Augsburg on foot. He stopped in Nuremberg for an overnight stay with his friend Wenceslaus (Wenzel) Linck, who offered to join him as his legal counsel. Together, they arrived in Augsburg on October 7 and waited for a message from Cajetan.

"Martin, I cannot emphasize strongly enough that you are not to enter into a theological dialogue with the cardinal," urged Linck. "You are no match for him, and you stand to lose in front of everybody. Remember, the cardinal is hot-tempered. Keep your answers short—the best defense is to answer a question with a question. I also strongly advise you not to meet the Cardinal without first obtaining a safe conduct from Emperor Maximilian. You must insist on that—we don't want them snatching you and carting you off to Rome."

Martin smiled. "Elector Frederick gave me the same advice. But safe conduct is no guarantee, is it? It didn't do Hus much good. As I remember, he burned at the stake despite having one."

"True, but his safe conduct came from the Church. You must insist that yours come from the emperor himself. We are in Germany; Maximilian can't afford to renege on his word here."

The next day, Martin was visited by a man who did not bother to introduce himself.

"Father, Cardinal Cajetan orders you to appear before him at the hour of eleven."

"And who might you be?"

"I am Urbanus Serralonga, lawyer and orator for the cardinal."

"Well, now, Mr. Serralonga. I have been forbidden by Elector Frederick to meet the cardinal without a safe conduct from Emperor Maximilian."

"But why? Why turn such a simple matter into a long, tiresome one?"

"It's Rome that makes it long. Not me."

"Look, why don't you simply say '*Revoco*,' and this whole business will be over?"

"Revoco means recant, does it not?"

"Yes, it does."

"Sir, then I don't think that this discussion will lead to a solution. I have made up my mind and will wait for the safe conduct. You might as well inform the cardinal."

"That won't help a bit, you know."

"Just tell him."

Serralonga came back two days later. "The cardinal wants you to come with me right now."

"And you know my answer to that."

"Do you seriously think that Elector Frederick will take up arms for your sake?"

"No, that will not be necessary."

"Then where will you go if the elector no longer protects you?"

"I'll stay here, under the heavens."

Serralonga scratched his head and looked at Luther. "I am curious; what would you do if you met the pope and his cardinals in person?"

"I would show them all the respect and honor due to them."

The Italian made a contemptuous gesture of biting his index finger, and then he left. He returned the next day with a safe conduct signed by Emperor Maximilian, and Martin promised to meet with Cardinal Cajetan at Augsburg Cathedral the next day.

That evening, Martin received a pleasant surprise—Johann von Staupitz, his mentor from Wittenberg, knocked on his door. "I just came by to wish you well and strength. We will be there with you," Staupitz said quickly, and he disappeared into the night.

The short visit brought tears to Martin's eyes.

The next morning, the cathedral was packed to standing-room-only capacity—princes, bishops, mayors, politicians, and even the emperor and his entourage were present. They mingled and talked among themselves while waiting for the proceedings to begin: "I haven't seen you in ages!" "Good to see you. Have you read the theses?" "I wonder what he looks like." "The pope has to learn that he cannot fool around with us. I think ..."

A sudden hush came over the crowd as the large doors opened, and Luther entered, with the cardinal's orator, Serralonga, at his side. People deferentially stepped back, opening a path for the two men to walk through. Necks strained to see the man they all had come to hear. As Luther and Serralonga walked to the front of the church, the path closed behind them as they went. Martin looked straight ahead and saw no faces. He felt alone. At the front of the church, he stood and waited. Without turning his head, he could see Emperor Maximilian sitting to his left and the electors to his right; Frederick the Wise was seated among them. Martin felt a bit relieved by Frederick's presence. He looked at the covered table before him, which had a massive opened Bible upon it, with feather pen and inkhorn off to one side.

A side door opened, and the silent crowd looked on as a Dominican monk with a paper under his arm entered and slowly walked to the table. He took a seat on a low stool close to the feather pen and inkhorn. A bishop came in next and stood at the other side of the table. The assembly waited again, longer this time, and then, with the great dignity, Cardinal Cajetan walked in and sat on a pillow-covered chair behind the table. He carefully removed his red hat with two hands and handed it to the bishop, who hung it on the wall behind the cardinal for everyone to see. The proceedings were about to begin.

Cajetan gave a small nod to the imperial figure to his right, and Emperor Maximilian approached the table. The bishop handed Cajetan an ornate helmet and a dagger, awarded by the pope as the symbols of the Protector of the Faith, which Cajetan presented to the emperor. Maximilian did not know what to do with the helmet, which was much too small for his large head. Cajetan motioned for him to put it on, and he complied, but he felt ridiculous as he walked back to his seat.

Cajetan turned to his left and nodded to Elector Frederick to come forward. Pope Leo X knew that the emperor and the elector were archenemies, so he could not award only one of them. The bishop approached Cajetan once more and handed him a rose with golden petals set with sapphires—the Golden Rose, blessed by the pope on the fourth

Sunday of Lent. The cardinal presented the Rose to Frederick, who was visibly pleased to receive this precious gift from the Holy Father.

Finally, the cardinal looked at the lone, thin figure before him.

"You are the monk Martin Luther?" It sounded more like a statement than a question.

Martin took three steps forward and prostrated himself on the cold, gray flagstone floor. Cajetan rose from behind the table and extended his hand to help Martin up. As he did so, he whispered in his ear, "*Revoco.*" Martin abruptly straightened. People seated near the front could see him ball his fingers into fists.

The cardinal returned to his seat behind the table, sat up straight, and imperiously addressed the crowd:

> To all men gathered, we now proceed with the examination of the monk Martin Luther over the book. We ask of you, Martin Luther, to do three things:
>
> Retrace your wanderings and come to your sober senses.
>
> Promise obedience in times to come.
>
> Abstain from all actions that may disturb the peace of the Church.
>
> What do you say to this?

"Will Most Reverend Father deign to point out where I have erred?" Martin asked firmly.

"In your seventh thesis, you state, 'Observe, no one can receive the grace of the sacraments without faith.'"

"I will never recall this point, because it is impossible for someone without faith to receive the grace of the sacraments."

Cajetan decided to leave the issue and move onto his second point. "In the fifty-eighth thesis, you assert that the treasure of indulgences does not consist of the merits and the sufferings of our Lord Jesus Christ." Cajetan allowed himself a small smile of satisfaction and continued. "However, in his bull *Unigenitus*, Pope Clement VI clearly enunciated that the merits of Christ are a treasure of indulgences."

"I will recant, Reverend Father, if the *Unigenitus* said so."

Cajetan thought he had bested Luther. He eagerly flipped through the *Unigenitus* to the page he had marked days before. "It says right here that Christ, by his sacrifice, acquired the treasure."

"True, but that is not what you said," Martin replied quickly. "You just said that the merits of Christ *are* the treasure. The book says he *acquired* the treasure; that is not the same. I question the authority of the Pope Clement VI, who was a human being."

A murmur, starting at the front rows, moved like a giant wave through the assembled audience.

Cajetan, suddenly red-faced, looked at the page, looked up, and realized that he had grossly underestimated his thirty-six-year-old opponent. He now knew that he had best not debate with the man. "My son, I am not here to argue with you. I am fully prepared to reunite you with the church."

"That is, if I recant. Correct, Reverend Father? I should not be condemned without being heard. I am not conscious of violating the scriptures, the fathers, the decretals, or sound reason. But I am against a decree issued by a human pope about indulgences that are not mentioned in the scriptures."

"Remember, that the pope is the only infallible interpreter of the scriptures," Cajetan stated authoritatively. "The pope is above a council, above everything in the Church."

Luther felt his courage rise. "His Holiness abuses scripture. I deny that he is above scripture."

"Leave!" Cajetan suddenly yelled at him. "Leave, and don't come back unless you are ready to recant, to say 'Revoco!'"

That evening, the cardinal had dinner with Staupitz. "I didn't get far with him today, did I?" Cajetan said wearily.

"No, you didn't."

"How am I going to get him to recant? You know him best of all. Can you convince him?"

"My friend, I have tried, but his command of the scripture is much better than mine. He is not only stubborn, but he also has a phenomenal memory. Don't tackle him on scriptures. He will beat you every time."

"I won't. So you will not ask him to recant?"

"No, that is your task. You know that the pope demands it, and you represent the pope here."

That night, Cajetan sent a messenger to Pope Leo X, informing him that Luther had questioned the authority of Clement VI.

Despite Cajetan's parting words to Luther, the two combatants met again the next day. The cathedral was only half full, and Emperor Maximilian was absent. Cajetan remembered how Martin had tripped him up the day before with just two words—"are" and "acquired"—and he proceeded cautiously. He concentrated his argument on the authority of the pope and the church, while Luther quoted from the scriptures to support his case, to which the cardinal rarely had a good answer. Cajetan emphasized that the pope and the council were above scriptures and had the power to interpret them authoritatively. Luther insisted that they were only men, who, being human, would make mistakes, whereas the scriptures were infallible. The second day ended in a stalemate, as did the third. By then, the cathedral was nearly empty. In the end, an exasperated Cajetan lost his composure and impotently screamed at his adversary, "Revoco! Revoco!"

Martin was convinced that eventually, a death sentence would hang over his head. He resolved to flee Augsburg before the gates in the town wall closed for the night and sealed him in. That evening, he was in his room at the inn, bundling his notes and books, when Staupitz and Linck suddenly entered.

"You're too late," said Staupitz with an air of urgency when he saw Martin packing. "The gates are already closed, and there are guards everywhere. I fear they will arrest you, despite your safe conduct. Wenzel and I are leaving Augsburg as soon as the gates open in the morning. Somehow, you must get out tonight, but first, as vicar general, I hereby release you from your vows of obedience as an Augustinian monk. I hope that may help somehow. Here are five gold pieces. Take them; you may need them. Go with God's speed, son."

Martin was close to tears after they left. He sat at the edge of his cot and remembered a story Staupitz had once told him: "Son, when I was a young preacher, I once gave a sermon on the torments of Job. It was a long and dreary sermon, and my boils were bothering me. You know what I did? I said, 'I am stopping now. Job and I are both glad.'" Momentarily heartened by this memory, Martin smiled, got up, and went downstairs to see the innkeeper.

"I need to leave tonight for Nuremberg," he said to the stout man.

The innkeeper shook his head. "Impossible, Father. For some reason the city gates closed early today. You'll have to wait until … uh-oh, perhaps I may be able to help you after all." He saw a gold coin in Martin's half-opened palm. He wiped his hands on his apron, opened his palm, and asked, "Do you have your things together?" He shoved the gold coin in his pocket.

"I'll go up and get them right now."

"Just a moment. When you come back down the stairs, don't come in here—there are too many eyes. There is a little door halfway down the steps on your right. It's a bit narrow, but you can fit through. One of my sons will be waiting for you on the other side." He started to walk away, but he remembered something and turned back. "Of course, if you give him some coin, he will be happy."

"Thank you. Do you think I can get a horse?" A second gold piece changed hands.

"That can be arranged. God bless, Father, and thank you."

The innkeeper's eldest son led Martin through the dark night to a thicket near the city wall. They crawled through a narrow break in the thicket, scraping their arms and faces as they went, until they reached a small tunnel in the side of the massive city wall. Few of the town's citizens knew of the tunnel's existence, and it was left unguarded. The two men slid through the opening on their behinds, dragging Martin's belonging behind them, until at last they reached the outside. Waiting for Martin was the oldest, most decrepit horse he had ever seen—but at least it had four legs, and it was not lame. Dressed in monk's robes, it was nearly impossible for Martin to mount the saddle-less horse without a lift and a push from the innkeeper's son. The old nag was quite swaybacked, which actually made sitting rather comfortable—at least, initially. Martin gave the boy some coin and headed toward Nuremberg.

Without stopping, he traveled on back roads through the night and arrived in Nuremberg in the late afternoon. He finally stopped at Wenzel Linck's house, where his friend was shocked to see him. Linck had left

Augsburg that morning on a healthy stallion and had arrived several hours earlier. The long ride on the ancient nag had taken its toll on Martin; he could not get off his horse without his friend's help. When his feet hit the ground, his legs buckled, and he fell to his knees; every bone in his body ached.

"Let me pass water before we go inside," Martin said to his concerned friend. "My God, that felt good," he said when he came back.

"I don't understand. Was something wrong?"

"It's this robe, that's what's wrong. Have you ever tried to mount a horse in one of these? It's impossible without help. I have been astride that animal for twenty hours straight. My bladder was bursting, but I did not dare stop, for fear that I would not be able to climb back on."

"How did you manage to escape?" asked Linck after escorting Martin inside and seating him on the edge of a cot. "But wait, don't tell me yet. I'll get you some soup and drink first."

When he came back into the room, he found Martin slumped on his side in a deep sleep. He took off his friend's muddy sandals, lifted his legs onto the cot, and covered him with a blanket. Martin rested a few days in his friend's house until he felt strong enough to walk the two hundred-plus miles back to the monastery in Wittenberg, where he was warmly welcomed by the brothers on October 31. At the urging of Staupitz and Linck, he immediately wrote a letter to Cardinal Cajetan:

> Highly esteemed in God the Father.
>
> I approach you once more, not in person, but in writing. Dr. Johann Staupitz has urged me to humble myself and my beloved brother, Dr. Wenzelaus Linck, has done the same.
>
> I now confess, Honored Father, that I have not been humble enough and that I have been too vehement, not treating you with sufficient reverence. Although I had good cause, I now know that I should have been more gentle and treat Your Eminence with more respect; however, it is done and I admit that it is not always wise to answer a fool according to his folly and thus become more like him.

I am very much regret all this now and plead for mercy. With God's help, I shall henceforth be more careful in how I speak.

Your Excellency's submissive son,

Martin Luther, Augustinian

Although he tried to make the letter contrite, he could not resist jabbing Cajetan a bit with his reference to fool and folly.

Cajetan did not respond. Instead, he wrote to Elector Frederick, complaining that Staupitz and Luther had ill used him during the examination at Augsburg.

It is only in respect of your Highness that no evil has been done to that fraterculus. This grave and pestilent matter will linger on after this meeting and they will undoubtedly prosecute in Rome. However, I have washed my hands of it. I am certain that you will not wish it to be a spot upon your glory.

I speak the absolute truth and I will be a slave to the rule of Christ according to which "you shall know them by their fruits." I urge you to send Luther to Rome or at the very least eject him from your territories."

The cardinal left Augsburg the same day. He had failed in his two missions—obtaining an indulgence for the crusade against the Turks and forcing Luther to recant.

On December 8, the elector responded to Cajetan:

You obviously have no idea how serious the situation is in Germany. You were wrong to force Luther to recant before he was heard. Many German intellectuals see no wrong, nothing heretical, in Luther's opinions. I will in no way expel Dr. Luther from my dominions.

He sent a copy of this response, along with Cajetan's letter, to Martin, who had to smile when he saw himself referred to as a *fraterculus* ("little monk," or "ass of a monk") but was furious with the rest of Cajetan's missive. The letter copies, along with Luther's narrative of what happened in Augsburg, leaked out in no time, and in the outside world the people's eyes opened.

When Leo X learned that Luther had questioned Clement VI's authority in the *Unigenitus*, he decided to issue his own bull about the doctrine of indulgence.

> The Roman Church, the Mother of all Churches, has handed down by tradition that the Roman Pontiff, the successor of St. Peter, by the power of the keys—that is, by removing the guilt and punishment due for actual sins by indulgence—can for reasonable causes grant to the faithful of Christ, whether in this life or in purgatory, indulgences out of the superabundance of the merits of Christ and the Saints; can confer the indulgence by absolution, or transfer it by suffrage. And all those who have acquired indulgence, whether alive or dead, are released from so much temporal punishment for their actual sins as is the equivalent of the acquired indulgence. This doctrine is to be held and preached by all, under penalty of excommunication, from which only the Pope can absolve, save at the point of death.

Elector Frederick was not impressed. "What legal gibberish," he growled to Spalatin. "His lawyers must have had a field day with it." The fact that the pope felt it necessary to issue a special bull justifying indulgences proved to him that Luther was right.

13

Erasmus Under Attack

1517–1520

Tension at Louvain - Comma Johanneum - Edward Lee, from friend to foe - Revises his New Testament translation - Reads the Ninety-Five Theses - Corresponds with Luther - Maintains neutrality - Attacked by Henry Standish - Death of John Colet

In the sixteenth century, no one had any idea what caused the frequent outbreaks of the plague. Erasmus, however, suspected that it had something to do with the lack of hygiene in cities, towns, and villages. There was no running water or gutters, so fetid water pooled in the streets. It was common practice for people to empty chamber pots from their windows directly onto the street below, with the shout of "coming down!" Manure from horses and cattle lay everywhere, and waste piled up, creating a haven for rats, stray dogs, and feral cats. At times, the stench was unbearable.

Erasmus absolutely hated it. "It must be bad for one's health and a source of infection," he reasoned. He advocated personal hygiene, starting with a bath once a week. He also advised people overnighting in roadside inns to make sure that their beds were clean and free of bed bugs. He further believed that people should avoid lice by keeping their hair short and well brushed and that men should stay away from prostitutes and loose women because they frequently harbored venereal diseases. Unfortunately, very few people other than Erasmus thought that there could be a connection between lack of hygiene and diseases.

Physically, he was not a strong man. "I am always in delicate health, and I must avoid people who have colds at all cost," he explained. "Fish does not go well with my stomach, so I cannot join others in fasting, which taps my strength too much." He was one of the world's greatest hypochondriacs and typically burdened others by enumerating his every symptom in minute detail. "The most miserable of all men, the thrice-wretched Erasmus," he called himself.

He was also delicate in his behavior. He avoided controversy, fled from fights and was considered by many to be a coward. He rarely accused someone to his face, and seldom, if at all, used a coarse word. He tended to be somewhat feminine in his speech and behavior, as well as in his letters, although he did not hesitate to use his pen as a rapier when enemies attacked him. He desired a quiet, peaceful existence and sought it in Louvain.

Living at Louvain University suited him well. There, he could study and write in peace, and he would have been perfectly happy, were not it for certain members of the theological faculty, which was divided between the conservative Dominicans and the more liberal humanists, including Erasmus. His relationship with his fellow faculty members varied from outright hostility from some to warm friendship from others. For the most part, the theologians at Louvain treated him with respect. Erasmus, on the other hand, found, *"They are the dreariest of all men. They write little or nothing that is useful, certainly not in an academic way, and they dominate all conversation with their idle talk."* A few faculty members were jealous of his brilliance. The fact was that Erasmus was one of a handful of scholars, fewer than five, who could speak and write Greek. More than once during debates involving the scriptures, Erasmus argued that in order to fully understand the subject of discussion, one should learn Greek. He often called them *the antibarbari* and accused them of suppressing the ancient literature of authors such as Plato. This did not sit well with his detractors.

The conservative faculty at the Department of Theology at Louvain always was on the lookout for a new reason to attack Erasmus. They were in an uproar when the dean of the university appointed Erasmus to find scholars to fill new faculty chairs in Latin, Greek, and Hebrew for the new *Collegium Trilingue*, which had been established through a gift bequeathed by Jerome Busleider, a friend and admirer of Erasmus's. The prospect of Erasmus filling faculty positions was too much for the conservatives, and they went after him. "He will help create a new kind of theology," they clamored.

"All I try to do is revive good literature," Erasmus countered. "Without fluency of these three ancient languages, you leave a vacuum in your knowledge."

"You are a traitor to the writings of the fathers of the Church," they accused.

"Not true," he retorted, "but hearing all your rhetoric, let me remind you that one goes a lot further with courtesy and moderation than with clamor."

Erasmus followed Thomas More's advice and spent his time in Louvain working diligently at revising his translation of the New Testament. One day in late 1517, he received letter from Georg Spalatin, who wrote:

> An Augustinian ecclesiastic, who greatly admires you, has asked me to draw attention to the fact, that in your interpretation of St. Paul you had failed to conceive the idea of justitia correctly and had paid too little attention to original sin. The ecclesiastic suggests that you might profit by reading Augustine.

Erasmus filed the letter away in his "do not pay attention to" drawer. Although he knew that Spalatin was the secretary of the powerful Frederick the Wise, he felt no need to respond to the suggestion of an unknown ecclesiastic—he already had a large collection of such letters. Instead, he returned his attention to his own studies.

He was particularly interested in the history of two clauses, known as the *Comma Johanneum* (Johannine Comma) that were included in all Middle-Ages Bibles:

> 1 John 5:7. For there are three that bear record in Heaven; the Father, the Word and the Holy Ghost; and these three are one.
>
> 1 John 5:8. And there are three that bear witness; the spirit and the water and the blood; and these three agree in one.

In his extensive research, which included examining manuscripts from the Vatican's collection, sent to him by his friend Paulus Bombasius, the Vatican librarian, he confirmed that there was no evidence that the passages existed in the original Gospels, and he theorized that they had somehow crept into the New Testament during the early Middle Ages. It was reason enough for him not include the *Comma Johanneum* in his translation.

One afternoon, while walking the hallways of the university, Erasmus, to his delight, met a young Franciscan who addressed him in English.

"Father Erasmus, permit me to introduce myself. My name is Edward Lee, and I believe we have mutual friends in Sir Thomas More and Dean John Colet."

"Well, now, I am more than pleased to meet you," said Erasmus warmly, grasping Lee's hand. "Friends of my friends are my friends. May I ask, are you in Louvain to study?"

"Indeed, I am, sir. I learned the rudiments of Greek in England and wish to become more fluent in that ancient language, in conversation as well as in reading."

"I am pleased to hear that, for I have always believed that without knowing Greek, one cannot fully appreciate and understand the Bible."

From this initial meeting they proceeded to visit each other and shared what they were working on—Erasmus on his never-ending revision of the New Testament and Lee on his annotations of the Bible. Lee even undertook to assist Erasmus in his work, and they shared notes and ideas.

Revising the New Testament was a three-year undertaking. When Erasmus finished his research in the spring of 1518, he gave draft copies of his work to the leaders of the conservative faculty at Louvain University, asking for their input and critique. To his pleasant surprise, nearly all of them declared their general support for the draft revision. His main adversary, Nicolaas Egmond, made some nasty comments but, when pressed, admitted that he had not read the work.

Edward Lee was the only faculty member to put his critique in writing. It was obvious that he had read the entire draft and put a lot of effort in his review. Lee strongly objected to the exclusion of the *Comma Johanneum*, and he must have shared his view with the leaders of the conservative faculty. They changed their initial opinion and joined Lee in strenuously objecting to the *Comma*'s omission, saying, "It threatened the doctrine of the Trinity."

Erasmus was intensely annoyed with Lee, and their relationship began to deteriorate. He later wrote:

> For a time, we proceeded agreeably, but then he began to include too many needless cutting remarks, so it seemed to me. A few times, I added slight remarks that casually came into my mind. Finally, when it appeared that he was becoming unnecessarily angry, I wrote him, "Remember that you are assisting a man with advice, but you yourself are only a man." From that day on, he no longer sent me his notes and stopped meeting me.

Sometime later, they met by chance in St. Peter's Church.

"Why have you changed so much, Edward?" Erasmus inquired.

"This is not the right place to discuss it," Lee replied rather brusquely. He turned and walked away with a quick step.

Perhaps resentment was the cause of Lee's change in attitude toward his much-older colleague. Lee charged that Erasmus used his ideas without giving him credit, and Erasmus did later admit that he'd included several of Lee's suggestions in his work. Shortly before Erasmus planned to leave for Basel to oversee the printing of the second edition of his New Testament, Lee handed him many sheets of comments, including ten conclusions. On the day before Erasmus's departure, Lee approached him.

"What do you think of my conclusions?" Lee asked hesitantly.

"I'm sorry, but I didn't receive them," Erasmus brushed him off. He, who hated people who lied, lied himself. He had received them, but he had not found the time to read them.

"But I worked so hard on them," Lee cried out. "I did it to help you."

"Sorry, I must go now," Erasmus said. He abruptly turned around, but over his shoulder, he added, "I'll look at it on my way to Basel." He left Lee standing, something for which the Englishman would never forgive him. Their short-lived friendship had turned into a relationship filled with hostility.

The next day Erasmus traveled to Basel to personally supervise the printing of his revised edition in Froben's shop. It was eventually published in 1519 under the title *Novum Testamentum* (New Testament) and dedicated to Pope Leo X, who had gratefully accepted the honor with one proviso—that Erasmus put in the *Comma Johanneum*. With this important push, Erasmus finally complied.

While in Basel, he received the news that an Augustinian monk named Luther had nailed a list of wrongdoings committed by the Church and the pope to the door of the castle church in Wittenberg, Germany. It did not take long for copies of Ninety-Five Theses to reach Basel. Erasmus read Luther's Theses and immediately sent a copy to Thomas More. Erasmus considered the Theses a part of the ongoing debate between old-time theologians and the younger generation. He agreed with Luther that there was no need for indulgences, for priests as intermediaries between man and God, or for sacraments, with the exception of baptism. He occasionally said a good word about the Theses to his friends, but he did not support them publicly or in writing.

Erasmus realized, however, that the Theses would create trouble between theologians, and he wrote to Frederick the Wise to express his support of Luther, be it limited. He urged, "Luther needs protection from the Dominican rogues who do not understand his writings—they [the writings] need corrections rather than destruction."

In response, Frederick invited Erasmus to visit him in Wittenberg. "I am eager to have your opinion," he wrote. "Has Luther erred?"

Erasmus declined the invitation but answered, "Luther has erred on two points—he attacked the tiara of the pope and the bellies of the monks."

When Frederick read this, he burst out laughing, and his ample belly shook. "Luther will be attacked from many corners," Erasmus continued in his letter, "but what the world needs is a fair, open and impartial hearing of Luther by the learned men within the Church, not by some hotheads."

Erasmus spent the summer of 1518 in Basel taking the opportunity to publish not only the New Testament but also several works on divinity, moral and religious issues, and a new edition of *Enchiridion militis Christiani*. He also published an updated edition of his *Epistolae* (Letters), which were first published in 1515 but had received little attention. Eventually he would publish a dozen editions of the *Epistolae*, the last one in 1536, the year of his death.

On the return trip from Basel, he had a remarkable encounter in Boppard, a small town where the Rhine River makes one of its sharpest loops. Erasmus told the story of the encounter in a letter to one of his friends:

I was taking a stroll along the banks of the river, when someone recognized me and excitedly told the customs officer who I was. Would you believe that the officer—Christopher Eschenfelder is his name—jumped with joy when he learned who I was. He dragged me into his small house where I saw several of my books lying amidst customs papers. He was so excited, he called his wife, his children and his friends, and kept on saying, "This is the famous Erasmus." Pointing to the books, he added, "This is the man who wrote those books I keep talking to you about."

When the captain of our boat sent two sailors to get me, Mister Eschenfelder sent them back with two tankards of wine, and another two when they called for me again. "Tell your captain that on his return trip, I'll forgo the toll because he brought me the eminent Erasmus."

He was deeply impressed that the simple customs officer could read Latin and had read his books. After his return to Louvain, he wrote a special letter, thanking him.

> Dear friend,
> What a delightful surprise to find such a friend at Boppard! A customs officer who cares for the muses and good learning … While most officials spend their time thinking what they shall eat and drink, Eschenfelder divides his hours between His Imperial Majesty and his books; I am lucky if the sight of me has not spoiled your dream. That red wine of yours found favour with the captain's wife, a full-breasted bouncing woman with a fine thirst, so much so that she became quarrelsome and nearly slew her servant-girl with a mighty ladle. Then, she went on deck, attacked her husband, and almost toppled him into the Rhine. That's what comes of your wine.
>
> Farewell, Erasmus of Rotterdam

They continued their friendly correspondence for many years, and in 1535, near the end of his life, Erasmus dedicated his interpretation of Psalm 14 to Eschenfelder in his treatise, *De puritate Ecclesiae* (On the Purity of the Christian Church), which was his last work.

Upon his return to Louvain in the fall of 1518, he discovered that there was a storm brewing among the members of the faculty. Every professor had read a copy of Luther's Ninety-Five Theses, as well as the report of his disputation in Heidelberg during the German Augustinian Congregation. The next morning, the discussion at the faculty meeting was dominated by the Dominican professors, who had the majority. They declared Cardinal Cajetan the clear victor over Luther at the Diet of Augsburg and could not wait for Pope Leo to issue a bull against Luther. The Augustinians did not want to rush their opinion. Someone proposed that the faculty vote to officially condemn Luther.

During the discussion, Edward Lee kept his eye on Erasmus, who, with slight amusement, was observing the maneuvering Dominicans.

"Brothers," Lee called out. "We haven't heard from Brother Erasmus. Let's hear it, Brother, or are you afraid to speak out?"

"Speak, speak, speak," the majority chanted.

Erasmus's enigmatic smile silenced them. "Brother Lee, you seemed to forget that you only heard a one-sided report. Would you not also want to hear Luther's side?"

"Listen to that heretic's foul lies? Never!" Lee sneered as he looked around for support.

"The bastard has already been banned," several voices called out.

"I do not think so, but you should go right ahead," Erasmus encouraged calmly.

The vote for the condemnation of Luther carried. Erasmus abstained.

Erasmus adopted a strictly neutral position and avoided taking a public stance on the Luther controversy. Some of his private writings, however, reveal that he was not entirely neutral. He had earlier written to Elector Frederick the Wise, urging him to protect Luther. In addition, on October 17, 1518, he had written to Luther's friend John Lange, reporting that he heard that Luther was supported by the best sort of people and that his book, *Conclusions*, pleased everybody, except those who were unwilling to see purgatory wrested from their hands. Finally, he wrote to a mutual friend of his and Luther's: *"I fear that Martin will be the victim of his own uprightness."*

Martin was pleased when he received word that that Erasmus had been writing about him. He admired Erasmus and his works, and he reached out to the great man, hoping to receive his support.

> Martin Luther to Erasmus of Rotterdam, greetings.
> Many times have I spoken with you and you with me [he writes figuratively], and as yet, we are not mutually acquainted … For who is there whose entire inmost thoughts are not dominated by Erasmus? … Therefore, I congratulate you, because, while you please all good men

in the highest degree, you nonetheless displease those who desire to be only great ones and have an excessive wish to please. But how foolish I am to approach such a man as you without any reverent and decorous face, as if I am one of your most familiar acquaintances, when, in reality, I am speaking as one stranger to another …

And so, dear Erasmus, amiable man that you are, recognize me if you see fit as your little brother in Christ, one who is truly most devoted and attached to you, but meriting by his ignorance nothing more than to be buried in a corner … I am fittingly conscious of my poor powers. I am compelled to my deep shame to have my ignominies and my unfortunate ignorance exposed and paraded even before learned men … May the Lord Jesus preserve you for all eternity, dearest Erasmus. Amen.

Brother Martin Luther
Wittenberg, March 28, 1519

He hoped that Erasmus would reply and wondered what his response would be. Would he ignore, berate, salute, or support him? Would he acknowledge Martin as one whose ideas were similar to his own?

Erasmus did none of these. Instead, he procrastinated drafting a response and left Luther waiting. In the meantime, he wrote a letter to Frederick the Wise, urging him to give Luther's theological thinking the same objective consideration he gave to that of others. Then, on May 18, 1519, he wrote a very long letter to his English friend Cardinal Wolsey and included the following paragraph:

Luther is as unknown to me as the veriest stranger; nor have I had time to read more than one or two pages of the man's work. Not that I dislike them … And yet some people think that I have helped him with writing them … And even if I had time to read him, I could not pass judgment on the writings of so great a man … Finally, a swarm of pamphlets appeared: no one saw me reading them; no one ever heard me either praising or censuring them. For I am not so rash to praise what I have not read, nor so hypocritical as to condemn what I know nothing about.

Not long thereafter, he wrote a similar message to the archbishop of Mainz: *"Luther is as unknown to me as the veriest stranger, nor have I had time to read his books beyond here and there a page."*

Finally, after two months had passed since he'd received Luther's letter, Erasmus wrote a noncommittal reply:

> Erasmus of Rotterdam to Father Martin Luther, Greetings.
> Dearest brother in Christ. Your letter was most pleasing to me, showing as it does the keenness of your mind and your Christian spirit. I can hardly tell you what commotion your writings have occasioned me. So far, I have been unable to pluck the most unfounded idea from the minds of some that your works have been written with my assistance, and that I am the ringleader of your faction ... I should never have believed anyone who said that theologians are insane
> I have asserted that you are the veriest stranger to me, that I have not read your books, and that, as a consequence, is why I have neither censured nor approved anything that might be in them. I have only advised some not to be so spiteful about books they have not read and not to bring matters before promiscuous assemblies. But it was all to no purpose, for up to the present, they rant and rave with their one-sided and notorious disputes. The theologians place no trust in books; their only hope of victory lies in their calumnies. Towards you, they are becoming a little milder; as for me, they fear my pen.
> There are persons in England, and they in the highest positions, who think very well of your writings. Here too, there are people among them the Bishop of Liége, who fan

your followers. As for me, I keep myself as far as possible neutral the better help the revival of learning. And it seems to me that more can be gained by such courteous restraint than by violence … It is better to disregard the violent contentions of some people than to refute them. We must be careful not to say or do anything tending to arrogance or partisanship … I do not, however, admonish you to do these things, but advise you to do always what you are doing.

I have read a few pages of your *Commentaries on the Psalms*; they please me exceedingly. There is at Antwerp a prior of his monastery who loves you greatly. He says that he was once a pupil of yours. I have written to Melanchthon. May the Lord Jesus give you every day more and more of His spirit, to His own glory and the public good. When I was writing this, your letter was not at hand. Farewell.

Louvain, May 30, 1519

A visibly angry Martin burst into the cubicle that served as an office for his friend Spalatin. "Look at what that arrogant man wrote!" he yelled and threw the letter on his desk. While Georg read the letter, Martin stomped back and forth in his office.

"Well, isn't that a piece of shit?" Martin asked with a sneer.

"Not really. Martin, this is by far the most beautiful example of fence-sitting I have ever seen. Erasmus obviously doesn't want to commit himself."

"He could have done that in one sentence," Martin fumed.

"Martin, slow down and sit." Spalatin tried to calm his friend. "You wanted him to give you his outright support, and you are disappointed. But look at the problems he is facing in Louvain. He is surrounded by fiercely conservative theologians who dare him to come out against you, and you must admit that he hasn't done that."

"I think that he is a coward."

"Oh, come on now; don't be so harsh. Not everybody is as impetuous as you are. All he did was to write you a very civil letter and he paid you a compliment about the psalms. It looks to me that Erasmus wants to change the Church from within, and that takes time. He has a lot to lose. You, on the other hand, want to see change right now, and you have little to lose."

"Only my neck, remember?"

"Only your neck. Right, but don't blame Erasmus for that."

"So, Georg, you want me to write this off as another disappointment. Is that it?"

"In not so many words, yes. You shook the world with your Ninety-Five Theses and the world is still absorbing it. In the meanwhile, Erasmus advises you to 'do always what you are doing.' In other words, he does not discourage you. As a matter of fact, you should publish this letter. Can you imagine what people will think when they read about the support you have in England and from the bishop of Liége?"

Martin got up from his chair, took the letter from the desk, carefully folded it and put it in his pocket. "Thank you, Georg. As always, you give me sound advice."

Érard de la Marck, bishop of Liége, was furious when his secretary handed him a published copy of the letter. Contrary to what Erasmus had written, the bishop did not support Luther.

"I thought that Erasmus was your friend," the secretary stated.

"He was. Do you remember his letter of January last year?"

"Yes I do." The secretary leafed through some papers. "Here it is—January 7."

"Read the part where he talks about himself."

"You even underlined it. *'In me there is nothing to be seen: or if there is, it is represented by my books. The best part of me is there, and the rest would not sell for a nickel.'*"

The bishop thought for a moment and slowly shook his head. "That's something one would only write to a friend. So why does he embarrass me so much in his letter to Luther?"

"Maybe he didn't mean for it to be published."

"That makes no difference. He wrote it in the first place, and he knows very well that I do not support Luther. He has put me in a very awkward position."

A few months later, Erasmus published a revised version of his letter, in which the bishop of Liége was not mentioned.

Back in Louvain, Lee and Erasmus continued to get under each other's skin, and Erasmus eventually showed his uglier side by starting a letter campaign against Lee. In a letter to his friend Hermus Buschius, he wrote, *"The man is a laughing stock; he is the anathema to all men of sense. His is hissed off the stage, and yet he obstinately remains pleased with himself."* In another letter, he said, *"Edward Lee has stopped at nothing to secure my undoing, but so far he has had no success. He tries to drive a wedge between me and my friends."*

Lee, in turn, wrote to Erasmus: *"You are always engaged in bringing suspicion upon others. How dare you usurp the office of a general censor and condemn what you have hardly ever tasted? How dare you despise all but yourself?"* In a later letter, he continued along the same vein: *"You keep on saying that if you were guilty of even the smallest of my accusations, you wouldn't dare sit at the Lord's Table. Who are you to judge me, a servant who stands or falls before my Lord?"*

Their relationship continued to deteriorate until one afternoon, as they approached each other in one of the many hallways of the university, Lee tried to stop Erasmus, but he merely shrugged his shoulders and walked on without looking up. Lee hastened after Erasmus, poked a finger in his chest, and snarled, "It was you … you, Erasmus, who laid the egg of the Reformation." Erasmus calmly removed Lee's offending finger, faced his attacker without flinching, and replied, "Yes, for once, Dr. Lee, you are correct. I laid the egg, but it was for a hen. It was Luther who hatched a gamecock from it."

In the same year, during a short trip to England, Erasmus was attacked by another Englishman, Bishop Henry Standish. The bishop, who was supported by Lee, was very critical of Erasmus's New Testament. In a sermon before a packed congregation at St. Paul's Church, Standish maintained that Erasmus had corrupted the Gospel of St. John and that the Christian religion faced destruction unless all new translations of the Bible were instantly destroyed. Standish should have known better than to attack Erasmus in St. Paul's, which was a center of humanism.

Later that evening, John Colet hosted a dinner at which both Standish and Erasmus were present. One of the guests turned to Standish and said, "I am delighted to hear that a godly man like you found the time to read Erasmus's *Commentaries*."

Standish smelled a trap. "Maybe I have read all I have a mind to read," he said with slight hesitation.

"Dear Bishop, I have no doubt that you have read him, for today you explicitly criticized a passage in his notes on St. John," the man persisted. Everyone noticed Standish's veiled discomfort.

"I may have read the book," Standish acknowledged.

"Splendid, for I long to know on what arguments or on which authorities Erasmus based himself. For there can be no doubt that he must have had something to go on when he boldly altered the passage."

Standish had fallen into the trap. "I care nothing for the authorities or the reasons of that man," he replied rather meekly. "I am content with what St. Augustine says, that the Son of God is more properly denoted word for word than by reckoning, *verbum* not *ratio*, although *logos* in Greek means both."

"I agree about *ratio*, but what has that to do with *sermo* for 'word'? Erasmus says that *sermo* and *ratio* mean the same thing."

"You show a lack of decency, Bishop," a second guest added. "You publicly attack the reputation of a man who has done so much on the subject. Yet you have not read the passage and do not understand the point."

By now, Standish was completely flustered. His still-full plate sat untouched. "Whatever I have said was prompted by genuine conviction. But I cannot remember any passage in Holy Writ where the Son of God was called *sermo*."

John Colet, who hosted the affair and had observed the heated exchange with amusement, approached the table. "Gentlemen, shall we retire and join the others?"

Erasmus related this Standish story to his friend Buschius, adding, "Believe it or not, that's exactly what happened. I haven't changed a word"

Shortly after Lee left the faculty of Louvain, Erasmus wrote a second letter to Luther.

> To the Reverend Martin Luther, the eminent theologian, greetings …
> Edward Lee has stopped at nothing to secure my undoing, but, so far, he has had no success. He tries to drive a wedge between me and my friends, while he loses his own. Another madman is Bishop Henry Standish, who during a dinner at the English court, fell on his knees in front of the king and queen and called out loud, "Majesties, I beseech you to follow the example of your ancestors and crush the heresies and schisms that Erasmus's books breed."
>
> Thomas More asked: "Can you produce any passages you call heretical?"
>
> Standish: "First, he abolishes the resurrection; second, he makes nonsense of the sacrament of marriage, and third, he is all wrong about the Eucharist."
>
> More: "Can you now prove the points you just made?"
>
> Standish: "Where we read, 'We shall rise again,' Erasmus reads, 'We shall not all sleep' and he thus abolishes the Resurrection."
>
> More: "That is just plain lunacy." And the people laughed.
>
> The king, who not infrequently writes to me, recently asked me what I thought of you. I replied that you are too good a scholar for men with little learning to be able to

form an opinion about you. The king wishes that you had written some things with more prudence and moderation, an opinion shared by all who wish you well. If an upheaval is required by the state of things, I would rather someone other than myself accepted the responsibility.

I beg you not to bring my name and those of my friends into what you write in an unpleasant way, as you did in your answer to the condemnation at Louvain and Cologne, because you deprive your friends of any power to assist you by casting suspicion on them. Undoubtedly, it harms me and does your cause no good. You have already had quite enough controversies with Eck.

Your commentary on the Psalter reached me six months late, but what I have read so far, I like very much indeed. Give my greetings to Melanchthon and your colleague Karlstadt.

Farewell, dearest brother in the Lord

In the same month, Erasmus received a letter from his friend Ulrich von Hutten, a thirty-two-year-old knight and one of the authors the *Epistolae Obscurorum Virorum*, which had helped bring an end to the Reuchlin Affair five years earlier. Two years previous, on February 22, 1518, Erasmus had written to his friend, the French scholar Guillaume Budé: "I am truly glad that you like Hutten, as I was myself singularly delighted with the man's character." Hutten had become an ardent follower and defender of Luther, and his letter to Erasmus expressed his disappointment that his friend had not publicly defended Luther:

To Desiderius Erasmus of Rotterdam the divine, my dear friend,

I want to tell you something, which I can only say in full reliance on our friendship. When the Reuchlin business was at its height, I thought you showed more weakness than worthy of you in your respect of the other side. And over Luther just lately, you did all you could to persuade his opponents that you had not the faintest intention of defending the common cause of Christendom, while they knew all the time that your real feelings were quite different. I did not think this did you much credit.

I say this, because I know the friend I am writing to, and how wrong and unlike you it would be to take my criticism in bad part. I didn't enjoy what people were saying, but I stood up for your reputation, even though I was not pleased myself with you on that score. So, please do this for me: do not put out anything in an unguarded moment like what you wrote in Luther's case and Reuchlin's. If you are afraid of burdening yourself with any unpopularity, do grant me this: do not let the fear of anything force you to make light of it– better pass it over in silence. I know what harm can be done me by one word from your pen.

I have written this frankly, as one friend to another. With best wishes from the stronghold of the Hutten family.

15 August 1520

Normally, Erasmus would react immediately when he was criticized, but when he read Hutten's letter a second time, he realized that Hutten was sincere and had opened his heart to him. For once, he did not respond in a negative way; however, neither did he respond in a positive way—he did not respond at all. He continued to maintain his strictly neutral position and continued to deny that he had any connection to Luther.

It seemed to Erasmus, however, that the more he denied supporting Luther, the more rumors continued to spread that he not only approved of Luther but had somehow helped him in his writings. Erasmus found himself in a bind, but unfortunately, he could no longer rely on his closest friend in England for advice. Less than a year earlier, he had received the sad news that John Colet had died on September 16, 1519. All of England mourned the loss of the great humanist scholar and educator. Thomas

More, who distributed compliments sparsely, said of Colet, "None more learned or more holy had lived among them for many ages past."

During their two-decade-long friendship, Erasmus had known that he did not equal Colet's purity of life, while Colet had known that he could not match the magic of Erasmus's pen or the power of debate that made Erasmus stand out among his fellow men. Yet it was Colet who had made Erasmus aware of certain shortcomings of St. Augustine and St. Thomas Aquinas and who had made statements about them that bordered on heresy. It was Colet with whom Erasmus had long discussions about the need for the Catholic Church to reform itself. It was Colet who did not hesitate to tease Erasmus for his cloying begging. Erasmus later said that when he listened to Colet speak, he imagined hearing Plato. "I never have conversed with him without feeling the better for it, or at least without feeling less wicked."

Erasmus wished that he could once again turn to his friend in this difficult time—the Reformation had been set in motion, and there was no return.

14

━━━◆━━━

The Leipzig Debate

1518–1519

Holy Roman Emperor Maximilian - Election of a new Holy Roman emperor -
Leipzig Debate - Johann van Eck - Decides to translate the Bible into German

Holy Roman Emperor Maximilian was not feeling well in the late summer
of 1518. He had been a good soldier, ruled well, and cared for his people,
who genuinely loved him. He was highly regarded, and many stories
circulated about his benevolence. It was reported that he once rode up to
an army camp follower who was preparing food for the soldiers. Leaning
forward in his saddle, he said, "Good woman, have you some food for me?"
She looked up and, seemingly unimpressed by his magnificent outfit and
his entourage, filled a wooden bowl with her soup and handed it to him.

"Let me taste it for you, my lord," a young knight eagerly volunteered.

Maximilian waved him back with his arm. "Where do you come from,
good woman?" he asked.

She turned and pointed to a forest in a distance. "From Augsburg,
Your Splendidness." Her choice of address elicited some snickers from the
emperor's staff. Maximilian straightened up and glared at them, and they
slunk back. He leaned forward toward the woman again with a warm smile.

"Well now, from Augsburg," he said loudly for everyone to hear. "Then
there is no need for a taster, for the citizens of Augsburg are God-fearing

people. It is only in my court that tasters are needed." He downed the soup and returned the empty bowl to the woman, along with a gold coin. As he looked on with amusement, the woman carefully examined the coin, spit on it, and rubbed it against her skirt. When she saw how shiny it became, she hurriedly tucked it away in her deepest pocket. She looked up to the emperor and, with a slight bow of her head, said, "May the good Lord keep you safely, Your Splendidness."

"Thank you, good woman. May the good Lord look after you too." He spurred his horse and galloped away, followed by his staff.

In the summer of 1518, Maximilian was at the ripe old age of fifty-nine, but whereas the succession of his huge worldly domain was secured, the succession of his title of Holy Roman emperor was not. He remembered clearly the turbulence that surrounded his own election after his father, Emperor Frederick III, passed away. The electors could not agree on a successor, and several rounds of heated debate and negotiations ensued, with Maximilian as one of the candidates. In the midst of the turmoil, old Elector Albert of Brandenburg collapsed and died. The shock of his death put an abrupt end to the opposition to Maximilian's candidacy, and he was elected on the first ballot.

Members of the House of Habsburg had held the title of Holy Roman emperor since 1273, and Maximilian hoped to continue the tradition by having his grandson, King Charles V of Spain, elected as his successor. King Francis I of France, however, wanted the crown for himself. Moreover, Rome was opposed to Charles's election—he had recently conquered Naples and his election would unite that kingdom with the crown of Germany, which was forbidden by the papal constitution. Maximilian remembered that Pope Innocent VII had been opposed to his own election, and as a result he had a strong antipathy against Rome. Moreover, he was not about to let a young interloper from France take the imperial legacy from his family.

It was time to do some politicking, and Maximilian proved to be good at it. The new emperor would be elected by the majority of a body of seven electors: the Margrave of Brandenburg, Frederick the Wise, the king of Bohemia, Count Palatin of the Rhine, and the archbishops of Mainz,

Trier, and Cologne. Maximilian arranged for them to meet in Frankfurt in March 1519—that would give him some time to secure votes for Charles.

His first target was Elector Joachim I of Brandenburg. Maximilian promised him the hand of his granddaughter Catherine, along with a large amount of silver. Joachim's younger brother, the archbishop of Mainz, was already beholden to Maximilian, who had helped him obtain his archbishopric. With the promise of a little extra money, the archbishop's vote was secured. Archbishop Hermann von Wied of Cologne was won over with presents and pensions for his brothers. Count Palatin assented when the emperor cleared up a misunderstanding between them with the aid of a considerable sum. The king of Bohemia, was closely connected with the House of Habsburg; his vote was secure. The remaining two electors could not be persuaded: elector of Trier was solidly in the camp of King Francis, and Frederick the Wise refused to meet Maximilian's deputies.

Maximilian had his majority, and Charles's election seemed certain. Before the scheduled vote could be held, however, the old emperor fell ill and died on January 12, 1519.

Luther closely followed the electioneering back in Wittenberg; he had much at stake. The election of King Francis would undoubtedly cause him great problems in view of Francis's close connection with Pope Leo X. They would put a price on his head, and he would likely end up in Rome, even though Frederick and the Germans would do all they could to prevent it. Fortunately for Luther, it appeared that Maximilian had laid enough groundwork for Charles's election.

On January 20, 1519, a few days after the emperor's death, Martin wrote a short letter to his friend Spalatin and signed it *Martinos Eleutheros*. "Why did you sign your epistle like that?" Georg later asked. "Is it intended as some sort of joke?"

"No, it is not," Martin said rather indignantly. "It comes from the Greek word *eleutheros*, and it means—"

"I know it means *free*, but what has that to do with you?"

"Well, I like it. I feel like a free man." Martin felt a little miffed that Spalatin did not take his new signature seriously.

"And it has nothing to do with the fact that your name happens to appear in the middle of *e-leuther-os*, does it?" Spalatin smiled.

"All right, Georg, you've made your point. I just wanted to try it."[25]

With Maximilian's sudden demise, Charles's election was no longer a certainty, and King Francis had a second chance at the crown. Count Palatin could still be bought for France. Cologne was close to the French-German border and, fearing the unpredictable Francis, Archbishop von Wied wavered. The archbishop of Mainz fancied the job of legate of Germany, which required approval from Rome, and Francis saw to it that such approval was granted. After Maximilian's death, the promise of his granddaughter's hand to the son of Joachim I of Brandenburg was no longer secure. Knowing this, Francis immediately promised him Madam Renée, daughter of Louis XII and Queen Anne. She would bring a huge dowry as well, and as a result, Joachim listened. Francis was sure that he had a majority.

Charles, however, was not finished, and he had cash to spend. His first target was the archbishop of Mainz, who was promised so many concessiones that he quickly switched back to Charles's camp. Count Palatine was also easy; he fell for more silver than Francis had promised. The elector of Trier was safe, but that was as far as Charles got. He enlisted the Austrians to work for him, but even they could not turn Joachim of Brandenburg, and Frederick simply refused to meet with them. Altogether, Charles had spent or promised over three hundred thousand florins of his own money. Fugger's Bank made an additional five hundred thousand florins available, but Charles was still one vote short of a majority.

In the middle of June, the seven electors met for preliminary discussions. By centuries-old tradition, the elector of Trier presided as chairman. He knew that his vote would be in the minority. He simply looked around the table: "Who wants to start?"

"Why don't we talk about the qualifications of the two candidates?" suggested the archbishop of Mainz. "Traditionally, the Holy Roman emperor has been a German, and I see no reason why we should change that."

---

[25] The letter was discovered in 1983 by Hans-Walter Krumwiede.

"Well, the king of France certainly is no German," said the king of Bohemia.

"And neither is Charles. He is a Spaniard," the chairman pointed out.

"Only by marriage. He became king of Spain through his union with a Spanish princess," contributed Joachim.

"That is not entirely correct," the chairman pointed out. "He was the son of Philip and Joanna of Castile, but he was born in Ghent, in Belgium."

"Yes, and let's not forget that he is the grandson of old Maximilian, may the Lord bless his soul. He can speak German. I heard it myself," added the archbishop of Cologne, eagerly. His ears must have betrayed him, however, as Charles barely knew a word or two in German—he spoke Flemish.

"Francis is trying to buy our vote," added an elector who already had accepted a huge sum from Charles.

"What's wrong with money?" Count Palatin questioned.

"It's not the money; it's the principle."

Joachim of Brandenburg put his two cents in. "And I don't appreciate the pope butting in." With one exception, the others nodded affirmatively.

It was then that Frederick, who hadn't said a word thus far, shoved his chair back, stood up, and looked around the table, briefly catching the eye of each of his colleagues. "I intend to vote for Archduke Charles *of Austria* when we meet again," he declared, his emphasis serving as a reminder of Charles's roots.

The sudden announcement came as a complete surprise to the other six electors. They all knew that Frederick had refused to be influenced by either candidate and had not received their gift-bearing deputies. Frederick's vote could not be bought. With all those Saxon silver mines, he did not need more money. The electors had the deepest respect for their colleague but were confused by his announcement. Perhaps there was intrigue afoot. A rumor spread that Charles had annulled his sister Catherine's marriage contract to the House of Brandenburg and contracted her to Frederick's nephew, in exchange for the elector's vote.

The next day, the elector of Trier moved the discussion in another direction, noting the fact that King Charles reigned over widespread territories and, if elected, he would likely be absent from many meetings.

This prospect prompted the electors to vote on several resolutions limiting the power of the emperor, including:

Our official must be German.
The emperor cannot create new taxes without our consent.
Only Germans can fill public offices.
No diet can be called without our approval.
No declaration of war without our consent.

Lastly, the electors stipulated the creation of a representative constitution, which they considered necessary for the times when the Holy Roman emperor would be absent from Germany for prolonged periods of time.

On June 28, the *tocsin*, a special bell, announced the start of the official meeting of the electoral body of the Holy Roman Empire, and a large crowd began to gather on the square before the Church of St. Bartholomew. Guards kept a walkway clear to the church door. After an hour of ringing, the elector of Trier led a procession of electors from the home of the bishop of Frankfurt to the church. They wore the scarlet robes of their office for the occasion. The tocsin stopped ringing after the last elector entered the church. The hushed crowd waited.

In their conclave, a small chapel behind the choir, there was to be no further discussion leading up to the electors' vote. They read a letter dated June 24 from Pope Leo X, in which he approved Charles, the king of Spain and Naples, as a candidate for the office of Holy Roman emperor, thus reversing Rome's earlier position. In a second letter, the pope announced his appointment of Elector Frederick of Saxony as the regent of the empire in northern Germany. The other six electors congratulated Frederick, but they did not quite know what to make of the news. They wondered whether his new appointment was prearranged. Was it the reason behind Frederick's sudden announcement about his vote? The heavy air in the small room hung somberly.

Following ancient tradition, the elector of Trier cast the first vote. Without hesitation, the one man who, until that moment, had appeared solidly in support of the king of France, declared, to everyone's surprise,

"I vote for Archduke Charles of Austria, Prince of Burgundy and king of Spain." Only Frederick noticed that the elector did not use the title "king of Naples."

The vote was unanimous. The electors opened the door of the conclave, a guard nodded to another guard standing at the front of the church, and the tocsin rang again, whereupon a jubilant crowd outside began to dance and sing. Their excitement increased tenfold when the result of the election was announced—the House of Habsburg had prevailed again. Choruses of *"Unser Karl"* (Our Charles) rang out. Their Charles, however, had yet to take his first step on German ground.

Martin was much relieved when the news of the election result reached him. Earlier that year, he had been looking forward to some peace, but his peace was short-lived. As the new emperor was being selected in Frankfurt, Luther was in Leipzig, fending off a new attack that had been launched against him by Dr. Johann Eck.

Eck was born Johann Maier in 1486 in Egg; he became known as Johann Egg and eventually, Eck. He was a bright student and obtained both his doctorate and a professorship in theology before the age of twenty-four. The Duke of Bavaria subsequently invited him to the University of Ingelstadt, where he became a teacher and vice chancellor. He remained there for the rest of his life, battling for the righteousness of the papacy and the order of the Roman Church. After reading the Ninety-Five Theses, he became Luther's most pugnacious and untiring opponent.

In response to Luther's Theses, Eck wrote the *Obelisks*, twelve theses in which he defended the authority of the pope and of the Church. He called Luther a Hussite, a follower of the despised heretic Jan Hus, who had burned at the stake. Luther briefly answered Eck in his booklet *Asteriks*, in which he stated: *"I cannot agree that the Roman pontiffs do not err and that they alone can interpret Scripture. Christ said, 'Thou art primate' and not 'Thou art Peter.'"* He then challenged Eck to a public disputation in Leipzig, which Eck eagerly accepted, believing himself to be the superior debater. Eck expected a large audience and worried that the auditorium in the university would not be large enough. Thankfully, Duke George of Saxony offered the use of a large room in his castle.

Eck traveled lightly and was the first to arrive in Leipzig. Luther, by contrast, traveled with a large contingent, which was led by a horse-drawn cart driven by Dr. Andreas Karlstadt, who brought with him an enormous amount of books and documents. Although he was not a fluent orator, he was scheduled to open the debate in defense of Luther's position and was determined to be accurate in everything he would say. Next came a cart with Luther, Philipp Melanchthon, and the Duke of Pomerania, followed by two hundred students from the University of Wittenberg traveling on foot, armed with pikes and halberds.

Just before the meeting was to begin, Luther proposed that each side retain two notaries to ensure accurate record-keeping. Eck objected, to which Martin teased, "Are you afraid?" Duke George, who considered himself the arbitrator, sided with Luther.

Eck, in turn, proposed that the theological faculties of the Universities of Erfurt and Paris decide the winner of the debate.

"That's preposterous," responded Martin. "This is not a game."

"I think that it is a good idea," interjected the duke. "I will arrange it."

It was agreed that on the first day of the meeting, Drs. Karlstadt and Eck would each give a two-hour presentation in the form of a sermon.

On June 27, 1519, the meeting opened with a long, boring, and largely inaudible discourse by old Dr. Peter Mosellanus, a humanist from Leipzig. The next day began with the sermon by Andreas Karlstadt, who had little experience in public speaking. Thinking that the notaries would have trouble following him, he spoke very slowly. He interrupted his sermon to check references in books and documents so many times that Eck could no longer stand it. "Stop looking at that stuff," he interrupted. "This is supposed to be a sermon, not a study."

"I just want to be accurate," replied Karlstadt defensively.

"Well, I object to this practice. I refuse to debate against a library."

"I agree," said the duke. "Doctor, you can no longer check your references."

Poor Karlstadt struggled from then on and could not finish his presentation in the allotted time. Surprisingly, Eck let him stumble on.

Martin left the sermon early to take a walk. He noticed a Dominican monastery and out of curiosity, he entered. One of the brothers met him in the small entrance hall.

"Does Dr. Tetzel live here?" asked Martin, inquiring after the notorious indulgence-seller.

"Yes, he does." The monk looked with some suspicion at the Augustinian gown.

"Do you think it possible that I could speak to him?"

"Eh … no, I don't think so. You see, Frater Tetzel is dying from cancer."

"I am sorry to hear that. Could you please read him a note from me?"

"That I'll do."

Martin wrote: *"Do not reproach yourself. This affair began by one other than you."*

June 29 and 30 were holidays, as was July 2. Karlstadt finally finished his presentation on the third of July, and Eck took over. He spoke succinctly, without notes, and utterly destroyed Karlstadt. It became apparent that the debate would last many days—too long for the Wittenberg students who had to go back to the university to resume their studies. When it was finally time for the main debaters to take the stage, it quickly became obvious that the two disputants could not be more different. Dr. Mosellanus reported afterward:

> Luther is medium-sized and so thin that one can count every bone in his body. He has a high, clear voice; he is polite and friendly and comports himself well at all times. His only failing is that, in rebuttal, he is a little more intense and biting than is appropriate for someone who wants to open new paths in theology and who wants to be regarded as taught by God. Eck is large and tall with a strong, broad body and a big, proper German voice. He lacks the intellectual power to see deeply into matters and to render sharp judgments.

Martin was first to speak. He surveyed the hall and acknowledged the duke. "Before I start, I must say that I am amazed and pleased that the many who have called me a heretic are not here. By them, I mean the Dominicans who so often interrupt meetings. Out of respect for the pope and the Roman Church, I would have preferred not to bring up the question of primacy. However, Dr. Eck obliged me to do so. Regarding primacy, I simply cannot accept that Roman pontiffs cannot err or that they alone can interpret scripture. Christ said, 'Thou art the primate.' He did not say, 'Thou art Peter,' as every pope claims."

"What does it matter whether the pope serves by divine right or by human right? He is still the pope, isn't he?" Duke George asked.

"Precisely. You are quite correct, thank you. In denying the divine origin of the papacy, I am not advocating the withdrawal of obedience. It doesn't matter whether there are ten popes or a thousand popes. There still will be no schism."

"Does the Reverend Father forget the everlasting dissention between the English and the French?" asked Eck. "And what about the French's hatred for the Spaniards? Look at all that Christian blood spilled in the wars over Naples. As for me, I confess one faith, one Lord Jesus Christ, and I venerate the Roman pontiff as the vicar of Christ."

"Your three examples deal with earthly matters, dear Doctor. They did not result into a schism within the Church," Martin pointed out.

"Don't interrupt me, please." Eck held up a few documents. "I have here letters from a first-century bishop who states that the Holy Roman and the Apostolic Church obtained primacy not from the apostles, but from our Lord and Savior himself. The priestly order began directly after our Lord Christ committed the pontificate that he Himself had exercised to Peter."

"That's humbug!" cried Luther. "Some letters from a bishop who didn't live at the time of Christ are worthless as evidence. You can stop waving them around. Nobody will ever persuade me that the Holy Pope and Martyr said that. Anybody can dig up letters like those you have. There are no doubt numerous around."

"I see that you are following those damned and pestiferous errors of John Wycliffe. Didn't he say, Dr. Luther, that it is not necessary for salvation to believe that the Roman Church is above all others? And you are also not advocating the pestilent errors of that Bohemian, Hus, who claimed that Peter was not the head of the holy Catholic Church." As he spoke, Eck noticed that he had gotten under Luther's skin.

"No, no, no!" Martin shouted. "Dr. Eck, I never, ever agreed with Hus. Even though his Bohemians had divine right on their side, they should not have left the Church, because the highest divine rights are unity and charity."

"I believe that it's time to adjourn," Duke George interjected. "We will continue the debate tomorrow morning."

From the reaction of the crowd, it was clear that Johann Eck held the upper hand that day.

"You can do better than that," admonished Melanchthon as they walked back to the university quarters where they were staying. "The first rule of debating is to always keep your temper down. By the way, did you notice that Eck left with Duke George?"

After dinner, Martin went to the university library and delved into literature about the condemnation of Hus. He was ready when the meeting resumed the next day.

"I want to go back to what Hus said or what he is alleged to have said," a confident Martin began. "I don't care whether it was Hus or Wycliffe who said that it is not necessary for salvation to believe that the Roman Church is superior to all others. The Greeks do not accept that the Roman Church is superior to their Orthodox Church. It was the papacy and the council that wrote that article, but neither had the power to make it a holy writ; they cannot construct new articles of faith nor can a council. Jan Hus wrote several Christian and evangelical articles that the Church cannot condemn. I can't believe that the Council of Constance condemned all of them."

"They are recorded in the reliable history of St. Jerome," said Eck.

"Did Jerome not live in the fourth century, and was Hus not burned in 1415, Dr. Eck? Let me remind you that the Council did not say that all articles from Hus were heretical."

"But none of them were called Christian and evangelical," argued the clearly agitated Eck. "If you defend them, then you are heretical, erroneous, blasphemous, presumptuous, seditious, and offensive to pious ears."

"I doubt that many here understood all those words you just threw at me," Martin said calmly. "I will speak in German from now on, so that there is no misunderstanding. I declare that councils have sometimes erred, will sometimes err, and have no authority to establish new articles of faith."

"How dare you say so?" Eck spit out. "That is heretical." He also switched into German.

"You already used that word earlier, Dr. Eck. You are wrong. Have not councils contradicted previous councils? Did not the recent Lateran Council reverse the claim of the Councils of Constance and Basel that a council is above the pope? Neither the pope nor the Church can establish articles of faith. They come only from the scripture, and for the sake of scripture, we must reject popes and councils."

During this session, Luther was the stronger debater; Eck never had a clear rejoinder to his solidly supported assertions. Eck rambled on about Luther's misinterpreting scripture and councils. Despite Luther's assertion that councils had reversed the errors of previous councils, Eck declared, "If you say that a legitimately called council errs and has erred, be then to me as a heathen and a publican."

"Doctor, if you won't hold me for a Christian, at least listen to me as you would to a Turk and infidel." Martin was completely relaxed but took care not to look triumphant.

"I certainly will," said Eck. "Now let me take up purgatory. I read from 2 Maccabees 12:45, 'Wherefore he made the propitiation for them that had died that they might be released from their sin.'"

"You forgot the word 'godly' after 'them that had died,'" Martin corrected him. "Moreover, 2 Maccabees belongs to the Apocrypha and is not part of the canon of the Old Testament. Therefore, it has no authority."

The correction completely flustered Eck. The debate continued to drag on, and at one point, Eck asked, exasperated, "Are you the only one who knows anything? Except for you, is all the Church in error?"

Eck's questions failed to unnerve Luther. "I'll tell, good Doctor, what I think. I am a Christian theologian, bound not only to assert but to defend the truth with my blood and death. I believe what I want. I will be no slave to the authority of anyone. I will confess what appears to me to be true, whether it has been asserted by a Catholic or by a heretic, whether it has been approved or reproved by a council."

When the debate entered its eighteenth day, Duke George had had enough—he needed his room for another occasion. He declared an end to the debate and left the room. And thus the debate ended, and the parties dispersed. The judging contingents from the Universities of Paris and Erfurt returned to their home bases to consider their verdicts. Luther returned to Wittenberg, and Eck traveled to Rome to inform the pope that Luther was a Saxon Hus. Before Eck left, he wrote to Elector Frederick and urged him to get rid of Luther. Frederick later showed the letter to Martin, who commented that Eck sounded like "Minerva's pig."

Erasmus had followed news of the debate from a distance. He called Eck foolish and declared that Luther was too honest, predicting that this was a quality for which Luther would pay, sooner or later.

After returning to Wittenberg, Martin and his friend Spalatin discussed the Leipzig debate.

"You know, Georg, this whole affair is a tragedy for the church and for the people."

"Do you think anything was accomplished?"

"Nothing. Eck only had authority on his mind. Authority of the pope, authority of the Church, authority of the councils, and all it means is that they think they are the boss and that others must obey or face the threat of condemnation and excommunication. That's what they live by. You should have seen Eck's face when I switched to German. He considered it sacrilege."

"Well, in the end, you survived this one. Now what are you going to do?"

"Oh, I'm sure that this won't be the last disputation. They'll be back with another one. But this one helped me to come to an important decision. On the way back here, I kept thinking about the general reaction when I began speaking German. Eck and the other church authorities were flabbergasted and so was the duke, but you should have seen the rest of the people. Suddenly, I had their attention—they could follow the proceedings, and they loved it. It made such an impact that I have decided to translate the Bible into German."

"Martin, what makes you think that you will succeed where Wycliffe failed?"

"The times have changed, Georg. People like Erasmus started it. He gets away with criticizing the Church, so why can't I? Wycliffe had only a few people to help him, but look how widespread our support is among the younger people. They have learned to read, my friend, and they deserve to have a Bible written in their own language. There is a need for one."

Spalatin drummed his fingers on the arm of his chair and supported his chin with his other hand as he looked at Martin. "I think you are right."

15

---⟫◆⟪---

Erasmus Under Pressure

1520–1523

*The difficulty of remaining neutral - Row with Egmonadus - Refuses to attack
Luther - Renews friendship with Jerome Aleander*

By the middle of 1520, the news about Luther's rift with the church had
spread throughout Europe like wildfire. Erasmus followed the controversy
but steadfastly refused to become involved and maintained his strictly
neutral position.

In March, he received a letter from an obscure bishop from Tuy, a
small town on the Minho River on the far northwest coast of Spain. The
bishop, Louis Marlianus, who was far removed from any university life,
was deeply concerned about the Luther controversy and advised Erasmus
to stay clear. It amazed Erasmus that news had already reached such a
remote corner of Europe, and he hastened to write back.

> You caution me against entangling myself with Luther
> and I have taken your advice. Luther's party has urged me
> to join him, and Luther's enemies have done their best to
> drive me to it by their furious attacks on me. Neither has
> succeeded … It is strange to me that the two factions goad
> each other on. I approve of those who stand by the Pope,

but I wish them to be wiser than they are. They may eat Luther boiled or roasted, for all I care, but they mistake in linking us two together ... I am surprised that Aleander is among them; we were once friends ... I have said nothing except that Luther ought to be answered and not crushed. They pretend that Luther has borrowed from me. No lie can be more impudent.

I would prefer that things should be quietly considered and not embittered by platform railing. I have not deviated in what I have written one hair's breadth from the Church's teaching ... Many great persons have entreated me to support Luther. I have answered always that I will support him when he is on the Catholic side. I recommended Luther himself not to write as a revolutionary ... I caution everybody against reading libelous or anonymous books, books meant only to irritate; but I can advise only; I cannot compel.

Although he clung to his neutrality, Erasmus could not help but admire some of what Luther had done. However, he took issue with Luther's methods. On July 6, 1520, he wrote to Spalatin:

May Christ direct Luther's actions to God's glory and confound those who are seeking their own interest. In Luther's enemies, I perceive more the spirit of this world than the Spirit of God. I wish Luther himself would be quiet for awhile. He does himself no good, while morals and manners grow worse and worse. What he says may be true, but there are times and seasons. Truth need not always be proclaimed from the house-top.

In public, he refused to either support Luther or condemn him, and he continued to maintain that he had not read Luther's books. Although he was familiar with the Ninety-Five Theses, he purposely avoided reading any of Luther's other works because he needed ignorance as a defense against the people who urged him to take a stance. Despite the pressure put on him, he refused to attack Luther. To Leo X, he wrote, "I hesitate to attack an eminent man." Elsewhere, he proclaimed:

> How, while there are persons calling themselves bishops and professing to be the guardians of the truth, whose moral character is abominable, can it be right to persecute a man of unblemished life, in whose writing distinguished and excellent persons have found so much to admire? … If we want truth, every man ought to be free to say what he thinks without fear.

Luther could not have found a better, though unwilling, defender.

After Edward Lee left Louvain, the role of chief attacker against Erasmus was taken over by his fellow Dutchman, the Carmelite monk Nicolaas Egmond, who was named after a town on the North Sea coast. He was educated in the Abbey of Egmond, the most important monastery in Holland during the Middle Ages, and had been appointed the inquisitor for Holland by Emperor Charles V. Egmondanus, as he preferred to be called, was a powerful member of the university faculty, and he despised Erasmus, taking the side of the Dominicans against him. He was not satisfied with Erasmus's neutral position on Luther and wanted him to speak out against the upstart German monk. Matters between the conservative Dominican faction of the faculty and the frail Erasmus became so contentious that the rector of the university decided to put an end to it. He summoned Egmondanus and Erasmus to his office.

"I have called you two together because you no longer appear to be able to talk without common courtesy. That's not good for the university, and I want it stopped. We have no audience in this room, so you can both speak freely without being dramatic about it." He turned to Egmondanus. "I know that Brother Erasmus is not happy about what you preach in some of your sermons. Why don't you begin, and I will listen?"

"I have injured no one in my sermons," said Egmondanus. "If Erasmus deems that he has been hurt, I am here to answer him."

"What can be a more atrocious injury than to say untruths in a public sermon?" Erasmus said.

"Why do you traduce us in your books on divinity?"

"Your name does not appear in my books," replied Erasmus.

"Neither was your name mentioned in my sermons."

"You lied about me publicly by saying that I favored Luther when I have never favored him in the sense in which the people interpret your statements and as you yourself imagine."

"You are the cause of all this trouble!" Egmondanus shouted furiously. "Turncoat and crafty fox that you are, there is nothing that, with that tail of yours, you cannot twist to your purpose!"

"Brother Egmondanus, there is no need to shout," the rector reminded him.

Erasmus turned to the rector. "He calls me names, and I could do the same, but that is unworthy of men and scarcely of women. Let us deal with the facts. Imagine that I—"

"I am not imagining," Egmondanus interrupted. "I do not wish to imagine. That is your forte. You poets imagine and falsify everything."

"If you do not want to imagine, then grant me—"

"I will not grant."

"Well, then, suppose it to be the case."

"I will suppose nothing."

Erasmus tried again. "All right, put it this way."

"I will not."

"Let it be thus."

"But it is not thus."

"What do you want me to say, then?" an exasperated Erasmus asked.

"Say, it is so."

"Say that it is true that I have written some things in my books other than I should have, in order to satisfy your personal animosity? It is not your place to abuse the privileges of a sacred edifice under the authority of a solemn sermon or to abuse the credulity of simple people. It is not so much me that you injure but this whole university, this entire community, as the office you hold of preaching the divine word, which is dedicated to far different uses."

Egmondanus did not quite follow what Erasmus had said. For loss of an answer, he switched to another subject. "*Ja*, you would like to have a similar privilege."

"What privilege? That of preaching?"

Egmondanus nodded his head.

"I used to preach, and I feel that I can say more worthwhile things than some of the things I hear you utter."

"Why don't you then?"

"Because I deem that I can do better work in writing books."

"Wherein do you merit better?"

"Most people admit that I have done some service to good literature."

"*Ja*, so you call it. But it is bad literature."

Erasmus ignored him. "And in sacred literature, I have restored a great deal."

"Yes, and in your *Novum Testamentum* you have falsified a great deal."

"Then why did the Roman pontiff approve it in his brief."[26]

"*Ja*, a brief, but who ever saw your brief?" Egmondanus insinuated.

"Do you think I carry it around with me? I showed it to Atensis, and Dorp also saw it."

"*Ja*, Dorp—" Before he could say another word, the rector restrained him.

"You may see it yourself, if you wish," Erasmus said with a wave of his hand.

"I do not want to see anything of yours," Egmondanus said stubbornly.

"Why do you then condemn me? Why does the pope's authority count so much with you when it is condemning Luther but have not the slightest value when approving my writings?" The fruitless bickering went on until Erasmus finally exclaimed, "Is there anything else you want?"

When Egmondanus did not reply, the rector stepped in. "You must answer the question."

"That you restore to us our good name, which has been injured by you."

"Where? In my *Epistolae*?"

"Yes."

"Those letters have already been published. How can I do what you desire?"

"Withdraw what you have said," Egmondanus persisted.

"How?"

---

[26] A brief is a papal letter, less formal than a papal bull.

"Write that there are theologians at Louvain who are sincere and upright."

"That I have never denied, but if those whom I have criticized will furnish me with proper material, I will write magnificently about them."

Egmondanus became angry again, while Erasmus, with his ever-present smile, kept cool.

"If you furnish us the opportunity to speak well of you, we will do so," Egmondanus growled. "You have a pen; we have a tongue. You accuse us of barking behind your back, but I am speaking to your face."

"It would not be surprising if, with your manners, you were to spit in the face of a good man."

"Brothers, we are supposed to be discussing Luther," the rector reminded the two combatants. "Since he was the cause of this trouble, talk about him."

"All right," said Egmondanus. "You have written for Luther; now write against him."

"I have not written for him. Besides, it would smack of cruelty, were I to give free rein of my pen against a man who is already prostrate and conquered."

"Write just that," Egmondanus exclaimed. "Write that Luther has been overthrown by us."

"You, overthrow Luther? Others have already tried to do that, way before you, and have failed. But why is everybody urging me to write against Luther? Why me and not someone else? Why all this discord? I have never broken off a friendship with anyone because he is either more inclined toward or against Luther than I am. I can even love a Jew, provided he were, in other respects, an agreeable person."

Egmondanus stood up. "Why you? Because you have the most authority in Europe." He turned to the rector. "Did I not tell you that we would accomplish nothing? As long as he refuses to write against Luther, just so long shall we consider him a partisan of Luther."

"By the same reasoning I shall hold you to be a partisan of Luther, since you have not written against him," Erasmus reminded him.

Egmondanus stomped out with a wave of his hand to the rector but not to Erasmus, who also was not happy with the outcome of the meeting. True, his opponent had been rather churlish, but he had left undefeated. If anything, Erasmus could expect more attacks to come from him and the Dominicans. When Egmondanus died six years later on August 23, 1526, Erasmus wrote: "Here rests an Egmonder, a useless burden of the earth. He loved madness; hopefully, he will have no rest."

Erasmus began to feel isolated in Louvain and was concerned about the opinion of the rest of Catholic Europe. He wondered whether the belief that he favored Luther was locally confined or widespread. He did not have to wait long for an answer—Lord Mountjoy wrote him to convey the news that people in England considered Erasmus to be part of the Lutheran camp. Too late, Erasmus realized that his acrimonious letters about Edward Lee had had little effect and had possibly been misconstrued—his attacks against Lee had been interpreted as a defense of Luther. Lee was well regarded in his homeland, and people listened to him. To Erasmus's surprise, Mountjoy, his friend and staid beneficiary, also advised him to write against Luther. Erasmus felt lonely.

He maintained his neutral position about Luther. His sense of fairness told him not to write of a man whom he had never met. However, was it wise not to read at least one book that the man had written? Erasmus took a walk through Louvain to clear his mind. Deep in thought, he did not see a man coming toward him until he bumped into him. "I'm sorry," he mumbled, his head down and his shoulders bent.

"Father Erasmus! What a pleasant surprise," the man exclaimed.

Only then did Erasmus look up. "Aleander, is that you? What are you doing in Louvain?"

"I can't tell you that on the street. Why don't we have supper together? My treat."

That evening, while they sat eating and drinking, they reminisced about their time together as friends in Venice.

"Do you remember how you used to put your cold feet against me when we slept in that narrow bed?" Aleander laughed.

"No, but I recall how your sharp elbow hit me in my ribs."

"You know, we were such good friends." Aleander turned serious. "I do not know whether to blame myself or you, or maybe both of us, for neglecting our great friendship. Neither of us wrote a single word after we parted." Aleander paused, and Erasmus remained silent.

Aleander, with a wry smile, continued. "On a serious note, I would like to hear your frank opinion about Luther. How far has his movement reached, and where will it go?"

"It has gone much farther than I thought," Erasmus replied, and he told Aleander the story about the Spanish bishop from Tuy. "Also, Luther has a lot of followers in Holland, and I understand that the same is true in Switzerland."

"Do you think it can still be turned around?"

"Honestly, after the Leipzig debate and the papal bull, I don't think so. But the Church could have handled him a lot better."

"How about you? Can you stop it from spreading further?"

"Aleander, why does everybody think that one man can stop it, especially a man who has no leading position in Rome?" Erasmus replied wearily. "Now let me ask you something. Do you think that Rome will ever offer a rapprochement to Luther? Will the Holy Father retract his bull, or will Rome continue to be hard-nosed?"

"I admire your frankness, Erasmus," Aleander replied after a pause. "But I doubt that a bull, once issued, will ever be retracted by this pope."

"Do you have any idea how miserable some people make my life here? The Carmelite Egmondanus preaches against me, and just this morning, the Dominican Vincent called me an enemy of the church in his sermon and vowed to continue attacking me in the same vein."

"I'm sorry to hear that. As the papal nuncio, I'll order Vincent to stop preaching like that. While I was in Cologne, I heard that some monks there, as well as some here, are preparing a pamphlet against you. They cannot publish it without asking my permission, and I promise you that I will not grant it."

They continued talking and drinking well into the night and parted as friends once more. Not long afterward, Erasmus left Louvain. He first traveled to Anderlecht, Belgium, where he stayed for three months before moving to Bruges and the court of Emperor Charles V, where he acted as an imperial councilor. He lived quietly, wrote, and published. It was a very comfortable life.

16

---◆◆◆---

Luther's Excommunication

1519–1521

Condemnation from Cologne and Louvain - Pope Leo's bull -
Excommunication - Emperor Charles and Jerome Aleander - Diet at Worms -
The emperor's condemnation - Kidnapped on the road

Although the Leipzig debate had ended, its repercussions were far from
over. Johann Eck was sure that he had prevailed, but the Universities of
Paris and Erfurt had not yet declared a winner. Erfurt was Luther's *alma
mater* and not about to rule against him; Paris had appointed twenty-four
judges and insisted that each have a copy of the debate proceedings—its
decision would take nearly two years. Eck, however, could not wait; he
decided to obtain the judgment of experts from other universities and then
take his case to Rome.

In July 1519, the dean of the University of Heidelberg called all faculty
members to a special meeting. He walked on stage, accompanied by a
heavyset man with shoulder-length hair and dressed in a long gown and
a soft cap. He was clean-shaven but for a small moustache, and he had
a firm chin, a long sharp nose, and bulging eyes. "Brothers, it does me
great pleasure to introduce the illustrious Johann Eck, the man who so
successfully debated Martin Luther in Leipzig last month."

A beaming Eck stepped forward, took his time to arrange his papers on the lectern, and surveyed the audience. He then nodded to the dean and began.

"Thank you, sir, for your kind introduction." Turning to the audience, he continued. "Brothers, it is indeed a pleasure to bring you a report of the disputation that recently took place in Leipzig. I consider myself the champion of the papacy and of the Church order, both institutions that the heretic Martin Luther has so vilely attacked. You should know that I had personally challenged him to a public debate, and he had made the decision—unfortunately for him, I might add—to accept my challenge." Eck lied; it was Luther who had challenged him.

The audience laughed. Eck continued to relate in detail his version of the debate, but he failed to add that the arbitrators had declined to announce a victor.

"And so, my dear brothers, I leave it to you to decide who was the victor—me or the heretic. Should you decide in my favor, then I urge you to issue a condemnation of Luther that I will then personally hand to our Holy Father, our beloved Pope Leo X."

The faculty members and the students jumped to their feet, applauded, and exclaimed to Eck, "You are our victor!"

Flushed with his success in Heidelberg, Eck then secured a condemnation of Luther's Theses from the theological faculties at the Universities of Cologne and Louvain. The faculty of Cologne needed no persuasion; it was solidly Dominican. Louvain's faculty was less solid, so just in case, Eck sent Jacob Hoogstraten to Louvain to influence their decision. On November 7, 1519, the University of Louvain condemned forty-five of Luther's Theses. In late 1519, Eck arrived in Rome to give the pope his report, carrying with him condemnations from Heidelberg, Cologne, and Louvain. He was sure that this would be enough to convince Pope Leo X to declare him the winner at Leipzig. Unfortunately for Eck, the pope refused, preferring to wait for the outcome of the official judges from Erfurt and Paris.

When Martin heard about the condemnations that Eck had obtained, he commented dismissively, "Those are like the words of a delirious, drunken woman. I'll pay no attention to them." His detractors, however, were not dismissive and continued to urge Luther's protectors to bring him into line. Cardinal Raphael Riario, whom Erasmus had befriended in Rome in 1509, wrote to Elector Frederick:

I think it the part of friendship to write to you concerning the common good of Christendom and the everlasting honor of yourself. I am sure you are not ignorant of the rancor, contempt, and license with which Martin Luther rails against the Roman pontiff and the whole Curia. Wherefore I exhort you, bring this man to admit his error. You can if you will; with just one little pebble, the puny David killed the mighty Goliath.

Frederick merely replied that the case had been referred to the archbishop of Trier.

In March 1520, the general of the Augustinian order wrote to Staupitz:

The order, never previously suspected of heresy, is becoming odious. We beg you in the bonds of love to do your utmost to restrain Luther from speaking against the Holy Roman Church and her indulgences. Urge him to stop writing and let him save our order from infamy.

Staupitz promptly resigned as vicar general.

In Rome, the Vatican council met four times to discuss the matter of Luther. Dominicans, Augustinians, and Franciscans were equally represented at the meetings. In addition, four outsiders were present: Luther's enemies, Eck, Cajetan, Prierias and the general of the Augustinian order. As the attendees milled about before the meeting began, Cajetan saw Eck enter and growled, "Who let that beast in?" Cardinal Accolti called Tetzel a *porcaccio* (a type of sow) and reprimanded Prierias for his hasty preparation of his *Dialogus*, the Church's response to the Ninety-Five Theses. Eventually, everyone settled down, and the meeting officially opened. After the first day, Pope Leo, who had a streak of humanism in him, left for some *a soliti piaceri* (atonement in solitude). When the meetings resumed, the Dominicans urged condemnation of Luther in the form of a bull, while a few cardinals, who were better informed about the conditions in Germany, warned against it. The sessions eventually closed with a unanimous condemnation of forty-one of Luther's Theses.

From his hunting lodge, Pope Leo X issued a bull, *Exsurgio Domine* (Arise, O Lord), against Martin Luther. It read, in part:

Arise, O Lord, and judge thy cause. A wild boar has invaded thy vineyards. Rise, O Peter, and consider the case of the Holy Roman Church, the mother of all Churches. Rise, O Paul, who by teaching and death hast and dost illumine the Church and teacher of the faith. Arise, all ye saints and the whole universal Church, whose interpretation of Scripture has been assailed. For now a new Porphyry rises, who wrongfully assails the holy pontiffs. We can scarcely express our grief over the ancient heresies which have been revived in Germany. We are the more downcast because she was always in the front of the war against heresy. Our pastoral office can no longer tolerate the pestiferous virus of the forty-one errors. We can no longer suffer the serpent to creep through the field of the Lord.

The final witness is the refutation, rejection, and condemnation of the errors by the universities of Cologne and Louvain, most devoted and religious cultivators of the Lord's field. By the authority of almighty God, the blessed Apostles Peter and Paul, and by our own authority, we condemn, reprobate, and reject each of these theses as heretical, scandalous, and against Catholic truth.

The books of Martin Luther that contain these errors are to be examined and burned. As for Martin himself, good Lord, what office of paternal love have we omitted in order to recall him from his errors? We have even offered him a safe conduct and money for the journey. And he sent a rash appeal to a future council although our predecessors, Pius II and Julius II, subjected such appeals to the penalties of heresy.

Now, therefore, we give Martin sixty days in which to submit, dating from the time of the publication of this bull in this district. Anyone who presumes to infringe our excommunication anathema will stand under the wrath of Almighty God and of the apostles Peter and Paul.

Dated on the 15th day of June, 1520

It took three months for Martin to receive a copy.

Leo X wrote to Frederick the Wise, informing him of the bull against Luther and urging him to return the monk to sanity and to receive his clemency. If Luther persisted in his madness, Frederick was to take him prisoner. The elector put the letter in a drawer. The pope and the cardinals surrounding him knew little about the religious developments in Germany. Frederick, however, knew that Luther's following was growing by the day and that his popularity lay not only among the common people. Many church leaders, including bishops, had become his adherents. The Italian-dominated leadership of the Roman Church remained deaf and dumb to this development.

Frederick had corresponded with Erasmus in strict secrecy about Luther and the bull, and Erasmus, who was, by nature, less aggressive than Luther, advised Frederick that *"although Luther was too sharp in his criticism of the Pope and Rome, he had only knocked the crown off the Pope's head and had given the monks a firm kick in their bellies."*

In October 1520, Luther published a small booklet titled *On the Babylonian Captivity of the Church*, in which he examined the seven sacraments of the Catholic Church. He rejected outright five of the sacraments—confirmation, penance, anointing the sick, holy orders, and marriage. He noted that these five did not appear in the Bible, and he claimed that they were a misuse of the word "sacrament." With these five rejections, Luther irrevocably broke from the Roman Catholic Church, which maintained that all seven sacraments were instituted by Christ. The publication caused an uproar and renewed calls for Luther's banishment.

Pope Leo's sixty-day deadline for Luther to recant had long passed, and, under intense pressure from the Dominicans in Rome, Leo officially excommunicated him on January 3, 1521. He was to be taken prisoner and executed. Ultimately, that responsibility rested with the new Holy Roman emperor and ruler of much of Germany, King Charles V of Spain and Naples, who spoke only a few words of German and had never stepped foot in Germany.

The problem of Luther landed on Charles's doorstep when his secretary announced the arrival of the newly appointed papal ambassador, Jerome Aleander, who was a friend of Erasmus's. The twenty-year-old Charles motioned to a chamberlain to let the ambassador enter.

"Your Esteemed Majesty, I bring you greetings and best wishes from the Holy Father."

"Thank you, Mr. Ambassador."

"As Your Majesty may already know, the Holy Father has issued a bull against the renegade monk Martin Luther. The Holy Father wishes you to ratify the bull and to dispose of the monk."

"Does the pope *ask* me to ratify, or is his wish an order?"

Aleander hastened to correct his error. "The Holy Father sincerely *requests*, Your Highness."

"Very well, I'll consider the request, Mr. Ambassador, and meanwhile, you are welcome to stay as our guest."

Charles had not forgotten that Leo X had strenuously maneuvered against his election as Holy Roman emperor. He considered the news about the pope's bull and realized that it presented him with an opportunity to finally spend some time in Germany, his new country. Upon his arrival, his first visitor was Elector Frederick.

"The pope wants me to arrest Luther," Charles informed him.

"I had no doubt that he would do that. However, as Your Majesty pays his visits throughout the country, you will soon learn how popular Luther is among your people."

"I have already noticed some of that during my travels here. What do the nobles think of him?"

"Quite a number are supporting him, and his following is growing by the day. Even some bishops and priests are siding with him."

"Do you have any suggestions as to how I should proceed?" Charles respected the elector's opinion.

"I believe that calling a diet would be the best way for Your Majesty to meet the princes and bishops. You could have Luther appear as well."

"Only if he promises to stop writing against Rome."

"He'll agree to that; I'll make sure of it. And will he come under safe conduct?"

"Yes."

"I also recommend a meeting between Your Majesty and the electoral body."

"I will consider it." It was Charles's first contact with the elector, and afterward, he understood why people called him Frederick the Wise.

Immediately after the meeting, Emperor Charles invited Luther to appear at the Diet of Worms, scheduled for April. The ink on the letter was barely dry before Aleander appeared before him.

"Majesty, Luther is under excommunication and, with respect to Your Majesty, you cannot give him another hearing. The Holy Father has already condemned him."

"And why was I not informed of that?" Charles asked angrily. "Does the pope not think it necessary to tell the emperor when he condemns one of his citizens?"

"Your Majesty, this is strictly a matter for the Church to decide."

"And who has to carry out the bull? Who has to arrest Luther? Does the Church do that too?"

"The arrest is a temporal matter, Your Majesty."

"Indeed, it is, and the pope seems to rule over that too."

"Majesty, Luther's books have already been burned by the Universities of Cologne and Mainz."

"But not in Louvain," the emperor quickly added.

Aleander realized that this discussion was leading nowhere. Young Charles was tougher than he had been led to believe.

"Your Majesty, it is your duty to arrest the monk," he repeated firmly.

"Are you now telling what I must do, Mr. Ambassador?" Charles leaned forward and glared at Aleander.

Aleander realized that he had gone too far. He stood up, bowed to the emperor, and humbly asked permission to retire.

Charles, satisfied with the points he had made, waved him off.

Over time, however, Aleander could not fail to notice Luther's rising popularity and began to rethink his position. He came to believe that arresting and executing Luther could lead to a revolt and irreparable damage to the Church, and he warned Rome and Charles accordingly. Elector Frederick had come to the same conclusion. Upon hearing that Charles had decided not to take his advice to meet with electoral body, Frederick called a meeting of his colleagues, and a majority of the electors then notified Charles that the arrest of Luther without a hearing would result in riots and, possibly, a revolution. If Charles wanted Luther arrested, he would have to do it himself.

In the meantime, Charles had another serious headache to contend with—the Turkish army had come perilously close to the borders of his new empire and needed to be driven back. To do so required an army, and raising an army required the support of the German princes. Charles could ill afford to alienate them over a mere monk; he decided that Luther would get his hearing in Worms, along with a safe conduct. He even went a step further to include the princes in the process.

"I want the official notice for Luther to appear in Worms, written in the form of an edict coming from the estates, not from me alone," Charles ordered. "And Luther must know that he is coming to the diet only for an examination, not for a condemnation."

While Charles's lawyers and scribes were working on the edict, Aleander, on behalf of Rome, put pressure on Frederick to prevent Luther from going to Worms. The official church position required Luther's arrest without any further hearings, but the old elector didn't budge.

It took few days to produce the final version of the edict, which, in the end, was unusually brief.

> Honorable, beloved, and esteemed Martin Luther,
> Both we and the estates have proposed and decided to ask you to come to Worms under safe conduct to inform us regarding your books and teaching. We desire that you set out and that, under our protection, you will appear among us and not stay away.

> March 6, 1521   Carolus V, Emperor

Aleander exploded when he saw the letter. "The man is a heretic! He cannot be addressed like that!"

The emperor remained calm. "I remind you that it is Rome that considers him a heretic. This is Germany, and here, thousands call him a hero."

"But the Holy Father declared him a heretic."

"Without giving him a fair hearing, as I remember. We do things differently here. The edict will go out as it is."

What Aleander did not know was that when the electors chose Charles as the new Holy Roman emperor, he had accepted his title under their newly created oath, which read in part: *We shall and wish to under no circumstance, permit anyone, whether of high estate or low, elector, prince, or otherwise, to be placed under ban and double ban for any reason without a hearing.*

"You know, Martin, that with an edict like this, you no longer have any reason not to go," advised Georg Spalatin after they shared an evening meal. "Besides, the elector really wants you to."

"I know, Georg, and I plan to go," Martin said warily. "But only if they give me a chance to defend myself."

"What do you mean? The letter says that they intend to do so."

"It is a letter and only that, Georg," Martin said firmly. "Rome has sent some powerful people to Worms, and you can be sure that they will try to influence the electors while we are on the road. When I walk into that room, if the first thing they do is tell me to recant, I am out of there."

"Well, I'll be there if you need me."

In the meantime, Aleander and his crew were doing exactly what Martin had predicted. They continued to remind the electors that the pope had declared Luther a heretic, a man who had brought enormous harm on their good Christian people. "Every day that he is free, he will do more harm. You must wipe him and his followers from your estates. He must recant or die in hell."

It took Martin and his two friends Melanchthon and Spalatin thirteen days to travel the 250 miles from Wittenberg to Worms. They traveled in a typical Saxon horse-drawn cart with a canopy and two wheels. Their first stop-over was Erfurt, where Martin preached in the church of his old monastery, the Black Cloister, before an audience of locals and the faculty of the university. He spoke in German. "The devil is constantly lurking around patiently waiting for his chance to snare you. Do what I tell him: 'Go wallow in your own shit and stuff yourself with it. And when you're finished, gorge yourselves on the shit of pigs.'" His audience loved it. He also preached to large crowds in two other towns and from there, all along the road to Worms, people stopped to wave at him. "You are becoming very popular," observed Melanchthon to his emboldened friend.

Ten miles outside of Worms, they received an escort of one hundred imperial soldiers, and outside the East Gate, they were met by a herald carrying the imperial shield, who led them through a massive crowd that had gathered to cheer their hero. Elector Frederick was staying at the Schwan Inn, and Spalatin had reserved a room for Martin in the inn's annex. When he walked into the dining room, Martin was pleasantly surprised to see his friend Hieronymus Schurff, a distinguished professor of canon and imperial law at the University of Wittenberg.

"What are you doing here?" asked Martin.

"Waiting for you to have dinner with me."

"That's very nice, but what is the real reason?"

"The elector has asked me to assist you during the sessions. I'll keep an eye on you and make sure that they don't pull something over on you."

"Thank you. Let's eat. I am starved."

The diet was scheduled to take place the following afternoon in the audience chamber of the archbishop of Worms's palace. Another escort of soldiers and a herald guided Martin to the palace through narrow side streets in a vain attempt to avoid the crowds. When they arrived, Luther and his escort had to fight their way through the packed room. Emperor Charles sat under a canopy at the far end of the chamber. Marshal von Pappenheim was standing next to him, and the electors were seated, evenly divided, to his left and right. At the front of the chamber stood a table with a chair on either side: one for Luther and one for his examiner. There were extra chairs behind them for their advisors. Another table against the wall was loaded with books.

The only person of importance missing was the papal nuncio, Jerome Aleander, whose presence would have endorsed the illegal examination of an excommunicated heretic. He had spent the previous day with Johann von der Ecken, chancellor of the archbishop of Trier, who was to be Luther's examiner. "You must keep the examination short," Aleander advised. "Don't allow Luther a chance to give a long speech. He is very good in evading the issues at hand and can turn things around to his advantage almost effortlessly."

"I intend to ask him only two questions," replied Ecken knowingly. "Whether the books are his and whether he will recant."

"Excellent. We should finish this in less than an hour."

The emperor signaled to Pappenheim, who called the meeting to order. "Dr. von der Ecken, you may proceed."

Ecken stood, gave his salutations to the emperor, and began. "Martin Luther, you appear before His Imperial Majesty to answer two questions." He pointed to the books on the table. "Do you recognize these books published under your name as yours and—"

"Objection," Schurff intervened. "You must read the title of each book to enable my client to reply to the question truthfully."

"Is that necessary?" Ecken asked Pappenheim.

"The monk has the right to hear the titles. You must call them off."

It took several minutes for Ecken to read out loud the thirty-odd titles. "Are you now prepared to recant part or whole what you have written in those books?"

Martin began to rise from his chair, but Schurff held him back. They held a whispered conversation.

"These are indeed my books, and I have written several others. Your second question touches on God and His word. It affects the salvation of souls. Did not Christ say, 'He who denies me before men, him I will deny before my father?' If I say too little or too much, I may put myself in danger. I beg you; give me time to think it over."

Martin had spoken in German, which all those present understood, except the emperor. For his sake, Martin repeated his reply in Latin. Ecken and his advisors were not prepared for the request and held a side conference. Charles became impatient. "Dr. von der Ecken, are you prepared to grant the monk more time?"

"Only with your permission, Majesty."

"Permission granted."

"Martin Luther, His Majesty had gracefully granted your request. However, I must say that it surprises me that a learned professor such as you does not know what he has written."

"If you, Dr. von Ecken, had written more books, you would understand," Martin said dryly.

The audience roared with laughter. Ecken's face turned the same shade of purple as his gown. "You have twenty-four hours." He spit the words out and turned away,

Later that day, in the dining room, scores of well-wishers came to Martin's table. That evening, three princes visited his room to express their support—William of Braunschweig, William of Henneberg, and Philip of Hesse. The meeting was scheduled to resume the next day at four o'clock, but the crowd was so large that it was postponed for two hours to allow the staff to set up a much larger room. The emperor motioned his marshal to begin. Ecken opened with a long, dry speech, to which nearly all in attendance, including an obviously bored emperor, paid little attention. The only one listening carefully, although from behind a door, was a furious Aleander.

Ecken finished by asking indignantly, "Do you recant or not? I want a simple answer."

Martin knew that his reply would to be the most important speech of his life. He had come well prepared.

> Most Serene Lord Emperor, Most Illustrious Princes, Most Gracious Lords,
>
> I beseech you to grant a gracious hearing to my plea, which I trust will be of justice and of truth. If, through my inexperience, I neglect to give to any their proper titles or in any way offend against the etiquette of the court in my manners or behavior, be kind enough to forgive me. I will be brief.
>
> I ask you to observe that my books are not all of the same kind. There are some in which I have dealt with piety in faith and morals so simply and agreeable with the Gospels that my adversaries are compelled to admit

they are useful and worthy reading by a Christian. Even the Bull, harsh and cruel though it is, declared some of my books harmless. If I should begin to recant, I would condemn truth that is admitted by friends and foes alike.

The second kind are writings against the papacy and the doctrine of the papist. No one can deny or conceal that the pope's laws and teachings trap the consciences of the faithful and that their goods and possessions have been devoured by tyranny without end in a shameful fashion, especially in Germany. If I recant, the only result will be to add strength to such tyranny.

I have written the third kind against private individuals who have defended the Roman tyranny and who overthrow the piety that I have taught. I admit that I have been harsher against them than befits my religious vows and my profession. However, I cannot recant them because that would contribute more tyranny and blasphemy and cause them to lord over those whom I defend.

Since I am a man and not God, I cannot provide my writings with any other defense than that which my Lord Christ provided for his teachings. He said, "If I have spoken evil, bear witness of the evil." If the Lord Himself did not refuse to witness against His teachings, how much more ought I, scum that I am, to seek and to wait for any who may wish to bear witness against my teaching? And so, through the mercy of God, I ask Your Majesty and Lordships to defeat them by the writings of the Prophets or the Gospels; for I shall be most ready if I be better instructed to recant my error and I shall be the first to throw my books into the fire.

He bowed and sat down.

Ecken rose to his feet with all the dignity he could muster. "Your answer is not to the point. There shall be no more taking into question matters on which condemnation and decisions have been passed by councils. Martin

Luther, in plain language, without subtleties and sophistry, answer this question: 'Are you or are you not prepared to recant?'"

Martin slowly rose from his chair and stood for a moment in deep thought. No one stirred; not a sound could be heard. Everyone looked at that monk standing as if on an island by himself, waiting. His head rose, and he looked at the emperor and said,

> Your Imperial Majesty and Your Lordships demand a simple answer. Here it is, plain and unvarnished. Unless I am convicted of error by the testimony of Scripture—for I put no trust in the unsupported authority of the pope or councils since it is plain that they have often erred and contradicted themselves—or by manifest reasoning, I cannot stand convinced by the Scriptures to which I have appealed and my conscience is taken captive by the Lord's words, I cannot and will not recant anything, for to act against our conscience is neither safe nor open to us. God help me, Amen.[27]

Everyone except Charles understood the speech and all that it implied. Martin was emotionally drained, but when asked, he recited his speech a second time in Latin for the benefit of the emperor. When he finished, Charles ordered him an escort back to the Schwan Inn.

Elector Frederick was troubled by the affairs of that afternoon. He said to Spalatin, "Dr. Martin performed very well this afternoon in the presence of the emperor, the princes, and the estate, but, especially near the end, he was too bold for me."

The emperor met with six members of the electoral body—the seventh member, the king of Bohemia, was absent due to illness. A number of electors told Charles that they were not convinced either way about Luther and his excommunication. "Very well," said Charles, who had shown only distant interest during the proceedings. "Then I'll give you my opinion." He looked around the room before declaring,

---

[27]   On a wood print of the proceedings, the artist added, "Here I stand. I cannot do otherwise." Aleander, who listened from behind a door, was the only person to record the quote. None of the official recorders mention it.

My family has always defended the Catholic faith and when a single friar goes against all Christianity, he must be wrong. Not only I, but all of you of this noble German nation, would be forever disgraced if by your negligence not only heresy but the very suspicion of heresy were to survive. After hearing the obstinate defense of Luther, I regret that I have so long delayed acting against him and his false teaching. I will have no more to do with him. He may return to Wittenberg under safe conduct, but without preaching or making any tumult. After that, I shall proceed against him as being a notorious heretic and I ask you now to declare yourself as you promised me.

The electors were impressed. The young emperor had spoken passionately, although he did not take the position that they were hoping he would. They did not quite know how to react. After a long pause, the archbishop of Trier broke the silence.

"When does Your Majesty think that the official edict will be ready?"

"I cannot say precisely. Two or three weeks."

"May I suggest that we reconvene after we have read the edict?"

"Thank you for that suggestion, Archbishop. Gentlemen, I will call a meeting as soon as the edict is ready."

Charles charged Aleander with drafting the edict. As Charles had assumed when he gave the electors a two- to three-week timeframe, Aleander prepared several draft edicts and sent them to Rome for input and approval. The edict was not ready until May 7, and Charles reconvened the electoral body. Not all of the electors had waited in Worms in the meantime, however. As expected, Frederick and Count Palatin had already returned home, leaving only four electors to approve the edict. The edict provided Luther a three-week grace period to recant, after which he would be considered a convicted heretic. The edict did not become final until May 26, partially because a special scribe took his time in rendering the edict a piece of art by adorning it with curls and flourishes.

On April 26, Martin left Worms, accompanied by his colleague Nicholaus Amsdorf and a young friar. Traveling with them were an imperial herald and a handful of soldiers to assure safe conduct. When the party reached Friedberg, fifty-five miles to the north, Luther convinced the herald that he had entered safe territory and dismissed him and the soldiers. In Hersfeld, he preached to the monks of the local monastery, and on May 1, he spoke before large crowd in Eisenach, in both instances ignoring the emperor's condition to his safe conduct that Luther could not preach while his on his journey home.

It was in Eisenach that Spalatin caught up with him. "I have a message from the elector. Martin, you are not safe anywhere for the time being. You are now a condemned heretic on the run and, surely, there are people out to arrest or kill you. They will not wait for your three-week grace period to expire."

"Dear Georg, are you not exaggerating? I am safe here with my people."

"No, you are not," Spalatin insisted. "Besides, by law the elector has to arrest you if you enter Saxony. He wants you stashed away where it is safe."

"And how does he propose to do that?"

"Well, where are you going from here?"

"Tomorrow I'm visiting my uncle in Möhra, and the next day, I'm going to Wittenberg."

"All right, this is the plan. Somewhere along the road, you will be kidnapped by a bunch of ruffians who will take you to a place that is completely safe."

"Did you come up with that plan, Georg?"

Spalatin showed mock indignation, asking, "How dare you ask such a foolish thing?" Then he grinned.

Luther and his companions traveled down a narrow country road in the forest on a beautiful May afternoon. The young friar held the reins while Martin and Amsdorf dozed in the cart. Suddenly, four horsemen appeared from among the trees and blocked the road.

"Highwaymen!" yelled the friar, and he dove into the bushes.

"Sit still," Martin ordered Nicholaus. "They are friends. Just pretend."

"Which one of you two monks is Luther?" one of the horsemen demanded.

"I am," said Martin.

The horseman grabbed his arm. "Off you go."

Martin half stepped, half fell from the cart.

"You," the ruffian yelled at Amsdorf. "Turn this cart around and skedaddle, if you know what's good for you." He jerked his thumb toward the friar in the bush. "And take that idiot out there with you."

"You can't do this!" Amsdorf yelled. "Do you know who this is? This is Martin Luther. You're making a big mistake, gentlemen."

"You hear that, boys? He called us gentlemen. Look, for all I care, this fellow could be the pope himself." He pulled a knife from his belt and pointed it toward Amsdorf. "How would you like a poke with this between your ribs?"

Amsdorf threw up his hands. "I'm going, I'm going." He turned the cart around, collected the shaking friar, and sped off.

Two of the ruffians grabbed Martin by his arms and galloped off with him hanging between them. The other two followed. They did not stop until they were around a bend in the road where an extra horse was waiting. They rode hard into the late evening hours to reach their destination: Wartburg Castle, the official residence of Elector Frederick. Built in 1069 on a 1,230-foot precipice overlooking the town of Eisenach, it could be reached only by a single road that crossed over a bridge.

Once inside, a servant led Martin to a room three flights up. It was furnished with a bed, a desk, a chair, and a closet. Martin was pleased to see that there was a window.

"Please do not leave this room, Father. I will bring you some food and beer for now. I will be your servant during your stay in the castle."

The sun was already up when Martin woke the next morning after a fitful sleep. The servant brought him breakfast and not long thereafter, George Spalatin stepped into the room. "Welcome to Wartburg Castle, Martin. How do you like your room?"

"The room is fine, and the view is magnificent. I suppose you are here to tell me what's going to happen next."

"Right. To begin with, you'll never see the elector. He is in residence and knows that you are here, but as long as he does not officially see you, he can deny your presence. The servant and I will be your only contacts with the outside world. You must grow a beard and let your hair grow to hide your tonsure. Then, in about two months, you will be able to leave this room and walk around the grounds, and we will give you a new identity."

"You've got it all figured out, haven't you?" Martin laughed.

"Yes, I have. Now, get rid of those monk's robes. We are going to transform you into a knight and give you a new name—Junker Jörg."

Martin smiled at the prospect but then looked more serious. "Georg, how long do you think I will have to stay here?"

"I am sorry, Martin, but I think at least a year."

"That long? Well, then, I may as well use the time for a good purpose. I'll need a Bible, lots of paper, and a pen."

"What are you going to do?"

"Translate the Bible into German."

17

⟫◦⟪

Junker Jörg

1521–1522

*Confined in Wartburg Castle - Translates the New Testament - Election of
Pope Adrianus - Masquerades as a knight - Triumphant return to Wittenberg -
The Reformation in full swing - Aids Katie von Bora*

Martin spent his long days in confinement working on his German
translation of the New Testament. He based his work on Erasmus's Greek
translation, rather than Jerome's Latin Vulgate, which was the official
version used by the Church. Although Martin had a masterful command
of the German language, his Greek was far less strong. He made a plan
to ask Philipp Melanchthon for help once he was free to leave Wartburg.

As soon as Martin's beard and hairstyle passed inspection, Spalatin
allowed him to leave the confines of his room and roam about the grounds
of Frederick's castle. He wore his new knight clothing and introduced
himself to the castle staff as Junker Jörg. He befriended the gamekeeper,
who showed him the extensive grounds and took him out hunting. There
was plenty of large game, such as deer, bear, wolves, wild boar, and foxes,
as well as fowl and rabbits. Martin did not like killing but knew that the

sport was necessary to provide meat on the table. On August 15, 1521, he wrote to Spalatin:

I followed the chase for two days last week to get a taste of the pleasure that fine gentlemen love so well. We caught two hares and a few deer. I managed to hide a poor hare under my coat, but the dogs discovered it and bit its legs through the coat and choked it to death. I have had enough of this kind of hunting and think it finer to slay bears and wolves and godless creatures such as these.

To his friend Wenzel Linck, he wrote. "I am a wonderful prisoner, for I sit here willingly, yet against my will." On November 21, he completed a booklet on the vow and dedicated it to his father. He sent his father a copy of the booklet with an accompanying letter, stating: *"God has redeemed me from my monkish vows and given me my freedom."*

While Luther was safely hidden in Wartburg Castle, all eyes of the Christian world were on Rome. On December 1, 1521, Pope Leo X, whose bull was the cause for Luther's confinement, died. The news spread throughout Europe, and all available cardinals traveled to Rome to elect a new pope. Of the forty-seven existent cardinals, only thirty-nine made it to the Vatican and walked in procession to the conclave in St. Peter's Basilica on December 28. They were dwarfed by the height of the magnificent Sistine Chapel and the new, masterful ceiling frescoes that had been completed by Michelangelo earlier in the year. All but three of the thirty-nine cardinals present were Italians. Fifteen were already beholden to Giulio de Medici, a cousin of Leo X, and of the twenty-three who remained, eighteen hoped to be elected pope themselves. After their first meeting, Emperor Charles's imperial envoy in Rome informed him, "There cannot be so much hatred and so many devils in hell as there are among these cardinals."

Cardinal Soderini, the leader of the French-Venetian faction, worked hard to stop his archenemy Medici from achieving victory. It was known that the king of France had threatened to break with Rome if Medici was elected. England wanted its Cardinal Wolsey to be the next pope, but on his previous visits to Rome, the Italian cardinals found him to be arrogant. A rumor circulated that the emperor favored his former tutor, Adriaan of Utrecht. The cardinals knew nothing about the man, other than the fact that he was the cardinal of Tortosa and the Grand Inquisitor of Spain—he had never come to their deliberations and was not present for the current election.

When Medici realized that he could not buy enough votes for his own election, he proposed Alessandro Farnese, a suspicious character nicknamed the Petticoat Cardinal. Years earlier, while Farnese was imprisoned for forgery, Pope Alexander VI had fallen for the charms of his sister, and he appointed Farnese a cardinal immediately after he was let out of prison. Farnese actually began to gain votes until the highly respected Cardinal Egidio, who himself would eventually became Pope Clement VIII in 1534, reminded his colleagues of Farnese's shady past, which included the fathering of numerous children. The votes went back and forth ten times without result until, finally, one of the exasperated cardinals suggested, "Let's retire for the day. You can cut the smoke in here from all those candles." It was bitterly cold outside and the chapel was so poorly heated that the older cardinals were shivering. They gratefully agreed to call it a day and hastened to their warm rooms.

That evening, Cardinal Sisto held a private meeting with Medici. Sisto showed him a letter in which the emperor expressed his support for Adriaan. "We have never seen the man and know so little about him," Medici pointed out.

"Doesn't that mean that he has no enemies in Rome?"

"True. That certainly counts in his favor. How old is he?"

"Sixty-three—and you are forty-four, aren't you?" said Sisto with a smile.

Medici realized what Sisto was implying, and he bent his head slightly and gestured with his left hand.

Cisto understood the gesture. "Look, I am authorized by Emperor Charles to offer you an emperor's pension of ten thousand ducats, as well as his support at the next election."

Medici lifted both hands. With a slight nod, he said, "I accept the emperor's generous offer and will bide my time."

Adriaan was born in Utrecht on March 2, 1459, the son of Floris Boeijens, a carpenter and cabinetmaker. His full name was Adriaan Floriszoon Boeijens. Father Floris and his wife, Geertruyt, lived in a small house in the Brandsteeg (Fire Alley). His father died when Adriaan was ten years old. The boy was studious and gifted; he attended the school of the Brothers of the Common Life in Deventer, where he befriended Erasmus. At age seventeen, he entered the University of Louvain, where he obtained a master's degree in arts.

In 1491, Adriaan was promoted to doctor in theology, and he became a priest in the Beguine House. It was in Louvain that he met Cardinal Bernardino de Carvajal, who, as the new papal legate, was on his way to Germany. The cardinal was acquainted with Margaretha of York, the sister of King Edward IV of England and widow of Charles the Bold. She taught the young children of Emperor Maximilian I and, having learned about Adriaan from Carvajal, recommended in 1507 that Adriaan be hired to tutor of Archduke Charles. On August 18, 1516, he was appointed bishop of Tortosa, a harbor town on the shores of the Mediterranean that he only had visited twice. Leo X also appointed him as Grand Inquisitor of most of Spain and, in 1517, promoted him to cardinal.

On Tuesday, January 9, 1522, it was time for the conclave of cardinals to hold its eleventh vote. Cardinal Giulio de Medici rose and spoke. "My esteemed brothers in Christ, it is clear that none of us has enough votes to be elected the next pope. Perhaps it is time for us to consider a cardinal who is not here. I propose that we elect the cardinal of Tortosa, an honorable man, sixty-three years old, whom many consider to be holy."

For a moment, the congregation sat in silent surprise, and then they proceeded to vote. The result was evenly split: fifteen for Adriaan and fifteen for the Spanish Cardinal Bernardino Lopez de Carvajal. Cardinal Cajetan, a kindly and highly respected man who had presided over the diet at Augsburg, quietly asked for support of Adriaan, and one after another, cardinals switched their votes. They paused when the total reached twenty-five and looked around the room. Cardinal Johannes de Cuppis raised his hand. "I also elect the cardinal of Tortosa and make him the pope." A two-thirds majority plus one had been reached.

"You idiots!" yelled the French-minded Cardinal Orsini. "Don't you know that this could mean the demise of France?"

Cardinal Sigismondo added, "You can practically say that the emperor is now pope, and the pope is emperor."

Senior Cardinal Cornaro of Venice opened the highest window of the chapel with some difficulty and leaned out, holding a long staff with a cross on top in his right hand and a long white flag in his left hand. He called out, "*Habemus Papam*, Adrianus Dortoniensis"[28] in his weak, elderly voice, but the crowd outside could not hear him clearly. Cardinal Lorenzo Campeggio then came to the window and called out the complete announcement in a much louder voice. "I announce to you a great joy: *Habemus Papam,* the most eminent and most reverend Lord Adrianus, cardinal of the Holy Roman Church." [29]

Outside in St. Peter's Square, the Italian crowd was angry. They hissed and screamed at the cardinals as they left the conclave. "You elected a Hollander, a barbarian," they yelled. Clearly, it was an insult to their national pride. Around Europe, reactions varied.

The king of France seethed with rage. "They made a pope out of Charles's schoolmaster."

Thomas More said matter-of-factly, "Adrianus will be the holiest of popes."

Erasmus declared, "The entire Christianity is to be congratulated. This tumultuous time asks for a strong captain."

Charles V remarked, "It pleases me more than my election as Emperor."

Severe winter weather and heavy snowstorms blocked all passes through the Spanish-French Pyrenees during the month of January 1522. Riding and walking day and night, a special courier managed to cross the Pyrenees and reach the mountain town of Vitoria in the early morning hours of January 22, just as Adriaan was ready to say Mass. Out of breath, the courier blurted out, "Your Holiness, you are the new pope!"

---

[28] Cardinal Cornaro added the word *Dortoniensis* to denote that the new pope came from Tortosa.

[29] Campeggio's announcement was incomplete. He should have added Adriaan's surname, but he did not know it. He also should have included the name by which the new pope wished to be known, but Adriaan was still in Spain, unaware of his election.

Adriaan, who was not known to be an emotional man, had some doubt. "If it is true what you have just told me, then I have every reason to be mournful and sad."

The courier was followed by a Vatican messenger carrying the official brevet of Adriaan's election, dated January 9. The first messenger was taken prisoner by pirates, but a second one safely reached the bishop of Logrono, fifty miles south of the Spanish-French border. The bishop wisely chose his younger vicar general, Blas Ortiz, to make the hazardous trip to Vitoria to deliver the Vatican's brevet, which finally reached Adriaan on February 9, a month after it was originally written. Not knowing that a courier had previously reached Adriaan, Ortiz was amazed and somewhat disappointed when the new pope showed little reaction and remained so calm.

A letter accompanying the brevet announced that three cardinal legates were on their way to Vitoria to ask Adriaan whether he would accept the papacy. Also included was a request that Adriaan not exercise his papal authority while he was still in Spain. When they arrived, Adriaan invited the tired legates to rest while he composed a letter to the Curia, accepting his new responsibility. Contrary to centuries-old custom, he kept his own name: in spoken Latin he would be called Adrianus, which would be written as Hadrianus. He was the sixth pope by that name and the first Nederlander.

During the month of February, he wrote letters, signed as "Adrianus Cardinalis" with his cardinal seal attached, to Emperor Charles V and King Henry VIII of England, stating that he was but a poor unknown man chosen to be the substitute of Christ: *"I am decidedly not happy and ask for rest and not for such an unbearable burden, but I will not insult God and the Church by refusing."* King Francis I of France did not get a similar letter, causing him to feel insulted by "that cardinal of Tortosa." Adrianus finally wrote him a quieting letter on April 21.

On May 9, he paid a visit to the new cloister in Saragossa and descended into the crypt of the church to view the mortal remains of St. Lambertus, a decapitated Christian slave. Years earlier, he had asked for a relic of Lambertus, but had not received one. Now that he was the pope, his request was readily approved. A monk removed, with some difficulty, a piece of the saint's mandible and handed it with much deference to Adrianus.

Getting the new pope to Rome proved to be a difficult matter. The Mediterranean was crawling with pirates, and it was not easy to assemble a fleet for the pope and his entourage. Venice refused to make ships available, and Genoa offered only two galleys. Rome sent a three-master warship and four ships. In the end, a flotilla of about fifty vessels was assembled, but their departure was delayed because they needed permission to sail close to the French coastline on their way to Italy. On August 5, the fleet finally left Spain, carrying the pope, hundreds of dignitaries, and two thousand soldiers. Adrianus sailed on the trireme *Donata*, a galley with oars on each side. On deck was a tent made of crimson velvet with the papal coat of arms on each side. The journey was an enormous undertaking, and it took Adrianus twenty-four days to reach Rome.

In the meantime, from January to August, Rome had been in total disarray. Three cardinals took care of church business each month and then another three the next, leading to poor leadership. The Church was involved in financing the war between Charles V and France, and there was an acute shortage of money. Tapestries designed by Raphael went to the pawn shop; the silver figures of Peter and Paul were taken from the Sistine Chapel and sold, together with tiaras and miters. The cardinals discovered, to their dismay, that the jewels of the tiara of Pope Paulus II had already disappeared on the market. The German and French cardinals were constantly at odds, and church vendors sold caricatures of the "Flemish-Spanish barbarian" and "Emperor Charles's schoolmaster." To top it off, there was still no news from the new pope. Rumors had spread that he was dead. The rumors finally dispelled upon Adriaan's arrival, and he was crowned two days later on August 31, 1522.

Sequestered in his castle prison, working on his Bible translation, Martin had to rely on others to bring him news from the outside world. Spalatin visited him in mid-January 1522 to bring him up-to-date with news not only from Rome but from Wittenberg as well. Dr. Karlstadt had performed the Christmas communion service wearing secular clothes. He had given it in German, wanted no confessions in his church, and proclaimed that secular priests should marry. "Just like you have said," Spalatin reminded Martin.

"Good for him. Secular priests do not belong to a religious order. They do not take a vow, so why shouldn't they be allowed to marry? But he is wrong to say that monks should also marry."

"Well, he married a young girl, Anna von Mochau," Spalatin continued.

"I know that girl. Isn't she a bit young?"

"I understand that she is fifteen."

"He must be at least twice as old as she is."

"He is thirty-six."

Martin laughed. "What else did the rascal do?"

"He removed all pictures and statues of saints from the church, and he lets the people take the bread and the wine themselves. I heard that some of this is now happening throughout Germany."

"And all the time I am rotting away in this castle," Martin said disgustedly.

"Rotting? Come now. You live here like a prince. By the way, how far are you with the translation?"

"Nearly finished, thank you."

"Good. Then you will be interested to know that I have saved the biggest news for last."

Martin looked up, questioningly. "Which is …?"

"We have a new pope. Leo died in December, and on January 9, the cardinals elected a Dutchman, Adriaan of Utrecht."

"Adriaan? Oh, he will have a tough time with those Italians. I do not envy him."

In late February 1522, the Vatican lifted Luther's ban. He was no longer a fugitive from the Church, although the Emperor Charles's ban was still in place. Luther was safe to travel, as long as he remained within Elector Frederick's territory. On March 1, he left the confines of Wartburg Castle to return to Wittenberg. A few days later, a young Swiss chronicler and his friend sought shelter from a storm in the portal of the Black Bear Inn in Thuringen. The innkeeper pitied the young men and took them into the main room, where a knight with a bushy black beard and clad in a scarlet cloak rested his head on his sword while reading. The knight introduced himself as Junker Jörg and invited the bedraggled travelers to his table to share a drink with him.

While waiting for their beers, their eyes fell on the knight's book. They stretched their necks and leaned over a little to read it, but could not make out the script.

"May I ask in what language your book is written?" one of them ventured to ask.

"This is Hebrew."

"Oh, wow." They looked as if they didn't believe the knight. "We are on our way to Wittenberg. Do you perhaps know whether Dr. Luther is there now?"

"I am quite sure he is not, but he will soon be."

The innkeeper, who had overheard their conversation, smiled to himself. After the storm passed and the youngsters were ready to leave, he met them at the door and said, "You know, that knight is Martin Luther himself."

"Impossible," one of them said. "Ulrich Hutten, maybe, but not Luther."

"No, believe me. He is Luther."

The knight overheard the innkeeper and laughed. "You two take me for Hutten and the innkeeper takes me for Luther. Maybe I am the devil."

Five days later, the young men saw the same knight preaching in Wittenberg. "You see that. It *was* Luther!" [30]

On the first day of Lent, Martin climbed the steps leading to the pulpit of the church in Wittenberg, and the congregation saw a changed man. Gone were his monk's gown and tonsure. He wore layman's clothes, and his hair was long—and, for this first day, he had kept his beard. The people welcomed him as a hero who had freed them from the burdens that the Catholic Church had laid upon them.

Martin was struck by the many changes that had taken place in Wittenberg during his absence: the secular priests had married, Mass was said in German, more than a dozen friars had left the priory, and churches had been ransacked and statues destroyed. In desperation, the town's council called on Luther to help restore order. Elector Frederick, however, did not want Martin in Wittenberg, for fear that his presence

---

[30] Credit for this story goes to the author Roland Bainton.

would incite further celebratory rioting. He told the city council, which informed Martin of the elector's position. He immediately sat down to write his protector a letter.

To Your Electoral Highness,

That Your Highness had the best intentions towards me is manifest and this is my answer. I have not received the Gospel from men, but from Heaven, through our Lord Jesus Christ, so that I may well glory in being able to style myself a servant and evangelist. I come to Wittenberg under higher protection than that of the Elector and I have not the slightest intention of asking for Your Highness's help. For I am more able to protect Your Grace than you can protect me and what's more, if your Gracious Highness could and would protect me, I would not come.

Therefore, he whose faith is the greatest will receive the most protection. So, as I see your faith as very weak, I cannot regard you as the man who could either protect or save me. I respectfully inform you that you have already done too much and now must do nothing at all. For God will not suffer our worrying. He wishes it to be left to Him and to no other, so let Your Grace act accordingly.

Seeing that I decline to follow Your Grace's advice, you are innocent in God's sight if I am taken prisoner or killed. Henceforth act thus regarding your duty towards me as Elector and support the authority of the Emperor. Should they command you to arrest me, then I shall say what to do. I shall protect you from injury to body, soul, and estate, whether Your Grace believes it or not.

I have written this hurriedly so that Your Grace may not be upset by my arrival. Were Your Grace only to believe, he would see the glory of God, but he has not yet believed; he has seen nothing. Amen.

March 5, 1522

The old elector smiled when he read the rather arrogant and overbearing letter. He still thought of Luther as somewhat of a rebellious youth. Fortunately, he was a forgiving man. He put the letter in the drawer next to the letter that Pope Leo X had written two years earlier, urging him to bring Luther to his senses.

Frederick was not the only nobleman to receive a sharply worded letter from Luther. One of his enemies, Duke George of Saxony, who had hosted the Leipzig Debate, inquired what Martin's immediate plans were, and Martin replied:

> Stop fuming against God for what I have done, you ungracious Prince. I have received your ungracious letter in which you complain that I have injured your soul, honor, and good name. For, however I may act or speak against Your Ungracious Grace, I am entitled to do so.
>
> If you didn't tell so many lies, you would not slander and persecute the truth so shamefully as you do. This is not the first time you have maligned me. Christ commands me to be kind to my enemies and, until now, you have had my prayers and service. If my Lord Jesus will, He can enlighten the heart of Your Most Ungracious Highness and turn you into a gracious and kind Prince to me.

With Luther officially free, the Reformation spread like a wildfire through Germany and the Netherlands. In Switzerland, Ulrich Zwingli, who had preached against the established Church since 1516, was deeply involved in the legislature with establishing a state church. Indulgences and pilgrimages were abolished; pictures, relics, and statues had been removed from most churches; and celibacy was rejected. Zwingli himself married the eight-months-pregnant Anna Reinhard. Luther was surprised to learn that even Martin Bucer, the Dominican monk who had congratulated him after the disputation in Heidelberg, had left his monastery and was a married minister in Landstuhl.

With the Reformation irrevocably set in motion, Martin turned his attention to his translation of the New Testament. He had completed a draft manuscript while confined in Wartburg Castle, and he asked

Melanchthon, who was a better Greek scholar than he, to help him revise it. The two men worked closely together for several months, and the German New Testament was ready for publication in September 1522. Martin intended to start on the Old Testament immediately.

Then something extraordinary happened in early April 1523—he received a note from a nun, asking him to help her escape from her convent. The note was from Katharina (Katie) von Bora, who was born January 27, 1499. Her father, Hans der Jüngere von Bora, owned modest estates at Lippendorf. After Katie's mother died in 1504, her father remarried and put Katie in a convent school of the Benedictine nuns. Three years later, he transferred her to a Cistercian cloister at Nimbschen, where a paternal aunt was a nun and a maternal aunt was the Mother Superior. The cloister was a wealthy foundation for the education of girls. Taking the nun's veil was gratuitous—granted without obligation—and Katie took it at age sixteen.

After five years, she grew dissatisfied with her life in the convent and became increasingly interested in the growing reform movement. Two years later, she and several other young nuns heard that some monks had left the Augustinian monastery in Grimma, and they decided to follow the monks' example. Katie sought the help of Leonard Köppe, a wealthy merchant who had a business relationship with the Nimbschen cloister. On the night of April 4, 1523, he and his nephew hid Katie and eleven other nuns in their covered wagon and drove them to Wittenberg, where three jumped off and went to their parents' houses. On behalf of the remaining eight nuns, Katie wrote to the famous Dr. Luther, pleading for assistance.

"What am I going to do with them, Georg?" Martin asked Spalatin.

"I don't know, but I am glad that it is not my problem," Georg said with a grin.

"I think that I am obliged to notify their relatives, don't you think?"

"Martin, that's the least you must do. Their families should be able to support them, and, if not, you can try to find husbands for them. Don't forget that they all come from good homes."

"True. One of them is Magdalena von Staupitz—a much younger sister of our beloved Johann. Listen, I cannot support them from my meager salary. Can you beg some money from your rich courtier friends? Maybe some of them will even be interested in marrying a few."

"I'll see what I can do," said Georg. He got up to leave. At the door, he turned around and said with a sly smile, "Why don't *you* marry one?"

Martin actually had his eye on Ave von Schönfeld, but she got married in no time to one of the many young Wittenberg knights who were looking for suitable brides. Katie von Bora was taken into the home of the rich burgomaster of Wittenberg, the Honorable Reichenbach. She stayed there for two years, during which time she had a love affair with Jerome Baumgartner, who broke her heart by reneging on his promise to marry her.

"Why don't *you* marry her?" Georg repeated. "This is your chance."

"Georg, the way I feel now, I'll never take a wife. Not that I am insensible to my flesh or to sex, for I am neither made of wood nor stone. However, my mind is averse to wedlock because I expect I will die the death of a heretic," he added somberly.

"Sorry, I forgot that, although you are free from the pope, the emperor's ban still hangs over your head," his friend replied. "But wasn't it only a few years ago that you gave a sermon on the estate of marriage? You even published it, if I remember correctly. You know all about marriage already."

"You don't have to be sarcastic, Georg. I just don't have the mind-set for it now."

"Martin, you are forty years old. Don't wait much longer, my friend."

18

━━▶◆◀━━

Erasmus and the Pope

1522–1523

A Dutch pope in Rome - Austerity measures and reforms - Erasmus reaches out - Secret correspondence - Erasmus declines an invitation to Rome

The newly elected Pope Adrianus VI finally arrived in Rome on the twenty-ninth of August, 1522, and was introduced to the members of the Roman Curia. They saw a slender man sitting upright in his chair, wearing a simple papal cap, the *camauro*. His face was well formed, his cheeks elongated and pale. His cheekbones were pronounced, and his dark eyes were small but lively, with heavy eyebrows. His nose was slightly bent, with flaring nostrils, and his lips were firmly pressed with a double crease at the corners. It was the strong face of a modest man.

The cardinals looked upon the new pope with skepticism. He was an outsider, and they considered him a barbarian. They were accustomed to conversing in Italian among themselves and with the previous popes, but Adranus could communicate with them only in Latin—although they had to admit that for a barbarian, his Latin was reasonably good. All in all, they were not sure what to expect from the new pontiff.

It did not take long for Adrianus to realize that the excesses and corruption of the Curia was the main cause for the decline of the Church. He immediately set about implementing a series of austerity measures. He reduced the *Apostolic Signatura*, the collegial court of cardinals, from forty to nine members. He banned the immoral Cardinal Innocentius Cibo, nephew of Leo X, from Rome and ordered the so-called palace cardinals to leave the Vatican. Of the one hundred footmen who had served Leo X, he kept twelve. When the cardinals asked him to appoint suitable personnel, he replied that he first had to pay the debts of his predecessor. There were no more lavish banquets or grandiose festivities. He dined at the simple table he was used to in Spain. "He only eats codfish and drinks beer," the cardinals snickered. His chosen lifestyle was very much a protest against the excesses of the Roman court.

Along with his austerity measures, Adrianus instituted a spate of reforms. He put an immediate end to the practice of granting indulgences. Cardinals were no longer allowed to give asylum to criminals and were prohibited from carrying weapons. Furthermore, they were ordered to shave their beards, as in Adrianus's opinion, "You look more like soldiers than priests." In a town famous for nepotism, he did not give a favored position to a single member of his family.

Although Adrianus worked diligently to reform the Vatican, he was strongly opposed to any reformation of Church doctrine. As a result, he firmly maintained the Church's strict anti-Lutheran stance.

Adrianus VI made no attempt to hide his criticism of the Curia from the outside world. In early 1523, he sent Bishop Francesco Chiergati as his nuntius to the Diet of Nürnberg, which had been called by Emperor Charles V late in the previous year. On January 3, the nuntius read aloud to the diet a letter in which Pope Adrianus first presented the errors and dangers of the Lutherans and then issued a *Confiteor*, a confession of the serious abuses of the Roman Curia and the spread of religious evil at all levels of the Church. [31]

Not surprisingly, the new pope was extremely unpopular with the Roman hierarchy, who felt that he blamed them for the many ills of the Church. Adrianus became alienated, and he did not help his cause by appointing Willem van Enckenvoirt as his closest advisor and Dirk van Heeze as his secretary and right-hand man. These two Dutchmen were

---

[31] During a visit to Utrecht on May 13, 1985, Pope Paul II reiterated the importance of this *Confiteor*.

new to Rome and completely lacked the necessary experience to deal with the procedures and bureaucracy of the Church. Pope Adrianus became a tragic, lonely figure; he was totally out of place.

Outside the Vatican, the Roman people, too, were dissatisfied, especially those who had business with the church and were directly affected by the new austerity measures. When Adrianus cut the enormous profits of the grain dealers, a dealer named Marco de Piacenza approached the pope with dagger in hand on February 25, 1523. Cardinal Campeggi stepped in between them and stopped the assailant, who then committed suicide.

Erasmus followed the news from Rome with great interest. The previous pope, Leo X, had protected him against the attacks by hostile theologians, and he was anxious to learn whether his childhood friend Pope Adrianus would do the same. He decided to send a letter to reassure the pope that he was not a supporter of Luther or Lutheranism. The letter became the first in a string of secret correspondence between Erasmus and Adrianus.

> Erasmus of Rotterdam greets His Holiness Adrianus VI, recently elected Pope of Rome.
>
> I have looked for a way that you will remember from the masses that applaud you, one not-so-dumb Erasmus. You were elevated to your high position by the will of God, not only as a person with the strongest moral integrity, but also the greatest authority, who could curb the wicked tumult in the Christian world. And alas, this tumult has already lasted too long and becomes ever worse … I wish you no luck with your worthiness. I also wish the country and the diocese that I have in common with you and to which now for the first time has its turn to have a pope of Rome, no luck. I do not strive for any advantages that our common origin or our friendship may bring. However, I do wish the Christian world luck, if you—and I have the fullest confidence—will fulfill your papal job in such a way that the world will finally understand that there is a pope in Rome for whom nothing is older than Christian honor. I bid that the Lord Jesus, the King of the Shepherds, will support you in this endeavour. Amen.

Basel, August 1, 1522

Shortly thereafter, he sent a second, much shorter letter, and included a note in which he dedicated to Adrianus his recently published translation of the *Psalm Commentary* by Arnobius of Sicca (died c. 330), a strong apologist of the Christian faith. This time, the pope responded with a long letter.

> Pope Adrianus VI to his beloved son Erasmus of Rotterdam,
> Beloved son, our greeting and apostolic blessing …
> You wrote that you feared that, as a result of hatred and whispers by some, we suspect you of Lutheranism. You have to trust us in this. In truth, your name has been dropped by some who are not favorably disposed to you. We do not like to listen to matters that are underhandedly told about learned and famous people.
> Because of your desire for fame and honor, we urge you to use your pen against the new heresies. You must believe that God has reserved this matter especially for you. You have great spiritual strength, wide learning, and fluency of writing like no other. You must use these many gifts for the honor of Christ and the defense of the Church. We therefore fervently wish that you will do so and thereby silence those who suspect you of Lutheranism. For Luther and his companions, judgment will not wait long and their doom will not be put off. Could you possibly refuse to sharpen your pen against such foolery? Remember, God has already damned them out of His sight. You can imagine how grateful God will be and how happy He will be for His true believer. After this winter, come to Rome as soon as possible. We will do everything to make sure that you will not regret it.
> Given at Rome by Saint Peter under the Fisherman's ring
> 1 December 1422, the first year of our pontificate
> (Drafted by Dirk van Heeze)

Erasmus had not enjoyed the atmosphere in Rome when he stayed there over a decade earlier, and he feared that if he went back, he would be trapped in the immense network of cardinals, bishops, and lesser clergy. He needed his freedom and his free time in order to be productive, and he felt that he would not have enough of either in Rome. He preferred to help Adrianus from a distance. In his next letter, he offered to do so in strict secrecy.

> Erasmus of Rotterdam greets Pope Adrianus VI,
> The whole world looks to you as the only person capable of restoring peace for the people. If Your Holiness asks, I will send in a private letter my advice of how this evil can be rooted out so that it will not easily return. In a heavy storm, even the best helmsman seeks advice from others. Moses did not refuse Jethro's advice, although I am not Jethro. If Your Holiness wishes to test my obedience, ask, and if I do not promptly react, then no longer count Erasmus among your friends.
> Basel, 22 December 1522

Adrianus needed more than the advice by letter from his fellow countryman; he was in deep trouble. The war against the Turks had gone from bad to worse, and neither the European kings nor Emperor Charles V offered to help. Cardinal Francesco Soderini, who had served previous popes, turned out to be a traitor who opposed Adrianus behind his back. Adrianus's health also caused him trouble. He had a chronic infection of his kidneys that caused him to have a constant low fever. In the midst of all these adversities, the plague broke out in Rome once again. In his next letter to Erasmus, he again urged his childhood friend to come to Rome.

> Beloved son, our greeting and apostolic blessing, …
> I am pleased with your offer to lend advice. We urge you in great earnest and in the fullness of your love to reveal your method and plan to remove this bitter evil from our people while it is still possible. Not because our authority and personal power are in any danger during

this fierce storm. It is because we see thousands of souls under our shepherdly care slide into devilish slavery in the hope of gaining evangelical freedom.

The sooner you reveal your advice, the better. Speed is important in view of the common danger; your personal secrecy, and your welfare is dear to us. We again extend our invitation to visit Rome, unless you are certain that you can do more for God and His Church from where you are.

Rome by Saint Peter under the Fisherman's ring

23 January 1523

(Drafted by Dirk van Heeze)

Erasmus took his time to consider and draft his reply. He cleverly explained that due to a gallstone, he could not possibly travel to Rome. He followed this with a long litany of the attacks he suffered from all sides of the Luther controversy, including from Rome. His advice came last, but its full extent is unknown to the world.

Holy Father, it would be better for us to discuss the affair in private. However, I am forced to listen to the laws of an extraordinary brutal tyrant by the name of 'Gallstone.' In the meanwhile, I will write my advice and no one will read this letter except us. I do not care for my hollow titles that only hamper me. But how much verbal abuse is thrown at me? What bitter pamphlets and threats do my enemies use? Some say that I agree with Luther and that I do not write anything against him. Luther, on the other hand, screams that I bitterly attack him … Germany is a large country. I hesitate to write how deep the feelings are of the people in favor of Luther and how much they hate the papacy. Many regions support him and the humanists do not remain silent.

I painfully tell this, Holy Father, and wish that these are false complaints, but they are not. I have very good contacts with all learned men and that alone makes me happy. I would rather die than lose so many friends and heap the hatred of the world on my head. In many letters and booklets, I have made it clear that I have nothing to do with Luther and his supporters. Publicly, I have advised against revolt, and privately I have urged people to temper their stands. At the same time I do this in Germany, I am slandered in Rome in ever more insulting pamphlets. In Brabant, I am no longer welcome at dinner tables and am called a heretic, a deserter, and a traitor. These offenders only strengthen Luther's party in their fanaticism. They scream that the pest in Luther's writing is also in mine, although they cannot find a single example. Now that Luther has come forward, they attack me for what I had written way before he was on the scene, writings that they had previously approved. Still, they will not chase me from my chosen course.

Your Holiness wants me to come to Rome. However, whenever I hear "come to Rome," it reminds me of the lobster that was told to fly, to which he replied, "Give me wings." And so I will say, "Give me back my youth and my health." You may rightfully say that until now you only heard complaints, whereas you expect wise advice. I see many who want to heal this evil with a strong hand, but the past has taught us that this is unwise. The affair would only end in a bloodbath. Already, this affair has so far advanced that neither knife nor fire will heal it. Truly, if you intend to suppress the affair with jails, beatings, confiscations, bans, condemnation, and death penalties, you do not need my advice. I know that you would rather heal than punish, but, unfortunately, the theologians will not let you. They demand that their authority must be honored, just as the monks will not let go of their easy living and royalty will stand by their own laws.

One must first go to the roots of the problem and start the healing there. I also wish, if possible, to limit the freedom of the printing press. Everybody shall breathe

again the sweet name of freedom that must be protected
in all possible ways that meet the safe keeping of piety.
Your Holiness will say, "What are those roots of things
that must change?" To find them, I believe we must call
from all corners honest, sincere, mild, and merciful men,
whose opinion …

The letter, as published in 1529 in Erasmus's *Opus epistolarum*, is cut
off in mid-sentence. There has been much speculation as to why. Was the
remainder of the secret letter too personal or too sensitive for publication?
Whatever the reason, the full extent of Erasmus's advice and how the pope
received it remains a mystery. Pope Adrian VI died on September 14, 1523.

19

———◆◆◆———

The Great Debate

1524–1525

Erasmus defends free will in De Libero Arbitrio - Luther condemns free will in De Servo Arbitrio - Erasmus and Luther debate

After Pope Adrianus died, his successor, Clement VII, also tried to persuade Erasmus to come to Rome, but he, too, was disappointed. *"I am simply too old and too weak to travel to Rome,"* Erasmus wrote. However, with two consecutive popes pressuring him to write against Luther, he began to waver. The final push may have been an unexpected letter from King Henry VIII, who urged him to take up his pen against the reformer. Erasmus realized that he was in danger of losing his English friends, something he never wanted. Without telling even his closest friends, he finally broke the neutral position that he had cultivated for so long and took up his pen.

He began work on a book in which he challenged Luther on the one question of theology and philosophy on which he and Luther were farthest apart: *Does man have a free will when it comes to doing good or evil, or has God predetermined the entire life of man and thus, a free will does not play a role?* Buried in a long letter to Pope Clement VII dated February 13, 1524, Erasmus revealed his project in one simple sentence that could easily have been overlooked: *"I will dedicate to the Cardinal of York the book* On

Free Will *against Luther, which I now have in hand.*" He wrote the same in a letter to Henry VIII to make sure that his English friends would hear about it.

Another person also heard about that one sentence—Martin Luther—and he immediately fired off a letter.

> Grace and peace to you from the Lord Jesus Christ.
> I have kept silent long enough, dearest Erasmus, expecting that you, being older and of higher station, would break the silence; yet, since I have waited so long in vain, respect compels me to proceed ... I was not much offended by the bitterness and acerbity with which you criticized me in many passages of your printed works. I am not the sort of man to exact from you that which is beyond your strength and capacity ... I have never desired that you should enter into my camp and forsake or neglect your own sphere. If your heart is not in the matter, then it is safer for you to serve the Lord in your own way. You may believe it or not, just as you like, though Christ is my witness.
> I am sincerely grieved for your sake that the zealous resentments of so many and such eminent persons have been aroused against you. Perhaps they feel that you have provoked them in an unworthy manner. Plainly speaking, there are some who cannot bear your acrimony and dissimulation. Hitherto, I have restrained my pen whenever you provoked me ... If you, my dear Erasmus, will abstain from your witty but bitter rhetorical sallies and if you cannot or dare not stand up for my teachings, then at least let me alone ... It is much more serious to be once gored by Erasmus than to be set upon by all the papists together ... Kindly pardon my poor way of expressing myself, and farewell in the Lord.
> In April 1524

Erasmus was dumbfounded. How anyone could read so much into one sentence was beyond him. "Why didn't Luther wait for my book to be published so that he could read what I wrote?" he wondered. In reply to Luther, he composed a rather meaningless letter that did not require a response.

The completed book was finally published on September 1, 1524, under the title *De libero arbitrio diatribe sive collatio* (Of the Free Will: Discourses or Comparisons) and was also known as the *Diatribe*. It was specifically written to address the Lutheran position on the subject of free choice and contained approximately 31,700 words on sixty-three pages. Luther answered one year later, attacking Erasmus's book in *De Servo Arbitrio* (On the Bondage of the Will), also known as his *Assertion*, which was four times as long, containing 118,000 words on 234 pages. Many theologians consider these two books to be, in essence, a long-distance debate on the subject of free choice.[32]

Erasmus and Luther never met in person, but if they had sat down to debate the merits of their respective books, one can imagine how their discussion might have progressed …[33]

The Debate

"As a way of preface to our debate, there is hardly a more tangled labyrinth in the holy scriptures than that of 'free choice,'" said Erasmus. "It has long exercised the minds of philosophers and theologians to a striking degree, though, in my opinion, with more labor than fruit."

"Your book struck me as so cheap and paltry that I felt profoundly sorry for you, defiling as you were your elegant and ingenious style with such trash," began Luther in his opening remarks. "Although you think and write wrongly about free choice, I still owe you no small thanks, for you have made me far more sure of my position by letting me see the case of free choice put forward with all the energy of so distinguished and powerful a mind, but with no other effect than to make things worse than before. It was my sheer disgust, anger, and contempt—or, to put it plainly,

---

[32]   Especially E. Gordon Rupp, professor at the University of Cambridge, and A. N. Marlow, senior lecturer at the University of Manchester.

[33]   The debate that follows is based on English translations of *De Libero Arbitrio* and *De Servo Arbitrio*.

my considered judgment—on your *Diatribe* that dampened my eagerness to answer you. It has, at length, come to me that my long silence has not been entirely honorable."

"My, my, you don't mince any words, do you?" Erasmus observed dryly.

"Why should I? I admit you are superior to me in powers of eloquence and native genius, all the more as I am an uncultivated fellow."

"Well, if that is your style, then I'll live with it. May I remind you that it was you, Martin Luther, who put out your *Assertion* about 'free choice,' and so violently stirred up the question. I'll try my hand to see whether the truth might be made more plain. However, I must warn you, I do not like assertions, and I have no fixed convictions, except that I think there to be a certain power of free choice. Quite frankly, after reading your *Assertion*, you have not persuaded me."

"Is it not the mark of the Christian mind to take no delight in assertions?" Luther replied. "On the contrary, a man must delight in assertions, or he will be no Christian."

"Is that your latest assertion, or is it a new dogma?"

"By 'assertion' I mean a constant adhering, affirming, confessing, maintaining, and an invincible persevering. Free choice is a pure fiction, for, like the woman in the Gospel,[34] the more free choice is treated by the doctors, the worse it gets."

"There are some secret places in the holy scriptures into which God has not wished us to penetrate more deeply. If we try to do so, the darker it becomes," Erasmus pointed out. "Didn't St. Paul say, *'O the depth of the riches and the wisdom and knowledge of God. How unsearchable are his judgments and how inscrutable his ways.'?*"

"Of course, there are many texts in the scriptures that are obscure and abstruse—I admit that—but not because of the majesty of their subject matter but because of our ignorance," Luther asserted. "Truly, it is stupid and impious when we know that the subject matter of scripture has been placed in the clearest light."

"Do you really think so? Well, in my judgment, we have learned what is needful to know about free choice, so let us go swiftly to better things—"

---

[34] Mark 5:25.

"I find that intolerable," Luther jumped in. "If you consider this subject unnecessary for Christians, then please quit the field. Then you and I have nothing in common, for I consider it vital. If it is irreverent and superfluous, as you say, to know whether God foreknows anything, whether our will accomplishes anything in things pertaining to eternal salvation or simply suffers the action of grace—whatever we do good or ill—then I ask you, what is there that is reverent or serious or useful to know? Erasmus, you go much too far."

"Not nearly far enough, Dr. Luther." Erasmus felt comfortable now that the debate was in full swing. "What could be more useless than to publish this to the world? Suppose for a moment that it were true, as Augustine says, that God works in us good and evil, and rewards his own good works in us and punishes his evil work in us. Who will be able to bring himself to love God with all his heart when He created eternal torments in order to punish His own misdeeds in His victim as though He took delight in human torments? For that is how most people will interpret them." His voice wavered slightly, just enough to reveal his emotion.

"I am surprised that you do not remember the point at issue and say, 'Where would free choice then remain?' My dear Erasmus, why are you so robust? Against whom are you speaking? Your admonition has nothing to do with me. If God willed that such things should be openly spoken of and published, who are you to forbid it? The way you talk, one must imagine the living God to be nothing but a kind of shallow and ignorant ranter."

"But what is the use or need to publish such things when so many evils appear to proceed from them?" Erasmus prodded Luther.

"Because God willed them to be published, and we must not ask the reason for the divine will."

"Must I remind you, dear Doctor, that in the holy scriptures, God is angry, grieves, is indignant, rages, threatens, hates, and then changes His mind and has mercy. To speak thus suits our infirmity and slowness. The same prudence I consider as befits those who take the task of interpreting the divine words. I prefer men to be persuaded not to waste their time and talents in labyrinths of this kind but to refute or affirm your views, Martin Luther."

"No, that is not the way it is. God hides His eternal goodness and mercy under eternal wrath, His righteousness under injustice. This is the highest degree of faith, to believe Him merciful when He saves so few and damns so many. To believe Him righteous, when by His own will He makes us necessarily damnable. Since that cannot be comprehended, there is room for the exercise of faith when such things are preached and published, just as when God kills, the faith of life is exercised in death."

Erasmus had had enough of the discourse about the prefaces of their books. "Now, let us move on to discuss the introductions to our disputation."

"The points you, dear Erasmus, raise in the epilogue to your preface do not impress me at all. You call our dogmas 'fables' and 'useless,' and you say that the scriptures have a language of their own."

"I do not recall having written an epilogue to my preface," said Erasmus. "And I did not use the words 'dogmas' and 'fables.' Is it possible that you did not read the first paragraph of my Introduction? I did use the word 'useless,' but that did not relate to your nonexistent dogmas. Can we now begin with our introductions? Since you do not acknowledge the authority of any writer and only listen to the canonical scriptures, I gladly welcome this abridgment of labor to stick to the scriptures and leave books out of it."

"Very well. I accept your promise not to discuss books. On my side, there were only Wycliffe and Laurentius Valla, but there remains only Luther, a private individual. Before we start, dear Erasmus, I have one request. Just as I will bear with your ignorance in these matters, so you, in turn, will bear with my lack of eloquence."

"If by lack of eloquence you include such language as cheap, defiling, paltry, and trash, as you used to define my booklet, and ignorance, as you did just now, then I must admit it will be hard to bear."

"*Ja, ja, ja.*" Luther held up his left hand as if to stop Erasmus. "I'll try to do better. Now, to come to the point, what is your definition of 'free choice'?"

"By 'free choice,' I mean a power of the human will by which man can either apply himself to the things that lead to eternal salvation or turn away from them. Free choice is supported in Sirach 15:14–17: '*God made man from the beginning and left him in the hand of his own council. If thou wilt observe the commandments and keep acceptable fidelity forever, they shall preserve thee. He hath set water and fire before thee; stretch forth thine hand for which thou wilt. Before man is life and death, good and evil; that which he shall choose shall be given to him.'* I don't think anybody will object to the authority of this work."

Luther remained in deep thought for a while, his chin on his chest. He lifted his head with a serious expression. "It is very prudent of you to give only a bare definition and not to explain any part of it, as others usually do. Perhaps you were afraid you might be shipwrecked on more than one point."

"You asked me for my definition. It is a simple one, and I feel no need to explain it. I'm sure that you'll do the wrecking."

"I am compelled to look at your definition anyway. I maintain that free choice belongs to no one but God alone. To attribute free choice to man in relation to divine things is too much. In the judgment of everybody, the term 'free choice' means that which can do and does, in relation to God, whatever it pleases, uninhibited by any law or sovereign authority."

"That last sentence befuddles me," said Erasmus with a frown. "What exactly do you mean? And who is everybody?"

"I mean that we cannot call man or angel 'free' when they live under absolute authority of God in such a way that they cannot subsist for a moment by their own strength. In your book, you make free choice a power of the human will, as if angels do not have free choice."

"I don't see what angels have to do with this, but go on."

"Let us come to those parts of your definition on which the whole matter hinges, namely 'apply' and 'turn away.' How are we going to define what this applying and turning away means?"

Erasmus could not resist saying, "It is plain to me."

"Don't interrupt me. You mention in the definition, 'things that lead to eternal salvation.' What is this all about?"

"I think you are nitpicking, my friend."

"You are to blame, sir. You gave the definition, not I, who is trying to understand it. For as the lawyers rightly say, if a man speaks obscurely when he could speak more clearly, his words are to be interpreted against him."

"My dear Luther, mine is just a simple definition, and I am afraid that you read far too much into it," said Erasmus, superbly at ease.

"Well, as I said earlier, you say less and attribute more to free choice than all others, in that you describe only part and not the whole of free choice, yet attribute everything to it." Luther continued to hammer his point. "When you say it can 'apply itself,' this means that you completely exclude the Holy Spirit, with all its power, as superfluous and unnecessary."

"May I remind you that I did not say apply *itself*. I said apply *himself*. However, I should add that free choice is only possible with the help of God's grace, which always accompanies human effort. Man's active motivation is required to accept or reject that precious gift."

"Thank you for that explanation. Although I could rightly reject your book, for the time being I will accept it so as not to waste time by getting involved in a dispute about the books received in the Hebrew canon. But let me reply briefly in your own words and say scripture is, in this passage, obscure and ambiguous, and therefore it proves nothing with certainty. We, however, as maintaining the negative, insist that you must produce a passage that shows convincingly, in unambiguous terms, what free choice is and can do." Luther relaxed after he said this. *So far, so good*, he thought.

"I am nearly a quarter through my book. How far are you?" asked Erasmus.

"I am at a third. We still have a long way to go."

"Are you ready for a break? I sure am."

"That's a good idea. I could stand a cold beer. How about you?" Luther stood up and stretched.

"I prefer a glass of wine," Erasmus replied amiably. "Care to join me?"

"Why not? We haven't come to blows."

"Where were we?" asked Erasmus when they resumed their dialogue.

"We finished with the free-choice dogma. You maintain that it exists, and I agreed to disagree."

"That's right, and I stipulated that divine grace is required. Actually, we speak of three graces. The first is implanted in man by nature and corrupted by sin. Since this grace is common to all, it should not be called grace, though it really is grace."

"Make up your mind, please," Luther interrupted.

"Just bear with me, dear sir. It will become clear as I go along. The sinner can reject this grace or accept it and begin to feel displeased with himself—he is aroused. The second is a distinctive grace that helps the sinner on his way to put off all the desire of sin. He regularly says his prayers, gives alms, goes to church, and, in general, behaves as a possible candidate for the highest grace. And if he continues to use the free choice that remains to him and puts his powers at the disposal of the divine, God extends to him the third grace, which they call pleasing grace. These three graces they think to be one. The first arouses, the second promotes, the third completes."

"I have listened to you patiently," said Luther. "And I wonder, my dear Erasmus, do you really know what you are saying? You seem to forget that until not long ago, I was a priest, and I have lived in a monastery at least as long as you have. Like you—or should I say, better than you—I studied the scriptures, and I never came across your three graces. I also noticed that during your presentation, you not once quoted a verse from the Bible in support of your three graces."

"Augustine wrote of the 'operative' grace,'" Erasmus replied.

"Augustine is not scripture. You proposed that we stick to the scriptures, remember? You said that free choice is a power of the human will, by which a man can apply himself to the good, but you now say that man without grace cannot will good."

"You're not quoting me correctly, Doctor. I said man can apply himself to the things that lead to eternal salvation or turn away from them. Please try to avoid incomplete quotes."

"Now it is my turn to use the word 'nitpicking.' What it comes down to is that you called your first grace not a real grace and, throughout, you speak of 'we' and 'they' without further explanation as to who you are talking about. You granted that man cannot will good without special grace. That means that it cannot apply itself to things that pertain to eternal salvation. He has lost that liberty and, perforce, is held fast in bondage to sin. There remains, therefore, an evil desire and an evil endeavor, the remnant of free choice without grace. Your first opinion denies that man can will anything good. The second holds that free will alone avails for nothing but sinning, which is also Augustine's view. The third and the most solid opinion is Wycliffe's and mine—that free choice is an empty name, and all that we do comes about by sheer necessity. It is with these two views that you quarrel in your book."

Luther had made some valid points. This time, it was Erasmus who did not reply immediately, and it was Luther who understood and waited patiently. After a while, Erasmus looked at Luther. "You know, Doctor, if you deny the scriptures to be clear on such a point about which so many great men have stumbled in darkness, our argument returns full circle. What it comes down to is that what people choose to claim for themselves is their own affair. If they say that Erasmus is an old vessel and is not capable of the new wine of the Spirit that they offer the world, and if they really rate themselves so highly, let them at least treat us as Christ treated Nicodemus. He didn't repulse him."

"I'll accept that. Now let's consider another issue," Luther suggested. "You quoted from Genesis 4:7, where the Lord says to Cain, '*The desire of sin shall be under thee, and thou shalt have dominion over it …*'"

"Wait," Erasmus interjected. "You left something out. The Lord says, '*If you do well, will thou not be accepted? And if you do not well, sin is crouching at the door. Its desire is for you and you must master it.*' Those six words—'And if you do not well'—make a whole lot of difference."

Luther chose to ignore the interruption. "It is shown here in your *Diatribe* that the motions of the mind toward evil can be overcome. That statement is ambiguous."

"Actually, it says, 'the motions of the will,' not 'of the mind,'" Erasmus corrected him again. "Let me remind you that I did not make that statement; it was God talking to Cain who said it. I also quoted what God said to Moses in Deuteronomy 30:15 and 19: '*I have set before your face the way of life and good, death and evil. Choose what is good.*' What could be put more plainly? God leaves man freedom to choose. It would be ridiculous to say 'choose,' if the power of turning one way or the other were not present."

"To all that, I say what is more plain than that you are blind here," Luther retorted. "By saying, 'choose,' do they then choose as soon as Moses says 'choose'? If that is the case, the Spirit is not necessary. How is it that you theologians spout drivel like people in their second childhood as soon as you get hold of an imperative word? Moses didn't say, 'Thou hast the strength or power to choose,' but 'choose,' as a command. Madam *Diatribe*, your reasoning is bad. In your blindness and carelessness, you only imagine that man's freedom to choose is proven."

"I must admit that you lost me there," said Erasmus. "You sure have a way of twisting a man's words. Let us now take examples from the New Testament. In Matthew 23:37, Christ weeps over the fate of Jerusalem after the killing of the prophets and the stoning of those He sent to them. *'I would have gathered you together ... and you would not.'* In other words, the people had a choice, and they chose not to come to Christ. And so the Gospel is replete with examples of free will."

"I'll grant for the moment that your proof is right and good," Luther said. "However, what, in fact, is proven by it? As I have said before, the secret will of the divine majesty is not a matter for debate. Human temerity, in its eagerness to prove this one point, must be called off and restrained from busying itself from the investigation of these secrets of God's majesty. When the will of the divine majesty purposely abandons and reprobates some to perish, it is not for us to ask why He does so, but to stand in awe of God, who both can do and will to do such things."

Erasmus noticed that Luther was really worked up. "Why is it that every time we reason about something, you fall back on the secret will of the divine majesty?" he asked. "I must admit that it is a clever way out, for there is no answer to your assertion. All right, then let's look at Paul and see whether he too assumes freedom of choice. In Romans 2:4, he said, *'Or do you despise the riches of His kindness and forbearance and patience? Do you know that God's kindness is meant to lead you to repentance?'* How can contempt of the commandment be brought against anyone when the will is not free? Or how does God invite to penitence if He is the author of impenitence?"

"If I may make an observation?" asked Luther. "First, you quote Paul and then you ask questions. Why don't you answer your own questions? You do that every time through your quotations of scripture. Christians are not led by free choice but by the Spirit of God, according to Romans 8:14."

"I believe that Christians are also led by sheer and inevitable necessity," replied Erasmus. "What is the point of praising obedience if in doing good or evil works, we are the kind of instrument for God that an ax is to a carpenter? But such a tool we all are, if Wycliffe is right. All things before and after grace, good equally with ill, are done with sheer necessity. Even you, Martin Luther, agreed. In your own words, you said, 'Wherefore it is needful to retract this article.' For I was wrong in saying that free choice before grace is a reality only in name. I should have said simply, 'Free choice is in reality a fiction, or a name without reality. For no one has it in his power to think a good or bad thought, but everything happens by absolute necessity.' These are your actual words, my friend."

"You will excuse me, please. I have to relieve myself," Luther pled, and he left the table.

When he returned, he did not answer Erasmus's challenge. Instead, he said, "You admit to our view in your *Diatribe* that the question of the will and determination of God is more difficult. For God to will and foreknow are the same thing. And this is what Paul means by '*Who can resist His will,*' and later, '*Thus the will of God, since it is the principal cause of all things that take place, seems to impose necessity upon our will.*' We can at last thank God that you have some sound sense."

"I'll take that as a compliment, dear Luther. However, I added that Paul rebuked the questioner: '*But who are you, a man, to answer back to God?*' Romans 9:20."

"There you go again. Like an eel, you wriggle your way out," Luther exclaimed, somewhat irritated. "What a beautiful evasion! Is this the way to treat the Holy Writ, pontificating like this on one's own authority and, in fact, corrupting the very clearest words of God?"

Erasmus smiled. "No, my friend, I am simply saying that God can, if He wills, do what He wills. In some cases, whatever God wills, He wills for good reasons, even though they are sometimes hidden from us."

Luther folded his arms across his chest and looked at his opponent with some resignation. "I admit that the question is difficult, and indeed, is impossible, if you wish to maintain at the same time both God's foreknowledge and man's freedom. This, then, is the place and the time for us to adore, not those Corycian caverns of yours, but the true majesty in His awful wonders and incomprehensible judgments, and to say, 'Thy will be done, on earth as it is in heaven.'"

"Amen. I could not agree more with you," said Erasmus with a nod to Luther. "You know, I am getting tired. Did you notice that it is already dark outside?"

"If by that you mean that you want to break up, that's fine with me. Shall we continue tomorrow morning?"

"Fine. I wish you a good night, my friend."

"And a good night to you too, dear Erasmus. Rest well, for I am not finished with you."

"Well, now," Luther began the next morning. "You mentioned that an oracle had spoken of Jacob and Esau that '*The greater shall serve the less,*' as Genesis 25 has it. Last night, I twice read what you wrote about these two and what Paul said subsequently, and I absolutely found no connection with our topic, free choice. May I perish if *Diatribe* herself knows what she is talking about."

Erasmus scratched his head and smoothed his hair. He turned to Luther. "You must have had a good sleep to be so sharp so early in the morning. You rightfully picked on that little chapter, for I must admit, it is a weak one."

"You were not at your best either with the next," said Luther. "The one about the potter and the clay. You yourself selected these passages that 'seem to oppose free choice.' You should have left this to your opponents, my friend. They do a much better job of it than you did."

"Well, then, let us examine how strong your arguments are against free choice. In your *DeServo*, you quoted Genesis 6:3. '*My spirit shall not abide in man forever, for he is flesh.*' You should have said, 'for that he is *also* flesh.' I take it to mean the weakness of our nature, which is prone to sin."

"I consider that a frivolity," Luther replied. "You also went back to Jerome, even though we had agreed to stick to scripture only. The man is not much more than a perverter of scripture."

"Those are your words, not mine," Erasmus admonished Luther. "You cannot deny the quote, '*My spirit will not judge these men forever, for they are flesh.*'"

"Moses said that," Luther interrupted. "Not Jerome."

"I know that, my friend. There is a clemency in those words. God gives man a chance to repent before he receives eternal punishment. And if no part of repentance depends on the will of man, but all things are done by God through a certain necessity, why is man given room for repentance? However, man does not get forever. God added, '*But his days shall be a hundred and twenty years.*'"

"A hundred and twenty years of being judged, that is," Luther said. "Since on the testimony of God Himself, men are flesh and have a taste for nothing but flesh, it follows that free choice avails for nothing but sinning."

"If that were so, why does God give man a chance? He can take it or leave it; it is his choice, his free choice. You take this flesh business much too literally. 'Flesh' is what God calls our created weakness, which is prone to evil. But this proneness to evil that is in most men does not take away free choice altogether."

Luther elected to change course. "Let us look at your example of the passage from Isaiah 40:2. *'She has received from the Lord's hand double for all her sins.'* You said that Jerome interprets this in terms of divine vengeance, not of grace given in return for our evil deeds. I see! Jerome says so; therefore, it is true! Didn't we promise to conduct our debate on the basis of the scriptures? What do I care what Jerome said ages ago? Let's not forget that 'she' in the passage is not a woman; it is Jerusalem. When Isaiah said, *'She has received from the Lord's hand double for all her sin,'* that means not only the forgiveness of sins but also the end of the warfare. It is as if God said when He referred to the soldiers, *'for I see they are unable not to sin, especially when they are fighting.'"*

"A point well taken," Erasmus acknowledged. "You also quoted Isaiah 40:6–8, *'All flesh is grass, and all that is glory is like the flower of the grass. The grass withers and the flower fades, because the Lord blows upon it … but the word of our God will stand forever.'* It seems to me very forced to apply this to the subject of grace and free choice."

"That's simple. By 'grass,' Isaiah means 'the people.'" Luther ignored Erasmus. "When he says 'all flesh,' what else does he mean but 'all the grass' or 'all the people'?"

"I repeat," Erasmus said patiently, "what is the connection with free choice?"

Again, Luther did not answer him and instead continued to talk about the flesh, adding numerous quotations from the Bible. After a while, Erasmus stopped him. "Dear Doctor, there is more to the human body than flesh. There is also a part called the soul and that which is called his spirit with which we strive after virtue."

When Luther did not pick up on the lead just offered him, Erasmus continued, "Why do I get the impression that you did not read the last chapters of my book? Did you read them?"

"No, I did not."[35]

"At least you are honest about it. However, be that as it may, I see no purpose in continuing our debate." He stood up from his chair.

The sudden move took Luther completely by surprise. "But we are not yet through with what I have written," he protested.

"My good man, what you have written is four times as long as what I wrote, and I read it all," replied Erasmus coolly. "In summary, I believe that man has a free choice, and you deny its existence. I may add that I have admired your courage when you nailed your Ninety-Five Theses on that church door, and I have followed your defense with great interest. You are a brave man, Martin Luther."

"And you too, dear Erasmus, are the brave man. It was only after I read your *Praise of Folly* that my eyes opened, and I published the Theses. Our debate clearly brought out how much we have in common." With a twinkle in his eyes, Luther added, "Why don't you join me in the Reformation?"

Erasmus laughed. "No, dear Doctor. Until I hear of a better Church, I'll stay with the one I have. I have said my piece; you have my opinion."

Luther replied, *"Non contuli, sed asserui et assero."*[36]

---

[35] E. Gordon Rupp, p.10. "Luther took no notice at all of the last three chapters of Erasmus, which are perhaps the best part of the work."

[36] "I have not discussed the issue but rather I have asserted and do assert."

20

❦

A Married Man

1524–1525

Marries Katie von Bora - Wedding gift of a cloister - The social structure of sixteenth-century Germany - The Peasants' War - Luther's disgrace

"So when are you going to find a wife?" old Hans Luder grumbled to his son during one of his infrequent visits to Wittenberg. The lines on his face had softened with age; he was sixty-four years old. He was a well-to-do man and was dressed in a fur-lined jacket, as behooved the owner of several mines and two copper smelters. His hands, which were once hard and dirty from working in the mines, were soft and clean. He had a full head of wavy white hair that extended to just below his ears. "Many of your friends already have a wives, so why not you? I want to see a grandson before I die, and your mother wants a granddaughter."

Martin laughed. "Father, I'm not against marriage, and I promise that when the right woman comes around, I'll marry her."

"Well, don't wait too long. I was twenty-one when you were born. You're not getting any younger, you know."

"I've heard that before," Martin half-heartedly replied.

Katharina von Bora told Martin's friend, Nicholaus Amsdorf, that she would only marry him or Luther. When Amsdorf held up both hands in reply, she began to make a habit of "accidentally" running into Martin around town. Martin fell for her tactic, and on June 13, 1525, they became man and wife at forty-two and twenty-six years of age, respectively. Their first home was an Augustinian cloister on the outskirts of Wittenberg, called the Black Cloister.[37] The complex was a wedding gift from Elector John Frederick, the son of Martin's protector Frederick the Wise. A boisterous crowd of guests and well-wishers escorted them to the heavy door of their new home. Martin opened it just wide enough for him and Katharina to slip inside and then needed all his strength to keep the rowdiest of his friends outside.

Once inside, the couple walked hand-in-hand toward the bedroom.

"I think I'll wash my hands, if you don't mind," said Katie at the door, and she turned to go to the kitchen.

"And I will make sure that all the windows are closed," said Martin. He took his time and when he came into the bedroom, she already lay on the bed with the covers drawn up to her nose. He undressed in a corner and slipped the long nightgown over his head. He went to the bed, lay down, and waited.

"Put the candle out, please," she said quietly.

Martin sat up, reached for the candle, and blew it out. It was pitch-dark in the room. He lay down again and turned toward his new wife. Suddenly, they were startled by the loud ringing of a bell.

"What's that?" Katie exclaimed as she bolted upright.

"The rascals are pulling the bell. Don't you hear?"

"Where is it?"

"At the door. Where else?" Martin threw the sheet off and got out of bed.

"Oh, come back, Martin. Let's ignore them, please."

"We can't. They'll keep doing it until I pay them off."

"Pay them off? You can't do that," she insisted.

"Wife, don't you know that it is a custom? They won't give us any peace until I pay their drinking money."

---

[37] Not to be confused with the Black Cloister in Erfurt, where Luther began his life as a monk in 1505.

With a candle in hand, Martin walked the long corridor to the door. The crowd let out a loud cheer when he opened the heavy door, and their chosen leader held out his hand. Martin gave him some coins.

"Now, off you go," he said, and they left, singing and laughing.

Just to be on the safe side, Martin lifted the bell from its hinge and took it inside.

"They won't be back again," he said, as he climbed back in bed.

They lay side by side. Neither made a move. Their hands met in the narrow space between them.

"Martin, what do we do now?" she whispered.

"Well, Katie, we … eh …" Martin cleared his throat.

"Hush," she said and moved over.

Martin was the first to wake up, early the next morning. With his hands behind his head, he gazed up at the low ceiling and its sturdy beams, thinking about the wonders of their first night together. He listened to his wife's soft breathing, and when he turned to look at her, he saw her face adorned with the trace of a smile. He gave a long, deep sigh and snuggled up to her.

Katie eventually bore Martin six children, two of whom unfortunately died at an early age. She farmed the lands of the former monastery, brewed beer, and bred and sold cattle—far more than was expected of a wife. Through it all, she maintained her sense of humor.

"The time will come when a man will take more than one wife," Martin teased her one day.

"Let the devil believe that," she shot back.

"It is simple, Katie. You can only bear one child a year while I can beget many."

"Didn't Paul say that each man should have his own wife?" she retorted, smiling.

"True, but he did not say 'his only wife.'"

Katie had the last word. "I'm not putting up with this. I'd rather go back to the convent and leave you with all the children."

"Just kidding, just kidding," Martin said, chuckling good-naturedly.

In the same year that Luther married, peasants throughout Germany were in open rebellion against the princes in a movement collectively known as the Peasants' War. Luther's reaction to the rebels would forever tarnish his reputation among the peasant class.

In sixteenth-century Germany, the top rung of the social ladder was occupied by the kings and princes. Their lands were subdivided into numerous secular and ecclesiastic entities, nearly all of which were ruled by noble dynasties, who stood on the second rung. On the third rung stood the lesser nobility, consisting mainly of knights who were lower-ranking army or navy officers. Although far richer than the lesser nobility, the patricians only rated the fourth rung. They were the descendents of the wealthy families, sat on city councils, and held the all-important administrative offices. The burghers stood on the fifth rung; they included merchants, guildsmen, and artisans. The lowest rung was for the plebs— the workmen, the journeymen, the landless, and citizens without rights. The peasants had no place on the ladder, and to make matters worse, everyone on the ladder exacted taxes on those below them, which meant that the brunt of the taxes ultimately fell on the peasants.

Peasants had severely limited rights. A peasant was not allowed to fish, hunt, or chop wood. When a peasant wanted to marry, he had to ask permission from his lord, who could, in turn, demand the right of the first night with the bride. The lord could cancel a farmer's lease at will or raise his rental fee. When a farmer died, his lord took his best cattle and anything else he wished and evicted his widow from her home to make room for another farmer. Last, when a lord or prince went to war, his peasants served as his soldiers. There was no redress from such injustice, because peasants were not permitted to enter a courtroom.

The latter half of the fifteenth century and the first quarter of the sixteenth century saw a marked increase in the technology and volume of shipbuilding in western Europe and England. Better ships and navigation maps made it possible for adventurous captains to sail to distant harbors. This led to an enormous increase in the availability of merchandise, which, in turn, led to the formation of a new class of merchants, who inevitably began to exercise a power never seen before by those standing on the upper four rungs of the social ladder; the middle class was born. The lower classes, too, benefited from the considerable wealth of the merchants, and common people began to discover their own strength. They spoke up, where before they had remained silent.

At the same time, the power of the printing press and the distribution of works such as Erasmus's *The Praise of Folly* and Luther's Ninety-Five Theses helped expose the wrongdoings of the church. Those standing on the higher rungs of the societal ladder were emboldened to speak out against the clergy. They opposed the privileges of the church leaders, which they perceived as unearned. People on the lower rungs found a new freedom of speech and writing, and it was only a matter of time before even those on the lowest rung felt free to speak out against those who occupied the rungs above them.

The peasants, however, experienced none of these newfound freedoms. They had no education, were illiterate, and lived their entire lives as serfs in a feudal society. Whenever a few peasants organized themselves, word would reach their prince, whose henchmen would put a brutal end to it. The hangman's noose was patient, and bodies were left swaying in the breeze.

Although no leader sprang from the ranks of the peasantry, their plight was taken up by Thomas Müntzer (c. 1489–1525), the son of a well-to-do family and who had studied Greek, Latin, and Hebrew at the Universities of Leipzig and Frankfurt. Müntzer was twenty-eight years old when Luther published the Ninety-Five Theses, and he added to them his own more radical views, such as rejecting all forms of baptism. He asserted that the persons who wrote the Bible could not be certain about the truth of what they wrote, nor could they prove it. He believed that only a divine spirit could interpret the Bible and maintained that Christian revelations were not only an experience of the distant past but were also revelations of the present.

"That man is much too radical for me," Luther preached. "He has swallowed the Holy Ghost, feathers and all."

"Luther is a Dr. Easychair, who basks in the favor of the princes," Müntzer shot back. As the new minister in the Saxon town of Alstedt, he gathered a large following around him. "I am ready to slaughter the ungodly," he called out, and his listeners hung on every word. In June

1523, Müntzer proclaimed himself a "messenger of Christ," a prophet. He married a former nun and lived in the kingdom of Bohemia, where he urged the citizenry to build an Apostolic Church. He used Luther's Reformation as a vehicle to create a political movement to rid the country of clericalism and feudalism. In March 1524, he led them to a chapel of the Virgin Mary. "No more false idolatry," he yelled, and he put a torch to the building.

It was too much for Martin. In August, he wrote to the court of Frederick the Wise, "*I am having a terrible time with the Satan of Alstedt. Kindliness and letters do not suffice. The sword that is ordained of God to punish evil must be used with energy.*"

In early August 1524, Müntzer moved to the small German town of Muehlhausen, where he was joined by a renegade priest, Heinrich Pfeiffer. The farmers and weavers of Muehlhausen, tired of being exploited, were in open rebellion against their princes, and Müntzer joined them in their effort. In the meantime, peasants in many other parts of Germany had risen in rebellion, and large numbers of plebeians joined them. These rebellions became known collectively as the Peasants' War. The leaders of the rebellion prepared numerous articles of complaints, all to no avail.

They sought Luther's support but did not receive it. He rejected their complaints and supported the right of the princes to suppress the rebellion. In his 1525 treatise *Wider die räuberischen und mürderischen Rotten der Bauern* (Against the Robbing and Murdering Hordes of Peasants), Luther infamously wrote:

> If the peasant is in open rebellion, then he is outside the law of God, for rebellion is not simply murder; it is like a great fire which attacks and lays waste a whole land. Thus rebellion brings with it a land full of murders and bloodshed, makes widows and orphans, and turns everything upside-down like a great disaster.
>
> Therefore, let everyone who can smite, slay, and stab, secretly or openly, remembering that nothing can be more poisonous, hurtful or devilish than a rebel. It is just as when one must kill a mad dog; if you don't strike him, he will strike you and the whole land with you.

Luther defended his extreme position through St. Paul's doctrine of the Divine Right of Kings in Romans 13:1–7, which he interpreted to say that the ruler is the minister of God, the power of God, and should not be resisted. Further, he claimed that the minister of God is a revenger who bears a sword to execute wrath upon those who do evil. However, he chose not to recognize as evil the rulers who exploited their power. Had his hatred of Müntzer clouded his judgment to the point that he sided with the princes against the common people?

In the meantime, Müntzer and Pfeiffer organized the citizens of Muehlhausen to overthrow the town council. Nearby in Frankenhausen, the citizenry and peasants surrounded their town. Müntzer joined them with three hundred fighters from Muehlhausen. Peasants from other townships came in droves to join them, and by May 11, 1525, approximately eight thousand fighters were camped out on the fields of Frankenhausen. They had no military training and were armed with only clubs, pitchforks, and sickles. When the superbly armed and trained armies of Hesse and Saxony arrived on the field, most of the peasants surrendered. On May 15, the Hessian and Saxon soldiers attacked the remainder of the peasants with cavalry, infantry, and artillery. Only six hundred were taken prisoners; the rest were butchered. By contrast, only six soldiers were killed in the battle. Müntzer and Pfeiffer were captured, tortured, and beheaded. Their heads were impaled on poles and put on display at the main gate of Frankenhausen.

Through the use of similar brute force, the princes crushed numerous other peasant rebellions throughout southern and western Germany, Switzerland, and Austria, and peace was eventually restored. An estimated one million peasants had been brutally murdered, many burned at the stake.

Luther's "smite, slay, and stab" treatise brought him disgrace for the rest of his life. The peasants of Germany called him a traitor and a double-tongued preacher. He never preached in farming communities again, other than those near his safe haven of Wittenberg.

21

---◆◇◆---

Luther - The Church Leader

1525–1535

Argues and reconciles with Andreas Karlstadt - Deaths of Johann von Staupitz and Frederick the Wise - The Augsburg Confessions - Dispute with Zwingli - The Marburg Articles - Melanchthon to the rescue - Meets with Bucer - A united German church

During the Peasants' War, an unlikely visitor rang the bell of the Black Cloister seeking refuge. Martin was surprised to see that Andreas Karlstadt, his former colleague and defender in Leipzig, had come to him for help. Luther and Karlstadt had had a dramatic falling out two years earlier after Martin's triumphant return to Wittenberg, following his year in hiding.

While he was confined in Wartburg Castle, Martin had received the news that Dr. Karlstadt had adopted numerous reforms in his church—he wore secular clothing, preached in German, and had removed all images of saints. Upon his return to Wittenberg, Luther was alarmed to discover that Dr. Karlstadt had become even more radical, going so far as to proclaim that newborns should not be baptized. "You are moving much too fast, Andreas," warned Martin, who had resumed wearing the black cowl of his Augustinian order. He looked Karlstadt up and down. "Look at you, dressed like that in civilian clothes. You are a monk, remember?"

"No, I am not a monk, and as far as I am concerned, I have never been one," said Karlstadt with great emphasis.

"Who gave you permission to preach against baptism?"

"Nobody, Martin. You seem to forget that while you were locked up for a year, the Reformation moved on. You are behind the times. You have some catching up to do."

"I will not tolerate disobedience in my Church." Martin moved chest-to-chest with the much smaller Karlstadt.

"What do you mean *your* Church?" Andreas's chin jutted out as he looked up at Luther. His voice trembled with indignation as he continued. "It is *our* Church, and we will completely break with the old one, not just in the interpretation of the Bible but also in the appearance of our churches—no more statues of so-called saints, you hear? We'll tear them all down."

"That's it!" Martin thundered. "You're out of my Church! Pack up your belongings and leave Wittenberg this instant!"

"I'm gone," Karlstadt said with a sneer. He turned abruptly and walked away, the picture of disgust. Over his shoulder, he yelled, "You can have *your* so-called Church!"

The break between the two friends was complete. Karlstadt moved to Orlamünde, where he became pastor in the parish church and immediately applied his reforms, including a ban on church music. He even went so far as to deny the physical presence of Christ in the church. "Christ has a *spiritual* presence within our communion," he preached, and his flock nodded in approval. However, if Karlstadt thought that Luther would leave him in peace once he left Wittenberg, he was wrong. Martin began an intense campaign against him, starting by denying him the right to publish. In July 1524, Luther published a "Letter to the Saxon Princes," in which he argued that Karlstadt was a sectarian, a revolutionary, and a danger to the authorities. It was the end of the irascible preacher.

A month later, Martin received a note from Karlstadt, asking to see him. Martin agreed, and Karlstadt appeared before him, hungry, disheveled, and without a penny to buy a meal. "Can you give me one good reason why I should talk to you?" said Luther sternly. "You are a revolutionary, just like Müntzer."

"Dr. Luther, I have always rejected violence in name of religion."

"But you joined Müntzer."

"No, sir, I did not. He approached me, but I rejected his invitation to join him."

"Hm." Martin looked at his former friend and softened. "Here, take this guilder and get yourself a good meal, but you must promise to write against Müntzer."

"Thank you. I will." Andreas backed out of the room.

Several months later, with the Peasants' War was in full swing, Luther opened the door of the Black Cloister and was confronted with the sight of a bedraggled Karlstadt and his pregnant wife, seeking refuge from Müntzer and his followers. Martin let them in his house. However, possibly to cover himself in the eyes of the world, he ordered Andreas to sign a retraction titled *Apology by Dr. Andreas Karlstadt Regarding the False Charge of Insurrection Which Has Unjustly Been Made Against Him.*

Karlstadt and his wife remained in the Luther household for six weeks, and during that time, their lost friendship was restored—enough so that Andreas later named Katie as godmother to his child. After leaving the Black Cloister, Andreas worked as a bartender, farmer, and peddler until 1529, when he moved Switzerland to become a minister. In 1534, he became the professor of Hebrew and dean of the University of Basel. He wrote extensively and significantly influenced Ulrich Zwingli and the Swiss Protestant movement. He died of the plague on December 24, 1541.

With the Reformation in its infancy, Martin Luther needed to find a way of promulgating the new Church as widely and as quickly as possible. Many German princes and theologians had already accepted the new Church and the German translation of the New Testament, but Luther knew that ultimately, his word had to reach those who could not read his writings: the farmers, laborers, and the commoners. The illiterate classes faithfully went to church to hear Mass given in Latin, which they could not understand. The younger generation, however, had heard Luther preach in German in Wittenberg and throughout Saxony, and they would become most effective in spreading Luther's word.

The mother of one of Luther's students at Wittenberg sent him a little lamb made of wax, with the words *Agnus Dei* cut into its side; it was meant to protect him from mishaps. The student wrote to her in reply:

> Liebe Mutter [Dear Mother], you should not be upset over Dr. Martin Luther's teaching, nor worry about me. Honestly, the lamb won't do me any good and I am sending it back to you because God's word teaches me to trust only in Jesus Christ. I don't thank you one bit less, but I pray God that you won't believe any more in sacred salt and holy water and all this devil's tomfoolery. Please do not give the lamb to my brother. I hope that father will let me stay longer in Wittenberg. Read Dr. Luther's New Testament; it is on sale in Leipzig. I am going to buy a brown hat. Love to my dear father and brother and sisters.

It was just the kind of support Luther needed to transfer his message from generation to generation. He continued to bring his word directly to the people through his daily preaching, his many writings, and the distribution of his German New Testament.

In late 1524, personal tragedy struck. Within less than five months, Martin lost the two people who had helped him most in life. Johann von Staupitz, who had recognized his potential, encouraged him to gain his doctorate, assigned him to take on important tasks for the Church, and stood by him during his inquisition, died on December 28, 1524. Frederick the Wise, who had sheltered him from danger and refused to arrest him when Pope Leo ordered him to do so, died on May 5, 1525. To make matters even worse, Georg Spalatin decided after the death of his employer that he was no longer needed at court. He married and assumed the role of occasional advisor to Frederick's successors. He took up residence as canon at Altenburg, visited the churches and schools in Saxony, and supervised ecclesiastical revenues. Although he was a regular visitor in Wittenberg, his general absence added to the great void that descended on Martin in such a short time.

Fortunately, Martin's trusted friend Philipp Melanchthon stayed by his side. The dwarfish, skinny man with hollow cheeks, somewhat bulging eyes, and a sharp hooked nose had a serene disposition. Only the best character qualities applied to him: he was honest, modest, noble, and generous to a fault. Without even trying, he had a calming influence on Martin. When, to the surprise of many, he married the mayor's daughter, the beautiful Katharina Krapp, Martin could not have been more pleased.

In early 1530, Melanchthon played an important role in the development of Lutheranism. On March 11, the electors received notice from Emperor Charles V, calling a diet in Augsburg on April 8. The leading evangelicals regarded the news with jaundiced eyes. "What does Charles have in mind this time?" the electors wondered.

"I think we had better be prepared for another round about religion," Elector John of Saxony, Frederick's successor, proffered. He ordered Luther, Melanchthon, Justus Jonas, and Johannes Bugenhagen to prepare a formal document explaining Lutheranism and a list of the ways in which Lutheranism differed from Catholicism. The four men were to meet Elector John with the result of their work on April 3 in his castle in Torgau. After reading their first draft, John looked up and commented, "Not a bad start." The group decided to call the document the Torgau Articles and continued to revise and refine it on their journey to Augsburg, two hundred fifty miles away.

Approximately one-third of the way through their trip, they reached the city of Coburg, and Elector John instructed Martin to stay there. "We are at the border of Saxony, and I can no longer protect you if you cross it. Remember, you are still an outlaw in the eyes of the emperor."

"I will stay in the Black Swan Inn, where you can reach me if you need me," Martin promised.

The remainder of the trip to Augsburg took twenty-nine days, during which time Melanchthon and his colleagues worked diligently on the official defense of Lutheranism. On May 11, a runner on horseback brought the draft to Luther, who approved it with minor changes. When they arrived in Augsburg, Philipp sought additional input from the bishop of that city, Chancellor Bruck of Saxony, and from the imperial secretary, Alfonso Valdez. On June 23, the final document was signed by Elector John,

Margrave George of Brandenburg, Duke Ernest of Luneburg, Landgrave Philip of Hesse, the Prince Wolfgang of Anhalt, and city representatives of Nuremberg and Reutlingen. Together, they represented a large part of Germany.

Elector John went to see the emperor. "Your Majesty, the documents explaining Lutheranism are ready for presentation."

"Good. You can present them to the diet tomorrow morning in City Hall," Charles said rather gruffly. He always felt like a stranger in Germany and yearned to go back to his palace in Belgium.

"We wish to make the presentation in German," Elector John added lightly, as if it were just a minor issue.

Charles leaned his right arm on the armrest of his chair and looked sternly at the man standing before him. "There will be no such reading, Elector."

Elector John stood his ground. "Your Majesty, I am authorized to state that the signers of the document will not hand it over without permission to read it aloud beforehand."

Charles sat thinking while the elector patiently waited. Then the emperor leaned far back in his chair with a bored expression. "You can have your reading, but it shall be in Latin, not German. You will be notified where the presentation shall take place." He raised a slack hand as a signal that the meeting was over.

On the morning of June 25, a huge crowd gathered on the square before the closed doors of the City Hall, where the diet normally was held. The people were in a festive mood, for this was the first time that a Holy Roman emperor had visited their town. They had no idea why he had come, and they didn't really care—they were there to enjoy the pageantry and get a glimpse of the emperor and his entourage dressed in their finery. After an hour of impatient waiting, a town clerk appeared before the crowd and announced, "The presentation will take place at the Episcopal palace."

"They tried to fool us!" yelled the people in front. "Let's go!" And in a mad rush, the crowd ran to the palace, only to be informed that the presentation would be held in the palace's chapel, which was just large enough to hold the party of presenters, the emperor, and his attendants.

The majority of the crowd dispersed, disgruntled that the emperor would not appear in public.

On Charles's signal, Saxon Chancellor Bruck stepped forward holding a Latin copy of the documents. Chancellor Beyer stood beside him holding a German copy. In a booming voice that could be heard not only by those inside the chapel but also the remainder of the crowd outside, Beyer began to read the German copy aloud. Emperor Charles's head snapped up, his face tight-lipped and furious—his plan had failed. He thought that by changing the venue of the meeting and forcing a reading in Latin, he could prevent the signers of the document from reaching the people. Instead, he had been duped, as Beyer read the documents in booming German for all to hear and understand. Bruck and Beyer handed the two copies over to Charles, who kept the Latin version and indicated to Beyer to give his copy to the imperial chancellor, the elector of Mainz.

Afterward, Melanchthon edited the first publication of the documents in both Latin and German, and they became known officially as the *Augsburg Confession*. The Confession consists of twenty-one Chief Articles of Faith, describing the principles of faith of the Lutheran Church and seven additional articles correcting the abuses of Christian faith in the Catholic Church.

The court of Charles V and representatives of the Vatican discussed at length how to respond to the Augsburg Confession. Although they finally came to an agreement in a document called *The Pontifical Confutation*, it was never published or formally presented to the Lutherans. Charles nevertheless demanded that the Lutherans respond to the Confutation by April 15, 1531. Melanchthon took up his pen for the Lutherans and defended the Augsburg Confession and dismissed the Confutation in a document called *The Apology*, which was published in German and made available throughout country.[38]

Article X of the Augsburg Confession states, "*Christ is truly present in the bread and wine of the Sacrament.*" This simple statement belies the firestorm of bitter disagreement over the true meaning of the sacrament that took place a

---

[38] Shortly before he abdicated in 1556, Charles made peace with the German princes and granted legal status to Lutheranism within the Holy Roman Empire in Germany but not in the Netherlands.

year earlier between two factions of the Protestant Reformation: the Lutherans in Germany and the Swiss-based Protestants, led by Ulrich Zwingli. The disagreement centered on translation of a three-letter Latin word—*est.*

Corinthians 11:24 states that at the Last Supper, Jesus took bread, gave thanks, broke it, and said, "*hoc est corpus meum pro vobis hoc facite in meam commemorationem* [take, eat: this is my body, which is broken for you: this, do in remembrance of me]." Luther believed in a simple, direct translation of *hoc est corpus meum* (this is my body). He maintained that the human body of Christ was present in all places. Therefore, His body is present in the communion bread, and the believer eats the body of Christ.

Zwingli took the same phrase and translated the word *est* to mean "signifies." As a result, he considered communion bread and the wine to be purely symbolic, representing the body and blood of Christ. Zwingli maintained that the human body of Christ can only be in one place at any given time; therefore, it is the spirit of Christ that is present when Mass is said, not His body.

Landgrave Philip of Hesse was deeply concerned about the division in the new Church, believing that it made it more vulnerable to the Holy Roman emperor. He invited the leaders of both factions to try to resolve their dispute in a three-day meeting in Marburg, beginning on October 1, 1529. Zwingli and Johannes Oecolampadius, a reformer in Basel who was also a friend of Erasmus, arrived in Marburg on September 28, and Luther and Melanchthon arrived the next day. Also attending was Zwingli's supporter Martin Bucer, the former Dominican monk who had congratulated Luther after his disputation in Heidelberg in 1518.

To the Landgrave's pleasant surprise, the two sides agreed on fourteen of fifteen major articles that had been prepared in advance. However, Luther and Zwingli refused to compromise on the fifteenth article discussing the presence of Christ in the Eucharist, and the parties left without uniting. The results of the meeting were published in the Marburg Articles, which contained the fourteen agreed-upon articles and a fifteenth article that included both parties' views. The end result was the formation of two different reformed confessions.

In the meantime, Luther continued to work on his German translation of the Old Testament. He visited towns and villages to listen to the language of the common people and use it as a basis for his translation. With the aid of five assistants, including Melanchthon, he completed the text in 1534. The Luther Bible, containing his previously finished New Testament and the newly finished Old Testament, was published in Wittenberg by Hans Lufft in 1534.[39] It contained 117 woodcut illustrations produced by the workshop of Lucas Cranach. The combination of the use of the German vernacular and illustrations brought the Bible to life for the common people. The Luther Bible was widely distributed throughout the land and greatly helped develop and unify the German language.

During the same year, Luther received news that Zwingli had been killed while leading Protestant Swiss forces against the armies of the Catholic Cantons in the Battle of Kappel. "He shouldn't have wielded a sword," Martin remarked dryly. Oecolampadius died not long thereafter, and Switzerland was left without a potent reformed church leader.

That is when Melanchthon stepped in. He began a behind-the-scenes correspondence with the only prominent figure left in the Zwingli camp, Martin Bucer, who was at that time a preacher in Strasbourg, Germany, on the River Rhine. In 1534, Philipp obtained permission from the Landgrave to meet with Bucer and make another attempt to settle the dispute over the Eucharistic controversy. Luther also gave his permission, but in his instructions to Melanchthon, he insisted that at the Eucharist, "the body of Christ is distributed, eaten, and chewed with the teeth."

Melanchthon met Bucer in December 1534. He was somewhat surprised when Bucer indicated that he was one of Luther's earliest admirers and was willing to meet with him. Melanchthon arranged a follow-up meeting between the two in Wittenberg.

"Dear Dr. Luther, I am so happy and so honored to meet with you again," said an exuberant Bucer, extending his hand.

"So am I, dear Dr. Bucer. So am I," said Martin, and they warmly shook hands. Turning to Melanchthon, he laughed. "How do you suggest we continue this conversation between us two Martins?"

Melanchthon threw up his hands. "I am not going to touch that. You two gentlemen figure it out by yourself."

---

[39] Lufft printed thirteen editions during Luther's lifetime, and over 100,000 copies between 1534 and 1574.

"Since I am younger, why don't you call me Junior?" Bucer proposed. The suggestion elicited a boisterous laugh from Martin.

"I like that, especially coming from an ex-Dominican," he said, with a friendly slap on Junior's shoulder. "Now that you have come more than halfway, how do you think we should proceed?"

"First, let me assure you that I have never preached that the bread and the wine are mere symbols of the body of Christ."

"Then what do you understand the bread and wine to be?"

"They are the soul, the spirit of Christ. When Christ indicated that although bodily He would no longer be with His disciples, He meant that spiritually He would remain with them."

Martin was deeply touched by the sincerity of his younger colleague. He walked to his desk, took the Bible from it, and opened it in front of them. "Brother Bucer, in Luke 22:19, Christ took bread and gave thanks and broke it, and gave it to them, saying, 'This is my body which is given for you: do this in remembrance of me.' You do believe in the Bible, don't you, Brother?"

Junior bent his head and slowly spread his hands out over the edge of the table and brought them together again. He then leaned back and folded his arms across his chest. He looked at the man he admired so much. "Yes, Martin, I do, and I also know that the Book says the same in 1 Corinthians 11:24, 25. And I have come to think that Zwingli was in error. But it is not easy to comprehend that the body of Christ is present in the bread."

"My friend—for that is what you are again—the body of Christ being present is not a myth. It is *mystical*, beyond human comprehension. It is a deep belief that sets us Lutherans apart, us Protestants separate from the Catholics. It is taken directly from the Bible, and we are true believers in what the Bible tells us."

Bucer slowly stood up out of his chair and moved around the table, his arms widespread. Luther too got up, and the two men embraced. A choked-up Bucer looked at his new friend and said, "I will join you as one."

True brothers again, Martin was jubilant. He opened the door and yelled as hard as he could, "Philipp, come back here! You succeeded!"

Landgrave Hesse was elated when he heard the news. Finally, all of Germany was united in one living faith.

22

———⟫◦⟪———

Erasmus—The Last Years

1526–1536

The Ciceronian - Beatus publishes the Epistolae - Oecolampadius and reform in Basel - Visit from Charles Blount - Henry VIII and his wives - Deaths of Wolsey, Fisher, and More - Lieve God

In 1526, Erasmus once more addressed Luther and the issue of free choice in his *Hyperaspistes*, a lengthy two-part volume[40] in which he summed up his position about his Church:

> I have never been an apostate from the Catholic Church. I know that in the Church, which you call the Papist Church, there are many who displease me, but such I also see in your Church. One bears more easily the evils to which one is accustomed. Therefore, I bear with this Church until I see a better, and it cannot help bearing me, until I shall myself be better. He does not sail badly who steers a middle course between several evils.

---

[40] Huizinga dismissed this work as "nothing but an epilogue, which need not be discussed at length."

His heyday of writing was over. He continued to publish but often spent time and effort on unimportant topics, such as *Ichthyophagia* (1526), a fifty-one–page personal colloquium about his hatred of fish-eating. He had long claimed that the eating of salted fish on fasting days was bad for his delicate nature. The previous year, he had pleaded his case with Cardinal Campeggio and obtained a dispensation from fast. This was followed in 1529 by a long essay *On Education for Children*, in which he lectures the Duke of Cleves on the education of his thirteen-year-old son, William. The essay is verbose, about fifteen thousand words, and says little: "Choose a good tutor for your son" was the best advice he gave the duke. The work was not a success.

His next essay, *De civilitate* (On Good Manners), published in 1530, was much shorter at 4,800 words, and it was an immediate success. Within one year, a dozen editions were published, and it was translated into several languages. He dedicated the essay to the eleven-year-old Henry of Veere, the son of his erstwhile benefactor, Anna of Veere, and his intended readers were "children of illustrious descent." His advice included keeping the eyes calm, respectful, and steady; and keeping the nostrils free of filthy mucus and refraining from wiping the nose on one's cap or clothing. He further instructed that when breaking wind in company, one should cover the sound with a cough. He reminded his young audience that the essence of good manners consisted of freely pardoning the shortcomings of others.

In 1528, Erasmus published a more substantial work, a classic satire as only he could write. In *The Ciceronian: A Dialogue on the Ideal Latin Style*, he criticized the self-proclaimed "pure" Latin scholars in Italy who lauded Cicero as their linguistic hero and considered any author who did not quote Cicero to be a barbarian. Erasmus lampooned them in a dialogue, using the same technique he employed years before in *The Praise of Folly*.

> My friends, it never ceases to amaze me how many people pride themselves on speaking correct Latin and how few really do. The trouble with that ancient language is that nearly every word is open to one or more interpretations and that in time several incorrect interpretations have crept in that are now considered correct by many. While

I was in Italy there was a large group of natives who maintained that only Italians spoke correct Latin. Cicero was their hero and they called themselves Ciceronians; together they formed a tightly controlled social club, not unlike the many snobbish clubs we see these days. People went to great length to become a Ciceronian. Let me illustrate that for you with the following story, which took place recently.

Three friends met in Rome and one of them, Nosoponus, who was clearly behind the time, said, "I pride myself in only using those words that can be found in the writings of Cicero and I will never read books written by other philosophers, especially not of the Greeks."

"I was recently invited to hear a speech by a noted speaker, who aspired after Ciceronian eloquence just like you, Nosoponus," said Bulephorus, the counselor. "His topic was the death of Christ. In attendance were Pope Julius II and rows of cardinals and bishops. He first sung the praises of Julius and then attempted to guide the audience through several emotions as a good speaker would."

"Did he succeed?" asked the third friend, Hypologus, who was not too bright.

"No, he never talked about the death of Christ."

"Who was that speaker?" Nosoponus asked.

"I prefer not to give his name. It is not important; it is the story that counts. He spoke beautifully; however, unlike Marcus Tullius, he avoided the topic. He turned out to be an extremist, a purist and ..."

"Marcus Tullius, who is that?" Hypologus interrupted.

"That was a famous lawyer and Roman senator, who often disagreed with Julius Ceasar, for which he was banned from the senate for a while. After Ceasar was murdered, he returned to the senate and spoke up against Antonio. He just could not watch his mouth and he, too, was murdered."

"I still do not know why you mention him," said Hypologus.

"My dear friend, Cicero and Tullius are the same man. Anyway, our speaker should have known that Cicero was a pagan who lived before Jesus Christ, before the Holy Spirit and before the Church existed and therefore could neither write nor orate on it. Our speaker, not having studied his topic because he could not find it in the writings of Cicero could not talk about it as a Ciceronian."

"But that means that we speak in a Christian way."

"Would you consider someone who does not understand his topic and talks around it a Ciceronian speaker, Nosoponus?"

"Of course not."

"Well, that is what happens if you only read Cicero. You cannot discuss events that occurred long after Cicero died in a Ciceronian way."

"But is it not true that when people sit in the sun they will become brown?" said Nosoponus. "And when one spends some time in a perfume shop one smells like perfume?"

"I don't know how that fits into our discussion, but that is true; however, the brown and the scent do not last long, while a good speaker leaves a lasting impression."

"Then what should I do? Throw Cicero away?"

"Of course not, but we must not try to imitate him all the time. A good speaker spends a long time in preparing for his speech in order to please the audience. He studies it in depth and he changes his style as he goes along. Always remember that a variety of spice makes a better meal that is not boring. That means that we must not solely concentrate on Cicero and instead also accept other worthy writers."

"But is imitation not essential for the art of speaking?" Nosoponus reminds him.

"I welcome imitation as long as it includes all good authors," replied Bulephorus. "Cicero may have been one of the greatest orators and writers; however, we now live in the sixteenth century and paganism ended long ago. We now are Christians and where can one find a better philosophy than our heavenly philosophy and the wisdom of Jesus Christ? Cicero would never have welcomed someone in his ranks who did not also study the basic principles of the Christian religion, embrace the Christian faith, and celebrate the glory of Christ. It is silly to try to join the ranks of these so-called Ciceronians, because it does not suit us. It is madness to pay so dearly and lose so much sleep for something which is hardly ever going to be of use to us. It is a sickness and I have every hope that you, Nosoponus, and you, Hypologus, will be cured of it.

"Oh, I got better long ago," said Hypologus.

"And I am nearly cured," added Nosoponus, "Except that I have had the disease so long that I still feel a few symptoms."

"My friend, those symptoms, too, will fade away with time and if necessary we will call Doctor Word again."

Erasmus expected and received much criticism from Italians, so much that he responded in jest, "Upon my word, I am going to change my style after Budaeus's model and become a Ciceronian."

Nearly every year, he updated his *Colloquies* and *Epistolae*, which did not require much effort on his part but brought him substantial revenue. His *Epistolae* were first published in a small volume produced by Johann Froben in August 1515, while Erasmus was living with the printer in Basel and working on his translation of the Bible. It was during that time that Erasmus met young Beat Bild (1485–1547), also known as Beatus Rhenanus after Rheinau, a small village on the Rhine River, where he was born. Beatus had studied in Paris and worked for Froben's partner, John Amorbach. When Erasmus and Rhenanus met, it was as if an invisible force pulled them together. Erasmus immediately felt comfortable with

Beatus and came to trust Beatus so much that, when he decided to publish a larger volume of his letters, he wrote to Beatus on May 27, 1520, saying:

> I am giving you authority to select, and even to make corrections, in case there should be anything that seemed likely to injure my own reputation, or seriously to embitter anybody's feelings … do what I should do myself … Act in every way as my second self, so that my absence from Basel may not be felt.

It is not known whether Beatus followed Erasmus's advice to "do what I should do myself." It is known, however, that Erasmus had edited the contents of his letters—both the copies he had made and originals that were returned to him. He did so in order to make them more suitable for publication, especially in those he considered too harsh. He also estimated dates when he had neglected to include them in original letters. He wrote to Beatus:

> Some secret natural impulse drove me to good literature when I was young and even when discouraged by my masters, I stealthily drank in whatever books came to my hand. I have either been led to my subject by chance or have undertaken some tasks with more regard to wishes of friends than to my own judgment. I advise you to treat your subject carefully, take your time, and revise your book frequently before you publish. I have never been able to swallow the tediousness of correcting.

In 1528, Erasmus was living in Basel once more and was delighted to receive a visit from Johannes Hussgen, who had been the editorial assistant and Hebrew consultant to Erasmus's first edition of the Greek New Testament.

"I hear you have a new name," Erasmus teased his former student.

"That's right. I am now Johannes Oecolampadius."

"I sense some Greek in that long name. Where did you get it?"

"You don't have to smile when you say that, Erasmus. You were fortunate when your parents named you Erasmus. You had no need to make a change."

"That's true. Now, in all seriousness, how did you choose Oecolampadius? That's thirteen letters."

Johannes leaned forward in his chair and looked at the tiled floor as his face became serious. "Well, you could say that the 'Hus' in my name could be a dialect for the German *Haus*, which means house. I took the liberty of changing the 'sgen' of my name to *schein* and that led to *Hausschein*, which means "House with a glimmer." I then translated that into Greek. Of course you know that *Oikos* is Greek for house, and a glimmer can come from a lamp, which is *lampada*. Then I put the whole thing together, and there you have it: Oecolampadius." He slapped his hands on his knees as he looked up with a smile.

Erasmus laughed. "It took a lot of work to come up with such a tongue twister, my friend, and I will smile whenever I hear it."

Oecolampadius was a compatriot of Ulrich Zwingli, the principal leader of the Swiss Protestant Reformation. While Zwingli worked in Bern, where he convinced the municipal council to accept the Reformation 1528, Oecolampadius worked in Basel and asked its city council to follow suit. The council initially hesitated, but when the citizens of Basel threatened a popular uprising, it relented. Catholics were banned from sitting on the council, convents were closed, and bands of Protestants used ropes to pull all Catholic images from their church pedestals and watch them clatter on the magnificent tiled floors. The old bishop of Basel was blessed that he did not have to witness the carnage that was inflicted on his religion and its churches; he had died in the previous year. The new bishop and the members of his congregation moved forty miles north to the German town of Freiburg.

Erasmus did not condone the revolt and decided to move to Freiburg with the bishop and his flock. On his last evening in Basel, he invited Oecolampadius to join him for dinner in his favorite restaurant. He always sat at the same corner table, from where he could observe the other tables, each festively decked with a single candle and a tablecloth in the red and white colors of the Swiss flag. He was friends with the proprietor, the waiters all knew him, and the chef had finally convinced him of the pleasure of eating fresh river trout, without salt.

"You know that I will always regard you as a dear friend," Oecolampadius said, confident in his role as the new leader of the Basel Cathedral.

"Thank you. I appreciate that very much. I'll never forget the time that we worked together in this beautiful town that is so dear to me."

"You know, of course, that you can stay, don't you?" Oecolampadius lightly patted his friend's hand.

"Johannes, let's be honest. I am a practicing Catholic in a town that has officially adopted the Reformation. There is no Catholic Church left in town, and I will not feel comfortable here." His voice wavered ever so slightly, betraying the conflict he felt deep in his being.

"I understand, but I foresee that after not too many years, both Protestant and Catholic Churches will bring succor to our people. And when that happens, please come back."

They shook hands outside the restaurant. "I plan to embark tomorrow morning. I will miss you, my friend," Erasmus said, and he walked away without looking back.

The next morning, April 13, 1529, he opened the front door of his residence and was surprised to see a large crowd, including the entire city council, waiting for him. "We will be honored if you, our revered Erasmus, permit us to escort you to the embarkation point at the Rhine Bridge," announced the mayor. He and the council members wore chains with the ornaments of their office around their necks. They were dressed in dark brown padded trunks, long stockings, and the square-toed shoes that had become popular in recent years. The ladies present wore long, predominantly red dresses.

Following a brief farewell address by the mayor, the huge crowd waited in silence for Erasmus to say a few words. He was barely able to control his emotion as he thanked the council members briefly, turned, and walked the up gangway. The captain rang the bell, and the people on the quay waved in unison. "Farewell, Erasmus!"

He replied with a little poem,

> *And now, fair Basel, fare thee well!*
> *These many years to me a host most dear.*

All joys be thine! And may Erasmus find
A home as happy as thou gav'st him here.

After Erasmus's departure, Johannes Oecolampadius continued his reform work, eventually siding with Zwingli against Luther in the dispute over the Eucharist at the Marburg Convention in 1529. Erasmus received a warm welcome in Freiburg, where the city fathers offered him temporary lodging in an unfinished house that was originally intended for Emperor Maximilian. He felt completely out of place in the large hollow rooms, and the noise made by the building crew distracted him.

In the summer of 1530, the diet met once again in Augsburg. Pressure emanated from all sides for Erasmus to attend, but he wanted no part of it. Yet his pride was hurt when Emperor Charles did not send him a personal invitation. He faulted Charles for being an absent leader who had no idea how solidly Germany stood in the camp of the Reformation. He nevertheless urged the diet by letter to formally condemn Luther and his writings.

He never regretted not supporting Luther or the Reformation, writing, *"I might have been a coryphaeus* [leader] *in Luther's Church, but I preferred the hatred of all Germany to being separate from the Church."* He was of the opinion that Rome's vehement reaction against Luther had put fuel on the fire of the Reformation, writing, *"Had both civil and Church authorities paid less attention to Luther, that fire would never have spread so violently."* He abhorred the conservatism of Luther and his followers, especially their neglect of the good literature: *"In their minds, everything is explained in the Good Book, in the Bible. They have become so narrow-minded that even Luther must now call his people back to the love of letters."*

Early in 1531, Erasmus bought a three-storied house with four steps leading to a heavy oak front door, situated underneath an ornate bay window—it befitted a man of his stature. There he lived with his ever-present students in his "great scholar's workshop."[41] The students researched manuscripts, took dictation, copied manuscripts, and assisted Erasmus with his prolific correspondence, especially with his letters to his friend,

---

[41] As it was referred to by Huizinga.

most senior assistant and sole heir, Boniface Amerbach, a teacher in Roman law at Basel University.

Erasmus spent most of his time writing his *Ecclesiastes* (On the Way to Preach), a work dear to his heart, as he had always regarded good preaching as the most important task of the clergy. What little time he had left in the day went to his correspondence. On March 1, 1531, he wrote a letter to Charles Blount, the fifteen-year-old son of his friend William Blount, in which he dedicated to the young boy his work on the recently discovered books by the famous Roman historian Livy. The letter is remarkable for what Erasmus writes about the boy's father:

> Your father has always been an insatiable glutton for history … I should not wish you to resemble your father too closely. His pouring over his books is wearisome for his wife and attendants and a cause of grumbling among the servants. So far, he has been able to do this without loss of health; still, I do not think it wise for you to take the same risk, which may not turn out as successfully … It will now be your turn to write me a letter. Farewell.

Erasmus had no other word or even a greeting for William Blount, his lifelong friend who faithfully continued to give him a pension of one hundred crowns annually.

Four years later, on a beautiful afternoon in July 1535, a young servant knocked gently on the door of his master's study and waited. Erasmus, who was then sixty-nine years old, had dozed off. With a second knock, Erasmus raised his head and mumbled something just loud enough for the young man to hear. He entered the study. "Sir, there is a gentleman to see you. He is from England."

"From England, you say?" Erasmus snapped awake and slowly managed to sit up straight, a tortured expression on his face. His gnarled fingers were the outward evidence of the rheumatism he had developed in recent years. Over his regular clothes, he wore a mantle with overly wide sleeves and a high collar. A soft cap covered his entire head from deep in the neck to just above his eyebrows. His face was even thinner than in his younger years, and instead of just one, there were now three grooves in his hollow cheeks.

"Well, show him in quickly, Hermann." His eyes popped wide open when a young man walked in. "You, young sir, so much look like William Blount when he was young that you must be his son Charles."

"I am indeed, sir."

"Forgive me for not getting up. These old bones no longer function as well as they used to do. Please do sit down." Charles picked up a pile of books from a wooden chair. "No, not that one. Pull that easy chair close by, please, and Hermann, bring us a bottle of my finest claret." He turned to his guest. "I was deeply saddened when news reached me that your father had died last year. He was only his mid-fifties, wasn't he?"

"Yes, sir. It began with a cold and soon turned into pneumonia."

"It's a shame. So you are now the fifth Lord Mountjoy. Ah, here is Hermann with the wine."

The servant handed a regular glass to the guest and a half-filled small glass to his master. "Unfortunately my tolerance has greatly diminished," Erasmus explained. "Please, tell me what is happening in England. From the snippets I get, I gained the impression that not all is well. By the way, what brought you here?"

"The king has sent me on a mission, and—you are correct—not everything is well in my country. If you permit me, I'll give you an overview of the situation, but to understand it fully, I will have to go back ten years or so and start from the beginning." Erasmus nodded, and Charles continued. "It all has to do with the marriage of King Henry. Queen Catherine has faithfully tried to fulfill her royal duty to produce a male heir to the crown. Her first pregnancy brought the proud king a son, but the infant died on the fifty-second day of his life. A second boy lived just one hour. She then had a healthy daughter, Mary, followed by a miscarried male fetus and a female infant who lived only a few days."

"How unfortunate. The poor woman must be devastated."

"She is. I should add that after six years of marriage, the king took a mistress, the beautiful Elizabeth Blount." Charles paused a moment and sighed. "Yes, I know what you are thinking; she is my cousin, and she was one of the queen's ladies-in-waiting. In any case, after five years, she bore him a son. Fortunately, Henry has acknowledged the baby as his and named him Henry FitzRoy. The king had proven that he could father a healthy son, and in the street, people sang, '*Bless'ee, Bessie Blount.*'"

"What are your feelings about it?"

"About her being his mistress? What can I say? Most kings are known to do such things, and many a father encourages his daughter in it, because it brings fortune and high positions to the family. Elizabeth happily married two or three years later, and in 1525, her place at court was taken by a hussy called Anne Boleyn. With the queen being forty years old, the chances of her producing an heir were small, and I doubt that the king entered her chambers any longer."

"Well, what about her daughter, Mary? Won't she inherit the crown and become the queen of England?"

"The king won't hear of that. By the way, I forgot to add that my father had been the chamberlain of the queen since 1512, years before my cousin came into the picture. But I digress. In 1525, the king ordered his lord chancellor, Cardinal Wolsey, to petition Pope Clement for an annulment of his marriage to the queen."

"So he wanted Clement to override Julius II's bull that allowed the marriage to take place in the first place?" Erasmus could hardly fathom what the young man had just said. He had not kept up with news from across the Channel.

"Crazy as it sounds, yes."

"On what grounds?" Erasmus simply could not believe his ears.

"On the grounds that Julius had no right to override the canon law."

"So first, King Henry overrode the law to get married and then, conveniently, he tried to void it. How nice."

"And my father had the unpleasant job of informing the queen." Charles drew a face, punctuating his dry tone.

"Do you know how she took it?"

"From what my father told me, she remained remarkably calm and said with great dignity, 'Thank you, Lord Mountjoy, for the kind words you added to your unpleasant message.'"

"She must be a brave woman. Was Wolsey successful with the petition?"

"My dear sir, you are not up-to-date in the world of politics, are you?" Charles said quietly. "Have you lost interest?"

"Not so much loss of interest as loss of effort." Erasmus smiled wryly. "I feel more and more removed from earthly matters. That's what old age evidently can do."

"Well, Pope Clement VII must undoubtedly be the weakest pope ever. He constantly changes alliance between Emperor Charles, King Francis, and various German dukes. You know, of course, that Rome was ransacked in 1527 and that Clement bought his life by paying a huge ransom and was then kept a prisoner in a castle. While he was expelled from Rome, he made an agreement with the emperor, and he has been in Charles's hip pocket ever since. Now, you should know that Charles is a nephew of Queen Catherine. You can well imagine what that meant. Pope Clement refused to annul the marriage, claiming that such an order had to come from Rome. He also refused to give our king permission to marry another woman in the meantime, which made him furious. He was convinced that Cardinal Wolsey was behind this last refusal, so he dismissed him from public office in 1529 and kicked him out of his home in York Place."

"I always thought of Wolsey as rather arrogant," said Erasmus. "A pompous man. I'm sure that Thomas More was happy to see him cut down."

"Despite all your denials, you have always been an astute politician. More denounced Wolsey in Parliament and asked the theologians of the Universities of Oxford and Cambridge to declare the marriage between Henry and Catherine unlawful, which they did."

"Most theologians have about as much backbone as have worms. I must say that I am disappointed in More," Erasmus quietly observed.

"Unfortunately, he has paid a price; however, that comes later in the story," Charles continued. "Another figure came to the foreground, a fellow called Thomas Cromwell. He is a lawyer with an adventurous background, and he has been with Wolsey for several years. I am afraid that most people underestimate him; he is smart, patient, and ruthless. Most important, he hates More, who became the new chancellor of the realm. He holds More responsible for the downfall of his beloved Wolsey."

"So, More became the second most powerful man in England?" Erasmus asked.

"He did indeed. As chancellor of the realm, or lord chancellor, he was the king's chief advisor. However, you must remember that he worked at the pleasure of the king and could be removed at any time. Henry and Anne got married in secret and, believe it or not, that day was likely the first day that they bedded together. She turned out to be a master in the art of intrigue and has become the power behind the throne. She made sure that her family's chaplain, a fellow by the name of Thomas Cranmer, was appointed as the new archbishop of Canterbury. After Wolsey died in 1530, she got Cromwell on her side, and two years later, she persuaded him to bring before Parliament a Submission of the Clergy Act and the Recognition of Royal Supremacy Act."

"What does that last act mean?" Erasmus was puzzled. "Henry is already the king of England. What can be more supreme?"

"It means that he is now the supreme leader of the Church in England."

"He can override the pope?" Erasmus was flabbergasted.

"Yes, he can. More resigned as chancellor immediately after that."

"I am glad. It was the decent thing to do.

Charles paused. He drank some wine, leaned forward, and gently patted the hand of the aged, frail man before him. "Brace yourself, dear Erasmus," he said. "For now comes the sad part. Cranmer created a special court that declared the marriage between Henry and Catherine null and void, and on May 18, 1533, that same court validated the king's marriage to Anne Boleyn, who was pregnant. On September 7, she gave birth to a girl, named Elizabeth in honor of the king's mother. Not long thereafter, Cromwell persuaded Parliament to adopt the Act of Succession in which Catherine's daughter, Mary, was declared illegitimate, thereby ending her claim as successor to the crown. Elizabeth was declared next in line of succession."

"Is it not amazing how easy it is to change matters in a kingdom?" said Erasmus in weary disbelief.

"Wait, there is more. All citizens were required to acknowledge the new act under oath. Those refusing would be imprisoned for life, and anybody who maintained that the act was invalid would automatically be declared guilty and punished with death. John Fisher refused to take the oath, and he was sent to the Tower of London last year on April 26. Your friend Thomas More was asked before a commission to swear his allegiance to the act and also refused. Last July, he was charged with high treason, found guilty, and sent to the Tower."

"Oh, my. Oh, my," Erasmus muttered, clearly agitated. "Don't tell me."

"Yes, dear sir, the worst happened. John Fisher was condemned to be hanged, drawn, and quartered. I'll spare you the details."

"No, Charles, I want to know what people were forced to witness." Erasmus's voice strengthened as he took a deep breath. The ligaments in his neck protruded as they stretched out with his rising tension. "I need to know how barbaric royalty and clergy can be."

Charles took a deep breath and let the air out slowly. "It takes place on the main square. The condemned is tied to a wooden frame and pulled by a horse from the Tower to the square. He is then hanged until he is near death. Then, they disembowel him, cut his genitals off, and burn this before his eyes. They then behead him and either cut his body into four parts or have four horses pull it apart."

"It is so gruesome," Erasmus said, shuddering.

"Fortunately, the king commuted the sentence to 'mere' beheading. I was there and witnessed how John Fisher met his death, calmly and with great dignity. Usually, the crowd is rowdy at a beheading but not this time. The people looked on in eerie silence. His head was then stuck on a pole and displayed on London Bridge."

"Don't tell me that this atrocity also befell Thomas More. Please."

Charles merely nodded sadly. "On July 6. At the foot of the steps of the scaffold, he said loudly to the executioner and his assistant, 'See me safely up. For my coming down, I can shift for myself.' On the scaffold, he kneeled, and before he put his head on the block, he declared loud enough for everyone hear, 'I was the king's good servant but God's first.'"

"I am grateful to God that He let them die in grace," Erasmus said solemnly as he made the sign of the cross.

"They took Fisher's head down and threw it into the Thames. It was replaced with More's, but his daughter Margaret Roper took it down before they could throw it into the river. Their bodies now lie side by side in the chapel of St. Peter ad Vincula."

"Thank goodness they had a decent burial." Erasmus paused, taking in all his guest had just told him. The images of his poor friends rushed upon him, disturbing him greatly. How had he missed all this? "Charles, thank you so much for taking the time to tell me what happened to my friends. Let us hope that this marks the end of this terrible time in history."

Charles managed a small smile. "There is one tidbit of news you should hear. Your former friend Edward Lee took Wolsey's place as archbishop of York."

"Well, good for him," said Erasmus, and he too smiled.

After Charles Blount left, Erasmus sat in his study, looking at the wall, his mind empty. When his student servant entered at nightfall to light the candles, he waved him off. Gradually, the enormity of the death of his two noble friends came to him. The way they had gone to their deaths—calmly, dignified, and self-chosen by their refusal to compromise their beliefs with insincere action—touched him deeply, for he knew that he would not have had the same strength or courage. He sat for a while in the darkness. After he got up, he no longer thought about any of it. The chapter was closed.

He finished the *Ecclesiastes* and left Freiburg for his beloved Basel— the unrest there had subsided and he felt comfortable there again—where he prepared the work for Froben's printing office. He found a heartfelt welcome at the home of Hieronymous Froben, who had taken over the management of the business after his father's death.

Erasmus grew weaker by the day. He was pleased when the new Pope Paul III begged him to take part in a council to restore the union of the church, but he knew that physically, he would not be able to effectively contribute, so he politely declined the invitation. On February 12, 1536, Erasmus started to make his final preparations. He sold his library to a Polish nobleman, Johannes a Lasco, whom he had befriended in 1523. To his will, he added detailed clauses, providing that the printing of his complete works should be done by Froben. His heir, Boniface Amerbach, already knew the other details of his charity.

And then, suddenly, he had an urge to leave Basel and return to Holland. To his friends, he explained, "I prefer to end my life elsewhere. If only Brabant were nearer." However, he knew that it would be impossible for him to make such a trip. On July 12, 1536, his friends Boniface Amerbach, Hieronymous Froben, and Nicolas Episcopius gathered around his couch and heard him whisper, "*O Jesu, misericordia; Domine libera me; Domine Miserere mei!*" (O Jesus have mercy; Lord deliver me; Lord have mercy on me.) They noticed the corners of his mouth move ever so slightly into a vague smile, and when they leaned over, they heard him say his last words in Dutch: "*Lieve God.*"

23

Luther—The Last Years

1536–1546

Happy domestic life - A doctor's warning - Katie speaks on behalf of women - Martin takes in students - Table Talks - Hatred of Erasmus - Banishment of the Jews - Anti-Semitic rage - Returns to the town of his birth - Katie the widow

Martin Luther led a happy domestic life. He considered himself to be the head of his family and expected his wife to please him and obey him. He loved her dearly and could not have expressed his love better than when he wrote: "*There is no more lovely, friendly, and charming relationship, communion, or company than a good marriage.*" Of children, he wrote that they should obey their parents and that any disobedience of the father was an offense to the majesty of God. His children brought him happiness, but whenever one of them would cry for a long time, he would yell, "This is the sort of thing that has caused the Church fathers to vilify marriage!"

Throughout his life, Martin was a mixture of concern, love, and insecurity, combined with a demanding nature. At times, he could be inconsiderate and offensive. Once, while on a six-week trip to Weimar, he wrote a letter addressed "*To my dearly beloved Katie, Mrs. Doctor Luther and Madam of the New Pig Market.*" The "Pig Market" referred to a parcel of land that he had recently bought, but he knew full well that "Madam" referred to the mistress of a brothel. He thought he was being funny, but

Katie did not appreciate that sort of humor. She did not write back. Two weeks later, he wrote again. *"I am not sure whether this letter will find you at Wittenberg or at the Pig Market."* Again, she did not reply.

Martin may have thought that he was the head of the family, but Katie's independence clearly showed who was the real boss. "If ever I have to find myself another wife, I'll hew myself an obedient wife out of stone," Martin once complained. Nevertheless, he was well aware that his Katie was far better than he was in financial matters and farm management; she even did the slaughtering herself. Sitting at dinner with Katie, with the children dutifully standing at the table, he once remarked, "Christ said we must become as little children to enter the kingdom of heaven," and smiling, he added, "Dear God, this is too much. Have we got to become such idiots?"

"If you don't slow down, you'll become a wreck," Kate warned him following the midday meal one day in April 1532.

"Nonsense. I'm as strong as an ox," he declared cheerfully, pounding his chest with both fists.

"Strong as an ox, eh? Martin, have you looked in the mirror lately? You look worn out," Kate said, unable to stifle the anxiety in her voice.

He looked at her inquisitively. When he saw how serious she was, he relented. "I do feel a bit tired. Maybe I'll lie down for a while."

When he woke up, he heard her working in the kitchen. He walked through the corridor leading from their bedroom to the kitchen, looked at her, and scratched his head. "That was a nice nap. What time is it?"

"Should be about nine," she replied.

"Nine? That can't be; it's still light outside."

She turned to him, wiped her hands on her apron, and smiled. "It's nine all right—in the morning!"

"*What?*"

"You, sir, slept for eighteen hours," she said and kissed him in his cheek. "You needed it. Now do you believe me?"

He looked at her a bit peevishly. "Yes, boss."

Halfway through his sermon that afternoon, he heard a buzzing in his head, felt dizzy, and could go no further. Two friends brought him home.

"I am calling the doctor," Kate immediately announced. Before he could protest, she ordered, "You lie down, right now."

When the doctor arrived, he sat down at Martin's bedside and had a good look at him. "You, sir, are grossly overweight," he announced.

"I have always been heavy," Martin protested.

"Nonsense! You seem to forget that I knew you when you were young and skinny. Now you are older and fat. I don't have to ask whether you were tired lately, because Frau Luther told me all about it. How about headaches? Do you have any?" He sounded officious.

"Well, *ja*, some in the back of my head."

"Any dizziness?"

"Sometimes but only lately."

"You didn't tell me about that," Kate protested.

"I didn't want to bother you," he said meekly.

"Any blurring of vision?"

"No," said Martin firmly, relieved that at last he could respond in the negative.

"How about chest pain?" The doctor posed his questions in rapid succession, not giving his patient time to equivocate.

"Only one time."

"Where and when?"

"It wasn't in my heart, if that is what you're worried about," said Martin. "It was here," and he pointed to the middle of his chest. Like most people, he believed that the heart was in the left side of the chest.

"I'll determine what is important, Dr. Luther," the doctor said gently. "And you didn't tell me when."

"Oh, that was last week, Doctor."

The doctor looked at Martin's rosy-colored face and then carefully looked at his eyes. He felt Martin's pulse— regular and strong … perhaps too strong? He put his ear on Martin's chest and listened carefully; he then listened at other locations on his chest and his back. He probed Martin's body and felt a moderately enlarged liver and strong pulses in the arteries of his feet, but he noticed no swelling. When he was finished, he sat down.

"Frau Luther, bring me a clean glass, please."

Kate handed him a glass, and he gave it to Martin.

"I want you to fill it with urine," he ordered.

While the doctor and Kate talked in the kitchen, Martin managed not only to fill the glass but also to contribute a good amount of the chamber pot.

"Well, now, let me see," said the doctor when Martin returned to the bedroom. He held the glass up to the light and studied it carefully. He then smelled the urine, put a finger in it, and put the finger in his mouth, tasting it. He wiped his finger on his coat and sat down. "You don't have to tell me about your work schedule, because Frau Luther already informed me of how hard you work." Martin was about to say something, but before he could, the doctor raised his hand and stopped him. "Please save your denials for later. I'll be blunt. Martin Luther, keep up your work schedule, and you'll drop dead one of these days. Slow down—and not just a little bit, mind you—and you'll live to a ripe old age, God willing, of course."

On his way out, the doctor remarked to Kate, "I see that you'll be doing business with old Gertrude again."

"Thank you, Doctor, for coming," she replied noncommittally.

"Who is Gertrude?" Martin asked her.

"She is Frau Stein, the midwife."

"I didn't know that you are with child again," Martin said.

"That's the trouble with you, Martin Luther. If you paid more attention to your own family instead of preaching all over the country, you would know," Kate said curtly, and she abruptly left the room.

Neither said a word during the evening meal. While she cleaned the dishes in the kitchen, he sat in a chair near the fire, without his customary Bible, pen, and paper, just staring and thinking. She came in, sat on her usual chair near the window, and started knitting. He looked at her and, after a long pause, said meekly, "I have been neglecting you, haven't I?"

"You've done much more than that, dear husband. You neglect all women." She was quiet and looked down at her knitting as she spoke.

"Can you explain that, please?"

She put her knitting down, brought him his pipe and tobacco, and took the chair on the other side of the fireplace.

"Uh-oh," Martin said, bemused. "This is going to be serious."

"Martin Luther, I have much to say to you." Katie was indeed serious. "Three years before we were married, I heard you give a sermon on the state of marriage. You said that God had created man and woman and said to them, 'Be fruitful and multiply.' And you said that when man resists the command to multiply, the urge remains irresistible and finds its way through fornication, adultery, and secret sins, for this is a matter of nature and not of choice. Therefore, you preached, 'priests, monks, and nuns are duty-bound to forsake their vows whenever they find that God's ordinance to produce seed and to multiply is powerful and strong within them.' Well, we have done that."

"Amen," Martin said softly. "Hallelujah."

"You also said that with respect to various stepsisters, there were no strict prohibitions against marriage, and you added that Tamar, Absalom's sister, thought she could have married her stepbrother, Ammon, and you quoted 2 Samuel 13:13. That upset me and the other nuns, because Tamar had refused to lay with Ammon. No such thing was done in Israel."

"She did lay with him," Martin reminded his wife.

"You call being raped laying with him?" Katie asked harshly.

"Tamar said, 'I pray thee, speak with the king, for he will not withhold me from thee.'"

"Yes, but just like so many preachers and priests, you only quoted the parts of 2 Samuel 13:13 that suited you. You skillfully omitted that she was ashamed and that permission from the king to lay with Ammon would lessen the shame. Did Ammon not kick her out of his house after he had ravaged her? Why is it that men think of themselves as so superior to women? Do you remember that you once said that in wedlock, fornication and unchastity are checked and eliminated, and that in itself is so great and good that it alone should be enough to induce men to marry forthwith. *Alone!* How vulgar!" She had reached a boiling point.

"Katie, we know all too well that the most terrible plagues have befallen lands and people because of fornication."

"How can you say something like that? Plagues occur because some people fornicate? Where is the proof of that?"

"It is the sin cited in Genesis 6, verses 1 through 13, as the reason why the world was drowned in the deluge." Martin was back on solid ground.

"You said that before, and I looked for the word 'fornication,' and I could not find it. Genesis only speaks of 'flesh.'"

"It is the devil who has brought this fornication about, and he coined such damnable sayings as, 'One has to play the fool at least once,' and 'He who does not do it in his youth, does it in old age.'"

"Husband, you have not convinced me. So, we women are good enough to stop men's fornication and to produce children."

"That's correct. Even when a woman bears herself weary—or ultimately bears herself out—that does not hurt. Let them bear themselves out. This is the purpose for which they exist." Martin mustered all his dignity as a preacher as he spoke.

"And is that still your opinion?" Katie showed herself to be a strong debater.

"Mind you, I do not wish to disparage virginity—"

"So, it's back to the virgins now."

"Please do not interrupt me, wife. In the worldly sense, celibacy is probably better, since it has fewer cares and anxieties. In itself, however, the celibate life is far inferior. A young man should marry at age twenty at the latest and a young woman between the ages of fifteen and eighteen."

"So, intercourse is never without sin? How dare you say so?"

"Psalm 51, verse 5, says: 'Behold, I was shapen in iniquity; and in sin did my mother conceive me.'"

Katie leaned against the back of her chair, tired and sad-looking. With closed eyes, she said softly, "I do not care what that psalm said. It is terrible to say that of loving mothers. I did not conceive your children in sin, Martin. It was done in love. Why do you always fall back on the Bible? Why do you never discuss the plight of women in any of your sermons? Especially poor women. Have you any idea how many women die in childbirth? Did you ever consider why poor women are so happy when they are giving their breast to their babies? It's because then, at least, they cannot conceive. Why do you think that rich women have a baby every year? It's because they can afford to pay a wet nurse. It is so easy for you to say that girls should marry when they are between fifteen and eighteen years old, because that is the world you live in—the world of the rich. Poor girls marry late because they have little to offer in the form of a dowry. Do you know that all too often they are sold off to well-to-do families as servants or to do day labor? Do you know what rich men say? 'Women and horses need to be well governed.' And do you know that when women talk, they say that the best marriage is the one in which the husband does not beat his wife?

"Why is it that women have to be so inferior, and why are they so little appreciated by their husbands? On an estate, a wife must supervise the servants and when her husband is away, she must run the estate. The wives of merchants usually manage the accounts. When the husband dies, the property goes to the oldest son, and when there are no sons, it goes to his nephew, because his widowed woman is not permitted to own property.

"Of course, you have never entered the municipal brothels that are maintained in almost every city, including here in Wittenberg. 'Their existence contains public disorder,' claim the city fathers. Do they realize that being a whore is a job that offers a roof over the head of poor women and provides food, medical care, and even some protection from abusive customers? Oh, Martin, if you only knew why so many poor girls enter the convents where they are only good for domestic work." Martin sat upright, ready to respond, but Katie stood up wearily. "No, dear husband, please do not speak."

She slowly walked out of the room. Martin, for once, was speechless. He did not give a sermon during the next three days, and when people wondered why not, they received their answer on Sunday morning when their Dr. Luther climbed to the pulpit. He did not open the Bible and did not quote from it. The entire sermon covered the plight of the poor and of women, in particular. And when he stood at the door of his church, waiting for his flock to leave, the women thanked him with heads held higher than usual. There were even a few smiles on the faces of the poorest. A beaming Katie stood next to her husband.

"What are you making?" Martin asked his wife one evening as they sat near the fire after the evening meal.

"A sweater."

"For me?"

"No, you have enough. It's for your son, Hans."

"Katie, I have been thinking. If I take the doctor's advice to slow down, I would have to give up preaching in faraway places. But if I do that, how will the Gospel spread? How will the Church grow?"

"Have you ever thought of letting the people come to you? You said yourself that your students will spread the Gospel. All you have to do is teach more students."

"But how?"

"Right here, in this house. Remember, it used to be a monastery, and there are many empty rooms where they can sleep. You teach them, and I will feed them."

"Just like that, eh?"

"Yes, Martin, just like that. Let it be known that you can take more students, and they'll come from far away, not just from Germany."

They discussed the matter late into the night. The end result was that Martin became a teacher at home.

The Luther household became a beehive of activity. They took in students who paid for room and board. They also took in four orphaned children and brought them up as if they were their own. They changed part of the cloister into a hospital of sorts, and not long after, Martin began to refer to his wife as "Dr. Katherine Luther." She hired extra maids for help with kitchen and housekeeping chores and menservants to do the gardening, feed the cattle, milk the cows, and tend to the fields.

Everyone was welcome at the cloister, and such was the reputation of Martin Luther that scholars came from far away to hear firsthand what he had to say. Martin instituted his famous Table Talks, which were held after meals in the great room of the former monastery. Luther and his guests sat at a long table that could seat twelve, and his students either stood or sat on the floor. While Luther dominated the Table Talk discussions, his friend Conrad Cordatus took notes and collected the notes made by others. Starting at Roman numeral I, the notes ultimately totaled VMDXCVI.[42]

Through it all, Luther could never shake Erasmus completely from his mind, believing that he was the only one who could still be a danger to the reformed church. "I hate Erasmus with all my heart," he said one day. "The man is as slippery as an eel. Only Christ can grab him." He referred to Erasmus as the vilest miscreant that ever disgraced the earth. In several Table Talk notes, Luther ranted about Erasmus, whom he regarded as his archenemy:

---

[42]   6,596

DCLXXV—Erasmus only looks after himself in order to have good and easy days and so he died like an epicurean, without any one comfort of God.

DCLXXVI—I hold Erasmus to be Christ's most bitter enemy. In his catechism, he teaches nothing decisive; not a word says: "Do this or do not do this." He only throws error and despair into youthful consciences. What I wrote in *De Servo Arbitrio* will never be confuted by Erasmus. If God lives in Heaven, Erasmus will one day know and feel what he has done. Erasmus is the enemy of true religion, the open adversary of Christ.

DCXCIV—I have cracked many hollow nuts and, yet, I thought them to be good, but they fouled my mouth. Karlstadt and Erasmus are mere hollow nuts and foul the mouth.

In his intense hatred, Martin once even went so far as to compare Erasmus to Moses. Erasmus chuckled when heard about it. "If I am Moses, who does he think he is? Jesus?" In 1525, in a very long letter to his friend and colleague Nicholaus Amsdorf, with whom he had traveled from Worms when he got "kidnapped," Luther wrote of Erasmus:

I attribute to him extraordinary thoughtlessness and emptiness of speech. He seems to treat sacred things slightingly, and to devote himself to little trifles and ridiculous levity with an eagerness not becoming to an old man and a theologian. I am almost to believe reports I have heard from wise and prudent men that Erasmus is insane. When I first wrote against his *Diatribe*, I was struck by his thoughtlessness, especially in a matter of such importance and I pricked him and accused him of being of the same opinion as Epicurus and Lucian, but I accomplished nothing except that I irritated the viper.

Our new catechism aims at this one thing that he may render his pupils doubtful and the dogma of faith to be held in suspicion. He brings before them the heresies and scandalous opinions only by which the Church has been vexed from the earliest times; and he almost insists that there has never been anything sure in the Christian religion.

There is infinity of such things in Erasmus, or, rather, that is his whole theology, as many before me have remarked and still observe more and more daily. Nor does he ever cease from adding to and publishing more widely his annotations, for his judgment is hasty and his perdition sleeps not. When asked why Christ descended from Heaven … he replies that He did so that thereby He might show Himself more perfect and absolute than the other saints … The wretched disturber of all things has thus assailed the Lord of Glory: Christ is merely more holy than others.

And yet it is difficult to meet him on account of his flexible talk and his slipperiness on which he wonderfully relies. He will not stay in one spot and he is skillful in avoiding the blows, like an irritated hornet. So it seems wise to me not to answer him, but I will leave my testimony about Erasmus for his own sake, so that he may at length be freed from that trouble he is always complaining of, namely, that he is held to be a Lutheran. For as Christ lives, they do him great injustice, and I must defend him against his enemies who accuse him of being Lutheran, when according to my belief and certain testimony, he is not a Lutheran but only Erasmus.

Erasmus did not defend himself. He only wrote the following:

Of Luther I will say nothing at present, except that I wonder why he should so rage at me, and should bring forward against me things which, even if I did not reply to him, he might know from my writings were most inane.

I did not lack arrows myself, nor did I lack friends who urged me to reply to him vigorously, but I preferred to merit the approval of the learned and the good. His letter has not injured my reputation; how much profit he may derive from it I know not.

Even in his old age, Erasmus could still use his pen as a rapier, but he made sure that his thrust did not quite reach his opponent, for he did not hate Luther, although he did acknowledge, *"Luther nurtures a homicidal hatred for me, and I do not know who he hates more, the devil or me."*

Luther's hatred was such that he was determined to pass it on to his followers and descendants. He once instructed his listeners during a Table Talk, "I charge you in my will and testament that you hate and loathe Erasmus, that viper." In a letter to his son, he wrote:

Erasmus is the right Momus, the god of mockery. When one thinks he has said much, he has, in fact, said nothing at all … I hold him for Christ's most bitter enemy. This have I, Martin Luther, written with mine own hand to thee my beloved son John, and through thee, to all my children and to the Holy Christian Church.

Aside from instructing his Table Talk listeners on the evils of Erasmus, Martin touched upon numerous other topics, both relating to the Reformation and otherwise. At times, he could be very coarse, at others, he spoke lightly:

The only portion of the human anatomy which the pope has had to leave uncontrolled is the hind end.

Germany is the pope's pig. That's why we have to give him so much bacon and sausage.

No good ever came out of female domination. God created Adam master and lord of all living creatures, but Eve spoiled all.

They are trying to make me into a fixed star. I am an irregular planet.

An officer in the Turkish war told his men that if they died in battle, they would sup with Christ in paradise. The officer fled. When asked why he did not wish to sup with Christ, he said he was fasting that day.

Table Talk discussions could go on and on for hours. One day when Martin paused to take a breath during one of his many impromptu diatribes, Kate interjected, "Doctor, why don't you stop talking and eat?"

"I wish," Martin snapped, "that women would repeat the Lord's Prayer before opening their mouths."

In August 1536, Elector John Frederick of Saxony ordered the banishment of all Jews from his territories and even refused them permission to pass through his lands on their way to other parts of Germany. The news of Elector John's ban was no shock to Luther; practically every European country had done so long before. Christian Germans believed that the Jews were responsible for the death of Jesus Christ, and Christian emperors, kings, and princes treated them accordingly to satisfy the Catholic clergy and the upright citizens. With Europe surrounded by water on three sides, the Jews had only direction way to go—east, to Poland and Russia.

Luther had not paid much attention to the Jews until that time, although early in his career he wrote, "*The Jews are blood-relations of our Lord. If it were proper to boast of flesh and blood, the Jews belong more to Christ than we do. I beg, therefore, my dear Papist, if you become tired of abusing me as a heretic, that you begin to revile me as a Jew.*" In a 1523 essay titled "Jesus Christ was born a Jew," Martin declared, "*I condemn the inhuman treatment of Jews and urge Christians to treat them kindly.*" He hoped that when he preached the Gospel, Jews would be so moved that some would convert to Christianity.

Unfortunately, it did not take much to turn him. One evening in 1528, Martin ate some kosher food for dinner, and that night he had diarrhea. "*They were trying to poison me*," he wrote to Melanchthon. From then on, he became suspicious of the Jews.

Several months after Elector John's ban, Luther received a letter written on April 1537 by a reformer, humanist, and friend of Erasmus, Fabritius Capito. Capito urged Luther to intervene with the elector on behalf of Josel Gershom of Rosheim, a Jewish money-exchanger and leader of the Alsatian Jewish communities, who hoped to gain an audience with the elector. Capito's letter came as somewhat of a surprise to Martin, as he and Capito had a strained relationship.

In the early 1520s, Capito was a sympathizer with the Reformation. When Luther found out that Capito tried to obtain a benefice in Strasbourg from the Catholic Church, he accused him of duplicity in a January 1522 letter. A year later, the letter was published without authorization, thus exposing Capito and forcing him to make a choice between the Reformed Church and Catholicism; he left the Catholic Church in 1524.

Martin remembered the unpleasant episode and still did not trust Capito. The fact that Capito was a friend of Erasmus did not help. He refused Capito's request to intervene and instead wrote to Gershom directly: "*I will not intervene because you and your people have so shamefully abused everything I have done. Christians regarded this damned, crucified Jew as the true God, while the Jews regard him as a heathen.*" He developed a sudden hatred of the Jews and not long thereafter, he recommended that all Jews be banned from Saxony. In his memoir, Gershom later wrote, "*Our situation was due to that priest whose name was Martin Luther—may his body and soul be bound up in Hell!*"

Although Luther was unforgiving when dealing with people of any faith other than Lutheranism—he mercilessly vilified them all—he was especially vitriolic toward the Jews. In 1543, he wrote a 65,000-word essay, titled "On the Jews and Their Lies." He explained that he had written it so that he would be among those who opposed the poisonous activities of the Jews and warned Christians to be on their guard against them.

A person might wonder why the Jews are so at enmity with the Christians above all others, for which they have no reason since we only do good to them. The Jews are base, whoring people, no people of God and their boast of lineage, circumcision and law are filth. They are full of devil's feces … in which they wallow like swine. The synagogue is a defiled bride, an incorrigible whore, and an evil slut.

Let me give you my sincere advice:
First—Set fire to their synagogues or schools … this to be done in honor of our Lord and of Christendom.
Second—Their houses must be razed and destroyed.
Third—Burn all their books and Talmudic writings.
Fourth—Henceforth, all rabbis must be forbidden to teach on pain of life and limb.
Fifth—Safe-conduct on the highways must be abolished for the Jews. If you princes and nobles do not close the road legally to such exploiters, then some troop ought to ride against them.
Sixth—Usury be prohibited to them and all cash and treasure of silver and gold be taken from them and put aside for safekeeping. When a Jew is sincerely converted, hand him one hundred, two or three hundred florins to help him get some occupation for the support of his poor wife and children.
Seventh—Put a flail, ax, hoe, spade, distaff or spindle in the hands of strong young Jews and Jewesses and let them earn their bread by the sweat of their brows.
To sum up, dear princes and nobles who have Jews in their domain, if my advice does not suit you, then find a better one so that you and we may all be free of this insufferable devilish burden—the Jews.

Although Luther's views were not entirely radical in his time, the Lutheran Church that he founded would eventually, rightfully, disavow them.[43]

---

[43]   In July, 1983, the Lutheran World Federation released a statement: "*The sins of Luther's anti-Jewish remarks and the violence of his attacks on Jews must be acknowledged with distress.*"
On April 18, 1994, the Evangelical Lutheran Church in America stated: "*We must with pain acknowledge Luther's anti-Judaic diatribes and the violent*

"Magdalena is sick," said a concerned Katie to her husband in September 1542, when he returned home after a three-day absence. "It started with a pain in her stomach, and the doctor said that there's nothing he can do."

Martin went to his thirteen-year-old daughter. She was feverish. Pearls of sweat dripped from her head to her pillow. He kneeled beside her and prayed. "O God, I love her so, but Thy will be done." He and Katie stayed at her bedside through the night as she became weaker and weaker. With the first sunlight, she opened her eyes and whispered, "Father."

Martin looked at her and took her hand. "Magdalenchen, my little girl, you would like to stay with your father here, and you would be glad to go to your Father in heaven," he said softly.

"Yes, dear Father," she said, her voice barely audible, "It is as God wills."

He took her in his arms and held her as she died. Katie collapsed in tears.

In January 1546, Luther was called to Eisleben, the town of his birth, to help settle a protracted inheritance dispute for the family of Count Mansfeld.

When he told his wife, Katie responded, "Eisleben? Why do you need to go there?" She pushed a strand of stray hair from her forehead.

"Oh, the old Count of Mansfeld has died, and there seems to be a question about the inheritance that needs straightening out."

"Does it have anything to do with your family's copper mines?"

"Probably. My family still owns some pits."

"Well, Eisleben is not the end of the world. You can get there in one day."

"Now, Katie, you know better. People along the way will want me to preach in their churches."

"Remember what the doctor told you—do not exert yourself. I want you back in good health," Katie said, concerned, as she plucked a little feather from his coat.

"I'll be back as soon as I can. Don't worry your little head off," Martin said, and he gave his wife a kiss.

---

recommendations *of his later writings against the Jews. We express our deep and abiding sorrow over its tragic effects on subsequent generations."*

He left home on January 17 and, traveling at a snail's pace, managed to cover the forty-eight miles to Eisleben in eleven days. He stayed at the home of the city clerk, Johann Albrecht, during the protracted negotiations over the count's will. On Friday, February 15, Luther gave four sermons. In the third one, Martin once more spewed his violent invectives against the Jews. He carried on for hours, unable to stop his rage.

The following Sunday, he did not feel well and spent most of the day in bed. Michael Coelius, the court preacher, prayed with him, and Dr. Justus Jonas felt his pulse. He frowned.

He put his ear on Martin's chest and listened intently. Then he straightened up and moved his left hand up and down his face, swiped his index finger along his eye, and looked at his patient.

"Are you just going to stand there?" Martin grumbled. "What is it?"

"Your heartbeat is quite irregular, Preacher, and much too fast. You must have absolute bed rest."

Luther looked at Dr. Jonas and then to Preacher Coelius and smiled wryly. "If I make it to Wittenberg, I will lay myself in my coffin to let maggots feast on the stout doctor."

His visitors left quietly. As they shut the door, they heard Luther shout, "Dr. Jonas and Herr Michael, I was born and baptized here in Eisleben. What if I should stay here?"

Against his doctor's orders, Martin insisted on having dinner with his friends at eight o'clock, as usual. After a few bites, he clutched his chest, clenched his teeth, and slowly blew out air. He sat with his head down while his friends looked on anxiously. After a minute or two, Martin looked up and said, looking at them, "Well, let's eat, shall we?" They finished their meals without much further conversation.

Martin went to his room, said a prayer, and lay down on the sofa. An hour later, he went to his bedroom and recited Psalm 31:6—"I have hated them that regard lying vanities: but I trust in the Lord." A sharp pain woke him up at one o'clock in the morning. "Oh, dear Lord, my pain is so great," he shouted. He moved to his sitting room, and his host swaddled him in warm blankets to ease the pain. "For God so loved the world that he gave his only Son," Martin repeated several times and went silent.

Dr. Jonas was called in and immediately noticed the cold sweat on Luther's face, he knew that the end was near. He motioned to Preacher Coelius and together, they asked, "Do you wish to die in the name of Christ and accept all His teachings?" Martin stirred and said for all to hear, "*Ja.*" He sunk back into the couch and died at 2:45 a.m. on February 18, 1546.

Katie was heartbroken, but she had little time to grieve in peace. Following Martin's death, she was ordered to vacate her home in the cloister. Having young children and no source of income, she refused to leave. Shortly thereafter, however, the outbreak of the Schmalkaldic War forced her to flee. She returned in July 1547 to find that most of the cloister had been destroyed and the land laid to waste. She managed to survive on small pensions from Elector John, the duchy of Anhalt, and King Christian III of Denmark. Five years later, an outbreak of the plague forced her to leave Wittenberg in the winter of 1552, and she traveled to Torgau The roads were bad, causing the wheel of her wagon to sink into a hole and Katie to be thrown into a deep pool of ice-cold water. She died of pneumonia on December 20 and was buried in Torgau.

"Martin Luther was not a saint," Melanchthon later said of his friend, colleague, and mentor. "He was a normal person who had rough edges."

Luther would have agreed. "I am a Saxon without good breeding, and I am thick-headed," Martin had often said of himself. To this judgment, his contemporaries added that he was short-tempered and extremely verbose, both in writing and in speech. Too often, he was not a pleasant man—he was steadfast in his opinions, and it was impossible to argue with him, for he never changed his mind. Perhaps it took a man with those qualities to take on the Catholic Church and its hierarchy and succeed.

Consulted literature

Allen, P. S. *Erasmus: Lectures and Wayfaring Sketches.* Oxford: The Clarendon Press, 1934.

Allen, P. S. *The Age of Erasmus.* Oxford: BiblioBazaar, 2007.

Augustijn, C. *Erasmus: His Life, Works, and Influence.* Toronto: University of Toronto Press, 1991.

Bainton, R. H. *Here I Stand: A Life of Martin Luther.* New York: Meridian, 1995.

Bijloos, J. *Adrianus VI: De Nederlandse Paus.* Bussum: Unieboek, 1980.

Dolan, J. P. *The Essential Erasmus.* New York: Meridian, 1983.

Emerton, E. *Desiderius Erasmus of Rotterdam.* Honolulu: University Press of the Pacific, 2002.

Desiderius Erasmus. *The Praise of Folly.* Translated by John Wilson. Hardpress.

Friesen, S. R. *Erasmus: Paradigm of Renaissance Humanism.* Padova: Piccin Nuova Libraria, 2001.

Froude, J. A. *Life and Letters of Erasmus.* New York: Charles Scribner's Sons, 1895.

Huizinga, J. *Erasmus of Rotterdam*. London: Phaidon Press, 1952.

Kittelson, J. M. *Luther the Reformer: The Story of the Man and His Career.* Minneapolis: Fortress Press, 2003.

Lull, T. F. *Martin Luther's Basic Theological Writings*. Minneapolis: Fortress Press, 2005.

Luther, M. *Three Treatises*. Minneapolis: Fortress Press, 1970.

Luther M. *Address to the Nobility*. Translated by R. S. Grignon. Oxford: BiblioBazaar, 2008.

Mangan, J. J. *Life, Character and Influence of Desiderius Erasmus of Rotterdam*. Vol. 1, 2. New York: The Macmillan Company, 1927.

Martin, M. *Martin Luther*. New York: Penguin Group, 2008.

Nichols, F. M. *The Epistles of Erasmus*. Vol. 1, 2, 3. New York: Russell & Russell, 1962.

Nichols, S. J. *Martin Luther's Ninety-Five Theses*. Phillipsburg: P&R Publishing, 2002.

Oberman, H. A. *Luther: Man Between God and the Devil*. New York: Doubleday, 1992.

Olivier, D. *The Trial of Luther*. Saint Louis: Concordia Publishing House, 1978.

Rummel, E. *The Reader Erasmus*. Toronto: University of Toronto Press, 1990.

Rupp, E. G. and Watson, P. S. *Luther and Erasmus: Free Will and Salvation*. Philadelphia: The Westminster Press, 1969.

Todd, J. M. *Martin Luther: A Biographical Study.* Westminster: The Newman Press, 1965.

Vansittart P. *The Tournament.* London: Peter Owen Publishers, 1984.

Verweij, M. *Pas de Deux in Stilte.* Rotterdam: Ad. Donker, 2002.

Winter, E. F. *Discourse on Free Will: Erasmus—Luther.* New York: Continuum, 2005.

About the Author

Barth Hoogstraten was born in 1924 in a one street village in Holland. At age ten, he was operated for a large tumor on his ankle, and the experience made him decide to become a doctor. He entered medical school in 1942. He became active in the resistance against the Nazis and, in early 1943, was forced to go underground. In 1944, he managed to go to England where he received a British officer's training. He served five years in the Dutch army, was awarded the Purple Heart and in 1949 started medical school all over again. In 1956, he immigrated to the United States and became a pioneer in cancer chemotherapy. He was an American Cancer Society Professor of Clinical Oncology at the University of Kansas Medical School. In 1971 he created SWOG, the world renowned multi-discipline cooperative cancer research group. In 1978-1979, he worked in Egypt and Kuwait as a Senior International Fellow of the Fogarty International Center. In 1988, he was elected a Fellow of the Royal Society of Medicine.